No Man's LAND

Donna E. Lane

Unless otherwise noted, all Bible verses are from the King James Version (KJV), Public Domain.

This novel's story and characters are fictitious. Certain historical events and historical figures are included for realism; however, when accounts of historical figures are given, they are fictionalized. With the exception of these historical figures, any resemblance to persons living or dead is entirely coincidental.

Reader alert: This book contains scenes of war and graphic violence.

ISBN: 979-8-9917357-5-9

For David

No man ever steps in the same river twice, for it's not the same river and he's not the same man.

Heraclitus

PART ONE

Winnowed like chaff in the blast

Chapter One

October, 1906

A great dust cloud the size of a Montana mountain approaches our station as if a giant hand reaches from heaven to stir the parched South Island dirt and fling handfuls of it into the air. I race up the steps by twos and across the veranda to the screen door.

"Pa! Pa!"

Pa's ruddy face appears beyond the screen like a ghost floating mid-air. "What is it, son?"

"Someone's a-comin'." I point to the ominous cloud.

Pa gazes into the distance, his hands planted on his hips. He chews the corner of his bottom lip, then disappears for a second and reappears holding his rifle. Stepping through the door, he pushes me behind him. "Run along inside, now. Find Manaaki and your brothers and head down to the cellar, and you stay there until you hear me call for you. Do you hear?"

"Yessir."

"Go along, then."

I scurry through our main room and down the broad hallway. "Ian. Buck. Where are you?"

Ma sticks her head out of the kitchen. "The boys e're out back gathering some eggs for me. What's wrong?"

"Some folks are ridin' up. Pa got his gun."

Ma wipes her hands on her apron and hurries toward the front door, while I race out the back toward the coop. "Ian! Buck! Come here!"

Buck calls back. "We're gettin' eggs for Ma."

"I know. Get out here right now."

Buck's cheeks and the tops of his ears are mottled red when he strides from the hen house, holding a basket half-filled with eggs. "You ain't my pa. Don't you be tellin' me what to do." Ian walks out behind him, his eyes wide, cutting between Buck and me.

"Holy Moses, Buck, it was Pa sent me to fetch you. We have visitors, and they don't look too friendly. Pa told me to go to the root cellar right away."

Buck nods once, and the two boys follow behind me to the large, wooden double doors along the back wall of the house. Buck takes one door, and I grab the other, and we heave them back, revealing a ladder leading into the underground darkness.

"Have you seen Manaaki?"

"I haven't."

"Me neither."

"Get on down there. I'm going to find him."

"Pa'll skin you alive if he finds you're not in here with us."

I huff a loud breath and fold my arms. "Pa told me to find Manaaki, so that's what I'm going to do."

Buck shrugs. "It's your hide."

Ian's eyes shine like white moons in the dark cellar. "Fin…"

"Don't worry. I'll be back before you can say shark n taters." I grip his shoulders. "*Kia kaha*."

Ian squints, nods, and fades into the pitch with Buck.

I close one of the doors, figuring my youngest brother needs a little light for comfort until I get back. Racing to the barn, I stick my head in the door. "Mani? You in here?"

The only answer I get is a blow and snort from Gypsy, Pa's favorite horse. I dash through the barn, and finding no sign of Manaaki, I run to the front corner of the house to see if I can spot him wandering in the fields.

Pa and Ma stand on the porch as tall and straight as mountain pines, their rifles trained on the horsemen churning dust in our yard.

"You outlanders need to stop sticking your nose in our affairs, ay?" The man's horse balks, twisting its neck against the reins. "If you know what's good for ya."

"Seems the good of the community *is* my affair since I'm a contributing member now." Pa shifts his rifle to the crook of his elbow.

The ruddy-faced man rubs his bristly cheek and growls. "Buying up all the land to give away isn't good for anyone."

"It's good for the Māori."

A man with bushy red hair urges his horse forward. "You think you're helping the Māori by giving them land? You're not." His lip curls above his teeth. "The only thing you're building is resentment toward them."

"You gentlemen seem to forget; the Māori were here long before you. And if the government hadn't stolen their land, I wouldn't be having to buy it back."

"They're not your kind."

Pa's brow wrinkles like when Buck says a word he doesn't like. "They're *human*kind, aren't they?" Pa's finger's getting twitchy on that trigger.

Manaaki leaps like a brown rabbit across the fields and through the yard, passing to the right of those crazed horses toward Ma and Pa. "Mister Clay! Mister Clay!"

Pa's frown deepens as the men's horses snort and stomp, and the red-haired man raises his pistol, pointing it toward Manaaki. Pa hefts his rifle on his shoulder.

"Don't shoot him!" I dash from my hiding place, gauging Mani's speed to set my angle to reach him, but my legs move like my feet are stuck in a bog.

Pa calls, "Findlay! No!"

I reach Mani, wrap my arms around his head like a wayward sheep, and twist him to the ground with a thud. A loud crack shakes the air around me as a puff of dirt flies in my face.

Pa's down the steps and by our side in a flash, standing over us like a lion guarding his kill, waving his rifle. "Get off my land. Now." His growl and his rifle against his shoulder brook no argument, so the men tug their reins and gallop down the path—save the red-haired man, who urges his horse closer, cocks his head, and sneers at us.

"This isn't the last of it." His horse rears as he holsters his gun. "You'll see us again. Real soon."

Pa fires, his shot skidding through the dirt at the horse's hooves, and the horse bucks and bolts, bouncing the man like a yoyo at the end of a string.

Ma's footsteps patter down the steps while Pa lifts me by my shirt collar. A swift slap and my ears ring like church bells on Sunday. "Of all the foolhardy…" He slaps again. "I told you to go to the cellar."

"I took 'em, Pa, like you said, but I couldn't find Mani."

"What were you thinking?" Ma snatches me from Pa's hand into a fierce hug. "You could've been killed!"

"That man was about to shoot Mani."

"Manaaki, *ke te pai koe*?" Pa takes Mani's hand and helps him to his feet.

Mani brushes dirt from his *maro*. "*Kei te pai ahau.*" He shakes his dark brown curls. "Whoa, those *weriweri* men come for ya, Mister Clay."

"They did indeed. But don't worry your head. They'll think twice before they return." Pa pops Mani's backside. "And if they do, you won't come running, do you hear? Go straight to the cellar with the boys."

"*Āe,* Mister Clay."

Pa's large hand rests on my shoulder, and I know I'm forgiven. "Well, it's over now. The two of you fetch the boys from the cellar. I'm ready to eat."

"Yes, Pa."

As Ma and Pa walk to the porch, their arms around each other and heads tilted close, whispering, Mani and I race around the house to the shed, the fear from the morning's events fading.

Buck stands at the top of the cellar stairs when we arrive. "What happened? I heard shots."

"Those men fired at Mani and me. We were almost killed." I puff out my chest. "But I saved Mani's life."

Buck sneers. "Sure you did."

Ian sticks his head out of the hole, his eyes wide. "You almost died?"

"Huh, those *ngarue* run scared from Mister Clay." He grabs Buck's arm. "Come, come. Time to eat."

Ma scrubs her hands down her apron as we stomp into her kitchen. "Wash up, boys." She glances toward Pa. "Maybe you should stop. They'll leave us be, then."

Pa shakes his head. "We're doing the right thing, Fiona. You know it." His face darkens. "I won't stand by and watch the same thing happen to the Māori that happened to the Lakota. It broke my pa's heart to watch them wither and dry up like flowers in the desert sun, and all of it started with the dirty *wasicu* stealing their land—same as here. And since the Māori can't purchase land legally…" He shrugs. "I'm their only hope."

"I know. But the boys…"

Pa squeezes Ma's waist. "I'll take care of you and the boys. But please don't ask me to stop buying land to give to the Māori." His eyes trail to the floor. "I still have a lot to make amends for."

Ian pulls his dripping hands from the sink. "What does 'make amends' mean?"

"It means to make right a wrong that's been done."

"What've you done wrong, Pa?" Buck's probably asking because of his long list of offenses, hoping there's some way out for him.

"Never you mind." Pa raises his head, clears his throat, and rubs his hands together. "Right. Who will lead our prayer this morning?"

For once, I don't raise my hand. My thoughts swirl like a dust devil in a prairie wind. Why are those men so angry? What's Pa ever done to them? Why would they want to shoot little Manaaki? He's no threat.

And why would Pa give away our land? Doesn't he always say protecting our land and family is the most important thing a man can do with his life? If those men are mad about him giving the land away, why would he risk his family to keep doing it? It doesn't make sense.

Pa's a mystery to me. He drops bits and pieces of his years living with the Lakota like corn kernels for the chickens, but he never finishes his stories, and he seems so sad afterward. Why would great adventures be so troubling to him? Instead, he wanders onto the fields, mumbling, "Never you mind."

The same thing happened when we lived for a spell in Montana. Pa would disappear for weeks at a time, and when he returned, he was diminished as if he'd left a part of himself out on the plains. I didn't understand it then, and I still don't understand it now.

But coming to the Island where Pa breathes deeper and laughs a lot more has put color back in his cheeks. Ma says he's become her Clay again. Maybe taking Manaaki into our home and helping the Māori has done that for him.

Now, these bad men from town threaten everything.

Ian leads the prayer, and I close my eyes but don't hear his words. I'm whispering a private prayer in my heart, hoping the Lord hears me, from one of those Old Testament psalms asking God to smite our enemies, and I don't feel a smidge bad for it.

"Why did those men shoot at you, Pa?"

"Those men, they got them *kino* cows. Always they want more land." Mani's face twists into a sour scowl. "Take everything, ya let 'em, I tell ya. Men like them that took my *mātua* from me."

All Mani's parents did was block land surveyors from coming onto their property, and the government men killed them for it and took their land anyway, leaving poor Manaaki an orphan.

Pa pats Mani's hand. "Well, we won't let them, then."

"Ya got it, Mister Clay."

Lines crease the space between Ma's brows as she spoons up our food in silence. Serving Pa last, she slams Pa's eggs on his plate like she's slopping a hog. The air sits hot and thick in my throat as I cut my eyes between her and Pa.

Pa's jaw ripples like the water in the river when it runs over stones. "I don't know why those men are so threatened by the Māori having land. There's more than enough to go around." He shovels a forkful of eggs in his mouth.

"Seems men are always fightin' o'er land." Ma tosses her head. "Scotland's history is rife with wars o'er it."

"But those men have land already like Manaaki said, plenty to graze their cows on. No one is taking their land away." Pa rips a piece of bread with his teeth as if he's biting hard taffy. "Why shouldn't the Māori have the same opportunity?"

"Why didn't you just shoot 'em dead, Pa?"

Ma's eyes widen as she pops Buck on the arm. "Barclay MacAlister, what a horrid thing to say. What does the Good Lord teach us?"

Buck's head drops to his chest. "Thou shalt not kill." He raises his eyes, his lower lip puffed out. "But they were gonna kill Mani. Don't that make a difference?"

"*Doesn't* that make a difference," Ma corrects.

"Well, doesn't it?"

Pa sighs. "Never you mind. I will protect my family, whatever it takes. Now don't worry your heads about it."

A slight rise in one of Ma's brows makes me wonder if she's the worried one.

"We have a full day, boys, so as soon as you're finished, get on your work clothes and meet me at the fence." Pa brushes his hands on his pants and pushes away from the table.

"What about their schoolin'?" Ma's brow lifts dangerously.

"They can do their schooling when the sun goes down. Today, we start the shearing."

Buck whoops and jumps up from the table. "You promised this season I could handle the shears."

Ma points a finger at Buck's chair and slams her other hand on her hip. "Sit yourself down and finish your meal, young man."

"Aw, Ma…"

"Boys who can't obey their mothers can't be trusted with the shears." Pa widens his eyes, then jerks his head toward Buck's seat.

"Yes, sir." Buck plops on his chair with a huff and starts moving his eggs around on his plate.

Pa nods. "This season, Fin, you'll take the sheep down and hold it, and Buck, you'll do the shearing."

Buck beams and slaps the table. "Ay, right."

"Ian, you and Manaaki will oversee herding the sheep down the chute. Got it?"

"Yes, Pa."

"Ay, Mister Clay."

"I'll gather the wool and prepare it." His thick brows knit together. "But before we go out, I'll hear your verses, and we'll have our prayers. Understood?"

"Yes, Pa."

Ma's face softens into a hint of a smile, then she quirks her mouth and shakes her head. "Go. Get on with ye." We don't have to be told twice. She picks up two half-empty plates as we bolt from the kitchen, slamming into each other and the walls as we race down the hall to our rooms.

After a quick stop around the fireplace to recite our memory verses and pray, Buck and I race each other for the pens, while Ian calls for Scotty, and he and Mani head to the fields.

Taking down and holding one sheep after another is hard, sweaty work, but it beats sitting with books and doing arithmetic drills all morning. Ma takes our learning seriously. She always says, "I'll not have my kin grow up to be a country dunce." Truth be told, I'd rather be dim than stuck inside all day.

Buck climbs atop the fence as we wait for the sheep, balancing on the boards like a *tuatara* until Pa barks dangerously, "Buck…"

"Yes, Pa." He leaps from the fence and kicks at the hawksbeard growing around the base of the post.

Scotty's bark signals us to take our positions. Ian, Mani, and Scotty guide the sheep into the pen, and the marathon is on. One by one, they send the sheep through the chute where I wrestle them onto their backside, and Buck drags the shears across their chests, stomachs, and sides. Then, I flip them, holding their face against the dirt while he shaves the thick fur off their backs. Pa bundles the fur into mesh bags, placing the containers into a vat for soaking.

The lowering sun colors the sky gold and red as we drag ourselves across the porch. Ma meets us at the door. "You'll not bring your filth into my home." She jerks her thumb over her shoulder. "Out back with ye."

Pa pulls the chain on the water tank while Buck, Ian, and I strip off our clothes and take turns standing under its flow.

Mani has a good laugh at us. "All those *taimaha* clothings, much trouble." He shakes the dirt from his *maro.* "See? No problems."

The three of us wrap towels around our waists, dump our smelly clothes in the laundry tub, and dash through the kitchen under Ma's critical eye. "We'll begin school straight away. No dawdling, now. Come along, Mani." I can hear his groan from the bedroom.

As usual, Ian the genius wins the arithmetic competition and races through his reading and writing, finishing well before Buck and me. Ma spends the time drilling Mani on his English words, which is always good for a laugh. Finally, Pa joins us, and we circle around the fire to share how we applied our memory verse during the day and to receive our new verse for tomorrow.

"I showed the fruit of the Spirit 'cause I was longsuffering and good while Buck and I waited for Fin to come get us from the cellar." Ian glows under Pa's approving gaze.

"You weren't none too peaceful, though," Buck grumbles.

"Barclay!" Ma wags her finger in Buck's face. "'Judge not that ye not be judged.'"

Buck swings his face toward Pa. "Can that be my memory verse?" He bugs his eyes like a hungry kitten and bats his lashes. "Ma says I need to learn it."

Pa closes his eyes and heaves a deep sigh. I shake my head at Buck's ploy, and then puff out my chest. "I showed love for Mani by saving his life from those bad men."

"Well, now, you did, that's a fact." Pa's face darkens. "But what about meekness and temperance? You could've been killed. Do you know what that would've done to your mother?"

I wince while Buck snickers behind his hand. Pa turns his fury on Buck, sparing me for the moment. "And what about you, young man? I haven't witnessed much fruit, but I've surely seen the works of the flesh in you."

"Sorry, Pa."

"It seems to me you two need wisdom, so your verses for tomorrow will be from Proverbs. Listen carefully:

> *When your fear cometh as desolation, and your destruction cometh as a whirlwind; when distress and anguish cometh upon you.*
>
> *Then shall they call upon me, but I will not answer; they shall seek me early, but they shall not find me:*
>
> *For that they hated knowledge, and did not choose the fear of the Lord:*
>
> *They would none of my counsel: they despised all my reproof.*
>
> *Therefore shall they eat of the fruit of their own way, and be filled with their own devices.*

Buck groans. "I can't remember all that."

"Do you understand what it means? If you do, it will help you memorize it." Pa lifts a brow, waiting for Buck's reply. His mouth opens and closes like a fish in a dry creek bed.

Maybe Pa will credit me as being meek if I help Buck out. "It means we can't expect to turn to God when bad things happen if during the good times, we won't listen to Him."

"In a way, yes." Pa sits back in his chair, his eyes trailing toward the ceiling. "I think it's a warning that bad things come because of not fearing the Lord or listening to His counsel. It's not that God brings bad things or wants bad things for us, and it doesn't mean He'll abandon us when we need Him most." Pa sits forward, his hands folded and his elbows on his knees. "But I know from experience, it's awfully hard to turn to God when you've been walking a wayward path and gotten yourself in trouble by it."

Barclay's brow creases. "Pa?"

"Yes, son."

"Do you think God will answer me if something bad happens?"

Pa's soft smile glows like the flickering flame in the fireplace, reaching deep into my chest to warm my heart. "Of course." He gathers us in his arms, even Mani. "He loves you, boys. And so do I."

Mani squirms beside me. "Mister Clay?"

"Yes, Manaaki."

"May I learn the words about the bad judge?"

Pa chuckles and rubs his dark hair while Buck and Ian roll on the floor laughing. Even Ma, who won't brook any frivolous treatment of the Scripture, giggles.

I elbow Mani in his side. "It's not about a bad judge, Mani. It means we are not to think bad things about other people."

His eyes widen. "Not even those *weriweri* men?"

Ma nods. "Not even those men."

His mouth opens into an O, matching his eyes. "Not even."

"Ian, why don't you help Mani with the verse about 'the bad judge', while Buck and Fin wrestle with the Proverbs." Pa grins. I think he loves torturing Buck and me. "I'll expect a perfect recitation in the morning."

"Yes, Pa."

"Now, snuggle down."

The four of us clamber under a large buffalo hide Pa brought with us from Montana. Ma waits for us to quiet down before she starts singing:

Aleluiah, Aleluiah, Aleluiah, Aleluiah.

Mo ghaol, mo ghràdh, a's m' fheudail thu,
M' ionntas ùr a's m' èibhneas thu,
Mo mhacan àlainn ceutach thu.

Ian's rasping cough startles me awake. The firelight flickers on the far wall—but wait, this isn't the main room, it's our room. And I'm in my bed.

I blink several times, causing tears to leak from the corners of my eyes. My throat burns like my knees when I scrape them climbing, and my chest is so heavy I can't take a breath. When I climb from my bed, the air thickens, smelling of spoiled eggs, turned dirt, and dead fish.

Someone laughs outside our window—a man with a harsh, throaty cackle. A shattering like a bottle breaking against a stone, a second laugh, then Ian coughs again, a shuddering, gagging sound.

Am I waking into a nightmare? A flame licks between the logs on the side wall, bringing awareness like a bright beam of sunlight into a dark night.

Our house is on fire.

"Get up!" I grab Ian by his ankles and drag him from the bed. His scream is interrupted by another, longer cough. Shaking Buck, I holler again. "Get up! Get up! The house is on fire!"

"Wha…?"

"Fire!"

I lift a crying Ian by the back of his shirt and run for the door, but when I open it, a spout of flame erupts with a whoosh toward our ceiling. I duck and roll out of the way, barely escaping with my skin. When I glance back, the hallway is completely engulfed.

"We can't get out this way!"

Buck stands in the center of the room, his eyes as white as a roped wild horse. "What do we do?"

What *can* we do? I'm not going to stand here and fry like a chicken, but I can't think. The fire pours through our door in a cascade, taking over the walls and growing closer and closer to my feet.

"The window!" Buck dashes to the window to open it but draws back just as quickly. "The fire's burning outside."

"Those men did this. I heard them out there." I crane my head left and right, looking for any answer.

There. The buffalo skin. Pa must've carried us in here still wrapped in it. "Buck, grab the hide!"

He drags it from his bed just as an ember lands on the mattress, and it catches up.

"Quick! Put it over your head and shoulders, then come wrap it around Ian and me. Hurry!" I set Ian on my hip. "Hold onto my neck."

For once, Buck does what he's told, and soon, the three of us are shrouded within the hide.

"Now, we're going to run. Run as fast as you can. Ian, don't you let go, you here?"

Ian blubbers something unintelligible but nods once.

"Ready? Go!" We bolt through the growing, encircling flames like we're running through an orange and yellow cave, racing blindly toward the main room, but the door and porch are engulfed as well, so we veer left and dash into the kitchen.

I lift the edge of the hide. The side walls are aflame but the fire hasn't reached the back door yet. "Here. Take Ian outside and run as far away from the house as you can. Hurry."

"What are you gonna do?"

"I'm getting Ma and Pa and Mani."

Buck nods, takes Ian's hand, and runs through the back door.

I wrap the skin around me tightly, then run back into the main room and down the other cave of fire leading to Ma and Pa's room. But as I throw open the door, beams from the roof crash into the burning room, sending the flames shooting into the night sky.

"Ma! Pa!" The burning air rushes into my open mouth, searing my throat and causing it to close like a *makahiya* plant. When I try to call again, the only thing that comes out is a rasping cough. Tears sting my eyes. Ice snakes down my spine and freezes my stomach.

Ma and Pa lie under those beams. If I can drag them out—but my legs won't budge. What's wrong with me? Go in there and get them. Coward. A monster digs its claws into my chest and squeezes my heart until it threatens to burst.

When the rest of the roof crumbles and falls into their room, my leaden feet finally move, but I'm too late. Too late. With a howl of anguish, I grab handfuls of my hair and yank as hard as I can. "Maaaa! Paaaa!"

Lord, help me. What are we going to do now?

I scrub my arm across my eyes. Pa would say, "Always keep your head, boy." He would tell me to protect Mani and my brothers and take care of things for him.

Mani.

I dash to the small addition Pa built onto the back of the house for Mani. He meets me at his door, as calm as a spring shower. "Come. We go." He takes my hand and pulls me into his room, where we climb out his window, already open, and drop to the grass.

Dragging Mani and the buffalo hide behind me, I run like a Montana antelope chased by a mountain lion. "Ian! Buck!"

"Over here!"

We find them tucked behind a large tree, shivering. I wrap the buffalo skin around them.

"Where's Ma and Pa?" Ian's voice trembles as if he already knows what I'm going to say. A single tear traces a shimmering path down his blackened cheek, glistening in the firelight.

I open my mouth, but it's Mani who answers. "I try to get to Mister Clay and Missus Fiona." He shakes his head. "Too late."

I glance from Buck to Ian, then lower my eyes, but I can't say the words. I won't. If I do, it will make it real.

CHAPTER TWO

October, 1906

My thoughts hang thick and ugly, like stirred silt from a muddy river bottom. Buck looks like he's bitten into a tenpenny nail. Ian's silent weeping wrenches my battered heart, but I can't make myself reach out to comfort him. After all, no one's here to comfort me.

It's as if I've swallowed an ember from the fire and it's catching in my chest. Everything burns, and the smoke rises within me like an impenetrable fog shrouding my mind.

Mani gestures toward the barn. "Fire spreads quick."

I blink twice, trying to awaken from my stupor. "The animals." I'm moving slower than a slug in snow. How could I forget the animals? Pa would skin my hide—if he were here. "We have to get them out."

Without a word, Buck shoves the buffalo hide off his back and Ian off his lap. He stands, brushes dirt from his clothes, and marches toward the barn like a soldier heading to the front lines. His stiff movements jar something loose in me, and at last, I force my limbs to work.

Mani runs ahead of Buck, and soon, I pass him, too, reaching the barn at the same time as Mani. The heat, soot, and cinders envelop the barn. Inside, the animals bellow and stomp enough to shake the boards.

I unlatch and slide open the heavy door as Buck arrives. We spread out, opening stalls and slapping and hollering at horses and cows to get them to move.

I understand. I'd rather curl up in this barn and let the fire take me, too.

Then, we try to herd the chickens from their coop, but those dumb birds keep running in circles. I'm vaguely aware of Buck's piercing, unrelenting scream, and Mani's clucking as he chases our prey.

Mani shrieks, pointing to a small flare in the hay. "Water!"

I rush to open the water tank and grab a bucket to catch the flow. When I return to the barn and douse the fire, Mani gestures. "Let water flow on dirt. Maybe stopping spread."

If I were thinking clearly, I would've thought of that. "Good idea." I race back outside and pull the chain to allow the water to run freely. Soon, the ground in front of the barn is sodden, and as Mani predicted, the fire stalls. As long as an ember doesn't hit the roof, the barn should be safe.

The remainder of the roof of the house collapses with a loud rumble followed by a thunderous clatter. The walls soon follow. Mani, Buck, and I stand as still as statues in the glow, staring at our lives disintegrating into smoke and ash. But as the final logs of our home fall, something inside me breaks, and my rage and confusion pour out like the water from the tank. I collapse to my knees and bury my face in my grubby hands. Sobs erupt from deep in my stomach, racking my body and stealing my breath until finally, I vomit my guts onto the muddy earth.

Mani pats my back once, then clears his throat. "Ian cries." He gazes toward the large tree where my brother crouches like a frightened, abandoned kitten.

I forgot about Ian. His keening pierces the fog and slices my soul to the quick. I left him alone—at a time like this. What's wrong with me? He's just a ten-year-old kid. "Come on, Buck." I sprint a few steps toward the tree, but Buck doesn't move. As usual, the boy does what he wants, no matter who suffers for it. "Come *on*."

Instead, Buck marches toward the remnants of our home, grabs a piece of log, and strides around the debris toward the front of the house.

"Where are you going?"

Buck's eyes are dead when he stares back at me. "I'm going to kill those men."

"You are not." Without hesitation, he stomps on, hefting his makeshift weapon. "Come back here. You'll get yourself killed."

True to form, Buck doesn't stray from his chosen course—not even a pause. With a groan, I dash after him, grabbing his shoulder. "Enough of this nonsense. We'll deal with those men later. They're likely long gone anyway." I spin him around and shove my hands on his shoulders. "We must take care of our little brother. Pa would say so."

At the mention of Pa, sparks shoot from Buck's eyes, and his lip curls above his gritted teeth. "You ain't my pa." He jerks away from my grasp and runs beyond the ruins, howling like a rabid wolf.

"If you get shot don't blame me." I throw up my hands and trudge toward Ian, where Mani already sits with his arms around my brother, comforting him in a way I could not.

My back tingles like when I used to feel Pa's disapproving glare following me. What must he be thinking? I'm the eldest, fourteen going on fifteen. He always told me I must set an example for the other boys, yet it was Mani's quick thinking that saved the barn. Mani braved the flames trying to reach Ma and Pa. Mani didn't freeze like I did. Now, Mani sits comforting Ian instead of me.

My throat closes over the realization I'm the man of the house now. A crushing heaviness floods my chest, knocking me to my knees like a raging river when the mountain snow melts in spring. It surges into my throat and vomits out in a rush of tears and choked sobs, pummeling me under its force until I'm drowning in it. Lord, help me. The burden of survival weighs on my shoulders, and I'm at a loss as to how to take even one step.

"Get up." Sometime during my torrential tears, Buck had returned. I force my eyes to meet his and find nothing but disdain. "We're going after those men."

A seething fury snakes through my gut, churning the flood waters and whipping them into a tumult. I swipe my arm across my eyes but do not attempt to rise.

"Get up!' Buck grabs my elbow to jerk me to my feet, and the flood inside me burns as red as the coals from the fire. I let him lift me as I swing my other arm in an arc and explode my fist into his jaw, sending him sprawling.

He leaps to his feet and jumps on my back, punching my ribs and growling like a Montana bear while Ian's piercing shriek shatters the night's grim reverence over our parents' grave.

"Stop!" Mani's small hands shove me to the dirt as Buck falls onto his back. "*Wairangi.* You have only the other." He stands between us, his arms wide as if to hold us apart. "You must not fight."

Buck snarls. "Baby." He spits toward me but hits Mani instead, who grunts in disgust.

"Idiot," I snap back. "What chance do you have against men with guns?"

"More than you sitting there and bawling." He drags himself to his feet. "What good does that do?"

I heave a sigh. "Not one thing." I push myself up, brushing my hands together. "But neither does going off half-cocked." My head aches, and my eyes burn as if filled with sand from the river bottom. "We need to think."

Buck's neck ripples like a cork bobbing on a lake. "I don't want to think." He clenches his fists, spins, and strides into the darkness of the field beyond.

Mani watches until Buck disappears into the low-hanging smoke. "We find horse. Go to Māori." He makes a scooping gesture with his hands. "They help kin of Mister Clay, that for sure."

I study the ground, chewing my bottom lip. Mani's right. The Māori are beholden to Pa. They wouldn't have land without him. They'll help us.

"I'll go collect the horses." I thrust my chin in the direction of Buck's disappearance. "You go find my brother." Not making the same mistake, I take Ian's hand. "Come on, Ian. Help me find the horses."

Ian's breaths come in ragged gasps as he wipes his nose on his sleeve. Slower than honey dripping from a comb, he trudges behind me like a beaten dog on a leash.

"Gypsy! Come here, girl." Ian and I search the area around the barn but find no sign of them. They must've run into the fields to get away from the flames.

As we move toward the darkness of the field, Ian's resistance to my pull grows stronger. "Come on, Ian. Hurry up." His high-pitched whine starts anew. "Don't start up again."

"I want Ma."

"I want Ma, too, but she ain't here, so we must get along without her."

With that, Ian throws back his head and wails, collapsing onto the dirt in a crumpled heap.

I groan and blow out a rumbling breath. "Very well. Stay here, then. I'm going to find those horses."

"Noooo." His screech sends an icy shudder up my back. "Don't leave me."

"Then *get up.*" A pinch squeezes my gut as I hear Buck's cruel words coming from my mouth. I wince, and closing my eyes, I kneel beside Ian and stroke his back. After a few moments of listening to his cries, I sigh. "I'm sorry. There's no call for me to yell at you. It's not your fault."

"When are they coming back?"

A cold fist punches my chest. Does Ian not know they're dead? "They aren't coming back, Ian. They're gone. The fire took them."

His cries stop abruptly, becoming snuffles and shuddering breaths.

"Do you understand?"

"They died?" I can barely hear his whisper.

"Yes." There's no going back. I've said it. It's real now.

"Are they in heaven?"

"Yes."

Silence descends and wraps around us, strangling my breath and clogging my throat. Why, God? Why did you take them from us? Why didn't you wake me sooner? Why didn't you stop those men?

Somehow from under the heavy shroud, Ian rises to his feet. "It's all right, Fin." His voice is soft, even calm—nothing like the bitter acid bubbling inside me. "Let's go find the horses."

We stagger through the thick silence, stumbling over clumps of hawksbeard and tripping over rocks until snorts and scrapes of hooves pawing the dirt break the quiet.

"This way." I tug Ian's hand, pulling him toward the unmistakable sounds. Fortunately, the horses remained together, so we gather all four quickly and walk them back to the barn.

"What about the cows?" Ian's eyes glow like a spring full moon.

"They'll be all right until morning. We can collect them then."

Soon, Mani returns to the barn, with Buck trailing behind him. "We have all the horses."

"*E tino pai.* We go now to my people."

Buck huffs and folds his arms. "We can't."

I blink at him, chewing the inside of my cheek. "And why can't we?"

"We can't leave the sheep. Those men might come back and steal them all. Plus, the cows will need milking and the chickens feeding." Buck waves his arm toward the barn and fields beyond. "This is all we have left. If we leave, we won't even have that."

"So, what would you suggest?"

Buck shrugs. "I say, we sleep for a bit, do our chores in the morning, then decide who's going to town and who's gonna stay here and guard the animals."

For once, Buck makes some sense. "Very well. We'll try to get whatever sleep we can until sunup, then we'll decide the next step."

"Manaaki goes to Māori now. Bring them back to help."

"No, Mani, I can't let you go alone in the middle of the night, and on foot."

"*Hamuti!* Walking hundred times to village. No problem."

"We don't know if those men are still lurking about."

"Ha! Better reason I go, get help quick."

Buck lifts his brow. "Mani has a point."

Sighing, I drop my chin to my chest. "Very well. Just be careful."

Mani doesn't hesitate. "Back quick, like lightning." He races across the field, melting into the darkness.

My legs feel as heavy as my heart, and my mind has gone soft. "Now what?" I glance at Buck.

"Well, one of us needs to sleep with the sheep in the fields."

Ian's face brightens—a welcome sight. "Like a real shepherd."

"Right." Buck scrubs Ian's curly hair. "Since Scotty's with them, we can call him, and he'll lead us straight to them. The others guard the horses and cows."

"I thought we'd wait until morning to try to bring in the cows. It'll be impossible to herd them in the dark."

Buck nods. "Whoever's in the field will probably hear if someone comes looking for the cows." His stare pierces through me. "So, the only question is, who sleeps where?"

I square my shoulders. "I'll take the field since it's more dangerous."

"I figured you'd want to protect Ian."

Ian frowns and plants his hands on his hips. "I don't need protecting."

"The horses, then."

Wrestling Buck over who's sleeping where is a waste of my breath, so I roll my eyes and sigh. "I'll stay in the barn." I reach for the horses' reins. "Come along, Ian."

"I was gonna ride Gypsy." Buck reaches for Gypsy's reins, but I shake my head.

"If Mani can run to the village, you can walk to the sheep." I pull Gypsy along with the other horses. "Get on with you, now."

Buck huffs but grabs the log he used as a makeshift weapon and strides into the field, swallowed by the night.

"Come along, Ian. Let's find us some hay to sleep in." I slide my arm around Ian's shoulders, who presses his head against my chest.

"Fin?"

"Yes?"

"I love you, brother."

Tears well and threaten to spill on my cheeks. "And I love you."

Oh, how I wish I were worthy of his love.

CHAPTER THREE

October 1906

The first rays of dawn glint off the dust swirling in the barn as if a million tiny dancing fairies flit about wreaking havoc before the humans awaken to interrupt their fun. I slip from my perch on a mound of hay, leaving Ian whose slow, deep breaths let me know he is still asleep. Moving as someone lost in a dream, I mount Gypsy and head to the fields to collect our cows, grabbing a rope from a hook by the door on the way out.

I spot Buck sitting with his back against a tree, his log across his lap and a piece of straw hanging from his mouth, with the sheep huddled nearby, munching on grass. Further down the slope, the cows gather near the small pond. The tree's limbs roll as the wind slips through them like a lazy river on a hot day. The fairies rest from their morning mayhem, perched in the winking sunlight reflecting off the leaves. I wave to Buck who lifts his hand in response, and amble down the hill toward our bell cow, making a lasso from the rope as I ride.

A sudden wave of nausea and cold sweat sends fingers of ice crawling up my spine as yesterday's memory jolts me from my trance—Ma and Pa are gone. This isn't another normal day of chores. No one will teach school. No one's making our morning meal. No bright "good morn" or "get on with ye". No new memory verse. No one asking how well I followed my verse yesterday.

What was my verse?

Something about fear and destruction coming upon us and not finding the Lord because we refused to listen.

Is that why Ma and Pa had to die—because we refused to listen to the Lord? My stomach lurches as my insides are swallowed into an empty, dark pit like the yawning mouth of some huge beast. I suppose it's true that Death is a monster. It barreled through like the whirlwind in my verse and left nothing behind.

The pastoral scene before me now takes on an ominous cast as if a storm cloud lowers over it. None of us have any idea what we're doing or how we're going to survive. Where does Pa keep our money? Did it all get burned in the fire like the guns, our clothes, and everything else we own?

How do we defend ourselves—with burnt logs? How do we protect the land and animals from thieves? What if those men return?

"What're you waiting for? Get moving!" Buck's thin voice drifts down on the breeze. Slowly, I turn my head to meet his eyes. Doesn't he know what we face?

My fairytale dream has transformed into a dark nightmare with monsters lurking behind every stone threatening to devour the few remnants of my life left behind.

Against my will, my hands circle the lasso, and my right arm slings it over the head of the bell cow. Then, Gypsy leads the cow up the hill toward the barn, prompting the rest of the cows to follow. I'm drug along for the ride, as empty-brained one of the cows.

"You take care of the milking and see if Ian can manage finding and collecting the chickens and maybe some eggs." Buck's voice sounds more like a retuning echo as if through a tin can along a string.

I nod dumbly. In some distant, watchful place, I'm aware he's baiting me, wanting me to argue back and demand he do his chores, but words won't form in my mouth, and I have no strength for a fight, so I ride past him without reaction.

Ian stands perched in the barn doorway waving when Gypsy returns me to the cow's pen. "Fin! Fin!"

My limp hand raises in reply.

"Mani's back! He brought some people from the village."

A square-shouldered older woman with a fierce scowl steps from the barn and stands behind Ian with her arms circling his shoulders. Two hefty men, one closer to Pa's age and the other more the age of the woman, stride from the barn carrying shovels.

Mani bolts from the barn and races to Gypsy's side. "See? I told ya. People come to help kin of Mister Clay and Missus Fiona."

Straining to find my voice, I croak, "I see."

"Come. Come." Mani tugs on my leg.

I stare blankly at the cows. "I should put the cows in the pen." I make no move to dismount.

"Them *kino* cows find their way. Come." He tugs again.

This time, I swing my leg over Gypsy and land with a thud on the packed earth, but my knees betray me, and I crumple in a heap. Sudden, hot tears flood my eyes as one of the prowling monsters bears down on my chest and grabs my throat in its clawed hands.

Mani jumps to my side, but I wave him away.

Time grinds to a halt. Garbled, unintelligible noises vibrate the air near my ears. Shapes move like spectres through a night mist. Soft, fleshy hands press my arms until I'm lifted into the air like a magician's trick to float into a stuffy semi-darkness where I'm deposited gently on a pallet of stiff hay. A cool, moist cloth slides across my cheek onto my forehead and lies draped over my eyes, blessedly blocking out all vision and thought. For a moment, I'm no one and nowhere. Perhaps I will sleep and never wake up.

Distant scraping noises invade my daze. A whiff of smoke. Voices chatter like cackling chickens.

No, that is definitely smoke. A wash of cold panic skitters across my flesh. Is the barn burning? Ian. Where is Ian?

"Ian!"

Ian's soft breath caresses my ear, and his gentle voice lilts like birdsong. "I'm here, Fin. I'm not going to leave you."

My words rasp in my throat. "Fire. Get out."

He pats my hand. "All is well, Fin. Missus Ata is cooking eggs and flatbread for us. She says it's called *takakau*."

My breath, frozen in my chest, releases in a gush.

"Can you get up? The food is almost ready."

I push myself to a sitting position, but a wave of dizziness clouds my vision, so I don't go further. I drop my chin to my chest and cradle my head.

"Don't worry, Fin. I'll bring it to you." Ian starts to rise, but I grab his arm.

"Don't leave."

Without a word, Ian sits down beside me, holding my hand like Ma used to when we were sick. My tears threaten to flow again.

Minutes tick by. The smells from the cookfire fill the barn. Outside, Buck returns from the fields. Mani and he are laughing together.

Laughing.

A seething rage bubbles in my stomach, turning into a tornadic fury when Buck bursts into the barn as if all is right with the world. "Come on, lazy bones. Are you gonna eat or should I finish your portion for you?" He stares at me, blinking, with his mouth cranked sideways. "Hey. What's wrong with you?"

I grit my teeth and hiss, "Get out."

Buck smirks and shrugs his shoulders. "More for me."

"Stop it, Buck." Ian's whisper is barely audible, but the edge in his tone is unmistakable. "Just stop."

"What? I ain't done nothing to him." He cranes his neck and peers into the darkness. "Are you crying?" Shaking his head, he folds his arms. "Don't be such a baby." He juts his chin. "Crying ain't gonna bring them back."

Ian must sense my body tensing because he presses hard on my shoulder. "You want to act like the tough guy, but I know you, Buck. You're running away, that's what you're doing. It's what you always do." Ian tosses his head and swipes his hand toward Buck. "You're calling out Fin for crying because you know you're too weak to let yourself feel the pain. Like Ma always said, 'Judgment going in is the judgment that goes out.'"

"Shut up. What do you know?"

Without thought, I leap from the pallet and run like a bull head first into Buck's chest. He slams onto the dirt with an "Oomph," but he doesn't have a second to recover his breath before I'm on him, my fists making mush of his face. All the rage, hurt, and terror pour out of me with each strike. Blood spurts from his nose and runs across his cheek into his ear, which infuriates me even more. I grab his shoulders, lift him slightly, and pound the back of his head into the ground.

"Stop! Stop it! Fin! Stop. You're killing him."

Ian's cry pierces the boiling red cloud engulfing me. I sit back on my haunches, gasping in mouthfuls of air and admiring my work.

Then, Buck begins to weep, and my heart cracks open like an egg. I can't look at him. Pushing my way to my feet, I sweep out of the barn, leaving Ian to dab Buck's ruined face with the cloth Missus Ata used to soothe my brow.

Mani stares at my bloodied hands as I stride toward the cookfire. "Where blood from?" He glances toward the open barn door.

"He got what he deserved."

Mani's eyes narrow. "You fight, with Buck?"

I don't answer.

"Must *not* fight." Mani lifts his head high. "This land now *tapu*. Sacred land. You fight, spill blood, you dishonor ancestors. Much bad."

Mani's words bring me up short. Dishonor Ma and Pa? Did I? I close my eyes, wincing. I know what Pa would say—that I'm the eldest and must set an example for the others. And Ma would be awful disappointed if she'd seen what I did.

Pa always called caring for the land a sacred trust. But now, it's more. It's the place where Ma and Pa are buried. Mani's right. The land itself is sacred now.

What have I done?

I spin on my heel and run back to the barn. Buck is still crying, bloody snot running from his nose, and Ian continues to try to comfort him, but when he sees me coming, Buck's eyes glow white in the darkness.

I drop to my knees beside him, showing him my open hands to calm his fears. "I won't hurt you again." I take the now-blooded cloth from Ian. "Here, let me wash this."

I race out to the water trough where Mister Ata has drawn water for the cooking, and dip the cloth, squeezing the blood from it. Running back to Buck, I press the cool cloth against his swelling nose and gently squeeze it to try and stop the blood. "I'm sorry, Buck. I am truly sorry." Closing my eyes, I shake my head. "I don't know what happened. Everything turned red, and I—lost my mind."

Buck's ragged inhale and snuffles are his only replies.

Lowering my voice, I lean close to my brother. "Mani says this land is sacred now. *Tapu.* Ma and Pa rest here, and we must show them the respect and honor they deserve. Always." I drape my arm over Buck's shoulders. "We can't fight anymore. Do you understand?"

Buck nods twice.

"We must act like they taught us to act. We must imitate them in everything we do. And we must love each other and defend each other, no matter what." I look from Buck to Ian. "Do you agree?"

"I agree," Ian whispers.

"Yeth." Buck's swollen lips muffle his reply, but his eyes aren't fearful. Now, they appear determined.

"Very well." I hug my brothers to my chest. "All of this is behind us. Never again. We are for each other, above all. Agreed?"

"Agreed."

"Yeth."

"It's what Ma and Pa would want." I squeeze their necks tighter for a second, then release them. "This is going to be a difficult—maybe impossible road. But if we don't have each other…if we don't stand together…we'll never make it."

Ian makes a fist. "Together!"

Buck envelops Ian's fist in his hand. I wrap my hands around the two and lift our joined hands high. "As one."

We sit in silence for several minutes. Images of Ma and Pa spin through my mind like a carousel, and with each passing memory, I make a vow to emulate what I see until Mani sticks his head in the door. "Ready for food?"

"Are you ready?" I look at my brothers in turn.

"I'm hungry, yeah." Ian leans his head against my chest.

"I could eat." Buck winces, touching his fingers to his lips. "I hope."

I stand and help the others to their feet. "Then, let's eat." I heave a deep sigh. "And afterward, we need to figure out what to do next."

Ian's wistful smile pinches my heart. "What would Ma and Pa do?"

"That's the right question." I close my eyes. "I pray we can find the answers."

Missus Ata hands each of us a piece of flatbread and scoops an egg onto it. "Eat." She waves us away, so we sit on a nearby stump, relishing the delicious bread. Mani squats on the ground nearby.

Mister Ata and the other, younger man dig through the rubble of our house, I suppose trying to find anything we could salvage. I thrust my chin toward the men. "I don't think they're going to find anything useful."

Buck raises his brows, then lowers his eyes. "They're looking for Ma and Pa."

Everything in me sinks into the hollowed pit in my stomach. I open my mouth but a choked groan is all that comes out. I turn away from the horrific scene, afraid I might see something I can never forget.

Missus Ata lumbers over to our perch. "*Haere mai. E haere ana mātau ki te kāinga.*"

"Missus Ata say we go to village."

Buck's mouth falls open, revealing a huge bite of bread. "We can't. We can't leave the animals." He shakes his head. "I'm staying here."

"Buck's right, Mani. We can't just leave the animals to fend for themselves. They're our responsibility."

"Missus Ata say boys cannot stay alone."

I straighten my back and lift my head. "I'm fourteen. I can take care of the others."

"Missus Ata say must…" Mani hesitates, his brow furrowing as he chews his lower lip. "*Ngaro.* What word?" He wrinkles his nose, then giving up the search for the right word, he shrugs his shoulders.

"We appreciate her help and will be glad for anything she can do for us. But we must protect our land."

He sighs and digs his bare toes in the dirt. "Those *weriweri* men come back."

Buck stands from the stump with his legs spread and his fists balled. "I'm not afraid of those men."

Lifting one brow, Mani quirks his mouth. "Should."

"Our pa wouldn't want us to run away or let those men take our land." I rise to stand beside Buck. "He would tell us to stand strong."

"Mister Clay say if *weriweri* men come, Mani runs and hides." Mani cocks his head. "Say same to you."

"But that was when he and Ma were here to fight them. Now, I'm the man of the house, so I must be the one to take a stand."

Buck shoots a glance my way and mutters, "Not the only man of the house."

"We stand together as one." Ian lifts his fist in the air, a reminder of our pledge.

"That's right."

"Missus Ata not gonna like it." Mani shakes his head.

Buck crams the last of his bread in his mouth. "Let's show her we can handle it. Come on, Fin. We'll milk and feed the cows. Ian, can you handle the chickens?"

"I do it all the time."

"Right."

"Next, we need to set up a living space in the barn to meet Missus Ata's approval." I rub my hands together. "I guess we need to set aside a separate space for the animals somehow."

"We can use some of the wool to make beds."

I shake my head. "No, we need that wool to sell. We need some way to make money. Straw will do."

"What about the cellar?"

Ian's simple question sends a jolt through my body. "Oh my. I completely forgot about the cellar. I wonder if it survived the fire?"

Buck grins. "If it did, we have food. And a place to store crops when we bring them in."

"And a place to sleep," Ian adds.

"Let's go find out." I bolt toward the two men busily shoveling through the remains. "You, too, Mani!"

I'm still reticent to look for fear of seeing Ma's bones, but I approach the men close enough to be heard. "Mani, ask them if they've found doors leading down into the cellar."

After frowning momentarily, Mani blurts out a string of words I don't recognize. The men look at one another, then the younger replies. He and Mani exchange a few more sentences before Mani looks at me. "They have not seen."

"Of course not. They're not digging in the right place." Buck points. "The cellar is closer to the kitchen. Come on!"

We scramble through the wreckage to the area that used to be the kitchen, now just charred rubble. Buck pushes aside some broken logs and soot-encrusted stone. "It should be around here."

Ian, Mani, and I jump in to help move the debris littering the area until I find a metal handle attached to a small piece of scorched wood. I hold it up for the others to see. "It looks like the doors didn't make it."

"But maybe they blocked the fire from going down the stairs."

Buck groans and collapses to his knees.

"What is it?"

He raises his head. "I found the opening." His head slumps to his chest again.

Ian and I walk to his side, leaning over him to peer in the hole.

The stairs and the floor above collapsed into the cellar space, carrying a lot of burning debris. From the looks of it, the fire consumed everything in the cellar.

"Maybe some of the canned food survived?" Ian's brows pinch above his nose.

"I think they would've exploded in the heat." I glance toward Buck. "Which means we're starting from scratch."

"And it doesn't solve the problem of where we're gonna sleep."

Mani, lingering beyond the edge of the rubble, clears his throat. "Going to the village now maybe?"

Buck leaps to his feet, his fists clenched at his sides. "Those men have stolen everything from us. *Everything.*" The red staining his cheeks deepens and spreads down his throat. "I won't let them take Pa's land." He points at me. "And you know the second we leave, they'll swoop in like vultures and take it all—the land, the sheep, the cattle, the horses. We'll never be able to come back here." He shakes his head, his red hair tumbling into his eyes. "I won't, I tell ye."

"Then, it's back to our plan of sleeping in the barn and living off the land until we can bring in some crops." I brush my hands down the front of my pants. "We have much work to do. Let's get moving."

But Ian's eyes well until a tear slides down his cheek. "What if the men come back anyway? What do we do then?"

All our guns were in the house, so we have no weapons, no ammunition, nothing to defend ourselves beyond tools, and we can't very well face a rifle with a rake. "Would Mister Ata be willing to loan us a gun?"

Mani shakes his head, his eyes wide. "Mister Ata no give gun to you. Danger."

"Then, we'll buy one." I drape my arm across Ian's shoulders. "Don't worry. After we take care of the animals, we'll prepare some wool. Buck, you'll stay here with Ian, and I'll go into town, sell the wool, and use the money to buy a gun." I swivel my head to the men digging in the ashes. "I don't believe those men will return if the Māori are here. I'll ask Missus Ata if they will stay until I get back."

Buck sneers. "Better buy some food, too, or we're gonna starve."

I toss my head. "I know that."

Ian swipes his hand across his nose with a loud sniff. "I miss Ma and Pa."

My jaw clenches as I swallow hard, forcing the pain back down my throat into my gut. It lies heavy as a stone and as scalding as lye. "We can't think about that right now. Ma and Pa would tell us to focus on the task before us. Remember?"

Ian nods, but his tears continue to cut white streaks through the filth coating his cheeks.

Buck raises his eyes to the bright, cloudless sky. "There's a time to be born, and a time to die; a time to plant, and a time to pluck up that which is planted; a time to kill, and a time to heal; a time to break down, and a time to build up; a time to weep, and a time to laugh; a time to mourn, and a time to dance." He tilts his head, turning his fierce gaze to Ian, whose tears dry up as his wide eyes meet Buck's glare. "Now isn't the time to weep and mourn. And it isn't time to laugh and dance either." Buck's teeth grind, and the muscles in his jaw ripple like the pond's surface after we've thrown a rock into the water. "Now is the time to survive." He swings his gaze to me. "And the time to kill."

CHAPTER FOUR

October 1906

It takes us the better part of the day to prepare a bundle of wool to sell. Missus Ata's wrinkled face folds like a crumpled napkin when I tell her I'm heading to town, but she says nothing.

I sling the sack of wool over my back and mount Gypsy while Buck holds her reins. "Stay off the roads. Those men might be lying in wait for you." He shifts from one foot to the other and gnaws his lower lip. "You should let me go. I'm better in a fight."

I heave a sigh and grab the reins. "That won't matter much if they're carrying guns." Shrugging one shoulder, I lean down to his ear. "Don't let Ian out of your sight. He's near breaking."

Buck nods, then slaps Gypsy's haunches, who gallops across the familiar, vast expanse of our land toward the town.

I don't see any sign of the men along the way, but I follow Buck's advice and remain some distance from the road, keeping to the trees or scrub brush as much as possible until I reach the edge of town.

The packed earth of the main road glows red in the lowering sun as I take a deep breath, square my shoulders, and ride down the center of town as if I belong. I head straight for the dry goods store.

The man behind the counter lifts his head as I enter, his eyes narrowing as he examines my face and stares down at my dirty clothes, then meets my eye. He quirks his mouth. "You're one of them MacAlister boys?"

"Yessir."

A long breath rattles in his throat. "Where's your father?"

"My pa…" The words dry up in my mouth.

"Speak up, boy."

Something about him calling me a boy sparks the white-hot rage I have toward the men who killed my parents. "My pa is dead, and I ain't a boy." I lift the package of wool and sling it onto the counter. "I'm here to sell you some wool at a fair price."

The rosy color drains from the man's cheeks as his eyes widen. "Dead, you say?"

"What will you give me for the wool?"

The man moves slowly around the counter, places his beefy hand on my shoulder, and leans down in my face. His hot breath smells of smoked beef and stale beer. "What happened to your pa, son?"

His sudden quiet kindness douses the spark of rage, and I must swallow hard to keep tears from flowing. But I won't show weakness, not in this town, not ever. So, I fan the guttering flame, baring my teeth as I spit, "Some men rode out to challenge Pa, but Pa put them in their place. That night, the cowards came back and set fire to our house." I toss my head. "Do you want my wool or not?"

"What about your mother?"

I shook my head, unable to speak the words without losing my resolve.

Slowly, the man rises, his eyes glazing as he stares out the store window—at what, I don't know. After a few moments, he shakes his head and mutters under his breath. "This is a bad business." He groans and presses his arm against my back. "Come on, son. We're going to pay a visit to the constable."

"What about my wool?"

"I'll buy your wool. But first, we must take care of something."

He ushers me from the store and down the street to a stone building on the next corner where we meet a burly, gray-haired man wearing a uniform. After a few whispered words exchanged between the two men, the constable shoves his hand in my face. "Constable Malcolm MacDougal at your service, young man. And ye are?"

His thick drawl reminds me of Ma, sending a wave of pain so sharp it causes my shoulders to slump. I grasp and shake his hand once as I'd seen Pa do a hundred times. "Findlay MacAlister."

Constable MacDougal's blue eyes sparkle. "I see the resemblance to your da in ye." The wrinkles across his brow deepen. "I'm sorrowful to hear of his passing. He were a good man." He motions for me to sit in front of his desk as he takes his seat and pulls out a pad and a pen. "I understand ye had an incident at your house that led to his death?" He raises his brows, poising his pen over the paper.

"Yessir. Several men on horseback rode out to our house yesterday. They were angry and accused Pa of siding with the Māori against the men wanting to buy Māori land. They had guns and threatened Ma and Pa. One man said he'd be back to take care of Pa." I swallow, my eyes trailing to the edge of the rough-hewn wooden desk. "That night, I woke up to the smell of smoke. That's when I heard the voices of at least two men outside. They were laughing and talking."

"What 'ere they saying?"

"I couldn't understand their words, but I heard them."

MacDougal nods. "Go ahead, son."

"The fire was already in our room, so I got my brothers out of there, and then I went to find my parents. But by then, the fire had spread everywhere, and I couldn't get to them. Mani tried…"

"Who is Mani?"

"Oh. Mani is the Māori boy who stays with us."

"I see." He makes a notation. "So, Mani also tried to rescue your parents?"

I nod. "He was there before I was, but he couldn't get in either."

"Then, Mani and ye got out of the house?"

"Barely. The fire spread toward the barn, so we worked together to stop the fire and save the barn and the animals."

The constable lowers his pen. "Ye were very brave."

I glimpse the man's gentle gaze and feel my tears threatening again. I blink them away. "Not brave enough."

He reaches out to pat my arm. "There's nothing more ye could've done, Findlay. The fire took them before ye could reach them." I pull back from his touch. He clears his throat. "Very well. Did ye recognize the men?"

"No, sir."

"Can ye describe them?"

I wince. "I was running across the yard to save Mani because one of the men was about to shoot him, so I didn't get a good look at them, except the one man who threatened Pa and the one who shot at Mani."

MacDougal lifts his brows. "One of them shot at the boy?"

"Yessir. He had thick, curly red hair. The other man's face was sunburned as if he worked outside, and he had a graying beard that looked like tumble thistle on his face."

"Tall? Short?"

"They were on their horses, so I couldn't tell." I shrug. "I'm sorry I can't tell you more."

"Ye are doing well." The constable sets his pen across the paper and folds his hands over it. "Now, Findlay, onto the business of who will care for ye and your brothers."

I straighten my back and lift my chin to meet the man's eyes. "I will care for them."

MacDougal squints his eyes and purses his lips. "No, son. I'm sure your da made provision for ye in case of such a tragedy." He stands and collects his pad. "We will speak with the banker. He will know your da's plans."

He grasps my arm, but I leap from the chair and dash toward the door. "You'll not take us from our land. I don't need no banker telling me what Pa wanted. He taught us our whole lives—protect each other and defend the land, and don't let no one take it from you. Ever. And I don't intend to."

"Wait, son…"

"I ain't your son!" I grab the knob just as the dry goods store owner grasps my shoulders in his sausage fingers.

"Hold on, there, now."

"Let me go!" Wrenching my back, I shove the man's rounded belly, but he wraps his thick, hairy arm across my chest. I writhe like a skink caught by its tail.

"Settle down. The constable's only trying to help you."

"I don't need anyone's help."

MacDougal towers before me, his broad chest filling my vision. "Findlay, ye may be in grave danger. How do you propose to protect your kin?"

I jut my bottom lip. "I'll buy a gun."

The shop owner chuckles, but MacDougal shakes his head. "No one will sell ye a gun, son. No one with any sense, that is. And how will ye feed them? What will ye do for money?"

"We know how to live off the land." I toss my head with a curl of my lip. "We don't need your help. And we don't want it." To emphasize my point, I spit a wad on his uniform.

"Ye be a feisty one, that's for sure and certain." The constable snatches my arm again. "But we'll be going to the bank, like it or not." With that, he drags me, kicking and yowling, out the door and down the street.

The bank towers above the other shops in the center of the town, stately and cold, with white stone walls, thick columns, and carved wooden double doors. Every few steps, the constable hisses, "Quit your yowling, boy," or some version of the sentiment, but as we enter the towering hall, I still myself. Ma wouldn't want me making a scene in so fancy a place as this.

Our footfalls echo across the marble floor like horse's hooves thumping on a hard-packed road. High tables staffed by silent workers line the corridor on either side. When we reach the end, MacDougal taps on a closed door.

"Come."

The constable swings the door inward, revealing a wood-paneled office and a balding, mustached man seated behind a large desk.

"*Kia hora*, Mister Williams." The constable holds out his hand.

The man behind the desk stands and shakes hands. "*Kia hora*, Constable. How may I help you today."

"This young man is the son of Clay MacAlister."

Mister Williams' eyebrows raise.

"He brings the sad news that his mother and father died in a fire on their station."

"I'm so sorry to hear that. Clay MacAlister was a good man."

"Indeed." After a moment of silence, MacDougal clears his throat. "Findlay here and his two brothers want to remain on the station, but I was hoping MacAlister made some kind of provision for his boys in an event such as this. Perhaps including contact information for a relative to care for the boys?" He shrugs one shoulder. "Did he leave instructions with ye?"

The banker rubs his hands together. "MacAlister has a deposit box and accounts at the bank. We can check his deposit box for a will or other documents, and his accounts list beneficiaries." He walks around the desk. "I will check on these things if you'll wait here."

After Williams leaves, I glare at the constable. "We don't have any relatives in New Zealand." I fold my arms across my chest. "And we don't need anyone to care for us."

"We'll see what Mister Williams finds." With that pronouncement, he sits in a small, rail-back chair that creaks in protest under his weight, but I remain standing, arms crossed and my back to the man.

Long minutes pass in stony silence. A wall clock ticks in beat with the pounding in my head, fuzzing my brain and confounding my attempts to plan an escape. Buck and Ian must be worried sick and starving by now, and I'm none too keen about riding the long path home in the dark with those men still ranging about, but the time marches relentlessly on.

My knees start trembling. This is taking too long. I must get home. MacDougal shifts his weight, and his chair groans, mirroring my frustration. My skin prickles and my feet shuffle until I'm propelled toward the door, just as Williams returns carrying a thick packet of documents.

The cold squeeze of dread grips my throat. Our fate might be outlined in those papers.

"Well…" Williams drops the papers on his desk. "As I expected. MacAlister planned for all eventualities." He taps the top document. "He has a signed last will and testament, a list of beneficiaries, a full accounting of his holdings, and a list of his relatives in the United States and their contact information. He designated his father and mother in Georgia as caregivers for the boys."

I don't wait for the rest, bolting from the stifling room, racing past the staring bank workers and clients, shoving through the double doors, and dashing down the steps to the street. I dart to the dry goods store where Gypsy waits tied to the rail.

What do I do about food? If I take the time to buy what we need, MacDougal could catch up to me and send us to America. But if I don't, what will Ian and Buck eat? And what about a gun?

I catch sight of MacDougal lumbering down the bank's steps out of the corner of my eye, so I swing my leg over Gypsy's back and gallop down the street toward home.

Home. At least for now.

I choose to keep to the road, despite the waning light and the constable's pursuit—better to get home quickly where we can all stand together—but I arrive without a weapon, without food, and with dire news.

Buck takes one look at my face as I ride up and blurts, "What happened?"

"We're in trouble. These men in town said Pa has a will that says we must go to America to live with our granda and granma. They're probably on their way now to get us."

Ian's face pales. "What'll we do?"

"I for one ain't gonna go." Buck brushes his hands on the front of his pants. "Where's the gun?"

"I didn't get it. The men wouldn't let me."

"The food?"

"I didn't have time to get anything."

Buck snorts in disgust. "So, all you accomplished is putting these men on our tail."

"Like you could've done any better." I jump from Gypsy's back. "I suggest you stop complaining and help me prepare for them."

I hurry to the barn and grab a pitchfork. Buck hefts a shovel on his shoulder, and Ian takes the shears. Looking around for a good hiding place, I point to the loft. "We could barricade ourselves up there."

"What good would that do us? They could wait us out, and we'd starve to death."

"You have a better idea?"

"Yeah." Buck swings his shovel in front of him like a sword. "Let's meet them head-on."

Ian's face blanches. "But they have guns."

"I don't think they'll shoot us. They want to send us to America, not kill us." Glancing around the barn, I gesture toward the bales of hay. "Those bales would make a good fort. We can ambush them from there."

"Good idea." Buck, Ian, and I drag and stack the bales in the field near the edge of the road leading to our house, arranging them to look haphazard while providing cover for our hideout. Then, we set up our makeshift weapons and wait.

The sun finishes its descent beneath the horizon and the last rays of golden light fade, leaving us in total darkness. Time drags by like a mud snail, but no sound of horses or sight of torchlight approaches from the west.

"I'm starving. What are we going to eat?" Ian squirms beside me.

"Quit your whining."

I poke Buck in the ribs with my elbow. "He's just a kid. Don't be so mean."

"You ain't my pa," Buck snarls.

"Besides, Ian's right. We must start thinking about food if we hope to survive, or those men will be right about us."

Buck heaves a great sigh. "But we can't leave our post."

"Maybe one of us should go to the Māori and ask for food?" Ian's pleading tone chafes like burlap clothes against my skin.

"And who would that be? You? You'd get lost in the dark. Fin? That leaves me alone to defend our land with a kid to protect."

"I'm not a kid."

Buck grunts his exasperation.

With as much authority as I can muster, in my best imitation of Pa, I lower my pitch and roar, "One problem at a time." When the other two quiet, I clear my throat. "We wait until morning. No one is going to starve to death before daylight. Then, if the men haven't come for us, we'll go to the Māori and ask for their help. They'll give us food and maybe even offer to defend us if the men do come." I caress my pitchfork like it's a security blanket. "In the meantime, we remember our pledge and stand together as one. No more arguing amongst ourselves."

"Buck…" Ian hurls Buck's name like an accusation.

Buck grumbles, "We stand together," under his breath.

"I mean it, both of you." Their wounded silence chastens me. "We're all tired and hungry—and grieving, most of all. So, let's not make things worse by taking it out on each other. We are all we have left." The truth of my words slams into my chest as if Buck had thrown a rock and hit me square on. Swallowing hard against the tears threatening to well up in my throat, I grip the pitchfork tighter. "I say we take turns sleeping so we don't all fall asleep at the same time. I'll take the first watch."

With a groan, Ian nestles alongside one of the bales.

"Wake me if you see anything." Buck grasps my shoulder and whispers, "I'm with you."

"I will."

As their breaths deepen and slow, the half-moon rises, its light glistening along the tops of the tall grass waving gently in the fields before me like always, as if everything is as it should be. But the blackened, broken beams, the piles of stones, charred wood, and cinders, and the silhouette of a half-standing chimney give lie to the grass's evening song.

Everything is not as it should be. And it never will be again.

CHAPTER FIVE

October 1906

Sunlight bathes my crusted-over eyelids in crimson too soon for my stiff neck and aching back, but I must set an example for my brothers, so I stand and stretch without complaint.

"No sign of the men." Buck, who took the last watch, leans against one of the bales chewing on a piece of hay, his shovel propped at his side.

I nudge Ian, who groans and rubs his puffy eyes with a huge yawn. "Come on, Ian. It's time to go to the Māori village."

He grasps his stomach. "Finally. Food."

We collect our things silently and hike to the Ata family's village. All our hopes lie with the people Pa sacrificed his life to defend. Why, then, does my heart pound in my throat and my stomach writhe like a *waitoreke* in a stoat's jaws?

What will we do if they refuse to help us?

As we mount the first rise, a sound like distant thunder and an approaching cloud of dust appears against the pale light of the early morning sky. Buck points. "They're coming for us."

"Get down."

We crouch in the tall grass and scramble over the hillock, lying out of the men's sight but still able to observe them as they reach the remains of our home. I recognize the constable, but the other two men with him I don't know—until the one wearing a brown bushman hat turns his face toward our hill.

Old thistle beard!

And he's in league with the constable.

They wander around the burnt ruins until they reach the barn, where two disappear. The constable continues onto the field, checking the paddock and the sheep pen. A faint call from the barn tells MacDougal we aren't inside.

The constable raises his hand to his brow and scans the area around our home. Pressing Ian's tousled blonde head into the thick grass, I whisper, "We must move." I eye the three men, waiting for them to look away. "Stay low and quiet. When you get to the bottom of the hill, run. Now!"

We slink the rest of the way down, careful not to stir up dust, then race toward the Māori at our best speed. Once I'm sure we're not being followed, I slow my pace, and Buck and Ian follow.

"We can never go back home now." Ian's sorrow wafts through his words like the low notes of a funeral dirge.

"That's not true." Buck's lip curls. "The men will see we're not there and leave. And when they come back, the Māori will be there to chase them away."

"You hope."

Buck's eyes widen and his mouth drops open. "And why wouldn't they, after all Pa has done for them?"

I shrug. "I hope they will, but the fact is, nothing is certain. Not yet."

"But they already fed us once," Ian protests.

"There's no guarantee they'll keep on feeding us."

Buck shoves me in the arm. "Now who's being a wet blanket?"

"I'm trying to be realistic is all." Ian's right. Discovering the constable in league with our attackers means we'll likely never go home again, so planting crops and selling wool to survive is off the table. That leaves the Māori or our grandparents. As our options are squeezed dry, I hold a thin thread of hope, but part of me is already resigned to living in America with strangers.

A wave of grief threatens to send me plummeting into deep waters to drown, but I can't let myself sink. Ian and Buck are my responsibility now. I tighten my jaw and lift my head as high as I can muster. "You're right. The Māori will help us. They must. They owe Pa."

We trudge the rest of the way in heavy silence.

As we reach the edge of the village, Mani scampers to greet us. "Good to come. Safe here." He leads us to the Ata's hut where Mister and Missus Ata welcome us, but their eyes appear wary, as if they already suspect I bear ill news.

Telling the Atas about our grandparents might land us on a boat across the ocean. "The men came back. And the constable was with them."

As Mani translates, the Atas exchange worried looks.

"We need your help. A temporary place to stay, food, and…" I pause, swallowing hard. "And help getting our home back."

When Mani finishes his translation, Mister Ata waves his arms and erupts in a stream of exclamations. Missus Ata shakes her head and barks a few words in reply. Mister Ata's fists ball at his sides.

I glance at Mani, my throat as tight as last year's pants. "What are they saying?"

"Mister Ata say no good fighting white lawman. Big trouble for Māori. Missus Ata say you only children, cannot fight alone."

"If we don't fight they will take our land, then they'll take back yours, the land Pa gave you." I clasp my hands before my chest. "Please help us as our pa helped you."

Missus Ata purses her lips. "*Me awhina tatou.*"

'Kahore," Mister Ata screams and marches from the hut.

"Mister Ata say no help." Mani squints and shrugs apologetically. "Risk great for the people. Little chance."

Buck roars his frustration. "After all Pa's done for them? They won't do nothing?"

"Must understand. Māori bad…um…*āhuatanga.* Great risk."

Tears brim in Ian's eyes, threatening to open the flood surging behind my throat. I choke them down. "Tell them we understand."

"I don't." Buck spits at Missus Ata's feet. "Traitors. Cowards. Forget you. We'll fight them on our own."

Mani grabs Buck's arm. "Missus Ata say you only children. Need help." He points to the moist spit wad shining in the light filtering through the open door. "Not fair."

Buck blinks, and his face reddens as he scuffs his toe in the dirt to cover his spit. "Sorry." His back straightens. "But you should help us."

Mani conveys Buck's apology; hopefully, better than Buck. Missus Ata nods. "Come. Food."

Ian breathes a sigh in relief. But her offer doesn't solve our problems, and we're down to one option. America.

I can't bring myself to say it to the others. Not yet.

We sit at a low table where Missus Ata spreads lamb, fruit, and *rewena* bread. Ian and Buck shove it in their mouths by the handfuls, but I barely manage a few bites. My stomach churns with the certainty of our fate. Not only that, but I must face the constable, knowing he's in cahoots with Ma and Pa's murderers, and beg him to contact our granda for us. The thought of that humiliation is more than I can bear.

"Eat." Missus Ata shovels more food onto my plate.

Not wanting to offend the Missus Ata, I force a hunk of bread into my mouth and chew slowly.

Through the mass of food in his mouth, Buck asks Mani, "Do you think the Atas will loan us weapons?"

"No weapon. Not safe."

"But we're not safe if those men come back. They could kill us."

"No go back."

Buck beats his fist on the wooden bench. "And just let them have our Pa's land, everything he worked and bled for?" Buck growls under his breath. "I won't do it."

"No choice." Mani shrugs. "Great sadness but true."

I heave a ragged sigh. "They're going to send us away, Mani. To America. We'll never see you again."

Mani's eyes widen. He murmurs a few words to Missus Ata, who shakes her head. Mani's mouth twists. "Nothing to stop *weriweri* men now. They take your land, our land, all land."

I slam my hands on the table. "Then why won't they fight with us? They'd be fighting for their land, too."

"Mister Ata fearing all Māori die. Like Mister Clay say Lakota die in America."

Buck's lip curls. "Better to die than to let them take your land. That's what Pa said."

"Die, they take land anyway." Mani opens his hands, palms up. "See? Cannot win against *weriweri* men."

My eyes trail down to my brogans under the Ata table, scuffed and dust-covered, with leather cracked along the sides and polish worn off on the toes and heels. How much longer will they last? How long before I'm walking barefoot through the brush?

Their condition accuses me. I've taken so many things for granted. Ma. Pa. How hard they worked. Everything they provided for us. It didn't cross my mind that if I ruined my shoes, I might never get another pair. I never woke up wondering if I would have food to eat, clothes to wear, or a roof over my head. I've wasted so much of my life on foolish games and childish whims while everything precious slipped through my fingers. I can never get it back. Never.

I push away from the table and plod from the hut onto the packed dirt of the central village square, watching my shoes with every step. Each contact with the earth shaves a few precious leather flakes from the sole. Each drag of my toe scrapes off another layer of polish.

No matter what I do or where I turn, all that's left to me is loss.

Rapid footfalls patter the dirt behind me.

"Where are you going?" Ian's question bites into my skin like Pa's razor. Where indeed?

"We gonna go back and fight those *weriweri* men?"

I skid to a stop and twirl to face Buck "With what exactly? Shovels and pitchforks?" I shove him in the chest with both hands, and he stumbles backwards and falls with a thump. "Grow up, Buck."

His eyes blaze as he scrambles to his feet and charges at me like a bull, his fists ramming me like horns. "Yiiiii!"

Now, I'm on my back, flailing side to side as his arms pummel my face, arms, and chest.

"Stop it! Stop!" Ian yanks Buck's shirt, and the sound of tearing cloth sends burning liquid into the back of my throat. "You're hurting him." Finally, Ian manages to pull Buck off me. "We stand together. Remember?"

Buck huffs, brushes the dirt off his hands, and stalks away.

"Are you injured?" Ian's grubby fingers paw at my face until I brush them away.

"Leave me alone."

I regret my words when Ian's huge, watery eyes fill my vision. He needs to grow up, too. He's not a baby anymore.

Closing my eyes against his hurt, I push myself up, lean down to check the condition of my shoes, then wipe dust from my clothes and march toward home.

Ian tugs my hand. "Where are you going?"

"We have no choice." If I say it… "Never mind. I'm going home."

"Where's Buck going?"

"I don't know. And I don't care."

"But we must stand together. We are all we have. You said so."

I blow out a heavy breath. "I did. But I can't change Buck. Ma always said he was wild as a buck rabbit." I stare at my shoes. "Poor Ma. We treated her terribly. We took her for granted. And now, there's no changing it."

"Ma loved us!" Ian's fierceness pulls me up short. I whip my head around as Ian hisses through his teeth, "Don't say that ever again."

Our eyes lock, his demanding a response. I imagine mine look as cold and hard as granite. "And now she's dead, and we're on our own, and Pa's will is sending us to America, and there's nothing we can do to stop it."

Ian's face collapses like tallow in the melting pot. His single sob sounds more like a dog's bark than a cry as tears gush down his cheeks. "Don't say that!'

"Well, it's the truth."

From the corner of my eye, I see Buck rushing toward me. "Leave Ian alone!"

"Oh, so I suppose now I'm the mean one. The bully. Not you."

"If the shoe fits."

My eyes glue to my scuffed shoes. They won't fit for long. "We have no choice now but to go to America." I've said it. Now, it's real.

"You're giving up? Without a fight?"

There's nothing more to say, so I turn on my heel and head toward home. If the men are still waiting for us, I'll tell the constable we'll agree to go. If not, I'll walk on to town and speak to him then.

I'm not concerned about Buck and Ian. They'll follow eventually. What choice do they have?

What choice do any of us have?

CHAPTER SIX

January 1907

The new year tightens the noose around my throat. MacDougal claims the last telegram promises my uncle's arrival any day now. Old Lady Appleton, who has kept us in her boarding house for the last three months at the constable's direction, has been fussing over us for days, demanding we bathe every day in case he should arrive. "I won't have anyone accusing me of not watching after you." I know the truth. Our Pa's gold has paid her handsomely for her "watching after."

Our Pa's gold has also paid for some clothes fit for travel and a new pair of shoes each.

I refuse to put them on.

To her credit, Missus Appleton has allowed us to walk to our land every day and care for the animals. We even bring eggs back to share with her other boarders. MacDougal promises, once he receives our uncle's approval, the animals will be sold and the proceeds given to our grandfather, but I trust him about as much as I trust a wolf guarding the sheep pen. He and those *weriweri* men perch around us like hawks circling before the kill. They'll have our land before the ship leaves the harbor.

I've still not let on that I know he's one of Pa's killers. That moment will have to wait.

I'm watching from the porch as Buck and Ian play in the yard when a carriage drives through the center of town, stopping before the constable's gray building. The man who steps from the carriage looks so much like Pa, I jump from the porch, screaming, "Pa!" before I have time to think.

Buck and Ian whirl around to see what's got me yelling. Quickly, I step between my brothers and the tall, red-haired man entering the constable's office to block their view so they won't go through the tumbling wave of feelings I just rode. Through clenched teeth, I whisper, "He's here."

"What are we gonna do?" Buck's eyes dart like mosquitoes in late summer.

Draping my arms across their shoulders, I herd them into the boarding house. "Pack your things in the sack Old Lady Appleton gave you. Then sit on your bed and wait for me. I'll come get you when it's time."

"Time for what?"

"Get on with you."

For once, Buck listens, and they scramble up the stairs. I race to the kitchen window with a good view of the corner and the constable's stone building and start packing all the food I can find—Missus Appleton's preserves and pickled vegetables, dried meats, and biscuits. I'm stealing, I suppose, but I believe Pa would forgive me.

When the constable steps onto the street with the young red-haired man on his heels, I hoist the sack of food and dart up the stairs.

"Get your bags. We're leaving."

"He's here?"

"Not yet." I eye the bedroom door. "Hurry."

Buck squints. "We're not going with him, are we?"

"Not if I can help it." I grab Ian's arm. "Come on."

"Where are we going?" Ian's face is pale with fear.

"Somewhere they won't think to look for us." I glance at my bed where my new clothes are folded neatly on the pillow with my unworn shoes carefully positioned on top. "Out the back way. Let's go."

We scamper down the stairs, keeping our footfalls light so as not to alert Missus Appleton, then race down the hall, through the kitchen, and out the back door. "This way." I scouted a route weeks ago, so Buck and Ian follow me through neighboring yards and down one lane side streets, ducking through hedges and jumping fences until we reach the outskirts of town. There, I dash to a stand of trees, and they follow, disappearing into the maze of trunks and underbrush.

We walk in the general direction of our land, staying off the main road. After a few minutes, Buck stops, his hands planted on his hips. "You're taking us home. That's the first place they'll look for us."

I growl under my breath. "Why don't you ever trust me, Buck?" Shaking my head, I face my obstinate brother, matching his stance. "We're going to free the animals. That's why we're going this way." I lean down and poke my finger at his nose. "I have a plan."

Buck raises his brows, then grins. "Freeing the animals will pluck Ol' MacDougal's tail feathers."

I return his grin. "That's the idea."

An uncharacteristically cool breeze carries the earthy, pungent aroma of approaching rain. God must be on our side. A good storm will slow the men down. No carriage can negotiate the path to our home when it's thick mud.

"Let's hurry and see if we can get there before the rain starts."

This time, I get no argument from Buck. I forge the now-familiar path through the trees with my brothers on my heels until we reach the open field marking the outer edge of our land. Then, we sprint full speed to the charred ruins of our home, the graves of our parents, and the barn where our animals are penned.

Buck pulls wide the barn doors while I open the stalls, and Ian runs to the pen to release the sheep. Once the cows and horses are out of the barn, Buck darts to the chicken coop to scatter the hens while Ian gathers the eggs, stuffing them in the bag with his clothes.

"We need to tear down part of the fence and herd them to freedom." I grab Gypsy's mane. "I'll ride Gypsy to lead the horses. Then, I'll take care of the cows. Ian, you get the sheep. Buck, you break down the fence."

"Got it." Buck rushes to the closest section of fencing. Ian starts his strange dance to herd the sheep, and the horses follow me riding their leader, Gypsy, without hesitation. By the time the animals reach Buck, the fence is destroyed. They move through the opening and scatter across the broad plains beyond.

I spin Gypsy around to gather the cows as distant thunder rumbles from beyond the mountains. Buck follows me to try to shoo the chickens toward the opening, but they prove more difficult. "They keep running in circles."

"Keep trying." The cows don't give me as much trouble as the chickens, but they're unpredictable and much slower than the horses, and time is running out. I should've had Buck ride one of the other horses to keep them in line. Too late now.

"Come on, you stupid cows. Hiya!"

Buck must hear the frustration in my voice, because he abandons the chickens and takes a position alongside the line of cows, slapping rumps and clapping his hands to keep them moving.

Once all the animals—minus the chickens—are on the open plains, I gallop Gypsy through them, pushing them farther from our land and closer to the ridge of mountains. I want them far away by the time the *weriweri* men come to retrieve them.

A metallic bite on the wind tells me the storm is close. I call to Buck and Ian with a sharp whistle, as we used to do when working in the fields, and we meet at the destroyed fence.

"This will have to do." I dismount and slap Gypsy's hindquarters sending her galloping to rejoin her herd. Buck, Ian, and I watch the animals for a few moments as they move slowly across the plains to disappear into the approaching gray sheet of rain.

A deep, piercing pang of regret stabs my chest, but I don't let on. "Now for the second part of the plan. Come on."

I lead my brothers back across our land, past the remnants of our home, and through the fields beyond, going in the direction of the Māori village. But before we reach the village, I veer off to the right.

"We aren't going to the village?" Ian glances longingly toward the Māori encampment. "Where are we going?"

"You'll see."

I lead them deeper into the bush. After a long hike through scrub and rolling hills, we cross a wide, shallow river with a rocky bed, then the land steadily rises as we get closer to the mountains. A mist of rain starts to fall on us. As we approach a large patch of evergreens near the base of the range, Mani appears, waving his arms.

"Here! Come! Come!"

Buck's eyes widen. "What's Mani doing here?"

"Mani agreed to help us. He's been staying out here for the last two weeks, setting things up." I wave at Mani. "*Teina*!"

We sprint the final distance to the tree line. Mani embraces each of us, then leads us into the dense forest. Thankfully, the intertwined limbs help keep us from getting soaked to the skin. After some time, we reach a clearing where Mani has set up a makeshift shelter, a tarpaulin to gather rainwater, a stack of firewood, and a bed of stones for a fire. He's even dug a hole behind a large tree for a privy.

"See? I make new home for family."

"This is perfect, Mani. Thank you." I wrap my arm around his head in a fierce hug. "You're the best." His giggles are muffled in my grasp.

Buck wanders across the clearing, his mouth hanging open. "How did you…where did you get all this stuff?"

"Borrow from Missus Ata and others in village. All want to help."

"That was very kind of them." Ian's gentle smile warms my heart. It's the first time I've seen him smile in three months.

The shelter is constructed using four standing wooden planks with stitched animal skins stretched across them and hanging down to form an enclosure. The skins are gathered and tied to a large tree limb at the top to prevent rain from collecting and causing the shelter to collapse.

"Let's put our things away before the storm comes in earnest." I carry the food supplies into the shelter while Buck and Ian bring their clothing bags and drop them next to the back wall.

Inside the shelter, Mani has a tarp spread on the ground and four pallets made of leaves, straw, and blankets. He also brought additional supplies stacked in one corner including more food, extra blankets, and some Māori clothes. "All things needed for living." The young Māori beams a toothy smile. "The people help with supply. Mani carries from village. No need ya ever return. No risk getting caught to be sent far away. No need ever fight those *weriweri* men."

"Thank you, Mani. And please thank the Māori."

"Village on land given by Mister Clay. Māori remember always."

Once we have everything stowed away, we put some dried meat on Māori flat bread and nestle on our mats to wait out the storm.

The wind picks up, rustling the sides of our shelter. I glance toward Mani, concerned, but he waves his hand. "Wood dug in deep. No worry."

Then, the bottom falls out. Rain pelts the animal skins, but the design works perfectly as the water flows in sheets down the sides, and we remain dry.

The storm lasts a couple of hours, but once it passes, Mani and I scour the area for more wood, knowing it may take days for it to dry.

"I run to town, see what white lawman and *weriweri* men are up to. Be back before sun fall."

"Mani, I'm not sure that's a good idea. They might follow you here."

Mani belts out a laugh. "*Weriweri* men slow, and poor trackers. They not catch Manaaki."

"Very well. But hurry back."

"Quick like lightning."

Mani bolts toward town as I pull back the flap and return to my brothers. Now that the running is over, my limbs feel like they've been battered by the storm. Buck and Ian seem worn out, too, as they crouch on their pallets, as silent as house mice.

I settle beside them. "Mani went to scout in town. He'll be back before nightfall."

Buck nods once. Ian's glassy eyes stare at nothing.

"Do you want something else to eat?"

Buck shakes his head, but once again, Ian doesn't respond.

I shrug and stretch out on my mat.

After a long silence, Buck breaks the heavy silence. "I don't know how you pulled this off…" He turns his eyes to meet mine. "But I'm forever grateful to you."

"Mani did most of the work."

"But this was your idea, I'll wager." Buck looks around the small shelter. "You know, we could have a good life here. Maybe, one day, once they stop looking for us, we could build a real cabin here. Maybe find our animals again."

I suck in a deep breath and blow it out. "One step at a time, Buck." I close my eyes. "One step at a time."

As promised, Mani returns as the sun slips behind the trees and the sky tints a soft rose. "Brother of Mister Clay very much mad, blames white lawman." Mani grins. "White lawman makes all *weriweri* men search for ya. Very mad to find horses gone." Mani shakes his head. "Whoa, I tell ya, white lawman boil like steam from hot spring, yelling at Missus Appleton, at chickens, at Māori, not matter." Mani twists his face into a mask of rage, pretends to yell, gestures with his hands, and thrusts his finger at imaginary people.

Buck throws his head back, laughing. "I wish I could've seen it."

"What did the Māori say to the white lawman?"

Mani chuckles. "Māori act like, who? What children? I never see no children."

"And he couldn't find our animals?"

Mani shakes his head and holds his hands open wide. "All empty fields."

Buck jumps up, rubbing his hands together. "What do you say we build a fire and cook some of that good Māori food to celebrate?"

"No fire. Not tonight while they're out looking. The last thing we need is for the smoke to lead them right to us."

Buck wrinkles his nose but bobs his head in agreement. "I guess it's cold meat, then."

While we munch on cold meat and hard biscuits slathered with preserves, I mull over each moment of the day, scouring my memory for any possible mistakes, missteps, or flaws in my plan. The next few days are critical. If they don't find us by then, maybe our uncle will go back to America, and the constable will give up. Maybe Buck's right, and we can build ourselves a cabin, collect the horses and cows, and make a good life here.

But if they find us, we're liable to take a beating, and they surely won't give us another chance to run away.

We must be careful and make no mistakes. Our future depends on it.

CHAPTER SEVEN

January 1907

The next day dawns bright and clear, and our moods match the weather. We haven't heard approaching searchers or seen any signs of the *weriweri* men roaming nearby, so we decide to risk a small fire to cook some of our eggs.

The wet wood means a lot of smoke, but I'm hoping the bright sunlight and distance from any settlements will protect us from being spotted. Still, as soon as the eggs are done, I douse the fire.

Buck and Ian are getting antsy sitting all morning in the shelter, so I send them out to collect berries and more firewood. "Don't range too far, though. And stay in the trees!"

Mani decides to return to the Māori village for the latest update, leaving me alone with my thoughts and concerns. The hardest part of all this is relying on Mani for all our information. It's too risky for one of us to sneak into town, to the Māori village, or onto our land. The constable will have lookouts posted at all the likely places, and even if they don't spot us, they could easily follow our tracks, particularly if we are running to avoid detection.

At the same time, I'm worried sick one of those *weriweri* men will remember Mani from the shooting and follow him straight here. Mani's smart and familiar with the ways of the bush, but he's young and tends to be impulsive. Like so many things in our lives right now, we have no choice but to trust him.

The biggest question is what next? Best case, we're left alone and can stay here, but how long will the Māori continue to provide us with food? We can't rely on them forever. Planting season is quickly passing by, and our sheep have already been shorn for the season. All the wool we gathered is in the barn—unless, of course, the constable's men have stolen it by now. Either way, we can't get to it or sell it.

All I bought us was some time. Ian and Buck are relying on me to devise a plan, but I'm as lost as a kiwi in the daylight. Boy, how I wish I could ask Pa what to do.

A distant scream jars me from my contemplations. I'm on my feet quicker than a pistol shot, running toward the noise. I'm afraid to call out. What if someone is close by and hears?

Then, Buck cries, "Help! Help!"

No more need for caution. "Buck! Where are you?"

"Over here!"

"Keep calling. I'm coming to you."

"Hurry. Ian is hurt."

My throat closes as if I've tried to swallow a stone. "How bad?"

No reply.

"Buck?"

"Bad. It's real bad."

Through the thick branches, I see a pale glimmer, like someone or something waving in the breeze and catching the sunlight. I dive through the underbrush in a beeline toward the movement.

Sure enough, I come upon Buck hovering over Ian, who lies on his back clutching his left arm. A smear of dark red on his shirt sends my heart racing.

"Ian!" I skid to my knees next to his prone body and paw over his head, neck, and chest.

"My arm's broke," he whimpers through brimming tears.

"How bad?"

Buck whispers in my ear. "I think the bone broke the skin."

A wave of dizziness and nausea forces my head between my knees.

"What are we going to do now?"

I close my eyes. A rumbling moan begins deep in my gut, rising slowly until it becomes a blood-curdling howl.

Ian bursts into tears. "I'm sorry, Fin. I'm sorry."

"Don't cry. I'm not mad at you." Breathe. Ian didn't get hurt on purpose. He's a kid. "Buck, what happened?"

"Ian was climbing this *feijoa* tree—the fruit was ripe for the picking—and he…"

"He what?"

Buck's eyes widen as he stares at me like someone face-to-face with a drawn weapon.

"Did you put him up to this?"

"No…I…"

"Whose idea was it?"

Buck's brows furrow. "Well, mine, but I'm too big to climb those branches, and Ian…"

"You hair-brained *porangi*! You didn't think we might need to be extra careful since we have no adults to help us?" My rage explodes like a geyser, and before I can think, I swing my fist and pop Buck across the side of his head, screaming, "You've ruined everything!" Buck twists like a coiled rope and falls, landing on poor Ian.

Ian shrieks in agony.

"Oh, no. Oh. Sorry. Sorry, Ian, I didn't mean…" I pat his shoulder, trying to calm him.

His sobs grow louder.

I snarl at Buck. "You stay here and keep him still. Do you think you can manage that?"

"Yes, but where…"

"I'm going to get help."

"You can't! You'll be seen!"

I poke my finger in Buck's chest. "You should've thought of that before."

'Where will you go?"

"The Māori. They'll know what to do."

Without another word or glance Buck's way, I vault into the trees, crashing through the brush toward the Māori village. I don't have time for caution or stealth. If I'm discovered, I'll send someone for Ian—either way, he'll get the help he needs.

Of course, Buck found a way to ruin my careful plans. He barrels through life like a rabid bull, destroying everything he touches, making problems for everyone else, and expecting others to clean up his messes. Now, we have no choice. We're going to end up stuck on some wee farm in America, living with people we've never met, probably sleeping in some outhouse and being forced into slavery as farm hands—or worse, spending the rest of our lives waiting on some crochety old folks.

I'll never forgive him for this. Never.

Mani must've seen me coming because he meets me at the edge of the village. "Why you come here? *Weriweri* men see you."

"I don't have a choice. Ian is hurt. He fell and broke his arm." Seething anger bubbles in my stomach. "It's bad. We need help."

Without a word, Mani scampers off to find Missus Ata. I weave my way between the huts, scanning the area for a lookout from town, but I see no one. As I approach the Ata's home, she walks out, carrying a bundle under her arm.

"Come. Quick." Mani pulls my arm, and we follow Missus Ata across the field and into the woods, where I lead her to Ian.

Buck paces beside Ian, wringing his hands while Ian moans and whimpers. Missus Ata opens her bundle, pulling out cloths, some kind of ointment, a small board, and some needle and thread.

"Shouldn't we take him to a doctor?" Buck eyes Missus Ata's bundle.

"Missus Ata is great healer. She fix up, real good." Mani beams. "No worry!"

As the Māori woman takes Ian's arm, she flicks her wrist and yanks, and the bone sticking through his skin snaps back, straightening the arm. Ian squeals like a hungry pig.

"*Noho*!" Missus Ata barks

Mani cocks his head. "She say to sit still."

Ian's whimpering starts up again, scraping like cat's claws across my skin. I can't even look at Buck, who feigns remorse and concern. He's never felt sorry for anything he's done in his life, and this won't be his first time.

Missus Ata brings out the needle and thread, and after smearing the ointment in the wound, she sews Ian's arm closed like she's making a new dress. Ian screams with every stab of the needle. Then, she sets the board behind his arm and wraps both tightly. Finally, she makes a sling out of some cloths, pointing and gesturing to Ian that he must leave it on.

"*Ngā mihi,* Missus Ata."

With a solemn stare, she nods once, then collects her things and leaves for her village.

"What now?" Buck's voice sends the hairs on the back of my neck to standing. I ignore him.

"Can you stand?" I reach down for Ian's good arm.

"It hurts really bad." Ian's scrunched up face fuels my anger with Buck. "I can't."

"Here, let me help you."

I take his arm, but he screeches, "No! I wanna go *home.*" His cry bounces among the tree trunks, echoing like tiny bells ringing.

"Come on, Ian. Tough it out."

As deliberate as a spider coming for a fly trapped in its web, I turn to Ian "You shut your mouth." My threatening tone silences even Ian's whimpers.

"He's acting like a baby."

"I said, shut up."

"Pa would tell him the same thing."

A red fire bursts over my eyes, and the next thing I know, Buck is on his back, his nose is bleeding, his cheek is bright red, and my fingers are around his throat. In a distant part of my mind Ian's muffled cries sound like someone talking through one of those new-fangled telephones.

Mani tugs on my shoulder. "You are killing him. Stop!"

I stand to the side, as if I'm watching myself choke Buck, knowing Mani is right. But my hands refuse to relent. Instead, I shake him, pounding his head against the packed earth.

Mani launches himself against my back, and he and I tumble away from Ian and Buck in a tangle of limbs. I rear back, my fist clenched, ready to strike. But Mani cringes, squeezes his eyes closed, and blocks his face with his hands as if I'm some kind of monster—as if he's afraid of me. A sickening wave of shame rolls over me until I'm drowning in it. I can't breathe. Lurching sideways onto my knees, I lean over and vomit until nothing but burning yellow liquid comes out.

I cover my face with my hands. What would Pa say if he saw the wreckage I left of my family strewn across the forest floor—Ian badly injured, Buck bruised and beaten, Mani scared out of his wits. I *am* a monster.

I can't meet Buck's eyes. "Take Ian to town." My throat rasps like Pa dragging a hand plow across rocky ground. "Go straight to the Constable and ask for our uncle. Have him take Ian to a doctor. Go." I don't wait to see if Buck complies or respond to his barrage of questions. Dragging myself to my feet, I stumble into the woods, letting the branches whip my face, neck, chest, and back. The more scrapes the better. It's the least I deserve.

The little shelter Mani built for us stands like a silent accusation. After all he did to help us…I repay him by threatening him. I stare at my still-bloody fist.

Monster.

And the plan—*my* plan—now in shambles, seems foolhardy in retrospect. It never had a spit's worth of a chance at saving us. Why couldn't I see it?

A monster *and* a fool.

Everything is destroyed. Pa's precious land is lost. Mani will be left as an orphan again. Who knows if Ian will recover. My brothers may never forgive me, and I can't blame them for it. My uncle will hate me for the humiliation I put him through.

I've failed at everything I've tried.

I collect the bags of clothing, including the Māori *maro* Mani brought for us, and sling them over my back. Their weight is nothing compared to the burden of shame I carry. I gather the food we took from Missus Appleton. At least, I can make amends for that thievery and return her goods. I'll tell Mani to get the food the Māori donated and give it back to the village—if he ever speaks to me again.

We don't need it anymore.

The light seeping through the tent's opening pierces my swollen eyes like flaming arrows, as if God punishes me for my transgressions. He should keep burning until I'm reduced to ashes. I deserve His wrath.

I reach for the flap, but my feet stick to the ground tarp as if it's covered in glue. They refuse to step from the shelter. It's like when I said Ma and Pa are dead out loud for the first time. If I walk out, leaving our home forever becomes real.

America. Buck and Ian don't remember it, but I do. I remember it as the place a dark cloud hung over our family, Pa would disappear for weeks and was miserably sad when he returned, and Ma threatened to leave Pa if he didn't take us away from that place. And now, we're forced to go back.

The nausea threatens to rise back up, so I shrug my packages higher onto my back, lower my head, force my tortured body through the shelter's opening, and march from the forest into the scalding midday sun.

Never to return.

CHAPTER EIGHT

January 1907

"I beg your forgiveness, Missus Appleton. I know it were wrong to take food from your pantry. You took such good care of us these past few months, and I repaid you by stealing from you. I'm deeply sorry." I deposit the sack of food at her feet. "We ate some of it, so as soon as I get money from the bank, I will repay you for the rest."

The deep lines on Missus Appleton's face remind me of Pa's maps of the trails through Wyoming and Montana. She folds her arms across her chest with a scowl. "Young man, I could have the Constable arrest you."

"I know, ma'am, and I wouldn't blame you if you did."

"Didn't your parents teach you, 'Thou shalt not steal'?"

"Yes, ma'am, they did."

She huffs and shakes her head. "You had us all worried sick, not knowing where you had gone."

"I know, ma'am. It were terrible wrong of me."

Her lips press into a thin line with a fan of wrinkles like a spider's web surrounding them. "Well then. I suppose all is forgiven since you've come back." She shakes her finger in my face. "But I hear little Ian was hurt because of your shenanigans. I hope you've learned a lesson from all this."

"Yes, ma'am. I have."

"Very well." She heaves the sack from the porch and carries it through the front door. "Best go find your uncle."

"Yes, ma'am." She slams the door in my face.

One humiliation down, two more to go. I drag my remaining bundles down the main street toward the Constable's office, watching the dust collect on my shoes until they're coated in gray.

Buck sits slumped in a corner chair, his face a mottled purple and red and his eyes swollen almost shut. If I weren't ashamed, I might laugh out loud, he makes such a comical figure. But his wounds scream accusations against me like a thousand knives slicing my chest.

He doesn't even look up when I walk in, which may be the worst knife of all.

MacDougal doesn't greet me. He doesn't say anything but grabs my arm and yanks me down the hall to his office, where the young red-haired man I assume is my uncle perches on the corner of the desk. His arms are folded, and one booted foot swings gently while the other taps the floor as if he's listening to a lively tune. A half-smile blossoms on his face when MacDougal shoves me toward the man.

"Aren't you a sight?" His blue eyes twinkle.

What do I say to that? "I…"

"May I have a few minutes alone with my nephew?" The man lifts a single brow and purses his lips, changing his request to a demand.

"Of course." The Constable mutters under his breath as he strides from the room like a petulant child being punished.

My uncle chuckles and shakes his head as MacDougal slams the door. "You've surely made an enemy of that man by making him look the incompetent fool he is. Findlay, right? I'm your Uncle Bear." He reaches his hand to shake mine, but I keep my hands shoved in my pockets.

"He was already my enemy," I mutter to myself.

"Here, now, let me look at you." He grasps my shoulders. "You are the spitting image of your Ma, like Ian. You both got her dark hair and eyes." He sighs gently. "Buck, on the other hand, from what I can tell, caught your pa's features." He chuckles again. "And his spirit, I'd say."

If he thinks I don't have my pa's spirit, he's mistaken. For the first time, I lift my eyes to meet his, giving him my best fiery glare.

But his eyes are soft, warm and caring like Pa's eyes when he looked at Ma. Everything inside me sags like melting butter. It's as if I've been sent back in time to meet Pa as a young man.

"I can't imagine how difficult all this has been for you. I would've probably run away, too, in your shoes."

My shoes. My battered, filthy shoes.

"But you're not alone anymore. You've got a huge family full of love with arms open, ready to bring you home."

My back stiffens. "This is my home."

"To a new home, then."

The words, "I don't need a new home," dance on my lips, but I gnaw them back into my mouth and swallow them down my throat. The truth is, I've proven I can't handle it on my own. I need them. These words taste bitter in my mouth.

"Where will we live?"

"Clay wanted you to live with my parents, your granda and granma." He beams a huge smile. "You'll love them."

I doubt it. Two crotchety old people don't sound pleasant. "Where do they live?"

"They have a large plot of land in the northern part of Georgia."

I breathe a shallow sigh of relief. At least it's not Montana. "Where do *you* live?"

"I live in California. That's why they sent me to fetch you home. I was nearest to you."

"What's going to happen to our land?"

Uncle Bear lifts his brows and nods his head. "I understand that's important to you. Your pa taught you what our pa taught us: value your land and don't let anyone take it from you." He presses his lips together. "Well, don't worry your head about it. We'll make sure your land remains in your names, and when you're grown, if you choose to come back here, it will be ready and waiting for you."

"What about the livestock? The planting?"

Uncle Bear smiles. "If you'd like, we can hire some folks to take care of the land and livestock for you until you decide what you want to do with it."

A sharp squeeze grips my chest. "You can't hire none of the men from around here."

"Oh?" He cocks his head. "And why is that?"

"The Constable didn't tell you how Ma and Pa died?"

"He said they died in a fire. That's the word he sent."

I grind my teeth and glare at the door. "He didn't tell you about the men who threatened Pa and shot at my Māori brother and came back to set fire to our cabin?" I snap my head back to stare at my uncle. "He didn't tell you he's in league with those men to try and take Pa's land and then claim the Māori land Pa gave to them?"

Uncle Bear's chin juts, his cheeks redden, and his eyes narrow as he chews on my words. "No. He didn't." An icy shroud descends over his eyes.

"What are you going to do about it, then? 'Cause I'm not leaving here until something is done, and if you won't do it, I will."

He stands from his perch. "First, I'm going to take care of you and Buck and Ian." His jaw ripples beneath his skin. "Then, I'll take care of Constable MacDougal and those men. Come with me."

He marches down the hall to the lobby without a word to the constable. "Come on, Buck." Buck still doesn't look at me, but he rises and shuffles with us across the street to the saloon, then up the stairs to the corner room. Ian is there, cleaned up and stretched out on the bed, a new cast on his arm. "Now, sit down and tell me everything."

I tell Uncle Bear all about the men and how they shot at Mani, then about waking up to their laughter and smoke from the fire.

"Who is Mani?"

Buck mumbles through his swollen lips. "Mani is our adopted brother. He was a Māori orphan before Pa took him in."

"Hmm." Uncle Bear frowns. "And where is he living now?"

I shrug. "He was going to stay with us in our shelter, but I don't know what he'll do now."

"Well, we can't have that, can we?" Uncle Bear rubs his hands together. "I've got a good bit of work to do, it seems." He grabs his holster and buckles it on his waist. "You boys stay here. I'll get the saloon owner to bring you some food, then I'll be back soon to let you know how things stand. In the meantime, please, don't go anywhere. Agreed?"

"Yessir."

He puts his arm across my shoulder and pulls me into a tight squeeze. "Everything is going to be all right. This I promise." He ruffles Buck's mussed hair and leans down to kiss Ian on the cheek, then dashes from the room, leaving the three of us staring at each other.

Ian breaks the cold silence. "Don't be mad, Fin. We didn't mean to ruin everything." Moisture makes his eyes glisten in the candlelight. "It was an accident."

I glance at Buck, who is studying the floor. I see no sign of remorse. "I'm not mad at you, Ian. It isn't your fault."

"I suppose it's mine, then," Buck snarls.

"Yes. It's yours."

Buck snorts. "That's right. I've always been a problem for you, haven't I?"

"You don't think, Buck. You plow forward like a bull chasing a fleeing cowhand and crash through everything in your path without any thought of the consequences." The side of my head pulses like a beating heart. "Then after everything's broken, you look around for someone else to blame and never own up to your mistakes. That's the problem I have with you."

"What do you want from me?"

As he screams his desperate question, Buck transforms into the frightened child he is underneath all his rage and bravado, and they're exposed as the lies they are.

"Nothing." I close my eyes and heave a deep sigh. "I don't want nothing from you. It doesn't matter now."

Ian blinks his large, round eyes. "So, we're going to America?"

"We have no choice." The stricken look in Ian's eyes pulls me up short. "It's probably for the best. Would've happened sooner or later either way." I pat Ian's unbroken arm. "It isn't your fault."

Buck mumbles under his breath, then swipes his bloodied hand across his nose. "Well, I ain't waitin' around for it." He's up and racing across the room before I can say boo.

I launch for the door, beating him to it by a split second, and block his exit. "Hold up. You're not going anywhere. We gave our word to Uncle Bear."

"I didn't give *my* word for anything." He wrestles against my arm for a few moments. "Get out of my way."

"Sit down!" The booming echo of my voice returning to me shocks me. I sound just like Pa.

It must shock Buck, too, because he backs away and sits on the edge of Ian's bed.

"We're going to honor our elders and hold to our promise, like Pa taught us. Do you understand me?"

Buck lowers his chin to his chest and nods once.

"And if going to America is our fate, so be it. MacAlisters make the best of a bad situation. We don't whine about it."

A hard silence descends over the room. It's as if the edge of a piece of heavy furniture has fallen on my chest. In their eyes I see the weight of what I said has fallen on us all.

It's decided. There's no escape, no going back, no more negotiating. We're leaving this place, like it or not. Better if we start accepting it.

Yet, deep in the darkest, hidden places, a part of me cries out like wailing women at a burial. So strong is my desire to remain on our land, I almost snatch open the door and run down the stairs myself, no matter what I promised. What restrains me, I don't know.

By force of will, I lean my back against the rough wooden door and fold my arms. "It's over." My eyes trail from Buck's to Ian's and back. "No more whining. No more crying. We deal with this like men and make Pa proud."

For the longest, the heavy silence is broken only by Ian's occasional groans, the sound of Buck's fidgeting feet scraping against the boards, and me padding across the room to stare out the window every so often, seeing if I can spot Uncle Bear.

A knock on the door causes all of us to jump. "Who's there?"

A man's muffled voice floats through the door. "I brought you food."

Opening the door, I take the tray from the grizzled man. "Thank you, sir." He grumbles about toe rags in his saloon as he stomps down the stairs.

I don't realize how hungry I am until the aroma from the stew hits my nostrils, and my mouth starts to water. Buck wolves down his bowl in minutes, sopping up the remnants with his bread and cramming the whole piece in his mouth. As usual, Ian is more delicate, taking his time and using the spoon provided.

The stew is watery and bland, but I eat it like it's a feast, wishing I could have more when my bowl is empty.

Still, Uncle Bear doesn't return. What is he up to?

The worm wiggling in my gut whispers I should go in search for my uncle, but I resist the temptation by reminding myself of my promise.

But as the hours pass, the worm becomes more insistent, making my skin itch like there's fleas crawling all over me. "I think I'll go see what's going on."

Buck quirks his mouth. "So, it's right as rain for you to leave, but I can't go anywhere, even though *you* were the one who promised to stay put." He shakes his head. "Typical Fin."

I gnaw on my lower lip. He's right, I can't make my brothers follow the rules if I'm going to break them. I pace to the window again, scanning the street for signs of Bear or MacDougal, or anything indicating something is happening, but the street is as quiet as a Sunday afternoon.

"Argh, it's so frustrating! I want to know what's going on out there."

"Most likely nothing." Buck fiddles with his crumpled napkin. "Why would Uncle Bear get involved in the mess going on here? It's not his land. He's got nothing to gain from sticking his nose in."

"But it was his brother they killed."

Buck tilts his head and shrugs.

"Maybe that's why he's been gone so long." Ian's soft voice carries the strained note of hope I'm trying desperately to cling to and failing.

"That's it, Ian. I'm sure of it."

Buck lifts one brow and smirks, as if he can see right through me.

The afternoon wanes, and darkness creeps into the corners of our small room. I light the oil lamp on the bedside table next to Ian, but its dirty globe emits a dusky light that doesn't even reach the four walls. And here we sit, wringing our hands and waiting for—for what? A reprieve to our sentence? Restitution? Justice? Vengeance? None of these are forthcoming.

At long last, the sound of boots on the stairs causes all of us to lift our heads. Sure enough, the door swings open, and Uncle Bear enters, looking sweaty, dusty, and disheveled.

"Boys?" He takes note of the empty dishes scattered around the room. "I see they brought you some food."

"Yessir."

"Are you hungry?"

I'm starving, but I'm hungrier for news than for food. "What's happened? Is there any news?"

Uncle Bear smiles and pats his hands in the air. "All in good time." He glances at Ian. "What do you say we go find ourselves a good, hot meal? Are you up for it, Ian?"

"Yessir, I think so."

"Good. Let's go, then."

The phantom fleas are running races all over my body, but I fall into step obediently behind Uncle Bear and my brothers. We leave the saloon, already filling with raucous men and unseemly women, and head down the street to a bright, cozy little restaurant with checkered tablecloths and pink and white flowers in glass bowls on every table. Several families dine at various tables around the open room.

I've never eaten at a restaurant before. Pa and Ma believed in being what they called "good stewards" of money, and Pa said, "Why spend extra money to be served someone else's food when we have good food we've grown ourselves?" But Uncle Bear seems right at home, speaking with the waitress as if they are fast friends and joking with the owner.

When the waitress says, "What'll you have?" I freeze.

Buck blurts, "Lamb pie. A lot of it."

Uncle Bear chuckles and points to a board on the wall. "The list of choices is up there. Pick one of those."

Lamb stew. Ugh, I've had enough of that today. Meatloaf. Yuck. Fish and chips. Hmm, that sounds promising. "I'll have the fish and chips."

"And you?" The waitress raises her brows and looks at Ian, who stares at me, wide-eyed.

"Tell her what you want." I tilt my head toward the board.

"Fish and chips?"

"Very good. And you?"

"I'll have the roast lamb with vegetables, and fruit crumble for dessert."

Leave it to Buck to choose the most expensive thing on the board and to add a dessert. I cut my eyes toward Uncle Buck, but he appears unfazed.

"And you, sir?"

"The roast lamb sounds delicious. Thank you, Irene."

"May I have fruit crumble, too?" Ian's voice is barely audible.

"Of course. Fruit crumble all around!"

The waitress smiles. "Very good, sir. It will be ready shortly."

I'm as nervous as a chicken when a stoat is raiding the coop. When is the shoe going to drop? When will Uncle Bear show his true colors? How did he spend the day and why won't he tell us what he found? What does he think of us?

"Well, boys." Uncle Bear beams an impish grin. "I've kicked the beehive."

"What do you mean?"

"I spoke with the magistrate and told him about the collusion between the men who murdered your parents and the constable to take your land. He directed me to ride to the closest district seat and bring a representative of law enforcement back with me." He places both hands on the table. "Seems the district attorney has had his eye on Constable MacDougal for some time and was thrilled to have something concrete to bring as charges."

"He believed you?"

"Oh, yes. He was eager to believe me. He and his deputies are questioning the constable right now before taking him to the district jail where he will be charged with accessory to murder." He rubs his hands together. "The district attorney is fairly certain the constable will identify his accomplices when the attorney threatens to charge him with murder in the first degree."

"And if he gives the names?"

"The district attorney promises to arrest the men and charge them to the fullest extent of the law."

I leap from my chair and envelop Uncle Bear in a bear-sized hug. Buck laughs uproariously and claps his hands, while tears stream down Ian's cheeks.

"The next step is to ensure the Māori keep the land Clay purchased for them. I have some feelers out with Canterbury legislators to sponsor a bill in Parliament to return the Māori's right to purchase land and to protect their land ownership from thieves like those men who killed your Pa." Uncle Bear's eyes gleam as he leans back in his chair. "In the meantime, I will hire several of the Māori who live near your home to work the land and tend the animals in your absence."

"What about Mani? We ain't leaving him behind." Buck's lip curls, a challenge for Bear to say otherwise.

"I'm working on it." Uncle Bear tilts his head and raises one brow. "And I'll do everything I can. But you need to be prepared for the possibility Mani might prefer to stay with his people, or he might not be allowed to immigrate."

Buck rises from his chair, his face reddening, but I put a restraining hand on his arm. "Mani's our brother. Pa adopted him."

"As I understand it, your pa never formalized the adoption legally. That's part of the problem."

"That don't matter. Mani is our brother, I tell ya." Buck slams his hands on the table.

Uncle Bear's tone is calm and measured. "Buck, lower your voice. Other people are eating and don't want to be disturbed by you yelling."

"I don't care! You gotta take Mani with us, or I ain't gonna go."

I hiss, "Shut up, Buck."

He turns his rage toward me. "You always side against me"

"Oh, boo hoo. Maybe that's because you're always *wrong*."

Uncle Bear raises his hand and opens his mouth to speak, but Ian interrupts him. "Please stop. Please. Both of you, *stop* it." His shoulders and chest heave, his breaths erratic and gasping. He covers his eyes with his good hand and sobs.

Bear drapes his arm across Ian's shoulders and pulls him to his chest, where Ian buries his face. "That's enough, boys. You're upsetting your brother when what he needs is for you to be strong and set a good example." His eyes narrow, and the corners of his mouth turn down. "I know your ma and pa didn't raise you to act like this. If you can't behave, I'll take you back to the saloon without your supper, and Ian and I will enjoy a grand meal, just the two of us."

I lower my head to cover my grin. Threatening Buck's food is the best way I know to get him to act like somebody.

But Bear isn't amused. "You think this is funny?"

"No, sir."

"Then wipe that smirk off your face."

"Yessir."

Irene rescues me by bringing our food. As she deposits the heaping plates, Uncle Bear takes Ian's good hand. "We'll bless the meal before we eat." His eyes pierce into my soul like burning arrows. "The two of you hold hands. And while we're at it, you can both ask the Lord's forgiveness for your deplorable behavior. Do I make myself clear?"

"Yessir."

"Yessir."

"Very well. Fin, you will lead us in the blessing. As the eldest."

I catch his meaning. He is laying the responsibility squarely on my shoulders for our behavior the remainder of our time together. Now, I must figure out how to keep Buck in line. "Heavenly Father, thank you for this food. Thank you for our Uncle Bear's success today with the magistrate and district attorney. Thank you for bringing justice for my family." To my surprise, my throat tightens, and the words stick in there like glue. Justice. I never thought I'd see it.

I repeat my prayer of gratitude in my heart, this time with depth of feeling. Then, I clear my throat. "Forgive us, Lord, for our quarreling. You say folks quarrel because of desires warring inside us. At least that's what Pa said You mean. If that's the case, Buck and I aren't mad at each other at all. We're really fighting ourselves. So, if you could help us remember that we're mostly mad at ourselves, we'll try to treat each other as Pa would want." I swallow hard. "And bless this food to the nourishment of our bodies, and us to Thy service. In Thy Holy Name we pray, Amen."

"We'll travel to the coastal port the day after tomorrow, and board the ship for home the following day." He shoots a glance toward Buck. "If you'd like, I can take you to your land tomorrow before I leave for the district seat. You can collect the animals and care for them, then say your goodbyes to your ma and pa." A gray mist tints his eyes like a cloud covering the sun. "I've hired a mason to create markers for their burial site. He is supposed to bring them around tomorrow afternoon. You can show him where they lie and supervise the placement of the stones."

"Yessir."

"This evening, I will speak with the Māori about managing the farm and ask about Mani. We'll see what they have to offer."

Ian's wide eyes blink rapidly. "We love Mani. He's my best friend. I hope he can come with us."

Uncle Bear offers Ian a warm smile tinged with deep sadness. "So do I."

CHAPTER NINE

January 1907

Uncle Bear rises early from his mat on the cold, hard floor, while Buck, Ian, and I share the sole bed in the room. He returned to the saloon late, well after we were in bed, so I don't know how his meeting with the Māori went.

"Good morning," he whispers, then points to the basin of water he's using to wash his face and hands. "It's still warm."

I slide from the bed as silently as possible, not wanting to wake my brothers, but Ian makes a soft, cooing noise in his throat and stretches his good arm above his head. Buck doesn't twitch a muscle.

"I'll go down and rustle up some food for you. Go ahead and get cleaned up and changed. We'll be heading for the farm soon."

As he slips through the door, closing it gently behind him, I touch Buck's shoulder. "It's time to wake up. We're going to our land after we eat."

Buck is uncharacteristically cooperative, jumping off the bed, and waiting behind Ian as he washes his face. I take my turn at the basin after Buck finishes. We've changed into our clothes and are sitting on the edge of the bed when Uncle Bear returns with eggs and bread.

I miss my ma's eggs. These feel like mush in the middle and hard, burnt edges on the sides. As usual, Buck gobbles down his eggs, and almost jumps up and down until we walk out the door.

"What did the Māori say about Mani?"

"They said it was up to him." Uncle Bear cuts his eyes down at Buck, who beams like it's Christmas morning. "Mani said he'd think on it."

"What about workers for the land?" I ask.

"They seemed happy with the opportunity to earn some money. Many have already committed, and some are saying they'll consider doing it. So, I believe that will work out well."

He rents an extra horse for the day for Buck and me to share. Ian shares the saddle with our uncle.

"I want you to remain either on the farm or in the Māori village until I return this afternoon. Once you've finished your chores, you can spend time with Mani."

Again, his eyes trail down to Buck. It's as if he knows something he's not saying, but if I had to guess, I'd say he suspects Mani will choose to stay with his people.

How will Buck react if that comes true? Maybe I need to prepare him so he won't go off half-cocked and ruin everything.

The trip to our land is quick and easy since we can follow the road without fear of those *weriweri* men. Uncle Bear helps Ian down, then remounts, and with a wave rides off in a cloud of dust.

"Let's find the horses first. Buck and I will search the plains beyond our boundary for them and lead them back to our pastures. Ian, do you think you could check on the chickens?"

"Sure, I can do that."

"If they're in the hen house, check the roosts for eggs. If they're still in the yard, feed them, if it's not too hard for you one-handed."

"It's not too hard."

"Very well. Once we collect the horses, we'll need your help with the sheep. You're the one they follow."

"And while you're getting the sheep, I'll herd the cows home." Buck puffs his chest a bit as if he's a real American cowboy.

I open my mouth to spew a mocking comment but manage to bite my wicked tongue before it's too late. "That'll be great. Buck. Thank you."

Working together like this reminds me of our life before…we lost Ma and Pa. It feels…almost normal. As long as I keep my eyes from glancing toward the charred remnants of our cabin, I can almost believe Ma and Pa are in the barn, spreading hay and churning butter. Almost.

Buck seems cheerful while we ride, chattering about the upcoming trip and how Mani will fare on a long boat ride. I grunt occasionally to let him know I'm listening, but I don't have anything to say.

My head pounds with the phrase, *this is my home*, repeated like a Māori drum beat. Uncle Bear is nice enough, and I'm sure the Georgia mountains are as lovely as he says, but we won't be *here*. Until I'm 18, I'll forever be a visitor, or worse, an intruder in someone else's home.

The horses have ranged far and wide, all the way to the base of the mountains in some cases, but we're lucky because the cows remained together, and we find them all during our search for the horses.

I loop the rope hanging on my horse's saddle around Gypsy's neck while Buck herds the other horses toward us. As expected, they follow their leader, and to make sure we don't lose any, Buck follows behind our little train to keep them going.

By the time we've secured the horses in our pasture, Ian has finished with the chickens and has started gathering the sheep, using a long stick to urge them along. Since he has the sheep in hand, Buck mounts Gypsy, and we ride together to herd the cows back home.

With the animals secure, we sit and wait for the stone mason. For me, this will be the most difficult part of the day. Uncle Bear wants me to say my goodbyes to Ma and Pa, but I can't bring myself to think about it.

Ian blurts a thousand questions. "How long will we be on the ship? What does their house look like? Are they nice people? Do you think they'll like us? What if there's a storm? Where will we sleep? Will they let us steer the boat? How big is it? Who's going to teach us? How will we get from California to Georgia? Do they have sheep? Will they let me sheer them?"

I repeat "I don't know" so many times, I want to spit by the time the stone mason arrives. He carries two large, gray stones, square on the bottom and rounded on the top, with the names "Fiona Kincaid

MacAlister" and "Alexander Barclay MacAlister" carved into the stone. Their birth dates and the cursed date of the fire are listed beneath their names. On Ma's stone, Uncle Bear chose, "Beloved Wife and Mother" and "Proverbs 31:10-31" for the epitaph, and for Pa, he picked, "Loving Husband and Father" and "Joshua 1:9".

Buck slides his fingers over the words etched in Pa's stone. "I don't remember Joshua 1:9."

I recall it because it's Pa's favorite verse, which he quoted to me often. "'Have I not commanded you? Be strong and courageous. Do not be afraid; do not be discouraged, for the Lord your God will be with you wherever you go.' I'm sure Uncle Bear knew how much Pa loved that verse. That's why he picked it."

"Pa was always strong and courageous." Ian leans down and kisses the top of the stone.

"Where would you have me place them?" the mason asks.

I gesture for him to follow, and we make our slow, solemn march to the spot where the Māori buried Ma and Pa. A searing bolt of panic grips my gut as I realize I don't know which mound belongs to which one. How can I not remember? Frantic, I dig through my memories, trying to visualize the men digging in the rubble and moving their bodies, but I can only grab bits and pieces—the first gleam of sunlight on a broken piece of bone, the men huddled around the newly dug holes almost as if they were trying to block our view, a glimpse of blackened skin—but nothing tells me which grave to mark.

I lean close to Buck's ear. "Which grave is Ma's?"

Buck pales, his eyes widen, and he shrugs. Suddenly, tears spring into his eyes. He dashes across the open space to the barn and disappears inside.

I must decide. The man is waiting. But my mouth hangs open like a dead fish. I can't say it. What if I get it wrong?

Ian's soft footfalls shake me from my paralysis. He moves to the end of their mounds and points. "Put the markers here, side by side, as close to touching each other as possible. Ma and Pa would like that."

He lifts his head high. A single glistening streak traces through the smear of dirt on his cheek from today's work. And in a voice as clear as crystal and bright as church bells, he starts to sing:

"A wonderful Savior is Jesus, my Lord,
A wonderful Savior to me;
He hideth my soul in the cleft of the rock,
Where rivers of pleasure I see.
He hideth my soul in the cleft of the rock,
That shadows a dry, thirsty land;
He hideth my life in the depths of His love,
And covers me there with His hand,
And covers me there with His hand."

Ma's favorite hymn. Out of the three of us, Ian is the strong and courageous one. He puts me to shame.

The mason places the markers as Ian directs as if they lie together in a single grave. It's perfect.

I move around the dirt to Ian's side, reaching out to touch Pa's headstone. "I will be strong and courageous, Pa, just like you taught me. I won't be afraid or discouraged anymore. I swear it." I place my other hand atop Ma's stone. "And I promise you, I will be back. I will work the land and rebuild what you built for us. And I will teach my children everything you taught us. Generations will be blessed by the work of your hands. I swear it."

"*We* will be back," Ian whispers. He places his hand on mine and bows his head. "Heavenly Father, we are grateful you gave us these parents for the brief time we had with them. We will honor them with lives lived well and filled with love and faith in You, the way they taught us. Make us strong so we can fulfill our promises. Amen."

"Amen."

At the end of Ian's prayer, the mason, still standing respectfully to the side with his hands clasped, mutters his amen, then collects his tools. I reach out my hand, which he grasps in a firm handshake.

"Thank you, sir. The headstones are perfect."

"You're welcome, young master." He touches the tip of his hat. "Give my best to your uncle."

"Yessir."

He mounts his wooden cart and urges his horse forward with a "Giddyap." The horse's brisk step down the path makes me think he's relieved he's no longer pulling those heavy stones.

Ian tugs my arm gently. "We better see to Buck."

"You're right." Arm in arm, Ian and I tread toward the barn, beside the ravaged ground where our peaceful home once stood. For the first time, I stop and really look at the ruins, the shattered shell of our lives, and as if in a dream, the stones rise to form a new, larger base, and the wood remnants reach high into the pale sky, forming angles and filling walls. "It *will* happen."

"What will, Fin?"

"'And I will restore to you the years that the locust hath eaten.'"

Ian presses his lips together until his mouth looks like a thin slash across his face, then nods once. "Yes." His jaw trembles. "I know it will."

When we enter the barn, we don't see Buck anywhere. "Buck?"

"Buck?"

Some stray pieces of hay sift through the rafters, catching the sunlight's gleam in their lazy spiral to the barn floor. I jerk my head toward the ladder into the loft. "He's up there."

Ian strides to the ladder and starts to climb, using his good hand for balance.

"Leave me be." Buck's insistent call is muffled as if he has a mouthful of straw.

"I'm coming up."

"Go away."

But Ian is already at the top of the ladder. He disappears from the opening in the loft floor, sending a few more hay strands tumbling down on my head.

I can't make out their muted conversation but after several minutes, the hay rustles, and Buck's bare feet take the first steps down the ladder. Ian follows more slowly.

I meet Buck at the base and gather him in my arms. "I'm sorry, Buck. I've treated you horribly. It's like I've been so busy trying not to feel my pain, I forgot you are hurting, too." I pull back, leaving my hands holding his shoulders, and duck my head until I meet his eyes. "At the same time, I've treated you like you're older than you are, putting burdens on you I should never have asked. Can you forgive me?"

Buck uses the back of his hand to wipe his nose. "I'm sorry, too. I know I've been a real *hōhā*. I…I just can't seem to help it."

"We are all struggling. And who can blame us?" I sigh deeply. "Everything is changing, all of it against our will. Sometimes I feel like I'm about to explode with it."

"Me, too."

"But Ian reminded me we have a responsibility to honor Ma and Pa by following their ways." I squeeze his shoulder. "If we don't, their legacy will die with them." After studying the straw-strewn barn floor for a few seconds, I drop my arms and ball my hands into fists. "I don't know about you, but I'm not going to let that happen."

Buck shakes his head vigorously.

Ian mimics my stance. "I'm not, either."

"Very well. From now on, we listen to each other instead of arguing. We try to understand each other instead of trying to change each other." I wrap my arms around my brothers. "And above all, we love each other through it all, the way Pa loved Ma, and the way she loved him."

Buck leans his head on my shoulder. "You know what, I realized something when Ian came to the loft to get me."

"What's that?"

"We are all we have left."

Ian pulls back, staring at Buck with his wide eyes. "But Uncle Bear says we have a whole, big family in America."

Buck frowns and shakes his head. "It's not the same. They have their own families. We'll be outsiders." He takes Ian's good hand. "But you…" He reaches for my hand and grasps it like he's holding on to a lifeline. "And you. You're my family."

I squeeze Buck's hand. "What do you say we head to the Māori village and find the rest of our family?"

"Let's go!" Buck pulls us toward the barn door.

"Wait. Your shoes?"

Buck chuckles. "I guess I'm gonna need them." He digs around in the straw near the base of the stairs, finds them, and slips them on. "Ready."

Buck gives the two mounds and new headstones a wide berth. I suppose saying goodbye is still too much for him to face.

The time passes slowly on the hike to the village. For most of the trip, we walk silently, except for a brief conversation about what Mani will choose.

But Mani isn't at the village. No one has seen him for some time.

"I bet he's at our hideaway." Buck crooks his thumb. "Let's find out."

So, another hike takes us into the trees and west toward the mountains. The crunch of our footfalls on the debris littering the forest floor makes a strange, rhythmic counterpoint to the sweet singing of the many birds and the shoosh of the breeze ruffling pine needles.

As we approach the campsite, pungent smoke wafts beneath the forest canopy, and the crackling of burning logs adds a new, quick beat to our little forest symphony.

Buck picks up speed. "Mani? You here?"

"*Āna*!" rings out from a distance.

So, we run the rest of the way to the site, relieved to find Mani sitting cross-legged beside a large fire, munching on some nuts. Ian wraps his good arm around Mani's neck from behind and squeezes him.

"Well? Are you gonna come with us or not?" As usual, Buck doesn't mince words.

Mani cocks his head, throws another handful of nuts in his mouth, and crunches them.

I flop beside him and cross my legs, warming my hands on the licking flames. He offers me some nuts, but I shake my head.

Buck plants his hands on his hips. "Well?"

"Much thought until Manaaki's head pounds. So…" He holds up his full palm. "Eating instead." He flips the handful in his mouth.

"But we're leaving tomorrow. You have to decide."

"Either way, much sorrow."

I place my palm on his knee. "We can't leave you here, Mani. It wouldn't be right."

"Not right leave Manaaki here. Not right Manaaki leave the people here." He sighs. "No right answer."

"Of course there is!" Buck stomps his foot. "You're coming with us. We're brothers."

"Brothers. Not blood." Mani pinches his arm at the wrist. "Māori blood."

"There's more to family than blood, Mani. Pa adopted you." I lift my head high. "You are a MacAlister now."

Mani frowns. "No! Name Manaaki. No other name." He stands, dropping his few remaining nuts into the dirt. With his fists clenched by his side, he widens his stance, bends his knees, and bares his teeth. "*Ka mate, ka mate! ka ora! ka ora! Ka mate! ka mate! ka ora! ka ora!*"

"Mani, what are you saying?"

"Manaaki is Māori. Always be Māori. Cannot change."

I close my eyes as my chin falls to my chest. "But you'll always be our brother. And that will never change."

"Cannot leave Māori people."

Buck howls like an injured wolf and bolts into the trees. One more loss he can't bear to face.

"Mani, please." Ian's pleading whine affects me more than Mani's decision. I swallow the ball of tears rising into my throat as Ian pulls on Mani's arm.

Mani swings around to face Ian. "Much sorrow."

"Where will you live, Mani?"

He gestures toward the shelter he built for us to share. "Plenty big room."

"All alone?" Ian's eyes look like two full moons on a summer night.

Mani shrugs. "Already alone much time. Manaaki not minding alone."

"But what will you do in winter? And how will you get food?"

"Brothers no worry for Manaaki. The people will help with food. Shelter when need comes."

Now, Ian's tears flow freely as he clutches Mani's hand. "You're my best friend in the whole world."

"Same for my world."

The two of them stand there, staring at each other, for what drags on too long. No one seems willing to say the final goodbye.

Finally, I break the tense silence. "Will you at least come to town to say goodbye before we leave in the morning?"

"Sure thing." He gestures to his fire. "Stay and eat. Until fire dies."

"Very well."

So, Ian sits beside me, and Mani disappears into the shelter for some of the food I left behind. Then, he sits between us, and we stare into the fire, eating *rewena* bread and fruit.

In the dancing flames, I try to picture memories of our time together and strain to imagine the new life facing all of us when the sun rises. But all I can see are flickers of light and darkness twisting around each other, weaving an inescapable web. And I'm trapped in its sticky strands.

CHAPTER TEN

January 1907

We discover Buck nestled among the twisted roots of a large tree, with his head buried beneath his arm, sleeping.

"Wake up, Buck. It's time to go back."

He moans, twists his neck, and stretches his arm above his head. "Ugh, my arm is tingling."

I reach out my hand to help Buck to his feet. "Uncle Bear is probably wondering if we've run away again."

"Nah." Buck yawns. "We'll be there before dark. He's probably not even back yet."

A fresh breeze cools the late afternoon air, making the walk to town somewhat pleasant, but I measure my steps as if it's a death march like the native people in America. Pa told us that story, about how his granda witnessed one such march, and how horrified he was by what happened.

Every step is one step closer to leaving. I'll likely never see these gnarled trees again, or the distant snow-capped mountains to the west, or my pa's beloved fields. All will fade from my memory—the crisp rustle of the grasses in the wind, the faint echo of the rooster's crow as the sun rises, the gentle lowing of the cows as they wander to the fields in the morning mist, the sweet, musky aroma of smoke curling from our fireplace, the serene quiet of day's end, the lilting music of Ma's voice calling us to the table.

A deep ache presses my heart through to my backbone, and the weight of it forces my feet to stop at the edge of our land. "One more step…"

"It's the last goodbye," Ian whispers.

Buck squats and digs up a handful of dirt. "Do you think we'll never return?" He massages the soil between his fingers.

"I hope we do. But nothing is certain." I look over my shoulder at the jagged remnants of our home, now fading in the rising fog settling over the fields. "Nothing is certain."

Buck stands, cramming the handful of dirt in his pocket. "I make my own destiny. Like Pa." He brushes his hands on his pants and strides ahead of Ian and me, his back as stiff and straight as a board.

Like Pa. Buck's right. Pa's life was a testament to taking the narrow road. Nothing he ever did was common or easy, from fighting for the natives in America to fighting for the Māori's rights. He was wild and free, refusing to take no for an answer at every turn. He explored the seas. He traveled across continents. Pa feared nothing.

What would he say if he could see my trembling hands?

It's time I acted according to his example. "Let's go, Ian." I lift my head, clench my jaw, and tramp after Buck, with Ian on my heels.

The sky glows purple and gold as we march into town and down the main street to the saloon, where we find Uncle Bear sitting at a large, round table, waiting for us.

"There you are!" He motions us over to his table. "Are you hungry?"

"Yessir."

He chuckles. "I bet you are. Would you rather eat here or at the diner?"

"Diner!" Buck shouts without hesitation.

"Very well, the diner it is." He pushes his seat back. "Maybe today they'll have roast pork."

The diner is busy, but Irene finds us a table in the corner. She giggles and flutters her lashes when Uncle Bear thanks her for taking such good care of us.

"I think she's sweet on you," Buck whispers after Irene takes our order.

Uncle Bear quirks his brow, his cheeks reddening. "She's a nice young woman."

The three of us have a good laugh at his discomfort.

"I have news. The representative for Canterbury will put forth a proposition allowing the Māori to purchase land. It might take some time to pass, but he is confident he can get it through."

I offer Uncle Bear my warmest smile. "Thank you. It would mean the world to Pa."

He lowers his eyes and nods. "I know." His brow furrows. "Oh, how I miss my brother. He was one of a kind."

"You're a lot like him."

Moisture films his eyes. "That's the finest compliment you could ever give me."

"Speaking of brothers." Buck heaves a deep sigh. "Mani decided to remain with the Māori instead of coming with us."

Uncle Bear's brows knit together as he pats Ian's hand. "I'm so sorry. I know how much you wanted him to come."

"Pa always taught us to make the best of every bad situation, so that's what we're gonna do." Buck juts his chin as if to challenge Uncle Bear to say differently.

"Very well." Bear tilts his head. "Although I would say there are worse things than meeting your family for the first time."

Buck's lips press into a thin line, and his jaw ripples beneath his skin, but he manages to hold his tongue.

Irene brings our steaming meals, and the aromas set my mouth to watering. I didn't realize how hungry I was. We woof down the food in record time.

"Do they have fruit crumble again?" Ian lifts his brows hopefully.

"Let's ask Irene, what do you say?"

"I say, yum!"

Uncle Bear lets out a hearty laugh. "Yum it is!"

Irene brings fruit crumble all around, this time swimming in cream, and we are moaning by the time we finish the dessert.

"We have a long ride tomorrow, so we'll need to rise early. I think we should all go to bed as soon as we get back to the room."

Did Uncle Bear assume we would balk at his suggestion? How he said it sounded tentative as if preparing for an argument. Have we made such a poor impression on him? I must remedy this.

"Uncle Bear, we appreciate everything you're doing for us. I apologize on behalf of my brothers and me for how we've acted. I wouldn't have you thinking our pa didn't raise us right."

"I don't think that at all." He shakes his head. "In fact, in my opinion, you've handled a difficult and painful situation brilliantly. The loss of your parents has been a devastating blow, but you've kept a stiff upper lip. I don't know how I would've acted had I lost my parents at your age."

"We promise to do better from now on."

He clasps his hands together on the table. "Making the best of it, eh?"

"Yessir."

"Very well."

After the day's hard work and painful goodbyes, I'm dead on my feet by the time we return to the room. But when we enter, I notice three piles of neatly folded clothes lying out on the bed.

"I did the best I could guessing sizes. I hope everything fits."

I finger the stiff shirt on top of the first pile. "Thank you, sir." Then, I notice the clean, shiny shoes with their toes stuck under the edge of the bed and rolled-up socks stuck inside. My body freezes.

"I figure you need clothes since…well, the fire."

"Yessir." No one moves.

Uncle Bear frowns and purses his lips. "I must say, this isn't the reaction I expected. Is something wrong?"

"Oh, no sir, they are very nice." I pull out one of the pants and hold them up to my waist. "They'll fit perfectly."

Ian paws through his pile. "Look, a jacket!" He swings it over his shoulder. "Thanks, Uncle Bear."

"Yeah, thanks." Buck picks up his pile and moves them to the top of the dresser. "Can we get some sleep now?"

"Of course."

I help Ian move his clothes, then I shift mine to the dresser on top of Buck's, and the three of us crawl into the single bed. Uncle Bear spreads out his blanket and stretches out on the floor.

After a few moments, his quiet voice drifts up to us, "Boys?"

"Sir?"

"Can I ask you something?"

"Yessir."

"What were some things your Ma and Pa did that were special to you? Like at bedtime. Did they read to you?"

The evening was almost normal, with laughter and good conversation—until the new shoes hit like a sharp arrow emphasizing our many losses. Now, Bear wants us to reminisce? I can't do it. I won't.

Once again, Ian proves himself to be the strongest of us. "In the evening around the fire, Pa would hear our memory verse and ask us how we applied it during the day. Then, he'd read Scripture, and we'd discuss what it means, and then he'd give us a new verse to memorize. After, Ma would sing to us." Ian's voice cracks. "That was my favorite part of the day."

Uncle Bear's soft laughter sounds like a gurgling brook. "So, he kept up the family tradition." His words catch in his throat.

Ian sucks in a gulp of air. "You and Pa did the same thing growing up?"

Why must he talk about Pa? He'll never ask us to recite our verses again. Why do I have to be reminded?

"We did, and that is surely something we can do from now on, although one of you will have to do the singing. What things were special to you, Fin ?"

"What Ian said," I mutter under my breath.

"My favorite was doing things with Pa. He'd always tell me stories of his adventures." Buck sighs. "Made me want to go on some adventures of my own."

"Well, you're about to embark on your own grand adventure. And your granda has a lot of stories he can share with you. He can tell you about Clay when he was growing up, and about the Lakota and the wars."

"What about you?" Buck asks. "You don't have any stories?"

"Nothing so grand as your pa's stories. Or my pa's." The floor creaks as he shifts his weight. "I live a pretty simple life."

"What's your pa like?"

Will Buck ever stop talking? I want to go to sleep.

"Hmm. How do I explain Pa?" Uncle Bear pauses long enough that my eyelids are drooping. "He's a strong man, the strongest man I know. He can be stern, and sometimes he withdraws into himself, and during those times, you need to let him be. But he's also very gentle and loving—you see it most with Ma." He sighs. "He's been through so much in his life, it's taken a toll. But it's also made him the wonderful man he is." A short chuckle rumbles in Bear's throat. "He'll adore the three of you, that's for sure and certain."

"What about your ma?"

"Ma is a rare gem, beautiful inside and out, with a heart so full of love it overflows on everyone. When the Scripture lists the fruit of the Spirit, it's describing my ma." He chuckles again. "But she won't take any guff off you, so don't think she's a pushover. She's as strong as Pa, and fierce."

"She sounds a lot like Ma."

Ian's quiet comment causes another wrenching twist to my soul. My imaginings of my new life suddenly take a hideous turn, where I'm surrounded by constant reminders of Ma and Pa who aren't them and can never be. I'd rather be dipped in lime-sulfur.

"Your ma was a special woman, too. She had to be, to put up with your pa." Uncle Bear giggles, and Ian and Buck join in.

"That's enough for tonight. We have an entire voyage to share stories, so let's get some sleep. Goodnight, boys."

"Goodnight, Uncle Bear."

"'Night."

The drowsiness I felt moments ago evaporates like morning fog on a hot summer's day. How can I face this living hell? My face burns as if I'm sitting too close to a fire. Needles prick my hands. An overwhelming urge to run suffocates me, but I can't move. Spit fills my mouth. Pressure builds in my throat until I fear I might scream.

I must get out of here.

But how? Uncle Bear lies between me and the door, and Buck will wake up and tattle as soon as I move an inch.

I'm trapped. My breaths start coming in short, wheezing gasps. "I...I can't...breathe." My chest is going to explode. "I can't...BREATHE."

Bear is kneeling beside the bed in an instant, stroking my head. "Calm down."

Sudden, hot tears burst out with an animal-like wail rising from deep in my gut. I'm choking on my own cries.

Uncle Bear gathers me in his arms. "Oh, son. I'm so sorry. I'm so, so sorry."

I'm dying. I must have air.

I wrench my body and jerk out of Bear's arms, tumbling to the floor, where I claw and scramble toward the door.

"Stop. Wait." Bear grabs my leg and pulls.

"Let. Me. Go." The burning scream erupts like a geyser, filling the room with my anguish.

"What's going on?"

"Fin? Fin, what's wrong?"

The futility of it all crushes my will, turning my muscles to jam, and I collapse on the roughhewn floor in a river of tears. Hands paw at me, bodies smother me, and babbling words pass through me without finding meaning. Gradually, I become aware my brothers are clutching me, crying, while Uncle Bear envelops all of us in his strong arms, trying to be a dam holding back the flooding river, but failing.

Sometime later—I don't know how long—my tears dry up and my shaking slows to occasional tremors. Uncle Bear lifts Ian in his arms and slips him into bed. He's asleep before the covers are tucked. Then, he reaches for Buck, who shakes his head, clinging to me like a life raft.

He doesn't know all the air is gone from me, and I couldn't hold up a blowfly. But I don't suppose that matters much. Like he said, we are all we have.

Eventually, Buck lays his head in my lap, and once he's asleep, I stretch out on Bear's pallet. My last vision of Uncle Bear is sitting in a wooden chair by the window, gazing out at darkness, with his chin resting on his hand, and the dim light from the moon shimmering on his wet cheeks.

When the first pale rays of sun hit our window, Uncle Bear is still sitting in the chair. Still staring at nothing. Still weeping.

CHAPTER ELEVEN

January 1907

I'm as washed out as ten-year-old pants when I get out of bed. Uncle Bear acknowledges me with a slight wave but doesn't turn from the window.

The water in the basin is cold. I splash my face, using a towel to wipe off the dried remnants of salt and sweat. "Get up, Buck, Ian. It's time to go."

As the boys stir, Uncle Bear rises, stretching his back. "We'll spend today riding to Timaru, spend the night there, and sail the following morning." Uncle Bear slides our new clothes, minus the ones we are to put on, into a travel bag. He leaves our dirty clothes in a pile on the floor, which I don't mind. They were hand-me-downs from Missus Appleton and mean nothing to me.

Then he tosses my shoes onto the pile.

"The ship will take around two months to reach San Francisco. From there, we take the rails cross country to Atlanta, which will take six days, then a wagon ride to the mountains and you are home." He closes the clasps on the bag. "I'm going downstairs to make the arrangements. Wash your faces, get dressed, and be ready when I return. We will have a quick breakfast and leave straight away." He walks stiffly to the door, shutting it with a loud bang.

"What's eatin' him?" Buck yawns and scrubs his eyes with his fists.

"Rough night." I toss him the towel. "Get cleaned up." I kick my new shoes farther under the bed, hoping Uncle Bear won't notice, and retrieve my shoes from the trash pile.

A sudden knock on the door makes me jump. "Who is it?"

"It is Manaaki."

Buck snatches the door open. "Mani!" He hugs him around the head. "I'm so glad to see you."

"Very glad catching you. Mister Bear say, go on up." His dark lashes flutter. "Wanting to say goodbyes."

"Yeah, I'm sorry about yesterday." Buck shrugs. "I don't know what was wrong with me."

Mani beams a toothy smile. "This day, all that matters."

Ian embraces Mani. "I'm going to miss you so much." He glances at me, his brows raised. "Do you think Uncle Bear would mind if Mani came to eat with us?"

"I don't think he'd mind."

Mani claps his hands together. "Much good news. Very hungry."

"We must wait here until Bear returns."

Mani's mouth quirks to one side. "Very hungry now. How long?"

"I don't know." I swipe my hand toward Buck and Ian. "And these lazybones aren't dressed yet."

"I'm gettin'."

They are slipping on their socks and shoes when Bear returns. "Mani. I see you found the room."

"Yes sir, Mister Bear. Easy."

"Ian invited Mani to eat with us." If Ian's the one asking for it, I doubt Uncle Bear will refuse.

"Very well. Come along, Mani, boys. We have a long journey ahead." His eyes trail down to my dusty, worn brogans, and his brow furrows. "Where are your shoes?"

"These are my shoes."

"Your *new* shoes."

I jut my chin and lift my head. "I like *these* shoes."

Uncle Bear's eyes close. His jaw ripples as he grinds his teeth. "Very well. But we'll not leave a perfectly good pair of new shoes behind. Where are they?"

My shoulders sag, but without a word, I retrieve them from under the bed and hold them out to Bear, who snatches them from me and marches out the door. Our somber little band follows behind him.

Bear stops to settle with the innkeeper, so it looks like we'll make one last visit to Irene at the diner instead of eating the eggs at the saloon. Thank the Lord.

Mani starts his usual chatter, asking about the ship and California and our new home in the blue mountains. Bear offers short or one-word answers—very unusual. Something *is* eating him. Is he angry about my breakdown last night? Did I offend him somehow? That's all we need, another angry caretaker.

A bright-cheeked Irene meets us at the door. "Hello again! The table you like by the window is available." She glances down at Mani. "How many?" she asks, her smile strained.

"Five."

Irene cuts her eyes toward the kitchen at the back of the restaurant, appears to check the other guests, then turns back to Bear, her eyes lowered. She gestures toward Mani. "His people don't usually eat here."

Bear rubs his lips together. "Are you saying he isn't permitted to eat here, or it's not common?"

Her eyes dart toward the back again. "I will have to ask."

"Don't bother." Bear's ire turns toward the young waitress. "This young man is my nephew. If he is unwelcome here, then I am not welcome." He spins on his heel and marches from the diner, slamming his fist on an empty table top as he leaves.

"I apologize." I bow slightly before the sweet, crestfallen woman before scurrying after Bear, with my brothers in tow.

Mani's chin sags to his chest. "Much sorry, Mister Bear, for messing up food time."

"You didn't mess anything up, Mani. The diner…well, I won't be giving them my business in the future, were I to return."

"Where will we eat now?" Buck's question takes on a whining edge. I wince because Uncle Bear is already in a bad mood and doesn't need us to start complaining.

"I guess we'll go back to the saloon."

"Missus Appleton serves breakfast to her guests. Maybe she would be willing to include us?"

Uncle Bear's mouth twists into a sneer. "I'm afraid you boys have burned that bridge."

"I apologized to her—when I came back." Hopefully, Bear will take that as a good reflection on us even if Missus Appleton is unlikely to serve us.

"I'm afraid the saloon is our best option." Bear offers a crooked grin. "Just don't order eggs."

We order bowls of Granose with warm milk, which blessedly is hard to ruin.

Through a mouthful of flakes, Buck asks, "Will we get to eat on the ship?"

Uncle Bear glances at him, his face solemn. "I'm afraid this is it. They don't have food on the ship. So, better eat up. It must last you two months."

Buck's saucer-shaped eyes and slack mouth cause Bear's lips to quiver, until he can't hold it any longer and bursts out in a guffaw. Buck slumps against his chair back. I don't know if he's embarrassed or relieved.

Buck's absurdity seems to break the spell hanging over Uncle Bear since last night. Giggling, we shovel our cereal like starving orphans, going along with the gag.

Buck shrugs. "Well, I didn't know."

"This ship is a little bit like riding on a train. Have you been on a train before?"

"Yessir."

Mani shakes his head no.

"Well, they have berths for sleeping, a grand dining hall, a promenade, even a circular staircase. It's quite lovely and comfortable."

"It sounds nicer than this place," Ian mutters.

Bear chuckles. "I think you will enjoy it." He glances at our empty bowls. "Is everyone ready to go?"

Mani's sigh quavers. "Time for goodbyes?"

"You could still come with us, Mani." Buck knits his brows. "Please?"

But Mani shakes his head once, his lips pressed tightly.

"Come, boys. Let's go to our carriage and say our farewells." Uncle Bear strokes Ian's back. "You will see each other again. I'm certain of it."

"Sure! You come back to live on your land. For now, Manaaki helps keep land ready."

My steps drag as we approach the stable. Is life a series of losses and that's all? I'm sick of it.

After Ian and Buck hug Mani and offer tearful goodbyes with promises of return, I pull him to my chest and clutch him so tightly that he starts squirming. "Listen to me. Don't you forget us, do you hear? It may not be for a couple of years, but I will be back." I scrub his black mop of hair as he wriggles from my grasp. "I leave you in charge of defending our land. Don't let me down."

"No *weriweri* men with them *kino* cows!"

"That's right." One more squeeze, and I hop onto Uncle Bear's carriage, climbing up to sit beside him on the box seat. Ian and Buck hang out the window, waving, as we ride away. The dust from the wagon wheels swirls around Mani, veiling him from our sight, but the boys keep waving nonetheless.

"Poor Mani. He has no one." I rub the coarse material of my new pants. "What will become of him?"

"I believe the Māori community will gather around him." Uncle Bear pats my other leg. "Besides, he seems quite a capable young man."

"Boy."

He nods once. "That's fair."

For a long time, the creak of the leather traces, the clomp of the horses' hooves, the gentle ringing of the bridles, and the grinding of the wheels against the axle are the only sounds. I must've nodded off for a while, because I wake to find I'm leaning against Bear's shoulder with my head almost in his lap. I jerk upright as stinging heat rises up my neck into my cheeks. Shame twists in my gut, winding around curling strands of resentment and melding into a simmering rage.

I've betrayed my pa. This man is a stranger, acting like he's my parent, and here I am, falling into his trap. I won't do it. I won't rely on him.

Besides, he's going to drop us off with the old Georgia farmers and leave us anyway. Another loss. Another goodbye.

I stiffen my back and turn my face away. No, it's like we said. Buck and Ian are all I have. They depend on me, and I, like Mani, must rely on myself.

Out of the blue, Uncle Bear murmurs, "I always looked up to your pa."

From the corner of my eye, I see Buck leaning out the window, his arms folded on the sill with his head resting on them. "Tell us some stories."

Ian's voice rises from the other side of the carriage. "Yes, tell us about him."

"He was strong as an ox and twice as bull-headed." Uncle Bear chuckles. "Ma and Pa could never quite contain him. He was always running off to go exploring, at first around the land beyond our farm, then as he got older, well into the mountains and beyond. By the time he was your age, Fin, he would be gone for days at a time. No one knew where." He sighs. "Ma always said he had a wanderlust. But she worried about him so, when he was gone.

"Then, when he turned seventeen, he up and told all of us he was leaving. Pa tried to convince him to stay, but he threw back in Pa's face that he had gone to war at seventeen. 'At least I ain't going to war,' Clay said. And that was that."

"Where did he go?"

"He'd write to us from time to time, mainly to relieve Ma's worry, I think. He lived for a spell with the Lakota. He fought on the side of the Sioux in the Messiah War and barely escaped Wounded Knee. After that, he traveled south and sailed for a spell with some men transporting goods from the Caribbean and Mexico to the Americas."

"Was he a pirate?"

Uncle Bear laughs. "Piracy was pretty much gone by that time, although he would've fit right in with them—according to the stories."

A mournful groan rumbles in Buck's chest. "I would've loved to see Pa as a pirate."

"Then, he traveled overseas to Africa where he hunted game, and to England, Ireland, and Scotland. That's where he met your ma."

"Did you ever meet Ma?"

"I did. Clay brought her to the farm to meet Ma and Pa. You were about one year old, Fin. She was a fiery woman, full of life. Perfect for Clay." A wistful smile curves his lips.

"So, I met you before?"

"Once. But I'm sure you don't remember. You were too young." He tilts his head. "They stayed with us on the farm for about a year, then he up and moved to Montana. Said he wanted to start a sheep farm." Bear shakes his head. "Where he got some of his hair-brained ideas, I'll never know." His brow furrows. "He ran into a lot of trouble with the cattle ranchers. Several times, they threatened his life. And with all of you, he didn't feel like he could stay there any longer. So, he bought the sheep station in New Zealand, where he said sheep were welcome, and moved you all there. You know the rest."

"Uncle Bear." I pause, almost afraid to ask. "Do you know why Pa would get so blue?"

Bear sits quietly, staring straight ahead, stroking the leather reins for several minutes. Then, he closes his eyes. "His experiences with the

Lakota broke something in him. It's like he lost all innocence and all hope at the same time, seeing such immense cruelty and slaughter for no good reason. See, the Sioux surrendered, and the soldiers killed them all anyway." He twists his mouth and wrinkles his nose as if smelling a foul odor. "He wasn't the same after that."

"Sometimes, Pa would disappear and be gone for a long time, like you said he did when he was a kid." I blow out a slow breath. "We never knew where he went."

"It was his wanderlust taking hold. Both a blessing and a curse, I suppose."

"Buck caught it."

Buck's bellow rises from inside the carriage. "Hey!"

"I meant no insult, Buck. I'm saying you're a lot like Pa."

"Oh." Buck settles back against his seat.

"Ian and I are more like Ma, I think."

Uncle Bear hums a few notes from a song I recognize Ma used to sing. "Fiona had a strength about her. I enjoyed getting to know her when they lived on the farm." His whistle through his teeth sounds like wind through our cabin's eaves. "What a fierce beauty. I can't imagine what she saw in my brother." A widening grin puffs up his cheeks. "But she surely could keep Clay on his toes."

Buck snorts. "She kept us on our toes, too."

"I bet she did." Bear tilts his head to the side. "I see her strength in all three of you."

All this talk about Ma and Pa tugs at my mood like thick mud along the riverbank. Why did Buck have to go and ask him to tell stories? I slump in my seat, fold my arms across my chest, and nod as if falling asleep, hoping Uncle Bear will take the hint.

Buck and Ian jabber made-up stories about Pa on a sailing ship, protecting the cargo with his sword, clinging to the mast while storms rage around him, and crying yo-ho-ho with his shipmates. Bear chimes in with tales of the big game hunter killing a mighty lion and almost getting skewered by a rhinoceros while protecting a damsel in distress. I want no part in their silliness.

The day wears on me like leather chaps chafing my skin, and by the time the sun touches the horizon and the dock comes into sight, I'm as antsy as I imagine Pa would get when stuck in one place too long.

"We'll stay in Timaru tonight. The ship is scheduled to leave early in the morning, so it would be wise to try to go to bed early." Uncle Bear urges the horse forward. "First, though, let's eat. Nothing but cereal and snacks all day has left me hungrier than a bear after hibernating."

Buck and Ian guffaw. "Uncle Bear's hungry as a bear!"

"Watch out, he might eat you!"

The leather seats creak as the two boys wrestle, growling and ripping at each other's clothes. I glance at Bear, wondering if he'll put a stop to it, but he's laughing at their stupid antics. I sink lower in my seat. If only I could disappear altogether.

Uncle Bear leaves the carriage at the stables, instructing the owner to sell the horse and rig and forward the earnings after subtracting any fees for the horse's care. Fortunately, it's a short walk to our lodgings.

This inn is nicer than the saloon where we stayed before, with a nice diner on the street level and rooms up the stairs. Uncle Bear checks us in, and we carry our meager belongings up to our room, which is more spacious than our last one, and even has two beds. Buck and Ian are still riled up from their roughhousing in the carriage, so they run straight to the beds, jumping on them and howling like the Māori before a hunt.

"Settle down, boys." Uncle Bear holds up his hands. "Settle down. You must remember, other people are staying in this inn."

"Yessir."

He rubs his hands together. "Now, who is ready to eat?"

"Me!"

"Me!"

"Very well. Let's see what they have."

I thought Irene's diner had good food, but it pales in comparison to this place. I choose the seafood platter, which has enough food on it to stuff a hog. Still, I manage to eat it all, even the chips. Ian gets the lamb shank, Buck picks the roast with potatoes, carrots, and peas, and Uncle Bear chooses a heaping plate of lamb chops with vegetables. I'm too full for dessert—until they bring out fruit cobbler drowning in ice cream, which I eat with relish.

After the meal, my stomach is as heavy as if I'd eaten a whole hoop of cheese. We drag up to bed, and I'm asleep about the time my head hits the pillow.

Uncle Bear rises before dawn, as is his practice, retrieving hot water for our basin. We wash up, don our travel clothes, then make our way to the docks.

A long pier lined with boats juts out from the dock. More boats and larger ships tied along the dock give the impression of a squat porcupine bristling with spikes. We walk to the far end of the dock, where the longest ship I've ever seen awaits. Its sides are painted black, while the upper portion is white and speckled with portholes. Two large, golden cylinders sit on top, billowing steam.

We stride up the long, wooden gangplank leading from the dock to the ship's deck as if we belong, but the other boarding passengers are dressed in finery like the wealthy city folk in Christchurch, so we stick out like pigs at an Easter parade.

We must descend to the lower decks to find our quarters, so our cabin is dreary with heavy, stale air, but I don't care, for once we drop our bags, we return to the decks to watch the ship pull away from port. The fresh, salty wind catches my hair and swirls it around my head. My clothes batter my body like a flag whipping against its pole. A fine spray of mist bathes me each time the ship digs through a new wave. The rising sun glistens on the deep blue water as if someone has strewn a million diamonds across its surface.

It's glorious.

The ship glides upon the water, the waves offering feeble resistance and causing no roll. I spread my arms like wings, as if I'm a bird skimming the sea, and shout into the heavens with an unfamiliar joy.

If I painted a picture representing freedom, it would look like this.

For the first time, I catch a glimpse of why Pa would go adventuring, and my heart finds grace to forgive his frequent absences. The stiff breeze carries away the dark cloud hanging over me, and the heaviness of my heart for the past few months evaporates, cleansed by the salt air, until a new awareness, foreign to my sensibilities and strange on my tongue, floats from within me on my bellowing cry.

I'm ready for an adventure of my own.

CHAPTER TWELVE

March 1907

A white mist flows along the foot of the pale blue mountain like a river, and as we ride into the fog, its droplets glow like tiny pearls in the horse's mane and moisten my hair until it hangs in dark ringlets around my face. The air hangs thick around me, making my breaths labored, unlike the fresh, dry air in New Zealand. My clothes cling to my skin like when the ship plowed through a wave, and a fine spray of salt water coated me.

No sounds pierce my ears—not s single note from a sparrow, no whisper of wind rustling leaves, not even the clomp of hooves, as a thick bed of pine straw deadens their plodding while we make our way up the mountain.

Someone named Chris brought horses for us, meeting us in Blue Ridge where we exited the train we boarded in Atlanta. Chris is my uncle, too, but he isn't a MacAlister by blood. My granda adopted him when he was a youth and gave him the MacAlister name. Chris married his wife, Emma, when Uncle Bear was only two years old.

"You'll have plenty of other children to play with." Chris ticks off each name on his fingers. "My son, Mac, is only two years older than Fin, and my Claire is Ian's age. Then, Liam's children…"

Uncle Bear interrupts. "Uncle Liam is your Pa's older brother."

"Right—Liam's son, Samuel is Buck's age, and Katy-did is Ian and Claire's age."

"Katy-did?"

Chris chuckles. "That's what we all call her. Katrina is her real name, but she prefers Katy. Thus, the nickname." He shifts in his saddle and glances over his shoulder. "Plus, you have several more cousins scattered across the country who you'll meet over time. Maisie and Bram's four children in Montana, Martin and Susannah's three children in Texas…"

Buck throws his hand in the air. "How am I going to keep all these people straight?"

Uncle Bear smiles. "It will be easier once you meet them. Maisie is your Pa's younger sister. She married Chris' wife's younger brother, Bram. Martin is Maisie's next-oldest brother. He married a Texas girl. Our other sister, Mary, lives in Atlanta with her husband, Jack, but they don't have any children."

"Geez, sure is complicated."

"I guess it is." Bear chuckles. "Big families often are."

"How many families live on this land?" My mind's eye imagines a cluster of cabins pressed against each other and a clog of people around all the time.

"I have my own land." Chris sits up straighter in his saddle. "Our cabin is in the valley by the river on the other side of the mountain."

"My parents, your granma and granda, live in the big house. Your Uncle Liam and his family live on the eastern slope." Bear leans over the saddle horn. "Believe me, you won't see each other unless you choose to."

"Uncle Bear?" Ian's quiet voice sounds weak and strained. "Will you be leaving soon and going back to California?"

"Not right away. But, yes, I will be returning to California."

"Why?" Buck blurts. "You said there's plenty of room here."

"Yes, but my home is in California now."

Ian groans and rubs his eyes. "Why can't we go with *you*?"

Chris looks over his shoulder again. "Just wait until you meet your granma, Ester. She's the kindest, sweetest, loveliest person I've ever met. You'll be thankful you are here, I promise. Meeting your grandparents was the best thing that ever happened to me."

Ian pouts his lower lip. "But I want to go with Uncle Bear."

Bear clears his throat. "Boys, do you remember when I first rode into town? What did you think of me then?"

The three of us glance at each other but don't answer.

"What did you do?"

"We—uh, we ran away." I lower my eyes.

"You didn't want to live with me then, did you?"

"No, sir."

"But we didn't know you!" Buck's brows knit together on his broad forehead. "We know you now."

Uncle Bear quirks his brow. "Like you don't know your Granma Ester or your Granda Mac?"

I already got his point, but I don't like it. "They're old." I spit to the side of my horse. "It will be like living with Missus Appleton again."

Uncle Bear chuckles, then lifts his chin, pointing it up the hill. "Wait until you meet them before you pass judgment. What do you say?"

"Yessir." But in my heart, a seed of resentment toward Uncle Bear burrows as deep as a mole, taking hold as a vow: I won't let myself get close to *any* of them, because all it means is another loss. And I'm done with losses.

Some adventure this turned out to be—living with two old folks, forced to take care of them and their farm, with a bunch of younger kids underfoot but no one my age to talk to, nowhere to go, and nothing to do but work, eat, and sleep.

"The way they live will be familiar to you," Bear continues, unaware of the black seed breaking open in my chest. "You'll memorize Scripture, like with your ma and pa, and share how you've applied them each day. You'll have school and chores…"

I pounce on his words. "They'll use us like slaves."

"I ain't no slave." Buck curls his upper lip over his teeth.

Uncle Bear's brow furrows. "You weren't a slave to your ma and pa, were you? They had you doing chores, the same as your granma and granda will."

Why can't Uncle Bear understand this? "This isn't *our* land! So, it's not the same at all."

Uncle Bear reins his horse and turns him across the path, forcing us to stop. "They are your *family*. And I know your pa taught you to take care of family above all else."

I meet Bear's stare with a glare of my own. I can tell Buck and Ian are watching, measuring Bear and me. I won't back down, and it doesn't look like Bear plans on it, either. But after a minute of uncomfortable silence, Ian breaks the tension with a sob. "*You* are our family, Uncle Bear."

The standoff melts with Ian's tears. Uncle Bear's face softens. "Yes, I am. And I always will be."

"So, why can't you take us with you?"

Bear sighs. "Ian, your pa was clear and very specific. He wanted you raised by your granda and granma, should something happen to Fiona and him." He shakes his head. "I'll not be the one to go against their wishes." He spurs his horse up the path.

"Come along, boys." Chris follows behind Bear.

I growl deep in my chest where the black seedling sprouts venomous tendrils. "Come on, Ian. Let's go." I yank on my horse's reins, my chest heaving, pressed in an invisible vise. "Buck, are you coming?"

Buck gives a barely perceptible nod.

It would be easy enough to ride into the fog and disappear in the thick woods. But Uncle Bear's admonishment to not judge, and the fact that Pa chose our grandparents as our caretakers keeps me following Bear and Chris.

I'll give it a week before I decide anything. If Granma and Granda are as nice as Bear claims, maybe I can make this work—maybe. If they act like Missus Appleton, I'll devise a plan of escape.

The trail curves around the mountain like a snake around a tree limb, squeezing me nearer to my doom. At the end of a sharply angled bend, we run out of the trees into a huge, open field of golden grain bending gently in the breeze. Our trail disappears into the waving stalks to emerge in the far distance near a set of stone steps and stained beams gracing the wide porch of a massive log home.

It might be four or maybe five times bigger than our cabin in New Zealand, based on what I can see.

Beyond the cabin lie more cleared areas rolling like waves on the sea, filled with grazing cows and horses. A huge barn and corral stand to the right of the cabin, and fenced areas for chickens, pigs, and goats to the left.

A thin woman stands framed in the doorway, her long, white hair swirling around her face like a waterspout. A thick, colorful blanket rests across her back, a sky-blue background covered with red and gold interlocking diamonds, black and red arrows, and a design of white and gray feathers in the center—definitely native. Her arms are folded against the chilly breeze, but when she spots our approach, she lifts her hand, causing the blanket to slip from her shoulder. The faint call, "Mac!" carries to us on the wind.

Then, a tall, rugged-looking man steps out behind the woman, dwarfing her with his broad chest and shoulders. His red hair is streaked with some white, but his full beard gleams like snow in the morning sun. The woman's smile is radiant as she waves, but the man's face remains impassive. He pulls the blanket up and tucks it carefully around her arm.

Chris and Uncle Bear urge their horses to a gallop, racing through the tall, billowing wheat toward the cabin. My horse strains against the reins, trying to follow, but I pull him up short. Ian and Buck stop on either side of me.

"This is it."

Buck leans on his saddle horn. "What do you think?"

Ian squints and lifts his hand to shield his eyes. "They look nice."

"Uh." It's all I can muster.

"Well." Buck heaves a great sigh. "Might as well have it over." He slaps his reins and starts up the long path to our fate. Ian follows behind him.

I can't make myself move. It's as if my horse and I are frozen at a single point in time. The way back is blocked by a huge, black, stone wall, and the way forward is a whirling tempest. My breaths catch in my throat, choking me. I'm exposed. Vulnerable.

Everything and everyone I've loved has slipped through my stiff, clumsy fingers. If I accept this family, they'll leave me, too.

My horse nickers, impatient to join his fellows and complete his journey. They're all waiting for me up there. Watching. Judging.

Ian and Buck are halfway to the stone steps. Chris and Bear are just ahead of them. It's too late now. Even if I gallop the whole way, everyone will be standing there staring, wondering what's wrong with me.

All that's in me wants to dash away into the trees and vanish. But the stone wall of time bars my escape. This singular moment is my last taste of freedom, and I'm loath to lose its sweetness.

By some mercy of God, Buck pauses on the trail, turning his horse to look for me. Ian follows his lead, and there they remain, with their backs facing our new guardians, waiting for me.

All we have is each other.

Somehow, their warm and understanding smiles thaw my icy heart enough for me to kick my horse, who bolts like lightning up the hill. Everything around me blurs. All I can see are my brothers patiently waiting for me. The stalks whip my legs as I race past. The horse's hooves pound against the packed earth, matching the beat of my racing heart.

Then, my horse skids to a stop beside them. Ian takes my hand, gesturing for Buck to do the same. Buck sneers and shakes his head, but when Ian raises his brows, he follows Ian's example, and the three of us, linked like a cord of three strands, ride the rest of the way with our horses shoulder to shoulder.

Granma Ester clutches her hands to her throat and squeals as we approach. "Welcome home, boys." She flutters her fingers like tiny butterflies. "I can't believe you're finally here."

"Ma." Bear jumps off his horse and darts up the steps two at a time to wrap his mother in a massive hug.

His pa beams a wide smile, clapping Bear's back. "Good to see you, son."

Chris also dismounts, taking our horses' reins. "Hop down, boys, and go meet your grandparents." He starts unhooking our bags from the back of his horse.

After a quick glance at Ian and Buck for confidence, I swing my leg over my horse and jump down. Buck and Ian follow. We meet at the bottom step, and holding hands again, we climb as if walking toward the gallows.

Uncle Bear extricates from his ma's hug and sweeps his arm toward us. "Ma, Pa, this is Findlay—goes by Fin—and this is Barclay—they call him Buck—and Ian."

Granda's stern countenance returns. "Boys."

Ester glides to the top step and pulls me against her thin, warm chest until I'm almost swaddled in her blanket. "You are most welcome." She holds my shoulders for a moment, examining my eyes. "It's a terrible loss for us all." Her clear blue eyes brim with moisture. "But you're with family now."

All I can do is nod once. Anything else threatens to start my tears flowing.

Ian nestles into her hug as if she's a warm fire on a cold winter's day. When she moves on to Buck, I spot a small, wet stain on the front of her dress.

Buck stiffens in Ester's arms. She draws back quickly, settling on patting his hand to show her affection.

"Let me show you to your rooms." Ester gathers her blanket close to her chest and, taking Buck's hand, leads us through the large oak door. "This is where we gather in the evenings to read and share—oh, everything."

The logs are stained a deep, rich, coffee color. Beams cross overhead below a vaulted ceiling rising two stories above us. Their stone fireplace is twice the size ours used to be. Granma leads us up the broad stone staircase that sweeps to the left of the large main room, which is filled with leather couches and chairs, dark wooden tables, and cases of books lining the walls on either side of the fireplace.

At the top of the stairs, a hallway extends to the other end of the house. Doors lead to rooms on either side of the hall down to the end, where a large door stands closed.

She points to the door at the end. "Mac and I sleep down there. This space is private. You will not enter our room without permission. Is that understood?"

"Yes, ma'am."

"Buck, you'll sleep here." She pushes open the first door to the left. The room houses a large bed covered with a hand-sewn, blue and brown quilt, a tall, double-doored wardrobe, a side table with a basin, pitcher, and towels, and a window overlooking the valley. Granma sweeps into the room and pulls back the curtains. "Do you like the view, Buck?"

"Yes'm."

"I picked out the colors and made your quilt myself." She giggles. "I don't know why, but I sensed you might fancy blue."

"Yes'm."

She pulls open the wardrobe door. "You may hang your clothes in here." Buck gawks at me, shrugging one shoulder, but Granma doesn't seem to notice.

When she grabs Ian's hand, I marvel at how delicate her fingers are. Ian's hands are almost the same size as hers. "Ian, come and see what we have for you. You'll be right across the hall from Buck."

Ian's mouth drops open. "We have our own rooms?"

"Of course." Ester opens the door opposite Buck's room. Ian's room is set up the same as Buck's, except his quilt is red, green, and gold. Ian's window overlooks the pastures behind the house.

"I can watch the horses and cows!"

"And the sunset." Ester beams and wraps her arms around Ian's neck from behind. "Do you like it?"

"Yes'm."

"I'm so glad."

We follow her as she flits down the hallway like a little fairy, her fluttering blanket acting as her gossamer wings. "Fin, your room will be here." She laughs and opens the last door on the right.

"Wow!" Ian rushes into the room, his eyes ogling like he's entered a magical land from one of his books.

The room is larger than Buck's and Ian's. My bed has spires on the four corners, like a castle. Maybe that explains Ian's awe. A thick, white coverlet adorns the bed, and folded across the bottom lies an animal skin, as dark as the log wall. Like Ian, my window overlooks the back pastures. I have a wardrobe, a dressing table, and a desk.

Ester caresses the animal fur. "Boys, this is buffalo hide." She lifts her brows and gazes intently into my eyes. "It is very precious to me. It belonged to my dear mother, a gift from Mac on our first Christmas together." She clasps her hands at her waist. "I'm trusting you with its care. Can you handle the responsibility?"

"Yes, ma'am."

"Very well." She moves to the window and perches on the wide ledge jutting from the base of my window. "If I lived in this room, I do believe I'd spend hours sitting right here, watching the sunsets and listening to the lowing of the cows. So beautiful." She smiles at me. "What do you think of your room?"

"It's fine, ma'am."

Ester chuckles and closes her eyes. " You may wait in your rooms while we bring up your bags, and then you can unpack your things and get settled."

Buck puffs up his chest. "We can get our own bags."

Granma tilts her head slightly, her lips quirked in an amused grin. "I'm sure you are quite capable of getting your bags. But you are our honored guests. Once you settle in and have a meal, you will be treated as the rest of the family and expected to help with chores. But until then, make yourselves comfortable and let us know if you need anything. Anything at all."

"Yes'm."

"I want you to know how thrilled we are to have you here with us." She presses her palm against my shoulder and squeezes. "I know the circumstances that brought you here were dreadful, but I hope our love will help you cope with your terrible loss." Clearing her throat and swiping a finger under her eye, Ester leaves us, closing my door behind her.

Buck walks over to the window and sits on the wide sill. "Well, what do you think?"

"It's so big." Ian spins, his arms wide.

"I bet they have a lot of rules. And who knows what Mac will expect from us." Buck frowns. "As big as this place is, I'm already feeling closed in." He shivers.

I understand his feeling. I've felt the noose tightening since Ester held my shoulders and stared straight through me into my heart. "We better get used to it. We don't have many choices here."

"It's nice to have our own rooms, though." Ian grins. "At least there's that."

"I guess so."

Footfalls thump on the stairs. "Better go to your rooms. Someone's bringing the bags."

Buck and Ian scamper to the hall. I press with both hands on the thick mattress. It sinks as if I'm pushing on a cloud. Everything about this place screams extravagance. I don't believe Pa would be pleased.

Then again, he was raised in this house. This could've been his room, for all I know.

I'll have to ask.

I move to the window and perch on the sill. Granma seems kind enough, but Granda appears to be a stern man. Surely Buck will test him. How is that going to fly? At least Ian seems content.

Through the glass, I can barely hear the melodious songs of the cows as they wander the green fields—a little taste of home in a foreign land. But no sheep. Ian will be disappointed. He loves shepherding and shearing.

A gentle knock propels me to my feet. "Come in."

The door cracks, and Chris sticks his head in. "I have your bag."

"Thank you."

He slides the bag along the rough-hewn floor. "Do you need anything else?"

"No. Sir. Thank you."

"I'll leave you to it, then." The door latches behind him.

What do I do now? Are there rules about how to store clothes? All my meager belongings are dirty from our travels. Where do I wash them? Do I take them to Ester, or will she expect me to care for them myself?

The paralysis threatens to return, so I leave the bag in the middle of the floor and return to the window seat. At least here, I can find some semblance of peace.

CHAPTER THIRTEEN

March 1907

"Food's on the table!" The loud call floating up the stairs yanks me from my reverie. How long have I been sitting here staring at nothing? The sun sits high in the sky now—has it been hours?

I'm like a lost fawn whose mother was shot dead, not knowing what to do or where to turn. I'm not hungry but figure I'm expected to eat now, so I head for the stairs, not realizing until I reach the bottom that I don't know where the kitchen is. Or do they have a separate room for eating?

Where are Buck and Ian? What if they didn't hear the call? I head back up the stairs and knock on their doors. No reply. "Wake up, it's time to eat." Nothing. Did they already go downstairs?

I go back down and listen for the sounds of conversation. I can always hear Buck, even if he's a mile away. Nothing.

It's as if I'm still stuck in my frozen moment in time, but everyone else has moved on—like time went on without me, carrying everyone with it. My chest starts to tingle and my stomach wrenches. Cold sweat pops out on my forehead. I open my mouth to cry out but nothing will come. I'm alone.

"What are you doin' just standing there?"

A wave of relief pours over me like a warm shower. I turn to find Buck with his head poked through a door behind the staircase.

"Didn't you hear them say there's food? C'mon."

I follow him like a sheep through what looks like a sitting room, and through another door into a large room filled with a heavy table surrounded by chairs. Granda Mac sits at the far end, with Ester at his right hand and Bear on his left. Ian sits beside Uncle Bear. Uncle Chris sits beside Ester, with a blonde woman, two young men, and a pretty little girl I don't know beside him. The little girl must be Claire, and one of the young men is probably Mac, named after Granda.

Another broad-shouldered man—Uncle Liam, I assume— sits at the table's end closest to the door. A lovely chestnut-haired woman sits at his left hand. Tucked on the corner next to Claire at Liam's right hand sits a girl who must be Katy, his daughter. His boy, Samuel, sits beside his mother.

Buck darts to the chair beside Samuel, so like a good sheep, I follow him and sit in the next chair beside Ian.

This is as close to my worst imagination as it gets—fifteen people pressed against one another, with everyone talking at once. What an odd sensation, as if I'm watching myself at the table with all these strangers—watching my hand pick up a serving spoon and dump some potatoes on a plate—watching Uncle Bear slide a slab of meat onto the plate—watching Uncle Chris' wife serve a spoonful of vegetables for me—watching my hand take a fork and shovel in beans. I can't feel the food in my mouth. It has no taste. What's happening to me?

Words fly past me too fast for me to capture them. There are introductions and conversations about planting and something about buying more horses. My body goes through the motions of eating, but I don't recall the food, the names, or the content of the discussions. All I want to know is if it will always be like this.

Wait, did I ask that out loud? Uncle Bear is chuckling at me.

"Family is always welcome at this table." Granda fixes his icy stare on me. "Everyone was excited to meet the three of you."

Ester lifts her napkin and coughs into it.

"Samuel and I are going to be great friends," Buck announces. How—and when did that happen?

"That's wonderful, dear." Ester beams at the two boys.

"The five of us can play together." Claire's eyes sparkle as she glances through her lashes at Ian and giggles into her hand.

Five of them. That excludes me, then. Very well. It's for the best. Who wants to play silly games with a bunch of annoying little kids? Perhaps Chris' son, Mac…but his glazed expression and preoccupation with Uncle Bear tell me he has better things to do than waste time with me.

So much for standing by each other. I knew this would change everything. Now, Ian and Buck are off after their new, exciting friends, and I'm left with no one. As soon as this nightmare is over, I'm returning to my room and hiding out for the rest of the day. Maybe the rest of the year.

"Fin, dear. Would you help me clear the table?"

"Yes, ma'am."

Ester stands slowly. "Bring them this way." She glides toward a door leading to the back of the house.

Starting with my plate, I move from chair to chair, stacking the plates to carry to the kitchen.

"You might want to make two trips," Chris suggests.

"I have it." I didn't mean to bark at him, but I find his concern insulting. I'm not some little kid. I know what I'm doing.

Granda's plate is the last one. Rather than help me by stacking it on top as the others have, he waits, his arms folded across his lap and his bushy eyebrows raised over his steel-colored eyes, forcing me to set the plates down and stack it myself.

"You have it?"

Is he taunting me? Making fun of me? "Yes, I have it."

"Very well." His eyes narrow slightly. "Take them to Ester."

The stack of plates reaches above my line of sight, so when I reach the door, I can't see that it has closed behind Granma. I bump into the door, causing the plates to wobble and rattle, but I manage to keep them from falling.

"You have it?" Mac asks again.

"I have it."

"Very well."

I balance the stacked plates on my hip with one hand while turning the knob with the other. The door is heavy, but I finally shove it open. As I push through, it swings back against me—hard—and I lurch to the left. The dishes teeter against my arm for a split second, then tilt and slide off my hip, landing with a deafening crash.

I can do nothing but watch in horror. My heart stops in my chest. Heat rushes to my cheeks then sinks into my neck. A cold silence descends over the room. The patters of Ester's tiny feet echo in the hallway. "What happened?" She pulls back the door and sees the shattered pieces scattered across the floor. "Oh, my!"

Every eye in the room is glued to me when I scan their faces to measure their level of rage. Buck's face glows beet-red. Ian's eyes bulge like tiny round moons. Uncle Bear's brow creases with pity. But it's Mac's expression that does me in. His face hasn't changed a lick, almost as if he *knew* I would fail spectacularly—like he *wanted* me to fail.

As my shoe pushes against the floor to bolt, a jagged piece of porcelain digs through my worn sole and into my foot. A high-pitched yelp escapes my mouth, but the pain doesn't stop me from limping out of there.

"Findlay." Ester's gentle call is almost worse than Mac's judgment. I hobble up the stairs, one-footed—tha-thunk, tha-thunk, tha-thunk—hoping no one follows me.

If I had dropped Ma's good dishes, Pa would've tanned my hide, and he loved me. What is *Mac* going to do to me?

I go to my room, slam the door, and shove the chair from the writing desk beneath the knob. Gingerly, I pluck the jagged glass from my sole. A tinge of red stains the white porcelain. I slide off my shoe and sock, revealing a cut in the ball of my foot, oozing blood.

I have nothing to use for bandages except the cotton cloth Ester left next to the basin. Will it be another unforgivable error to sully her washcloth with my blood? I don't suppose it matters much since I'm leaving.

The thought shocks me. When did I decide I was running away? The moment the dishes crashed? When Buck announced Samuel was to be his best friend? When I laid eyes on the overcrowded table? Was it when Ester announced we were honored guests? Or was it when she dove into my eyes and shared my pain?

My clothes bag still sits in the middle of the bedroom floor. If I leave now, I can walk out the front door without anyone seeing me. But how do I get Pa's money from Uncle Bear? And will I leave Buck and Ian behind without giving them the chance to choose to go with me? No, I can't leave Ian, and even with Buck choosing Samuel over me, I won't leave him, either.

So, I'll take my punishment, no matter how painful, and wait for the darkness to shield my escape. Meanwhile, I'll figure out how to get that money.

With my foot wrapped in the cloth, I limp to the windowsill and stare at the wandering cows and grazing horses, imagining myself riding one of the horses to freedom beyond the bounds of Mac's land. If I can get to our money, maybe I'll have enough to buy passage back to New Zealand, where our land awaits. The Māori are already working the land. I'm sure they'll be willing to continue once I return.

Then, I won't be alone because Mani will be there, and the Atas, and the other Māori from the village. They'll be glad to see me.

A light tap on the door stops my breath. Here it comes. I stiffen my back. "Yes?"

"May I enter?" It's Ester.

I exhale. "Yes, ma'am."

She opens my door slowly, looking around the corner before entering. "I would like to speak with you about the accident."

Dropping my head, I rub my offending hands on my pants. "I'm sorry about your dishes."

Ester blows a quick breath through her nose and waves her hand. "Oh, I don't care about those silly dishes. They are things. All things can be replaced or done without." She moves closer and grasps my shoulders in her delicate fingers. "I care about you." Her eyes fall to my wrapped foot, and her brow creases. "Do you want me to check your injury?"

"No'm, I took care of it."

Her eyes meet mine, and once again, I'm exposed. Peeled open like a boiled potato. Invaded. "Now, then. No need to be upset. It was simply an accident."

Of course, Granma doesn't know that Chris and Mac warned me not to try to carry all the dishes at once, and I ignored them. "I should've made two trips."

She smiles in her gentle way that feels like a warm caress. "So, now you know. Mistakes are opportunities to learn and grow. That's all." She moves to my side and takes my arm. "Come back downstairs with me and join the rest of us. We were going to have some dessert." The corners of her eyes crinkle. "It's quite yummy."

"No, thank you."

Her hand drops to her side, and her eyes trail to the bag of clothes left in the center of my floor. "You haven't unpacked yet?"

"No'm."

"Is there a reason?"

What do I say? Because I'm leaving tonight? Because I hate it here? Because I never had any intention of staying? "I…I didn't get to it."

"Very well." She presses her lips together. "We will miss you." She pauses with her hand on the knob. "Are you sure you don't want to rejoin the family?"

"No'm."

"We *will* miss you." Thankfully, she slowly opens the door. "I hope you will change your mind."

Is she talking about dessert or something else? Does she suspect something? "No'm."

"Very well." The door closes quietly behind her.

My feet remain glued to the floor, staring at the polished gold doorknob. Strange, how the little things leave me so out of place as if I've entered another world, one in which I don't belong. In many ways, Ester's kindness is worse than Pa's whippings. Dropping her dishes was no accident. As Pa would've said, "It's pride, plain and simple." Surely, she knows that. Yet, she expressed no disappointment or anger. Why?

Realization hits me like a slap in my face. She feels sorry for me, that's why. What on the surface looks like grace is pity. Well, she can look down on me all she wants, but I won't be here to take it.

I kneel beside my clothes bag, digging through its contents until I find the new shoes Uncle Bear made me pack. I yank them out and throw them one at a time against the wooden door, then stuff my clothes back in the bag and close it. Now, I'm ready.

Another knock sounds on my door. What now?

Without waiting for my response, Granda Mac swings the door open and strides into the room, his brow pinched above his nose, and his mouth turned down like a crescent moon. "Ester says you aren't coming downstairs." He folds his arms across his chest.

"No, sir."

His eyes narrow. "Well, son, in this house, we take responsibility for our choices, and we clean our messes. Are you going to leave your granma to sweep up the dishes you broke? Is that how your pa raised you?"

Shame folds my gut against my backbone. "No, sir."

Mac nods once, walks across the floor to my bed, and sits. "Come here, son."

"I'm not your son," I mutter under my breath.

"You might not have been born my son, but according to your pa, you're my son now. So, sit."

I drag to my feet, slink to the bed, and slump down beside Granda.

"Hard things happen in this life, Fin. I know firsthand how difficult it can be when you lose someone you love. But you need to decide if you'll let those hard things rule your life."

I raise a brow and cut my eyes toward Mac. "Seems I don't have much choice about it ruling my life." I gesture around the room. "I'm here, aren't I?"

He tilts his head and quirks his mouth. "It hasn't crossed your mind that you're the only one choosing to be miserable here? Buck and Ian appear to be choosing to make the most of it, so obviously, there is a choice to be made."

I turn my face away. I won't give him the satisfaction of seeing my reaction.

"And has it crossed your mind that maybe, just maybe, the Good Lord has a reason for bringing you to us? Perhaps coming here is His best redemption for your parents' deaths."

White hot rage races through my chest like a flaming arrow. I dig my teeth into my lip to keep from screaming.

"I had a family before Ester. I bet you didn't know that. I had a wife, a boy, and another baby on the way." Granda lowers his head. "They were killed, along with my whole tribe." He swallows. "I thought my life was over—I *wanted* it to be over." He turns toward me. "But the Lord still had something wonderful for me—my Ester, and the family we made."

Mac reaches over and grasps my hands in his oversized one. "Now, I know we can never take the place of your ma and pa, any more than Ester and my boys and girls could replace my first family. But what a redemption they are of my loss." He squeezes my hands. "Maybe we could be a redemption for you."

"I don't want a stinking redemption. I want Ma and Pa." My words strangle my throat. Tears gush up but I swallow them.

"I don't blame you. The grief is too near." He sighs. "But over time, you may come to see things differently." He slaps his thighs. "In the meantime, you can clear your mess and join the family for dessert."

The black seed of resentment now blossoming in my chest sends its tendrils to grip and squeeze my heart until hatred oozes out of me like tar. So much for having a choice.

I'll do as he says for now. But he'll witness my choice soon enough.

The family is arrayed across the sitting room, eating pie, playing games, or talking in small groups, except for Granma Ester, who is already sweeping when I return to the dining room.

"Granda says it is my mess, and I must clean it." My words grate in my ears.

Ester leans against her broom. "Why don't we do it together?" She holds the broom out to me. "You sweep, and I will hold the dustpan."

I'd rather do it myself. If she's holding the dustpan, I must be careful while sweeping lest she get glass in her eyes or cuts on her hands. Then, Granda Mac would beat me for sure and certain. But I take the broom with a sigh and continue sweeping.

Working together, we make short work of it, and while Ester carries the bag of broken pieces into the kitchen, I grab a piece of the pie and slip into the sitting room where I find a lone chair in the shadows of a corner to eat in peace.

The gathering lasts until late in the afternoon. Buck, Ian, Claire, Katy, and Samuel move from playing on the floor to frolicking outside in the field. Tom and Mac ignore me, talking instead with Uncle Bear. Uncle Chris and Uncle Liam have their heads together. I can't hear what they're discussing, and I don't care. Granda Mac falls asleep on the settee for most of the afternoon. Granma Ester, Emma, Uncle Chris' wife, and Julianna, Liam's wife, do needlework and talk boring women's talk. My misery is complete.

At long last, Julianna signals to Liam it is time to go home. Chris and Liam call the children from the field and ready them to leave while Ester gathers some leftovers for them to take home for dinner, and young Mac and Tom prepare the horses. After lengthy goodbyes and hugs at the door, Buck, Ian, and I are left alone with Granma, Granda, and Uncle Bear.

"Did you have a nice time, boys?" Uncle Bear ruffles Ian's hair. "It seems you hit it off with Samuel, Katy, and Claire."

"We had the best time." Ian beams his brilliant smile. "Claire is mighty sweet."

"Samuel wants to come over tomorrow after chores. Would that be acceptable?"

I've never heard Buck be so formal and—respectful. It's disgusting. He's play-acting to make a good impression on our new guardians.

"Of course, dear." Ester lifts one finger. "After chores."

"Fin, why don't you lay in a fire? Buck, Ian, you can help Granma ready our dinner."

"Yessir, Granda."

Uncle Bear glances my way. "What about you, Fin? Did you have a nice time?"

No, this day was horrible in every way possible. "Yessir."

Bear rubs his hands together. "Good! Let me help you with that fire before a chill gets on the room."

He and I carry armloads of chopped firewood in from the woodshed, I lay a fire, and Uncle Bear lights the kindling. Soon, golden flames crackle within the stacked stones, sending phantoms' shadows dancing across the log walls. I remain seated on the hearth, staring into the flames, while the rest of the family return to the dining room for warmed leftovers from lunch.

Minutes later, Ian arrives, carrying a plate of meat and biscuits. "I thought you might like some of the meat, at least."

"Thank you." Although I'm not hungry, Ian's right, it would be wise to eat something—before I leave. There's enough here to eat a little now and save the rest for the road.

"Are you well, Fin? You've not been yourself."

"I miss Ma and Pa."

His face sags. "Me, too."

"Here, come sit with me." I wrap my arms around his shoulders. "The fire is warm."

For a few minutes, Ian and I enjoy the familiarity of each other's company and the peace that comes with ease and comfort. It reminds me of home. I can almost imagine Ma and Pa sitting in their usual places, Pa holding the Bible, preparing to read, and Ma stitching a ripped shirt or knitting some sweater or cap to give to the Māori.

Then, Granda, Granma, Uncle Bear, and Buck storm our retreat, and our peace evaporates. Why must everyone talk at once? Their chatter buzzes in my ear like summer mosquitoes. If only I could swat them away.

"I understand your pa kept up our family tradition of memorizing Scripture." Granda slides a large Bible from the bookshelf beside the fireplace. "Who would like to pick a verse?"

Buck whoops and waves his hand. "I know one!"

Granda Mac grunts and chuckles. "Memorizing one you already know defeats the purpose, don't you think?"

Buck deflates. "Oh. Yeah, I guess so."

"I believe tonight I will pick one." Mac hefts the heavy Bible and opens it to the center of the book. "I'm fond of the Proverbs."

I wrinkle my nose.

"Oh, so you're not impressed with the wisdom of Solomon?"

"I prefer the New Testament."

"Very well. I know the perfect verses. II Peter 1:5-8." Granda flips the thin pages and clears his throat. "'For this very reason, make every effort to add to your faith goodness; and to goodness, knowledge; and to knowledge, self-control; and to self-control, perseverance; and to perseverance, godliness; and to godliness, mutual affection; and to mutual affection, love. For if you possess these qualities in increasing measure, they will keep you from being ineffective and unproductive in your knowledge of our Lord Jesus Christ.'"

Buck groans. "*Auē*, that's a lot. How can we remember all that?"

Granda lifts his hand. "First, tell me what it means."

Ian stands, as is our custom. "I noticed Peter assumed we will have faith because he tells us to add things to our faith in increasing amounts so we will know Christ better."

"Very good, Ian." Ester's smile is radiant. Is it her smile or the fire that makes Ian's face shine as if he's standing in the sun? "What else, boys?"

"He gives a whole lot of things to add." Buck fidgets in his chair. If I know him, he stopped listening after the first item on the list.

"Such as?"

"Good stuff. Like being good."

Granma purses her lips. "Well, yes, Buck, they are all good things. But I believe every word in Scripture is important. Does anyone remember the words he used?"

"Goodness. Knowledge. Godliness. Perseverance." I'm skipping some but I don't want to think about such things as self-control, mutual affection, and love. Not right now. Let them think I can't recall them.

"What else?"

"Love!" Ian shouts.

Ester's beaming smile returns. "Absolutely. Mutual affection and love."

"And self-control," Granda Mac adds.

Did he choose these verses to make a point, directed at me? My rage seethes as I glare at my shoes. What do I care if he's angry with me? I'm gone before the dawn.

"I'll read it once more, then in the morning, you can repeat it, and tomorrow night, you will tell me how you applied the verse throughout the day."

I turn away, staring deep into the flames, allowing my mind to be consumed by their movements and sounds to drown out his slow, repetitive reading. I won't be here to repeat it, so why memorize it?

"Off the bed, now," Granma Ester chirps. "We have a busy day tomorrow. We'll go over your chores in the morning, then we'll wash the clothes you have, but I fear tomorrow, after our meal, we must head into town to buy you more clothes."

Buck groans again. "But Samuel wants to come over!"

"He may come after chores and stay for the noon meal. We will go into town after that."

"Thank you, ma'am."

Ian hugs Granma, then Granda before running up the stairs. Buck glances my way, then follows Ian.

"Buck's not one for affection." I shrug. "Good night."

"Good night, Fin. Sweet dreams, dear."

I wait a few seconds for Granda's good night, but it never comes. All the better. I'll have no regrets when I leave.

Buck and Ian are camped out in my room when I arrive upstairs. I waste no time. "I'm getting out of here," I murmur. "Who's coming with me?"

To my surprise, Buck chews his lower lip. "I don't want to go."

"What?" Buck, who never turns down the chance to break a rule, decides now is the time to be obedient?

"Uncle Bear's right, Fin. Pa wanted us to come here. There must be a reason for it."

Ian blinks rapidly, looking from one to the other.

"You don't want to come with us, Buck? Very well. But Ian and I are leaving."

"I…I…" Ian stutters.

"Where will you go? You can't get back to New Zealand."

"Uncle Bear has the money Pa left us. I'm going to get it. It's probably in his room."

"But what if you can't find it?"

"Then we'll survive in the woods like we were going to do with Mani."

"Yeah?" Buck snarls. "And look how that turned out."

"Then maybe we'll ride to Montana, where we lived long ago with Ma and Pa."

Buck shakes his head. "You'll never make it."

"I can't believe you, Buck. You were the one most vocal about not coming to America. Now, you want to stay here?"

His head slumps to his chest. "Maybe I'm tired of fightin' all the time."

"Wait, Fin." Ian's face pales below his dark hair. "What if we give it a go? We could agree to stay for one month. If we don't like it, we can take our money from Uncle Bear and go back to New Zealand or Montana or anywhere you want."

"They'll never let us leave once we're settled. No, this is our one chance to get out of here."

Ian's wide eyes turn to Buck, who shakes his head.

"Fin?"

I don't answer him.

"I don't want to go."

I throw up my hands. "Then I will go it alone. Get out! Both of you!"

A sharp-edged silence shrouds the room. I'm afraid to move lest I shatter beyond repair. Buck and Ian, also paralyzed, stare at me wide-eyed as if I've become the monster growing within me. Time slows to a crawl.

"Fin?"

I cut my eyes to Ian, who holds his palms up as if pleading.

"All we have is each other."

Ian's words pierce my heart and burst the black growth into flame. Hot, bitter liquid oozes into my stomach until I wretch up the filth inside me. "I hate you both!" I spin like a whirling top. "I hate this place. I hate you all. They aren't my ma and pa. They're not my family. They never will be!" I spin on my heel and take off running into the hall to Uncle Bear's room.

Like mine, his bag remains packed, and the satchel he carried from New Zealand stands beside it. Do I grab the whole satchel? That leaves Buck and Ian without anything, which doesn't seem right. But when I try to open it, it's locked, and I can't get the mechanism to work with my trembling fingers.

So, I carry the satchel back to my room, where Ian and Buck remain, as still as statues. I fling the satchel on the bed. "Here. Open it."

After staring at the satchel like a poisonous snake ready to strike, Buck finally works his magic, breaking the lock and prying it open.

"Please don't leave us." Ian's eyes are awash with tears.

"I must. I can't bear it here." I grab handfuls of gold coins, stuffing them into my bag until it bulges.

"Then, Fin?" Ian heaves a shuddering breath. "I will go with you."

"No!" Buck yells loudly enough, I run to the door to see if anyone heard and is coming to see what's wrong. "You're not taking Ian. He's happy here, and so am I."

The hall remains clear. I walk to the bed and sit beside Ian. "Is that true, Ian? You're happy?"

Ian licks his lips, his eyes bouncing around like tiny balls. Finally, he squeaks, "At least we have family here."

"You, too, Buck? You say you're happy?"

Buck nods. "I figure it's better than scraping by on our own."

Nothing else need be said.

I sneak the satchel to Uncle Bear's room, positioning it beside his bag. Hopefully, he won't notice anything missing before I'm long gone. Then, it's back to my room to wait until downstairs is empty.

Our last hour together is spent in harsh, jagged silence punctuated by Ian's whimpering and snuffling.

Finally, the creak of footfalls on the hallway boards, whispered goodnights, and the click of closing doors signal the end of our mute vigil. The house falls silent. After several minutes, I stick my head out to check. No candlelight glows from under any of the doors.

"That's it, then." I sling my heavy bag over my shoulder. "Last chance."

No one says a word.

I don't look back.

CHAPTER FOURTEEN

March 1907

I creep down the stairs, treading along the edges to avoid making the boards groan under my weight, through the sitting room and dining room to the kitchen, and out the back door into pitch darkness. Mist douses my skin, making my clothes cling to me like thick spiderwebs. I grope my way along the unfamiliar path toward the barn. Of all nights for dense fog to cover the mountain and leave me blind, of course, it had to be tonight. That's my luck.

I open the barn door slowly and squeeze through the opening. Every noise sounds like a dozen sirens to my ears. It doesn't matter which horse I take, so I choose the first stall on my left. The horse stomps and strains against its tether, bobbing and shaking its head. He doesn't know me. None of them do. It's less than ideal, but I must make the best of it. What choice do I have?

Do I ride without a saddle, which means I must hold my bag the whole way, or take the time to tack up the horse, risking discovery? I can't see two inches in front of my face, so finding the gear will be impossible without some light, but if I light a lamp, it will be like a warning beacon in this darkness. Bareback, then.

I lead the horse from its stall, throw the bag across its back, and pull myself up by its mane. So far, so good. If I don't want to get off and remount, I'll have to leave the barn door open——again, less than ideal, but it'll have to do, so we ride through the door and toward the trail through the field of waving grain—and freedom.

I give the horse its head, figuring he knows the way, but he won't cooperate. How am I going to find the path in the dark? It's hard enough to see in the daylight among all that tall wheat.

Oh, well. I know which way is down, so that will have to do. I tug the horse's mane and give him a kick, sending him plowing through the stalks, heading downhill in the general direction of the town where we got off the train. I'm leaving an obvious trail for Uncle Bear to follow. My only hope is getting far enough ahead of any pursuer during the night so he can't catch up with me by morning.

An ominous thought floats through my mind, matching the eerie setting and my foul mood. I'm now a horse thief, which is a hanging offense. Not that I believe Granda would have me hung, but he did say in this family, we take responsibility for our choices and accept the consequences, so who knows? Would he go that far? Best I not get caught.

I urge the horse to go faster, but he tosses his head and slows his pace. Everything seems against me tonight. "Come on! Let's go." Still, he plods along, picking his way across the field like a lost, frightened lamb. At this rate, I won't make the town before daylight. And if I miss the train…well, they'll surely find me and drag me back to the farm. Who knows what Mac will do to me—chain me to my bed? Tie me to a chair? Make me sleep in the hayloft? Have me do everyone else's chores? Write II Peter 1:5-8 a hundred times?

Beat me black and blue?

Anything is possible.

We reach the tree line, and I can finally pick up the trail. I give the horse its head. He seems to relish running now that he has a wide, smooth path. We wind down the mountain and along the road leading into the small town of Blue Ridge, arriving well before sun up. I locate the train depot, tie the horse to the rail, and spread out on the little bench intended for passengers waiting to board, to doze until morning.

The streets are quiet for the most part, with the occasional drunken man stumbling by, perhaps heading home from a night in the saloon—such a contrast to the rowdy atmosphere of the New Zealand town, where men and women were about all hours of the day and night. I drift off easily.

Someone pokes my arm, startling me awake. "What're ya doin' out here, boy?"

"I…I'm waiting for the train."

"You alone?"

I cut my eyes left and right but see no one. "Uh…"

"Whatcha got in that bag there?"

I pull the bag against my chest. "Clothes."

The man juts his chin toward my horse. "That yours?"

"Yessir."

His mouth broadens into a cross between a sneer and a grin, revealing a set of black-coated teeth with several gaps. "Nice horse."

"Yessir."

He lifts one of his hairy black brows. "Mind if I take a look in that bag?"

"Yessir, I do mind it. It's no business of yours what I have."

He folds his arms. "No need to get persnickety about it. I was just askin'." He leans his head back and cuts his narrowing eyes down at me. "T'ain't right. Young boy your age sittin' out here alone. Waitin' for the train, ya say?"

"Yessir."

"Where's your folks?"

"They're coming. They'll be here any minute." My words rush out in a wave—too quick, because the man's eyes narrow further.

"That right?"

"Yessir."

He snatches the bag from my arms as quick as a cat and tries to pry open the lock. I leap toward him, wrapping my arms around the bag and hanging on for dear life.

"Get off." He shakes the bag, but I won't let go. He tries to sling me off, pulling my feet off the ground, but still I cling to it like a life raft in a stormy sea.

"Help! Someone help me!"

Then, he punches my nose with his fist. I crumple to the ground, my eyes filling with flashing light and my nose gushing warm blood. I can't see which way he runs away with my bag.

All my money. Gone. What do I do now? "Help! Thief! Thief!"

The sound of pounding feet followed by a strong hand lifting me up. "What happened, son?"

"A man. He hit me and stole my…my bag."

The figure touches my nose. I howl at the piercing pain.

"Yep, it's broken. Son, will you be OK if I leave you here to try to find your thief?"

"Um hm."

"Which way did he run?"

I shrug. "I couldn't see."

"Did you see what he looked like?"

"Yessir. He's a hunched, skinny man with a long, crooked nose, stringy black hair, bushy black eyebrows, and rotten teeth. He's missing a few, too."

"Hmm. I have an idea who that might be." He pats my arm. "You stay here. I will be right back."

He disappears into the night fog. There's nothing more I can do, so I sit on my little bench, pinching my nose to try and stop the bleeding.

I don't know how long I'm sitting and waiting before two men stumble into view, one pushing the other from behind. My bag falls at my feet with a loud clang of metal on metal.

"That your bag?"

"Yessir."

"Wait here, then. I'm going to get some coffee in Ol' Dezzy to sober him up before I lock him in the jail, but I will be back soon to sort this mess out."

Sort it out? What does he mean? Does he think I stole the coins? Is he going to force me to go home? Should I run?

The truth is, I'm pretty shook up. When I try to stand, my legs wobble like noodles fresh from a hot pot of water. Maybe this wasn't such a good idea after all. So, I sit down, my chin in my hands, and wait for the nice man who retrieved my bag.

As he promised, he returns in a few minutes. "Now, then, young sir. What has you out at such hours by yourself?"

"Well, sir, I…"

Horse's hooves clatter against the stones of the main street, skidding to a stop in front of the depot, and Uncle Bear leaps from his horse and runs to my side. "What happened? Are you hurt?"

"Sir, are you this boy's father?" The sheriff's eyes narrow as he studies Bear's face.

"No, Sheriff. I'm Mac MacAlister's son, Bear, visiting from out of state. This is his grandson, Fin MacAlister."

"I know the MacAlisters. Grandson? Huh. Very well." The sheriff quirks his mouth. "The boy got robbed. I was able to catch the thief, but Fin got a good punch in the nose for his troubles. Does Mac know his grandson is out here at all hours of the night by himself carrying a bag full of coin?"

"We just found out. I came as soon as I heard."

The sheriff purses his lips and nods knowingly. "A runaway, then."

"I'm afraid so."

The sheriff squats before me, bringing his face close to mine. "Son, running off with someone else's money is thieving."

"It's *my* money." I lift my head high and glare back at him.

"Is it your horse, also?"

My chest deflates. "No, sir." I meet his eyes. "I was going to leave it for them once I got on the train."

"I'm afraid that makes no difference. You stole their horse."

I lick my lips. "Yessir."

The sheriff turns to Uncle Bear. "Should I lock him up?"

"That won't be necessary, Sheriff. We found the horse, and you recovered the money, so all's well."

"All's well that ends well, eh?" The sheriff presses his large hand against my knee. "Fin, did you like getting robbed?"

My eyes bulge. "No, sir, I didn't."

"How do you suppose your family feels about you robbing them? Seems to me, it's worse to be robbed by someone you love than by a stranger."

Someone they love? If they loved me, I guess that would be true. I figured they'd be mad for a spell, but that's all.

I glance up at Uncle Bear. "Are you mad at me?"

"I'm just glad you're not hurt worse." He reaches out his hand. "Come on, let's go home."

"A firm hand might go a long way," the sheriff mutters.

"Thank you, sir. I'll take it from here." Uncle Bear thrusts his hand toward me again. "Let's go, Fin."

"No, sir."

The sheriff snorts in disgust as he walks away.

"Fin? Let's *go.*"

"I'm waiting for the train."

Uncle Bear closes his eyes under his wrinkled brow as he flops beside me on the bench. To my surprise, he sits in silence—no lecture, no questions, and no pleading. He laces his fingers and leans forward, his elbows on his knees, gazing up the track as if looking for the coming train.

In some ways, his silence is worse than punishment. I squirm in my seat, gnawing on the inside of my cheek, trying to imagine what he's thinking.

"I'm going back home. To New Zealand."

Uncle Bear continues to study the tracks.

"I left most of Pa's money for Ian and Buck."

A barely perceptible nod.

"I wasn't going to take your horse."

Nothing.

My breath whistles from my wounded nose. "I can't do it, don't you understand? I can't pretend to be happy. I can't pretend everything is great."

Uncle Bear turns his head slowly and meets my burning eyes.

"There's no *room* for me here!" This thought bursts from me like juice from a rotten fruit that falls from a tree. A tear leaks from the corner of one eye.

Uncle Bear's hand finds mine, squeezing ever so gently.

"To you, all these people are family. You've known them your whole life. But to me, they're strangers who want me to pretend I know and love them." My hands ball into fists and pound my thighs. "They don't know me. How can they love me?"

"You're right."

My breath catches in my throat. I don't know what I expected, but it wasn't that.

"We tried so hard to make you feel at home, we overwhelmed you, leaving you feeling like an outsider among strangers." Uncle Bear shakes his head. "Ma always says, 'We create what we most fear.' I guess we were afraid you wouldn't like us. I'm truly sorry."

My mouth opens and closes like a giant *kōkopu* skimming a pond for insects.

"Everything has happened so fast. I can't imagine what it would be like dealing with all that you've been through." Uncle Bear's chin lowers to his chest. "If you would give us another chance, I promise we will learn from our mistakes. We'll give you plenty of space. You can take your time getting to know us. And we'll get to know you—and, I'm sure, love you." He shrugs. "If you don't want to give us a chance, well…" He looks down the tracks again. "I'll make sure you get to New Zealand safely."

What did he say?

"You…you'll take me all the way home?"

"If that's what you truly want."

My body quivers at the possibility of going home—so why do I hesitate?

The ever-present black stone wall towers over me, bashing me at every hope or wish of going home, pushing me ever forward into the tempest. I dig my feet into the dirt beneath the bench. No, I won't give in. I won't let go of my one desire, even if the wall crushes me for it.

A thought like a wisp of cloud flits through my mind. *Is* it what you want?

To go it alone, trying to survive against the elements and our enemies in New Zealand? To be forever without my brothers? To never again know the warmth and affection of family?

With its final, devastating blow, the wall hisses in my head. "What do you think you'll find if you go back?" The voice lowers to an ominous growl. "There's nothing there for you, either. Your ma and pa are *dead*."

I wilt like a fragile flower in the midsummer heat, collapsing against Uncle Bear's chest. My shuddering gasps and sobs echo mockingly against the empty depot. If I could rip my chest open with my bare hands and pull everything out in a steaming pile, I would do it—anything to stop the agonizing, shattering pain. From deep within my gut, a volcanic howl boils up and explodes from me. My face burns. My chest folds until I'm tucked in a ball like a newborn babe.

Uncle Bear clutches me as if I'm about to fly apart, rocking me in his arms and murmuring unintelligible but soothing words.

I don't know how long we stay like this, but when the last of my tears are spent, and I look up at Bear, I see swollen eyes, a flushed face, and streaked cheeks.

A shroud covering my eyes lifts, and for the first time, I understand the pain this family—my family—has endured at the loss of their son and brother. Rays of the rising sun pierce my mind. My brothers and I are helping this family a little with their sorrow by being here. Bear's face says he knows my grief all too well. They must've felt so powerless, being so far away, unable to do anything for Ma and Pa. Maybe through us, they feel they are doing *something*—honoring Pa somehow. Is that what Granda meant by redemption?

And all this time, I've focused on my pain, as if I'm the only one who lost something beyond valuing.

Why run away from the only ones who truly understand?

"I'm sorry I ran away." My breath hitches.

Uncle Bear gazes down the tracks. "The train will be coming soon." He presses his lips together and says no more.

The steel rail glints like a ripple on the water, catching a beam of light. In the distance, a single eerie note echoes through the scattering fog. Bear's right. Time's up.

"I…"

Uncle Bear turns his head, his eyes penetrating my soul with the ache of unfulfilled longing. What *is* his desire? For me to remain with Mac and Ester? Bear won't be here, so what difference does that make to him? For his dear brother, whom he claims was his best friend? All the wishes in the world won't bring Pa back. To stay with his family? Then why doesn't he do it?

"Why won't you stay?" I meet his longing with a silent plea. "I can't bear to lose anyone else."

He closes his eyes. "I know."

"I don't understand."

"I know."

The tracks quiver, making the light dance along the rail, as if a tiny fairy glides along the metal on skates, spinning and hopping until it reaches the shadows. The vibration intensifies when a metal beast billowing black smoke comes into sight around the bend, belting another blast of the whistle.

Bear raises one brow.

"I think…I…I…" So much is on the line.

My uncle stares in silence.

"I guess…" I blow out a heavy sigh. "Let's go home."

"Home?"

"Yes." I nod once and jut my chin toward the blue-gray mountain rising above the river of white mist. "To the only home I have now."

He drapes his arm across my shoulders as he whispers, "Thanks be to God."

Chapter Fifteen

March 1907

"Who told on me?"

The horses' hooves ring against the stone-covered street. "Ian."

"Of course. Buck would never."

"He was terribly frightened. And it turns out, he was right to be."

"Yeah. I guess so." A jab and twist pinch my heart. "What's Granda going to do to me?"

Uncle Bear shrugs but offers no reply.

A growing sense of dread haunts the remainder of the trip to the farm. When we arrive, Buck and Ian perch on the bottom step of the front porch, Granma stands in the doorway wrapped in her usual blanket, Liam and his boys wrangle the horses and cows near the barn, but Granda is nowhere to be seen.

Buck spots us and hollers out, then Ian and he race down the path toward us. Ester lowers her head and clasps her hands before her chest.

"You found him." Ian slaps Bear's leg.

"I did."

Ian folds his arms and glares at me. "That was a darn fool thing you did."

Buck winces. "I told him not to tell."

"It's a good thing he did." Bear swings his leg off his horse. "Fin was robbed."

"Robbed?"

"It could've been much worse."

"What happened?"

"Later." I hop down and take the two horses' reins. "Where's Granda?"

Ian's mouth twists to one side. "In the house."

Time to take my medicine, whatever it may be. I lead the horses to the barn and hand the reins to Liam, who smirks beneath the lowered brim of his hat. "Welcome back." He takes off his hat and mops his brow, then gestures toward the main house. "Best apologize for worrying Ma."

"Yessir." I drag my feet through the trampled grass, kicking up dust as I go, doing my best to delay the inevitable, but I reach the bottom step way too soon.

Head down, I kick at the board and mutter, "I'm sorry, ma'am."

"Come here, young man."

Her voice is hoarse, as if she'd swallowed gravel. I clomp like a draft horse up those steps and proceed to study Ester's tiny shoes.

She gathers me to her like Pa clutching a sheep for shearing. No words are spoken, but I feel her thin shoulders heaving beneath my cheek and her heart fluttering as fast as hummingbird's wings. Shame floods me until I'm like to drown in it—and here I was fearing Mac's punishment. Granma's loving sorrow cuts deeper than any beating he could offer.

"Very well." She clears her throat and dabs her eyes with a delicate finger. "Come along, then." She herds me into the house. I glance over my shoulder to see Buck and Ian standing at the foot of the steps, wide-eyed. Dread grips my throat and squeezes it shut.

Granma directs me to go to the sitting room. "I'll make some breakfast for you." When I stop at the doorway, she flutters her hand. "Go on, now." Then, she disappears.

Taking a deep breath, I push open the heavy door. Granda sits in his overstuffed chair, a book open in his lap. He doesn't look up as I walk in and stand before him with my hands clasped at my waist. I chew on my lip as I wait for him to speak.

"Well? What have you to say for yourself?"

"I'm sorry, sir."

He purses his lips. "Sorry you were caught or sorry you left in the first place?"

"I'm sorry I left. It were wrong of me."

"Indeed." He sighs and folds his hands over the pages. "You worried your granma to death."

"Yessir."

"You scared little Ian half out of his wits."

"Yessir."

"You put Buck in an impossible position."

"Yessir, I did."

Finally, he looks me in the eye. "And what did you learn from this mistake?"

What did I learn? My mouth falls open as his unexpected question scatters my thoughts like leaves to the four winds.

"Well?"

"I…" Best to be honest. "I learned you and Granma and Uncle Bear and the rest of you are hurting as much as I am—maybe in a different way, but you suffered a terrible loss, same as me. As us. I learned I've been selfish and inconsiderate, thinking I'm the only one grieving, when all of you and my brothers are grieving, too." I inhale a deep breath and blow. "I figure you and Granma are hoping to honor my pa by caring for us, just like he wanted." I examine my dusty, ragged shoes. "I forgot Pa and Ma wanted us to come here, being too busy thinking about what I wanted."

When I look up, Mac's eyes have softened, his brows have lifted from their stern furrow, and his downturned lips have parted. "Is that all?"

I quirk one brow and shrug. "Yeah. I guess so." I glance out the big picture window at the row upon row of hazy blue mountains lining the horizon. Pressing my lips together, I clear my throat. "One more thing. I realize Ma and Pa are gone, and they aren't coming back. And going to New Zealand isn't going to change that fact." I will my tears to stay sitting in my throat. "This is the only family I have left." My throat tightens as I swallow hard. "I guess I learned I need my family more than I realized."

"Hmm. Very well." He stands slowly and hands me his open book. "I'd like for you to read this story. Pay attention to the father's responses." He gestures for me to sit in his chair, then leaves the room. The door closes with a muted click.

Is that it? Is he delaying my punishment? Or is he satisfied with my answers? I curl up in his chair and start reading at the top of the page. " Likewise, I say unto you, there is joy in the presence of the angels of God over one sinner that repenteth. And he said, A certain man had two sons: And the younger of them said to his father, Father, give me the portion of goods that falleth to me."

I know this story. Pa taught us from it many times. He called it the Parable of the Loving Father.

The one son sought his own way and squandered everything good that had been given to him. When he realized he'd wasted his life, he begged to return home, not as a son but as a servant. But the loving father welcomed him as a son and even had a party to celebrate his return.

Am I this ungrateful son? I suppose in taking Pa's gold and running away, I acted like him, headstrong, impulsive, and selfish.

Is Granda the father in the story? Is he trying to tell me he welcomes me home as a son? Or is there a deeper meaning he wants me to grasp?

Or am I the bitter, elder son, jealous of his younger brother and resentful of his father's celebration? I certainly did sulk in the corner during the family gathering, and I was jealous of my brothers' newfound happiness. Why, oh why didn't I join them in play?

Pa's voice whispers in my ears, "It's pride, plain and simple." Older or younger brother, my problem is pride.

Maybe I've been both brothers.

I close Granda's well-worn Bible carefully and place it on the arm of his chair, stroking the leather cover before kneeling in front of the chair and clasping my hands together in the seat.

"Dear Lord, you say there is joy in the presence of the angels in heaven when one sinner repents, so here I am, Lord. I repent of my wicked pride, my selfishness, my bullheaded will, and my stiff neck." I rest my forehead on my hands. "Please forgive me, Lord, although I don't deserve it. And…" My words dry up in my mouth. Can I thank Him for providing my grandparents to take care of us? Isn't that the same as saying thank you for taking Ma and Pa?

I can't thank Him for that. Not yet. Maybe not ever.

"And thank you for making Mac and Ester loving grandparents. Amen." It's all I can muster. And it's enough.

The grasping vine shrivels within me, its death reaching to the black seed until the whole bitter growth crumbles into a pile of dust and drifts away with my exhale.

Ashes to ashes.

Ester's voice clangs like a bell's song from the kitchen. "Come and get your breakfast, Fin."

"Be right there."

After patting Mac's Bible one last time, I race up the stairs two at a time and dash into my room. My abandoned new shoes, a gift from Uncle Bear, lay strewn where I hurled them against the door. I collect them, and, sitting on my voluminous bed, I slowly remove my old shoes and slip on my new ones. I align my old shoes neatly, side by side. Holding them in my hands like I held Granda's Bible, I march in four solemn strides to the wardrobe, open the doors, and slide them gently onto the back of the top shelf.

PART TWO

Dignity in tilling a field

CHAPTER SIXTEEN

October 1913

Crimson and golden leaves flutter in the wind racing down the mountain, bringing the first crisp taste of winter's approaching cold. But by midday, the sun will warm the air enough for shirtsleeves again. After all these years, I'm still not used to the strange weather in Georgia.

Everyone is up early this morning. Harvest time means long hours and hard work, but I, for one, look forward to it every year. I find gathering the fruit of our labor deeply satisfying.

Giggling like little children, Katy and Claire run past me down the front steps, dressed in dungarees and suspenders like field hands with their long, flowing hair tied up and their sleeves rolled to their elbows. Katy looks more natural in her picking clothes than in her Sunday finest, with her freckled face and untamed, curly red hair, and to hear her tell it, she prefers men's clothes to women's.

But Claire—well, Claire is as beautiful as a spring sunrise no matter what she puts on. Her golden, wheat-colored hair flows like a stream over a waterfall, and her cream-colored skin, as flawless as porcelain, makes the rose of her full lips glow like the red autumn leaves.

"Y'all best slow down. You'll use up all your energy before the picking starts."

Katy flicks her wrist dismissively, but Claire looks over her shoulder with a beaming smile, her blue eyes twinkling like sunlight reflecting off a mountain lake. "Is that why you're sitting in a rocker like an old man? Saving your energy?"

"I'm just saying."

She throws her head back and laughs, a high-pitched melodious aria rising and falling on the wind.

Ian steps onto the porch at that moment, gazing after Claire with a look of unbridled longing that brings heat into my cheeks as if he can hear my desirous thoughts. His sigh ends with a little groan.

"Happy birthday. You're still one year short of being a man." Teasing Ian soothes the ache in my chest.

"I'm one year *closer*. Besides, Granda went to war right before his seventeenth birthday. That's man enough for me." He plops down on the top step. "Granma's baking a cake."

"Of course she is. It's not like she has anything else to do, with the canning and pickling and making jams."

Ian runs his fingers through his dark curls. "I didn't ask her to do it."

"I know. I'm funning you."

"Have you seen Buck?"

I nod. "He's in the barn tending the horses and cows, I guess."

"He doesn't need our help?"

"Doesn't want it." I shrug. "You know how much he loathes this time of year. He's been out there for over an hour, chomping at the bit to get going and have it over."

Ian wiggles his fingers. "I'm in no hurry to blister my hands raw."

Uncle Liam and Granda stride onto the porch. Liam, as usual, is arguing with his pa. "Pa, you don't have to come into the fields. We can handle things. We have more than enough workers, what with the girls, and Fin and the boys, and me."

"When I'm too old to take care of my own farm, I'll give up the ghost." Granda growls under his breath. "Uppity young'un, tellin' me a couple of girls can keep up with me."

"I'm just trying to take care of you. Ma said…"

"I've taken care of myself for over fifty-three years, I'll have you know. And I've done a right fine job of it, too."

"Yessir. But at sixty-nine, don't you think it's time to slow down a might?" Uncle Liam gestures toward Ian and me. "Especially with all these able bodies ready and willing to help."

"More workers make for quicker work."

Liam heaves a deep sigh. "I give up." He cuts his eyes toward Granda. "You can deal with Ma, then."

"Your Ma and I understand each other." Granda lifts his chin with a curl of his lip. "She'd be on my side."

Ian clears his throat. "Uncle Liam, what about your harvest? Won't you need help bringing it in?"

"Thank you if you're offering, but no. Samuel and Mac are coming home from the university tomorrow to help me. We should have it covered. You three boys focus on helping your granda."

As Granda grouses under his breath about three worthless boys being more in the way than helping, Uncle Liam shakes his head and bounces down the steps to head toward the barn.

"So, what're you two lazy bones doing sitting here? Get on with ye."

"Yessir."

Ian and I bolt down the stairs and run to the barn, where we find everyone gathering their baskets and tools for the harvest. I watch Claire, graceful as a swan on the water, bending down to pick up a stack of baskets. When she stands, her eyes catch mine, and she winks.

My heart seizes in my chest as I whirl around to check if Ian saw anything, but he's with Buck, arguing over a knife, his back turned toward me. Thank the Lord.

Granda enters, and we fall silent, waiting for our assignments. "Ian and Claire—apples and pears." My heart sinks in my stomach as Ian grabs the ladder with a grin, and the girls heft their baskets. Ian has all the luck. "Buck, gather the pumpkins, cantaloupe, and butternut squash." Buck groans but cuts it short when Granda glares at him. "Is your back not strong enough to lift a little pumpkin, boy?"

"No, sir. I mean, yessir, I can lift pumpkins."

Granda raises a brow before continuing. "Katy, you can handle the beans and collards. Liam, you can pull the peanuts and gather the pecans. Fin, you bring in the cabbage, broccoli, and carrots. I'll be digging up sweet potatoes and gathering the yellow squash and zucchini."

Liam slams his fists on his hips. "Pa! Why don't you let me do the digging? You gave yourself the hardest job."

"As it should be."

"Granda, why don't I help you with…"

Granda's thunderous look stops my plea. "Enough. I've said my peace."

A piercing scream shatters the heavy silence. I stare at Uncle Liam, whose eyes widen as his mouth falls open. "What…?"

I spin to look at Granda. He's facing the double door, his hand on his brow to block the sun.

"Help! Help! Hurry!"

"That's Julianna." Uncle Liam races from the barn with Granda and the rest of us tight on his heels.

Julianna rushes onto the porch, waving her arms and screaming, her face as white as winter snow. "It's Ester!"

Granda passes Liam and leaps to the top step in one bound. "Where is she?"

"We were in the kitchen. She was making Ian's cake…"

Granda doesn't wait to hear the rest. He dashes through the door while Liam collects Julianna in his arms. "What happened?"

"She just—collapsed. I don't know what happened. She was well one moment, and the next, she's on the kitchen floor." Julianna's breath hitches as her tears begin to flow. "I tried to revive her, but I couldn't. Oh, Liam!"

No. No, not again. I dart past the rest of the clan and run straight to the kitchen, where I find Granda kneeling beside my prone Granma, clutching her in his arms. Her face is ashen, and her eyes are closed.

Granda whispers in her ear until he senses me approaching behind him. "Get some water and a cloth!"

I scan the kitchen, but the only water is boiling in a pot. So, grabbing a white towel, I race outside to the well and pump some cool water into a bucket. I douse the towel and run back inside, handing the soaked cloth to Granda and setting the bucket beside Ester.

The rest of the family files into the kitchen. Granda barks at them to stay back. "She needs air." He caresses her cheek and forehead with the wet towel. "Ester. Ester, my love. Come back to me."

Her eyes flutter as if at his call. "Oh. Oh, my." She dabs her finger at a droplet sliding down her temple. "Did I faint?"

"You did."

Her hands dance across her chest as she tries to sit up. "Don't make a fuss, now. I'm sure I got overheated. That's all."

"My love, you need some water." Granda's eyes command me without a word. I grab a cup, fill it from the bucket, and hand it to him. "Here you are. Drink it slowly."

Her delicate fingers rest lightly against the glass next to his as she sips the cool water. "Much better." She offers Granda a wan smile. "I'll be fine in a moment or two." A ragged cough rumbles from deep in her chest.

But Granda stands and lifts her in his arms, carrying her out of the kitchen to the stairs.

Liam follows him, carrying us in his wake. "Pa?"

"Fetch the doctor. Quickly."

Liam doesn't hesitate. He flies from the house, leaving us standing at the base of the stairs, staring at each other as Granda disappears with Ester.

Katy and Claire clutch each other in a tight embrace and begin to weep. Ian rushes to Claire's side, stroking her back and whispering empty promises that Ester will recover and all will be well.

I know there are no guarantees. If I learned anything in this life, it's that nothing is certain.

Julianna lurches over to a chair where she sits with her eyes swallowed in sunken gray pits, staring at nothing, and her fingers twisting as if she were at the loom.

Buck kicks the boards of the bottom stair, spins, and stalks out the door, so I follow him. He stares at the trail as if the force of his will can hasten the doctor's arrival.

"Do you think I should go check on Granda? See if he needs anything?

Buck wrinkles his nose and shrugs his shoulder but offers nothing.

"I don't want to be in the way. But I don't want him to be alone either."

"He's not alone. He's with Granma."

Buck's voice carries a hint of disdain. "Buck, what's wrong? Why are you so angry?"

He slams his foot against the tall wooden beam. "Because Granda looks scared."

"What?"

He throws his hands in the air. "Don't you get it?" His arms flail at his sides. "If Ester dies, it will change everything."

"None of us wants Granma to die. But why are you assuming she's dying?"

Buck's brows rise high into his hairline. "Granda is never scared. Ever."

True. Over the past six years, I've seen Granda come face-to-face with a raging black bear protecting its cub and walk straight past her without blinking an eye. I've seen him grab a copperhead that was threatening the girls in his bare hands without care. I've heard him speak before dozens of powerful men at the town hall, accusing them of stealing community funds without any thought for his safety, and then bending them to his will, so strong were his convictions.

Granda claims fear is from the devil. Like Pa, he taught us to never give in to our fears, to stand firm and be strong in the Lord. Maybe Buck has a point. If Granda appears frightened…

"What do you mean, it will change everything?"

Buck casts a sideways glance toward me with a sneer, then rolls his eyes and shakes his head. "Never mind." He bolts down the stone steps and runs toward the barn.

"Buck!"

He calls over his shoulder, "I'm getting me a horse!"

Running again, the same as when Ma and Pa died. I blow an exasperated breath and return to the house, where Ian continues to comfort the girls and Julianna still stares as if in a trance. I don't pause but race up the stairs two at a time, straight to Granda's and Granma's room, and tap gently on the door.

"Granda?"

No one replies.

I knock again. "Granda, do you need anything?"

After a long pause, Granda's breathless, hollow whisper echoes through the door. "Ester is resting. Leave us be."

"Yessir."

Buck's fears have attached themselves to me like a tick in summertime, spreading their poison through my veins. Images of life on this farm without Ester's calming hand flit through my mind like a horror house at the carnival. Granda growling at everyone all the time. Uncle Liam bossing us around and working us day and night with no reprieve. Aunt Julianna trying to be like Ester but breaking down in hysterics every five minutes. Claire and Katy—and Buck—running wild.

It's the stuff of my childhood nightmares.

There's nothing to do but wait, so I sit on the top step of the landing, cross my arms on my knees, and rest my head on my arms, counting the seconds and waiting for the sound of a carriage or the pounding of horses' hooves.

From the position of the sun, an hour or more has passed when Buck's roan horse gallops up the path, and he screams, "They're coming! The doctor is coming!"

I leap up and clamber down the steps, meeting Buck at the front door.

"They're here."

"Finally," I breathe.

A few minutes later, Uncle Liam, astride his horse, leads a fancy carriage up the path through the newly planted winter wheat. Liam swings open the carriage door and helps the doctor step down, then brings him into the main room, where I push forward to greet him.

"Granma is upstairs. I'll take you."

"Very well."

The doctor follows behind me up the stairs to the bedroom. I knock on the door. "Granda? The doctor is here."

"Send him in."

I'm desperate to follow the doc into the room, but instead, I only catch a quick glimpse of Granma, arrayed on their bed covered in blankets and quilts—including the buffalo hide that has long lain across my bed. Her face is the color of her bed linens. Her hair is uncharacteristically mussed. And as the doctor closes their door, a rattling, wheezing cough drowns out the conversation between Granda and the doctor.

"Please, God. Not Granma." I close my eyes. "If you must take someone, take me."

Pressing my ear against the door, I strain to make out the quiet murmurs between the two men, but I'm unable to hear anything beyond indistinct whispers and gurgling coughs, so I slink downstairs to join the others in waiting for the final word.

Silence blankets the main room, as if Ester were already gone, and we were in full-blown mourning. Nausea swirls in my stomach, and my chest tightens, sending a wash of spit in my mouth and tingles up my arms. "She worked herself too hard, with the harvest. That's all."

Am I trying to convince others or myself?

"It's exhaustion. A good rest and she'll be right as rain."

Aunt Julianna's pained eyes find mine. "I hope you're right. But when she collapsed…" She closes her eyes against the memory. "I believe she stopped breathing." She shakes her head. "We almost lost her."

"But the doc is here. He'll know what to do." I fold my lips between my teeth.

Ian groans. "If only she hadn't tried to make my stupid cake."

I suck in a quick breath. "Ian. I was only teasing you earlier. This isn't your fault."

"But it was one more thing, like you said."

Uncle Liam lifts his hand. "Boys, there's nothing to gain by trying to find fault or blame. You know Ma. She's always going to do exactly as she pleases, and no one can dissuade her from it. Just like Pa." He shakes his head. "I think they'd want us going about our day as planned. We aren't helping Ma by sitting here twiddling our thumbs."

My mouth falls open, and my eyes widen, but it's Buck who protests. "I can't just go about my business while I know Granma is suffering."

"The harvesting still wants doing."

What a cold, callous comment. "Well, you go ahead and get to work then, if you think that's what's important. I'm staying right here until I know Granma will be well again." I toss my head, throwing a side glance Liam's way, challenging him to argue with me.

"Suit yourself. But there'll be hell to pay when Pa comes downstairs."

"If he comes downstairs," Buck mutters under his breath.

Liam raises a brow at Buck. "Let's not assume the worst."

"What should we assume? Aunt Julianna said Granma almost died." Buck juts his chin toward Julianna.

Uncle Liam growls under his breath. "Come along. We can at least get things started."

Buck heaves a huge sigh. "Fine. I'll come with you."

"I'm going to go tell my Mom and Dad what's happened." Claire wrings Katy's hand. "They'll be upset if I don't let them know."

Aunt Julianna nods. "Of course."

"Do you want me to come with you, Claire?"

"I'd like that, Ian." Her long lashes flutter over her crystalline eyes.

Why didn't I think of that? But no, I backed myself into a corner by saying I wouldn't leave until I heard about Ester. So once again, Ian gets to be with Claire, and I'm left holding the bag.

Julianna rises as Claire and Ian walk toward the door. "I'll finish preparing luncheon for everyone."

"Thank you, dear." Liam kisses his wife gently on the cheek.

Which leaves me sitting, useless and alone, in the main room, feeling every bit the fool. But I refuse to back down now.

Pa's voice whispers in my ear. "Pride, plain and simple."

Will I ever learn?

Chapter Seventeen

October 1913

Shadows creep in along the edges of the floor, like dark spirits worming their way inside our home, while I sit, staring at the empty stairwell. Will the doctor ever come down?

"Fin?"

Chris' voice startles me from my reverie. "Oh!"

He stands in the doorway, his silhouette framed by an ethereal glow—a warrior angel to stand against the spirit of death. "Is there any word?"

"No, sir. No word."

"Very well." His head drops. "We're all praying for Ester."

"Yessir."

He breathes deeply and releases a sigh. "Ian and Claire have joined the others in the fields. Would you like to come with us?"

Chris' kind offer gives me a chance to save face, but I can't bring myself to do it. "No, I want to wait to hear what the doc says."

"Very well." A barely perceptible shake of his head tells me his view of my decision. "Come get us when the doctor comes down."

"I will."

Time grinds out its seconds in a slow, funereal march. The longer the doctor takes, the more likely the news will be grim. Dread builds a nest in my gut, wrenching and squeezing and clawing my insides to make space for its growing mass.

Too late, I realize my error. As the others distract themselves from foreboding with productivity and purpose, I'm bound in its clutches.

Then, a door creaks, footfalls thump on the stairs, and the doctor descends into view. Without a glance in my direction, he marches straight out the door.

I race to catch him. "Wait! What is it? What's wrong with Granma?"

"Son, you'll need to ask your grampa."

"Is she dying?"

"Ask your grampa." He disappears into the carriage, and the driver whips the horses into a turn, heading down the trail.

The dread blossoms into full-blown panic. I race up the steps by twos, dash down the hall, and burst into Granda's room, forgetting the one hard and fast rule Ester set for us on our first day.

Granma, propped on pillows, leans against the bed's headboard, while Granda perches by her side on the edge of the mattress. His head turns slowly, his eyes smoldering beneath his lowered brow. "You know better than to come in here uninvited." The words rumble in his chest like thunder. "Get out."

My legs stiffen, paralyzed by his fiery stare.

"No, no. Come in, Fin." Ester wiggles her thin fingers, gesturing for me to enter. "Come and give me a hug."

Mac's eyes soften. "Are you feeling able to receive visitors, my love? I'm not sure it's a good idea."

"Oh, pshaw. You and that doctor are like two fussy old women. I'm fine." She waves again. "Come on. I want that hug."

Keeping my eyes on Granda, I slink across the room to her bedside. She reaches her arms around my neck and pulls me down into an embrace.

"Now, go tell the others the excitement is over, and I am well. I'll be up in a little while to make your meal."

"Aunt Julianna is making it."

Granma's eyebrows rise "Oh. Well…I must…" She starts to swing her legs from under the covers.

"She said most of the preparations were already done by you." I hope my little white lie convinces Granma to stay upstairs in bed and rest. "She said it would be no trouble."

"The doctor urged you to remain in bed, my love."

"Poo. I'm not an invalid."

"No, of course not. But you must have your rest." Granda's worry leaks from him like sweat from a galloping horse. What are they not telling me?

"What did the doctor say?" I'm pushing my luck with Granda, but hopefully Granma will curb his reaction.

Ester tosses her long white hair and huffs. "A lot of nonsense about my heart being weak, causing fluid to collect around my heart and lungs." Gently, she lays her hand on her chest. "But my heart's strong beating tells me otherwise."

"You have the biggest heart of anyone I know." Granda strokes her arm to soothe her. "But you mustn't ignore the doctor's instructions."

"Granda is right." I pat her hand. "You work too hard. That's the real problem. If you'll take your rest, like the doctor ordered, you'll be well in no time."

"You all would have me bedridden, wasting away." She presses her lips into a thin line and sits up straighter in the bed. "If my heart *is* weak, doesn't it make more sense to work on strengthening it instead of giving in to its weakness? Isn't that what the Lord urges us to do in our spiritual life?"

"He also says His strength is made perfect in our weakness." Granda rearranges her pillows and gently urges her to lie against them. "Perhaps He wants you to rely on His strength during this time."

"'The Lord is my strength and my shield; my *heart* trusted in him, and I am helped: therefore my *heart* greatly rejoiceth; and with my song will I praise him.' There is nothing in there about remaining in bed."

"Ester, my love…"

Granma's clear blue eyes narrow, shooting arrows toward Granda. "Aidan MacAlister, I will not spend the remainder of my life, however short or long, confined to a sick room, shut away from my loved ones." Granda closes his eyes and lifts his hands, palms up in surrender.

Ester kicks the blankets off her bare feet. "Fin, if you would be so kind as to step outside, I'd like to get dressed and join the family for luncheon."

"Yes'm." I shoot a final glance at Granda to make sure I'm supposed to leave. He responds with a quick nod, so I back out of the room and slide the door closed behind me.

Behind the door, I hear the rustle of bedclothes and scrape of Granda's shoes on the wooden floor, so I dart down the stairs, out the door, and to the edge of the fields where everyone is working.

I wave and call to them. "Come inside. Granma is getting dressed and coming down."

"What did the doctor say?" Liam yells back.

"It's her heart."

Everyone drops their baskets, buckets, and bags in the field and sprints toward me. Buck reaches me first. He leans close and whispers, "Is it bad?"

I shrug. "Granda is worried. But Granma says the doctor is making too much of it."

"What do you think?"

"I don't know."

As the others gather around, my breath hitches. What do I say? What Granma told me to tell them, or what the doctor told Granda? Exhaling, I study their anxious faces. "Look, all I know is the doctor said her heart is weak, and that's causing fluid on her heart and lungs. His instruction is to rest. Granma says her heart feels strong to her and is insisting on going on with her life as normal." I quirk my mouth. "But Granda is very worried about her, I can tell."

Voices tumble one over another like an engorged river racing over the boulders blocking its flow.

"Then she should stay in bed and rest."

"I don't understand her. She fainted."

"For goodness' sake, why doesn't she listen to the doctor?"

"She needs to take care of herself."

Uncle Chris lifts his hand. "We all know Ester can be headstrong, but she's not foolish. We must trust her judgment. And Mac's. I'm sure they will make their decisions in her best interest."

I wrinkle my nose. "Granda wants her to stay in bed and rest."

Liam chuckles and folds his arms. "I wouldn't want to be caught in the middle of that fight."

"They'll sort it out. They always do." Chris gestures toward the house. "Let's go in. But I urge you all to be respectful of Ester's wishes and not argue with her. It won't do any good if her mind is made up." He catches each eye. "Mac will take care of things. Trust me. He would die before he'd let anything happen to his Ester."

Chris is right. If Granda believes she desperately needs rest, he'll forcibly carry her to her bed, if need be. "Come on. Aunt Julianna is making lunch."

We walk toward the cabin, but our steps are measured, some even dragging through the hard-packed dirt, and our moods somber. Liam and Chris remain at the back of the group, their heads bent together in whispered conversation. The girls are uncharacteristically silent. It's as if all the life has been sucked out of the family.

They all know the truth. Ester is the glue that holds this family together. Her joy and love soften Mac's hard edges, while Mac's devotion to her curbs his tongue and restrains his harsher judgments. It's Ester who brings Uncle Bear, Aunt Mary, Aunt Maisie, and Uncle Martin home for visits and keeps Uncle Liam and Aunt Julianna living on the land. By all accounts, Ester is the main reason Uncle Chris wanted to join our family. And all of us younger ones worship Granma.

When we enter, we find Granma already downstairs, seated in the sitting room with Julianna and Granda, awaiting our arrival. Her skin is almost translucent, except for dark smudges marring her eyes.

"Julianna has made us a lovely meal. Everyone, wash up, then let's have our prayer and go at once to eat."

"Yes'm."

When we return, Granma looks to Mac. "Would you lead the prayer today, my love?"

Granda clears his throat and nods. "Lord, hallowed be Thy name. I thank Thee…" His words catch in his throat. I glance up to find a fresh tear leaving the corner of his eye.

"I thank Thee for sparing the life of my Ester today." He swallows, then clears his throat again. "I thank Thee for our bountiful harvest, for the good food waiting for us on our table, and I thank Thee for the blessing of our wonderful family. In Thy holy name we pray, Amen."

"Amen."

"Amen, and pass the biscuits!"

Leave it to Buck to lift our moods and return us to a semblance of normalcy.

As we move into the dining room, Ester's melodic laugh dances across my heart like fingers over guitar strings. It's almost as if today didn't happen.

But in the deep places, the places I want to ignore, the looming, ominous threat of death lingers, waiting for its moment like a mountain lion ready to pounce, and its darkness casts a pall over my eyes as we dig into Julianna's meal with a fervor I don't feel.

The chatter focuses on the progress of the harvest, everyone studiously avoiding the topics of Ester's collapse and my failure to contribute to the workload. At a lull in the conversation, Granma, who has been listening quietly, turns to me.

"Fin?"

Is she going to correct me for not joining the others? "Yes'm?"

"I was thinking about Scotland."

If she had reached across the table and snatched my head sideways, I wouldn't have been more surprised. "Scotland?"

"Your mother was from Scotland, yes?"

"Yes'm, a little place called Aberfeldy."

A haze covers her eyes as she gazes through the large window at the rows of blue mountains. "Have you seen it?"

"I have, but I don't remember it. I was only two years old when we came to America."

"A shame." She sighs. "I would've so liked to visit Scotland."

Granda leans forward and takes her hand in his. "You never said a word."

Her wistful smile weighs down my heart. It's almost like she knows…no, I won't utter it, even to myself.

"Our life has been filled to the brim with blessings, and I wouldn't have had it any other way. It's…" She pauses, looking down. "Your lineage is from Scotland. I've always wondered if the MacAlister clan is still there. I would've liked to meet them."

Granda furrows his brow. "I don't know how I'd ever find them. I wouldn't know where to start looking."

"It's just a dream. A silly dream, I suppose."

Granda slaps his palms on the table. "We'll go. As soon as you're well and the doctor gives his permission, I promise, we'll go."

That melancholy smile, again.

I force enthusiasm into my voice. "I'll go with you. I'd love to see where Ma was born."

Buck chimes in. "I'll go, too."

"As will I." Ian's eyes mirror the troubled stirrings in my heart. Does he sense the same thing I suspect?

"That would be so lovely, boys." But her voice carries none of the excitement that rings in ours. "Maybe one day."

After an uncomfortable silence suffocates the room, Granda clears his throat. "Yes, well. You had better get back to the harvest, if there's any hope of finishing up before sundown."

"Pa, there's already a lot of work to be done in the kitchen with what we've picked already. Maybe we should spread it out over the next few days?"

Chris places his hand on Liam's arm. "I can fetch Emma to help Julianna."

Ester flutters her fingers in a dismissive wave. "Now, now, that's not necessary. Emma has her canning to do, as does Julianna. I am more than capable…"

Granda shoves his chair away from the table with a grating rasp. "There'll be no more talk of you working this day. Claire, call for your mother. Katy, you help Julianna in the kitchen. Boys, you'll continue your picking until the heat of the afternoon, then come inside and help as you can. Is that clear?"

We all agree, but Granma remains silent, staring venomously at Mac.

He stands and picks up his plate and Ester's. "Ian, I believe it is your turn to bring in the dishes?"

"Yessir." Ian takes the plates from Granda and begins stacking the others, while Granda helps Ester to her feet. Am I seeing things, or is she a bit wobbly? Is it her frustration or her condition? I pray I'm imagining things out of my concern.

"I'll help you, Ian." I collect the plates from the other side of the table, and we carry them into the kitchen, where Julianna meets us.

"Stack them in the sink, boys. I'll take care of the washing."

"Thank you for making lunch for us, Aunt Julianna." Ian gives her a quick squeeze.

"Thank you, Ian." Her mouth turns down as she studies us with her sober eyes. "We must do everything we can to help Mac and Ester during this terrible time."

Terrible? That sounds ominous.

"They're going to need all of us to pull together. No more running in the house. No more fighting amongst ourselves. No more shirking our duties." She wags her finger at us. "We must all show Ester a brave face."

Ian, looking as confused as I feel, glances at me with knit brows. I shrug.

"Run along, now, and get those crops in."

"Yes'm."

The first order of business is to bring in the filled baskets from the morning, so Aunt Julianna and Aunt Emma can get started. Then, keeping to the same assignments, with Uncle Chris taking over Granda's portion, we get back to work. No one complains, not even Buck.

By the time the sun heats the fields to an uncomfortable level, we are almost halfway done. The others agree that another two days should finish the job.

The hard work bolsters my mood until we carry the last baskets into the kitchen and walk by Ester, curled up in her chair, sleeping, her thin body and ashen face lost in the multiple blankets piled atop her.

I've rarely seen Granma sleep during the day, certainly not at harvest time. It's a grim reminder that our lives will never be the same again.

Chapter Eighteen

October 1913

The day begins for me before dawn, when the house stands as a mute sentinel overseeing the half-harvested fields and the darkness hides my solitary creeping through its halls. Grabbing a kerosene lamp and a piece of leftover bread from dinner, I head for the barn to gather baskets to begin the day's labor. When I reach the barn, the door is cracked, and high-pitched giggling drifts through the opening.

The girls must've had the same idea as me.

I don't want to startle them, so I slide through the door and tiptoe down the straw-laden threshing floor toward the dim glow in the back storage. I open my mouth to alert them of my presence when I hear a second, deeper whisper, unexpected but oh so familiar.

Buck.

What's going on here?

More giggling.

I shove the door open with a bang and lift my lamp to find Buck with his arms around Claire and his face buried in her neck under her long locks.

"Buck! What are you doing?"

Claire stares at me, wide-eyed, her mouth a small, rose-colored circle. Buck jerks his head up and thrusts Claire away. She stumbles and almost falls, but Buck reaches out and grabs her arm.

Rage seethes through my veins like fingers of a spreading fire. "How could you?" The words drip like venom from the end of my tongue.

I march up to Claire and lean close until my nose almost touches hers. "Go."

With a mouse-like squeak, she scampers out of the storage room and runs from the barn.

I turn to face Buck. "How could you do this to Ian?"

Buck's face glows bright red in the dim firelight, but he curls his lips in defiance. "Ian hasn't laid claim to her."

I punch Buck in the nose, and he drops like a stone. "You know Ian is madly in love with Claire. He's talked about marriage when he's of age." I stomp my heel in the center of his stomach.

"Oomph. Stop it."

"No more, do you hear me? No more."

"You're not my father!"

I fold my arms. "Oh, so you want me to take this to Granda and see what he has to say about it? Gladly."

"No!"

"Why not?"

Buck's jaw pulses as he cuts his eyes away.

"Because you know what he'd say, that's why. Like you know what you are doing is wrong." I spit at his feet, turn on my heel, and stalk to the door.

"What if she wants *me*?"

His weasely whine shoots a hot flash up my spine and neck into my face. I spin, and in two strides, I'm grabbing his throat and lifting him off the ground. "Don't you say that. Not ever." I toss him across the floor. "Claire deserves a nice person, a good and decent person like Ian, not a selfish dog like you who, in the end, will hurt her."

Buck scrambles to his feet, propping his fists on his hips as his eyes widen. "Ooh! I see how it is. You're in love with her, too."

"I am not." I jut my chin and jerk my head. "I would *never* do that to Ian."

Buck's cackling laughter follows my footsteps as I march from the storage room, grabbing a basket from the stack by the door.

"You'll have to find someone else to work with," I call back to him. "I can't bear your presence for one more second."

"Fine. I'll work with Ian and the girls."

My tenuous hold on my temper snaps. I throw the basket, dash back to the storage room, and with my head down, I charge into Buck like a bull after a rodeo cowboy. My fists are already flying before we land in a pile of bundled wheat. He tries to cover his face with his arms, but I pummel him mercilessly until my hands and his face are bloody.

"What in the Sam Hill?" Uncle Liam's gruff cry freezes my last punch in mid-air. "What's the meaning of this?" Liam grabs the back of my collar and hauls me off Buck. "Explain yourself."

"Take your hands off me." I wrench from Liam's grasp.

"You're both too old to be acting like this." Uncle Liam drags Buck up by his elbow. "Fist fights. Your pa would skin your hides, both of you."

I glare at Buck, the cause of it all, unwilling to meet Liam's stern stare.

"Normally, I'd march the two of you up to the big house and let you explain yourselves to my pa. But since Ma needs her rest, I'm going to send you to the fields without breakfast or lunch." He gestures toward the basket I threw down. "Get your baskets and get to work. Now."

Buck skitters away like a spider to get a basket while I pick up mine, sulking under Uncle Liam's gaze.

"And if I see either one of you lazing about, you'll be working through the night."

"Yessir."

"Honestly, of all times to be acting like fools. You two take the cake."

"Yessir."

"Now, apologize and forgive each other."

"No, sir. I won't do it." Finally, I meet Uncle Liam's stare. "Buck's behavior is unforgivable."

"And yours *is* forgivable? Beating your brother senseless?"

"He deserved it."

"So, you are now the judge of right and wrong, is that it?" With a scoffing snort, he presses me toward the barn door, then gestures for

Buck to follow. "Tonight, the three of us will have a long conversation about this. But I'd better not see your face before then. Get to work."

As we drag out to the fields, Buck murmurs, "I'll help Chris with the sweet potatoes and squash instead."

"Fine. Just stay away from me."

"Don't worry. I will."

He veers off toward the vegetable garden while I continue to the pumpkins. But my eyes are glued to him the whole way.

How can I ever look at him the same again? His betrayal cuts too deep. Will I ever recover from this terrible breach? What if Ian finds out? It will destroy him. How could Buck have been so stupid? And what about Claire? She was in the barn, too. Is she not accountable for her actions? My mind pulses with questions, but I can find no answers to soothe the ache in my soul.

Worst of all, Buck is right. I am in love with Claire. The only difference between Buck and me is that I will never act on it. The piercing ache wrenching my heart has less to do with Buck's betrayal than my own unfulfilled longing, and my chastisement of Buck is as much for my sake as his.

I must put Claire out of my mind and focus on the important things—Granma's health, the farm, what I want to do with my life…

Perhaps that's the problem. I don't know what I want to do. I'm like an untethered boat. When waves come along, I'm too easily swept out to sea.

A thought resurfaces, unconsidered for several years: I could return to New Zealand, take up caring for Pa's land, and make a go as a sheep farmer.

It means leaving the only family I have. Ian will never leave Claire, and Buck made it clear long ago that he has no desire to leave America. At this point, I wouldn't want him to come along anyway.

And then there's Ester, who has been nothing but gracious and kind to me. To leave her in her time of need seems cruel. Granda is getting older, too, and needs our help on the farm.

No, now is not the right time to leave. But the possibility of a different future where I am my own man, self-reliant and free of the burdens of others, makes the sky seem brighter and my workload lighter.

The day passes to dusk before I realize it, as my mind is filled with imaginings of this potential future in New Zealand. Everyone besides Buck has already quit for the night. They are probably eating the evening meal by now. My stomach grumbles at the thought of delicious stew made of venison, potatoes, and carrots I'm missing because of Buck's stupidity. Maybe Granma will take pity and make a plate to bring to my room.

I carry my last load to the kitchen and head straight to my room without a word to anyone. As I wash my battered hands in the basin, I picture Buck's swollen, bleeding nose and bruised face with secret glee. My only regret is I didn't permanently disfigure him so Claire would lose interest.

A quick tap on the door startles me out of my guilty pleasure.

"Yes?"

I expected Uncle Liam, but it's Granda who sticks his head through the opening. "May I come in?"

"Yessir."

Granda shuffles into the room and sits in the chair beside my desk. "I understand there was a commotion in the barn this morning."

So, Liam told Granda, despite what he said about Ester. "Yessir." Here it comes.

"Want to tell me what the fight was about?"

"No, sir. Not really."

Granda purses his lips. "Hmm. Very well."

Then, he sits there. And sits. And sits.

What does he want from me?

I stride to my bed and plop down on my belly, feigning indifference to his passive scrutiny.

Still, he sits, watching. Waiting.

I prop up on my elbow and cradle my head in my hand. "Do you have something you want to say?"

"Do you?"

A low rumble in my throat blows out in a huff of air. "No, I don't."

"Hmm. Very well."

I throw my head back, my eyes closed. "Just say it!"

"Say what?"

"How wrong I am. How Buck's my brother, and I should love him unconditionally. How sorry I'll be one day if I don't forgive and make amends."

"Do you believe those things?"

"No!" Do I? "Yes." But I don't want to. "I don't know."

Granda raises his brows and tilts his head as if asking a question, but he says nothing more.

"Buck doesn't deserve my forgiveness."

Granda's eyebrows lift higher.

"Well, he doesn't. He didn't admit he'd done wrong."

"Like you are not admitting your wrong right now?"

I knew he'd twist my words. "I don't want his forgiveness!"

"Hmm." Granda nods once, his lips disappearing into his white beard.

"He got what he deserved."

"Is that right?"

"Yessir. You don't know what he did. The awful thing he did."

"No, I don't." Granda lifts his palm. "You haven't told me."

"No, sir."

"What did *you* do?"

Like air from a punctured balloon, my resolve sputters and deflates. "I punched him in the nose."

"And?"

"And I beat him up pretty bad."

Granda leans forward, his elbows on his knees and his hands knit together. "What do you believe you deserve?"

I can't help myself. I sneer and narrow my eyes, daring him to disagree. "Congratulations." I hold my breath, waiting for the explosion.

Granda chuckles.

My breath stops in my throat, and my mouth hangs open for a second or two, then bitterness surges from my gut, drowning my confusion. "What are you laughing at?"

"Do you realize you're the same age as your pa when you were born?"

My brain bounces around like a kicked ball at the sudden change of topics. "No, sir. I never thought about it."

"He had been on his own since he was Ian's age and had been on many adventures before he met your ma." Granda lowers his head. "I'm afeared we've sheltered you too much. We did it because of your terrible loss, but I don't think we've done right by you." Granda slaps his hands on his knees. "Yes. It's time for you to grow up, become a man, and learn the lessons of life."

"What do you mean? I am a man."

Granda's eyes take on a sorrowful cast. "No, son. You're a boy who beats up his brother when he doesn't like something he's done and who pouts in his room when he gets in trouble for it." He breathes out a deep sigh. "A man works out his disagreements with his brother. A man accepts responsibility for his actions. And a man examines his motives before he judges the motives of his brother." He lifts one brow and fires an arrow into my eyes. "A man forgives. Seventy times seven."

"Even if what my brother did was truly cruel?"

Granda pauses, moistening his lips. "Let me ask you something."

"Yessir?"

"Have you ever been cruel to anyone?"

I open my mouth to say no, but the image of me riding off in the night with plans to run away to New Zealand wafts up from my memory. I left Ian when he pleaded for me to stay. I took the gold from Uncle

Bear's room and Granda's horse. I was selfish in believing I was the only one in pain, and I caused Granma sorrow and worry by leaving. All of that was cruel.

A flood of images follows on its heels: leaving Ian alone in the woods after the fire; all the times I took out my anger at Ma's and Pa's deaths on Buck; stealing from Missus Appleton after she cared for us; running away and hiding from Uncle Bear; making Mani promise not to forget us, and promising to return but not writing him even one letter…beating Buck up because I have a silly crush on Claire.

I chew on my lower lip. "I…I guess I have been pretty cruel."

"And all the people you've hurt with your cruelty, would you want their forgiveness?"

Recalling Ester's loving embrace, welcoming me home without question after I ran away, sends a flood of hot tears up my throat. My cheeks burn beneath their flow.

"We forgive because we have been forgiven so much." Granda claps his hand on my shoulder. "It's time to grow up, Fin, and become the man your pa would want you to be."

And with that pronouncement, Granda walks out, leaving me drowning in a pool of tears and sucked under in quicksand of shame with no way out.

As the crying wanes, I stand before the window, bathed in the moon's soft glow, and place my hand over my heart. "Pa. I promise you, I will be the man you were, no matter what it takes. From this day forward and forever, I will be like you. I will love like you loved Ma. I will give like you gave to the Māori people. I will lead like you led your children. I will be strong and stand against evil, the way you were strong against our enemies. I will serve others like you served everyone else, selflessly and with a willing heart. I will be independent like you. And I will be fiercely loyal to family and friends, just like you were, always. This I vow."

First things first. I must make things right with Buck. I tiptoe down the hall to his door and tap lightly, but he doesn't respond, so either he's asleep already or he doesn't want to speak to anyone. Very well, I'll take care of the rest of his picking. That'll make up for the beating he took.

I creep outside through the kitchen door, grab a basket, a knife, and a kerosene lamp from the barn, and follow the path to the vegetable garden. Buck made good progress. It should be a cakewalk to finish tonight.

I start with the rows of squash, cutting the vines and dumping the squash in my basket. I do the same with the zucchini. When my basket fills to overflowing, I hoist it on my shoulder and carry it to the kitchen. Then, it's back to the barn for another basket and a trowel to dig up the sweet potatoes.

I make short work of the sweet potatoes Buck didn't finish and carry them to the kitchen, dropping the half-filled basket in the cupboard before darting back upstairs, unseen. Once again, I wash my hands and face, but this time, I don't hesitate to look in the mirror.

CHAPTER NINETEEN

October 1913

A smug, self-satisfied warmth fills my chest when I spy Buck standing by the vegetable patch with one hand planted on his hip and the other scratching his head. I saunter up to him, fully prepared to receive his gratitude, but his confusion melts away when he sees me. In its place, a flush of red enflames his cheeks, his eyes narrow, and a distasteful snarl as if he's smelled something foul curls his lip.

"What are you doing here?"

"I came to tell you I'm sorry for punching you. I'm sorry for everything that happened."

He turns his back on me.

"I finished your harvesting to make amends." I sidle up to him. "I know how much you hate picking."

"I never asked you to do nothin'."

"I know. I thought of it on my own." When he doesn't respond, I touch his elbow. "Look, I'm the oldest, so I must set a better example for Ian and you."

Buck snorts. "You mean, Granda got onto you."

"He did, yes. And he's right. I was childish and foolish, and there was no call for it." I suck on my bottom lip. "So, I forgive you for what you did with Claire. I am asking your forgiveness for the beating."

"If Claire will have me, I'm gonna marry her."

My insides cringe against my backbone. What would a man say? "Well, that's between you and Ian, I suppose. But I urge you to consider his feelings before you plow over him and steal Claire."

"Steal her? I told you, Ian's laid no claim to her."

I inhale a gulp of air to quiet the pounding in my chest. "But he has. He told me his plans."

"He best tell Claire, then." Buck hoists his empty basket and turns toward the orchard.

Claire with Buck. It curdles my stomach to imagine it. "Have you told Ian you want to marry Claire?"

Buck stares at me like I've grown horns. "Of course not. Why would I give him the chance to ask her first?"

"He's your brother. It seems right to play fair."

"What's the saying? 'All's fair in love and war'?" Buck smirks and strolls toward the orchard with his head high, whistling a bright tune.

Everything in me wants to tackle him again. Instead, I call out, "Buck?"

He spins, his free hand on his hip. "What?"

"Please. You'll destroy Ian. Please think about it."

He throws his hand in the air and marches on, showing no signs of remorse.

When he's beyond earshot, I mutter, "Granda says I must forgive you, so I forgive you. But I don't have to like you."

Maybe if I'm around, Buck will behave. Dashing to the barn, I grab a basket and race to the orchard.

Ian, Katy, and Claire are already working. Ian, perched atop a ladder, tosses down apples to Katy while Claire picks around the lower limbs of the tree. Buck has positioned himself near Claire on the adjacent tree. I grab a ladder lying on the ground and carry it to Buck's tree, intruding into the middle of their conversation.

"Buck and I can handle the rest of this row. Why don't y'all head down to the last row, and we'll meet in the middle."

"Sounds good." The threesome finishes their tree, then they move on as I suggested.

Buck growls under his breath. "You think you're so smart."

"I'm protecting my brother. *Brothers.* You don't want to do something you'll regret."

He huffs. "You don't get to decide my life for me."

"You're right." I smile down at him through the laden branches. "But I can try to prevent you from destroying everyone else's lives."

Buck and I work in silence until the sun reaches its zenith. Ian, Katy, and Claire, carrying their filled baskets, wander up through the rows. Ian pauses beside my ladder. "We're going in for luncheon. You?"

"Tell Aunt Julianna and Aunt Emma we'll be up in a minute."

Buck balks. "I'm ready to go now. I'm hungry."

"Our baskets aren't full. We can finish this tree in no time and fill them."

Ian hooks Claire's arm, who leans closer to him as they walk up the trail. I can almost hear the steam boiling off Buck's head.

A low growl rumbles deep in his throat. "Hurry it up, then."

I've never seen Buck work so hard.

Buck mutters under his breath as we heave our baskets onto our shoulders and start the long climb to the big house. I keep my thoughts to myself, but a contemptuous sense of satisfaction blossoms in my chest. Hopefully, Ian has used the opportunity to make his intentions explicit to Claire.

Buck leaves me in his dust, almost running up the hill to try and catch Ian and Claire, who are long since out of sight. If I'm lucky, luncheon will be well underway, and Ian will be sitting beside Claire when Buck arrives.

Sure enough, when I finally enter the dining room, Ian and Claire are nestled together on one side of the table, and Buck, his face a mask of fury, hunches over his plate on the other side, shoveling in his food faster than a starving hound.

As I spoon Aunt Julianna's stew onto my plate, Ian stands and clears his throat. "I have an announcement to make."

Is this it? Has he asked Claire to marry him?

Granda lifts one brow. "What is it, son?"

"I've been writing to Mani, our Māori brother, and he's been keeping me updated on our ranch."

How did I not know Ian and Mani were staying in touch? A flush of guilt heats my neck. I should've been handling that communication, as the oldest. But I've not reached out to Mani in years.

"In his last letter, he shared that things aren't going well over there. It was a little hard to understand his writing, but I believe he was saying all the workers in the country are refusing to work. So, no one is making any money or producing any goods. Ships are standing in the ports waiting to be offloaded, but no one will do it. There's no food or other goods available anywhere for sale, and the Māori are suffering greatly. I don't think they are working our ranch anymore, although Uncle Bear is still paying them. His money does them no good if there's nothing to buy, so they're busy trying to survive. Mani's been trying to care for the sheep, cows, and horses, but it's been difficult without any supplies."

'Is Mani OK?" Buck's face is no longer buried in his plate. I check his widened eyes and furrowed brow with surprise. Buck, thinking about someone else for once. Who would've thought it possible?

"I don't know. Hard to tell. But that's why…" Ian pauses, looking around at the upturned faces. "That's why I'm going to return to New Zealand."

Granma's eyes close, and her pale face sags. A breathy gasp escapes Claire's open mouth. Glancing briefly at Ester, Granda rises slowly from his chair. "No."

Ian's head jerks back as if he's been gut-punched. "Sir?"

"No. You're too young." Granda presses his palms against the table and leans toward Ian. "Besides, we need you here."

Ian's head tilts to the right. His eyes narrow as he bites his lower lip. "I'm sorry, Granda, but the Māori need me more."

Granda's face folds into a thunderous scowl. "I'll not hear another word on the subject. The answer is no."

My eyes cut between Ian and Granda. A breathless hush falls over the room.

Ian presses his lips together and meets Granda's stare. His eyes gleam with confidence I've never seen in the boy. Finally, he blows out a breath. "Granda, I love you, and I respect you. But you'll not stop me from doing what's right." Ian's back straightens. "If Pa were here, he would tell me to take care of the people. And the Lord tells us to care for the poor." A sad smile softens his determined expression. "This is what I'm supposed to do, and I mean to see it through."

Granda's jaw pulses, his face reddens, and his neck bulges. He looks like he's a threat to launch across the table and throttle Ian, but instead, his voice lowers to a menacing whisper. "You'll not upset Ester. Do you understand me ?"

"I'm proud of you, Ian." Ester's quiet voice flows like a soothing balm over the tense room. "You are following your heart and doing what you believe to be the Lord's leading. No one could ask for more from you."

"Ester…"

"Leave the boy be, Mac." Ester is barely audible. She lays a gentle hand on Mac's arm.

Now, it's Granda's mouth that hangs open. He sputters. "But…"

She pats his arm. "My love, let him go."

"That's not all." Ian clears his throat and smooths his shirt. "Claire." He turns to face her, then kneels before her chair. Claire's hand flies to her mouth. "You know how I feel for you. I've made myself plain." Ian reaches in his back pocket and pulls out a small, blue box. "Claire, will you marry me?" He holds the box out toward Claire.

Uncle Chris studies his daughter's face. Tears rim Aunt Emma's eyes as she clasps her hands at her breast.

They knew about this! And Ian didn't let on a thing to Buck and me.

Claire takes the little box and opens it carefully. A silver ring rests on blue velvet lining. The band, carved with an elegant swirl, holds a small, deep blue stone that glistens in the candlelight.

Claire gasps and fingers the ring. "Ian, it's so beautiful. How did you ever…"

"Will you marry me?"

Claire's head bobs like a baby bird's. "Yes! Of course I will." She wraps her arms around his neck.

Cheers and applause erupt around the table—all except for Buck and Granda. And me. My heart writhes in my chest like a deer in the jaws of a mountain lion, slowly crushed and bleeding. I glance at Buck, whose face looks as yellowed as old parchment.

Be the better man. "Congratulations, you two." I paste a smile on my face. "This is wonderful news."

"Will you be taking Claire away to New Zealand?" Granda's harsh tone pierces their joy like a well-aimed arrow. Emma's pained expression and Chris's knit brows tell me this was not part of their understanding of the plan.

"No, Granda. We'll wait to marry until I return. It's not safe for her there right now." He grasps Claire's hands. "Are you willing to wait until I come back for you?"

Again, Claire bobs her head, then embraces him again. "Of course I'll wait for you. Just don't stay away too long."

"Once everything is settled there, I'll come back. We'll marry and return to New Zealand to work the ranch."

For a fleeting second, Claire's face blanches, a single line creasing her brows. Then, it's gone quicker than a hummingbird. Am I imagining things?

Chris thumps the table with his fists. "This calls for a celebration. What do you say?"

"We must celebrate their engagement." Emma claps her hands. "I will bake a cake."

Granda's eyes disappear into the dark gray puffiness beneath them as he examines Ester's face. "You'll not lift a finger."

Ester smiles weakly. "If we are having a party tonight, I must take my rest this afternoon." Slowly, she tries to stand. Granda grabs her arm and helps her up. "Phew. All the excitement has me aflutter."

"Come, my love." Granda supports her in his arms and carries her feather-like weight up the stairs as easily as he might carry a flower petal.

After we clear the table, Emma and Julianna put their heads together about the party, Chris and Liam head for the barn, and I grab Buck's arm and drag him into the hallway.

"That's it, then. Ian has made his intentions clear. No more talk of Claire."

Buck's lip curls in a surly frown. "We'll see. A lot can happen while he's away."

I snatch his arm sideways. "Look here. It's one thing to daydream about a single girl, but they're betrothed now. You'll behave, or I'll take you out behind the barn and beat you good."

"You ain't my Pa."

"No, I'm not. But I'll not have you shame Claire or this family." I toss my head and glare at him. "I'll send you away with Ian if that's what it takes. But you'll give me your word right now. Hands off Claire. No more flirting."

Buck sneers.

"I mean it. If you don't give your word, I'm packing your bags to go with Ian to New Zealand."

"Fine. I promise."

"You promise what?"

"I promise, hands off Claire."

I lean close to Buck's face until my nose is less than an inch from his. "The better man won."

He blinks, then turns away, and the satisfied feeling returns, filling my battered chest. At least he's hurting as much as I am.

The three of us work in the fields with Liam and Chris the rest of the afternoon while the women and girls prepare for the grand celebration of Ian's engagement and my broken heart. Buck is more surly than usual, but I'm too consumed with my pain to care about his. Ian seems oblivious, chattering about his love for Claire, their plans, and his upcoming trip.

"I'll ask Uncle Bear to help me arrange transport on a ship. Hopefully, he will let me stay with him in San Francisco for a few days before I leave."

"How will you get to the ranch?"

"I suppose I must buy a horse. Or maybe Mani could meet me and bring one of ours with him."

Buck snorts. "You made it sound like Mani can't handle anything more than what he's facing right now. And what if there aren't any horses because of the problems over there?"

"Then, I'll figure it out." Ian's contented smile burns like acid on my skin. "I'm doing the right thing, so I trust the Lord will provide."

"Like He provided for Mani."

I whip my head around to glare at Buck, but Ian is unfazed.

"I suppose *I'm* the Lord's provision for Mani."

Anyone else saying such a statement would sound arrogant and self-righteous, but Ian's shining goodness belies any false motive in his heart. Suddenly, an image of Buck and me tearing at each other's throats without Ian to soothe our constant friction sends a chill across my flesh.

"Ian?" I chew my lip as I fumble with picking the beans. "Would…do you think one of us should…go with you? To help Mani?"

Ian tilts his head, then frowns. "No. You're needed here to help Granda and Granma."

"But the harvest will be done." My mind screams *don't leave me,* but this is the best excuse I can come up with to justify joining him.

"There's still so much work on the farm, and Granda will be busy caring for Granma. Liam has his land to work, as does Chris. Who else is there to help Granda?"

Buck spits a wad in the dirt. "I'm not going. Leave me out of this."

Of course. He's banking on wooing Claire away from Ian while he's away. And he might succeed, too, based on what I witnessed in the barn, if I'm not here to stop him. "You're right, Ian. We're needed here."

Ian nods, whistling as he continues down the row. Buck and I trudge along beside him. Neither of us is whistling. When our baskets are full, we hoist them on our backs and hike up the hill to the big house.

"I think Claire will want a simple wedding, with family and her closest friends." Ian purses his lips, gazing into the cloudless sky. "Maybe right here on the mountain."

Simple? Claire? Does he know the girl? I figure she'll want the biggest wedding in the county.

"I can't wait to show her the ranch. We can build a new cabin where our old one was, and I can teach her how to shear…"

Claire, shearing sheep? What is Ian thinking?

"…and we'll raise horses and cattle and grow vegetables in our garden. It'll be perfect."

"Claire is sort of a dainty lass for such things." I don't mean to burst Ian's bubble, but I don't want him to go into marriage with Claire blind to her attitude about getting her hands dirty.

Ian chuckles. "Claire's a beauty, but she has a strong spirit. You'd be surprised."

I would indeed.

The kitchen reminds me of a big city train station, with overflowing baskets and stacked pumpkins vying for space with bustling women, heaping bowls of cake batter, simmering pots on the fire, and whispering, giggling girls. This party is putting the canning way behind.

Buck yells over the din. "Where do you want these?"

Aunt Julianna huffs and brushes her hair out of her eyes, leaving a smear of batter across her forehead. "Put them anywhere, just get them out of my way."

"Aye-aye, captain." Buck stacks his basket atop another in the corner, I wedge mine between a cabinet and the back door, and Ian plops his on top of mine.

"What's for dinner? Mmm, can I taste the batter?" Buck reaches his grimy fingers toward the nearest bowl, but Julianna swats his hand with a spoon.

"Get out, the lot of you." When Buck doesn't move, she wallops him, this time on his rear. "I said, get on with you."

Claire and Katy giggle at us as we scurry from the kitchen, with Julianna's bellow trailing behind us. "Don't traipse your filth through the house. Go wash up first."

So, we scramble back through the kitchen and out the back door to the pump to wash up. Liam wanders up from the barn.

"I'd stay out of Aunt Julianna's kitchen if I were you." Buck snorts. "She's in a tizzy."

Liam closes his eyes and groans as he sticks his hands into the bucket.

I glance toward the barn door. "Where's Uncle Chris?"

"He went down to his cabin." Liam rolls his eyes. "Probably wanted to avoid all the hullaballoo."

"I don't know why they're going to all this trouble. Ian and Claire ain't marrying yet." Buck's lip curls into a sneer. "Puttin' the cart before the horse, I'd say."

I give Buck a hard poke in the ribs.

"Hey, watch it." When he looks at me, I nod toward Ian, whose head is lowered and his cheeks flushed as he pumps water to rinse his hands in the flow.

"Listen. Dinner won't be ready for a while yet, and Aunt Julianna wants us out of the way." I nudge Ian with my elbow. "Why don't we go for one last swim at the waterfall. What do you say? The last swim of the fall."

"I'm game," Ian says.

"Me, too. Better than a bath." Buck laughs and splashes a handful of water at Ian, who draws back at first. Then, his shoulders relax, and he scoops water in Buck's face, giggling when he sputters.

"That does it." Buck rubs his eyes with his fists. "First one to the waterfall gets to dunk Ian." And with that, he's off like a shot.

"No fair," Ian calls, running after Buck. I take off after them, my longer strides catching the younger boys easily. As I pass by Buck, I swing my foot toward his ankle, making him stumble. Ian races ahead. "Looks like we'll be dunking Buck instead!"

"Not on your life."

I reach the edge of the falls first, and with a full-throated holler, I leap off the ledge, pinwheeling my arms and kicking my legs until I crash into the water at the base. Ian jumps in right behind me, with Buck bringing up the rear. With a cry of victory, Ian pounces on Buck's head. I join him, and soon, Buck is flailing under the water like a caught fish.

When we finally let him up, he spits a water plume at us. "Serves you right. Cheaters." In a flash, Buck is on top of Ian, dragging him under. Ian's hands grab Buck's hair, but it's too late. Buck has him good.

After a minute or so, Ian bursts through the surface, laughing, his dripping curls in his eyes. "Get Fin! Get Fin!"

"Oh, no you don't." I launch into the water, but Buck catches my leg as I try to swim away and pulls me back, then Buck and Ian are on me. Down I go.

Is this really it? Our final moments as children, playing together, free from the worries of the future?

Buck and Ian finally let me go, but I don't swim up right away. I'm not ready for it to end, for once it does, nothing will ever be the same again.

Against my will, my chest tightens, the pressure behind my eyes pulses, and my throat burns until I'm forced to surface.

We frolic a while longer, but the joy of it seeps away with the setting sun, and too soon we return home for the party that brings an end to all my hopes and dreams.

CHAPTER TWENTY

December 1913

Six weeks and a flurry of telegraphs with Uncle Bear and Mani later, Ian, Buck, and I, along with Uncle Chris and, of course, Claire, stand in the pre-dawn cold at the Blue Ridge railway station, waiting for the morning train to Atlanta. Ian said his tearful goodbyes to the rest of the family at the big house because Granda refused Ester's request to accompany us to the station, fearing she would "catch her death of cold."

Granma's frail, blue-veined arms clutched Ian and refused to let go while she wept into his curls. He cried on her chest, as he had done the first day we arrived at the farm, only this time, she was on her bed, propped up with pillows. It was all I could do not to bawl myself.

Afterward, Granda shook Ian's hand and ordered him to return before the next harvest. Typical Mac.

Now, Claire is a blubbering mess. The rest of us observe like silent sentinels while the two lovebirds cling to each other, the only survivors from a sinking ship.

Buck's mouth contorts like he's chewing a lemon peel as his hooded eyes shoot invisible arrows at his brother. Uncle Chris stands by, ready in case Claire collapses from her grief. If not so tragic, it would be comical.

With the best of us leaving, what will be left for Buck and me? Sickness and mourning? Will that be our fate?

Mani reports tensions are high between the Māori and the *pākehā,* the dock workers continue to strike, and food is hard to come by. Ian carries a steamer trunk filled with staples for the Māori, *if* the boat is allowed to dock. Who knows what the state of things will be when he finally arrives a month from now? Too many unknowns. Ian is taking a big risk for something he believes in. I admire, respect, and resent him for it.

A distant whistle tells us the train will be here soon. Chris peels Claire off of Ian and lets her collapse against his chest. "Bear will meet you at the station in San Francisco in four days." Chris shakes Ian's hand. "Be careful. And come home to us soon."

Claire points her nose to the sky and wails in tune with the train's whistle. So dramatic.

Ian collects his luggage while Buck and I lift his steamer trunk and carry it to the edge of the track to await the train. Now that he's free from Claire's clutches, Ian turns to Buck and me. "I'm sorry."

"Sorry? For what?" Buck's mouth still twists beneath his pinched nose as if he's swallowing down vomit.

"For leaving." Ian heaves a deep sigh. "I wouldn't go except I believe the Lord wants me to be there for Mani and the Māori."

I shake my head. "No need to be sorry. We understand. Right, Buck?"

"Sure."

"I'm not certain Claire understands."

Buck guffaws. "Probably not. You're supposed to be marrying the girl after all."

"Buck!" I punch his arm.

"So, you think it's a mistake? Me going?"

I narrow my eyes at Buck and give a barely perceptible, single shake of my head. "No, it isn't a mistake. It's…noble. Sacrificial. Claire should be proud of you."

"Mani is our brother."

"That's right, Ian. And you're going to help our brother while we stay here and help Granda and Granma. We are all making sacrifices."

Buck blows a hard breath through his nose. "Ain't we something?"

The tracks sing a piercing dirge as the train rolls slowly into the station. As it draws near, my throat tightens, and my heart starts galloping in my chest. It's here. It's time. Ian is really leaving. I stare at him, memorizing every curve and line of his gentle face. I should say goodbye, but I can't get the words past the knot choking my throat.

Red-capped men jump out and collect the baggage from us, and Ian turns to climb the steps into the train car.

At the last moment, my frozen limbs move, and I stride toward the steps, but before I can get there, Claire bolts past me and grabs Ian around the neck.

"Don't leave me! Don't go!" She sobs like she's standing over his grave.

"I'll be back before you know it. I'll take the food and supplies to Mani, check on the farm, then come right home. I'll be back before the harvest. Like I promised Granda."

"That might as well be forever." She wails her final word in one long, mournful note.

"All aboard."

I'm out of time. Will she ever let him go?

"Come away, Claire. The train is ready to leave." Chris strides up and takes her hand.

"Nooo." Another wail, but she finally drops her arms and falls to the concrete. Chris lifts her in his arms and carries her away.

Ian stands framed in the doorway as the train moves slowly down the tracks. Buck stares after Claire and Chris, his arms folded, missing Ian's final wave.

It's too late. I'm too late.

What am I doing? I can't just stand here.

I race after the train as if my life depends on reaching Ian. When I'm parallel to Ian's door, I wave frantically. "Ian! Ian!"

He sticks his head out the door. "Fin!"

"I love you."

Over the blaring whistle announcing the train's departure, I barely hear, "I love you, too."

The long ride home is somber. Buck continues to chew on his liver while Claire's sobs add a strange rhythmic counterpoint to the creaking leather and clopping hooves. A burning ache grows in my chest as if some unnamed beast gnaws a hole in me from the inside.

"We're all going to miss him," Chris murmurs, which only serves to increase the volume and frequency of Claire's shuddering gasps. "Bear will let us know when he arrives safely. Until then, let's not add to Ester's worry by moping about or moaning about him leaving. Agreed?"

"Agreed." Buck's response sounds more like relief than acknowledgement to me. Is he truly so heartless?

"But Pa, what will I do without him?"

"You'll make do. Focus on your chores and planning your wedding. That should make you happy."

But Claire tosses her curls and groans. "Thinking about the wedding makes me miss him more."

Buck shifts in his saddle and rolls his eyes.

Chris sighs. "With Ester sickly, there will be a ton of work to do helping Julianna and your ma. If you keep yourself busy, the time will pass quickly." He glances over his shoulder at Buck and me. "The same goes for you two. Granda will be busy taking care of Ester, so you need to pick up the slack and take care of the farm."

"Yessir."

"I'll help you as much as I'm able."

We drift back to the smothering silence while the creature within me tunnels its way through my chest. A single question repeats in my head like a steady drumbeat: *Will I ever see him again?*

The winding trail through the tall grass to the cabin sends my thoughts spinning like *kowhangatara,* the silvery tumbling sand grass of New Zealand: remembering our arrival, the first time we rode this trail, and how Ian made Buck wait for me; Ian's grateful tears staining Granma's chest; seeing Buck and Claire embracing in the barn and my red-hot rage; Ian's bright eyes as he proposed and Claire said yes.

First Ester, and then Ian, just when everything finally seemed settled…now, nothing but unknowns.

I offer to take care of our horses when we arrive at the barn, which Buck is more than glad to concede. He takes off for the back pasture, and once he's out of sight, my mood lightens. I untack the horses, brush them down, and give them food and water, then I care for the rest of the horses before turning them out to pasture.

I milk the cows and turn them out next, then gather the eggs and take them to the kitchen, where I find Katy and Julianna making biscuits.

"Eggs."

"Thank you, Fin. Breakfast will be ready soon."

"Thank you, Aunt Julianna."

Katy tugs on my arm. "How is Claire?"

I shrug. "You know Claire. She's making the most of her misery."

Katy snickers but gives me a little slap. "Stop that. You know she'll miss him terribly."

"We all will."

"Did Ian seem OK?"

I shrug again. "He seemed determined. Strong. But I could tell he was sad to be leaving."

"Of course." Katy hooks her arm through my elbow and pats my hand. "We'll make do, you and I."

I offer her a slight nod.

We wander into the dining room and set out the plates and silver, readying for the morning meal. While we work, Granda and Granma shuffle into the room. Granda takes his usual seat at the head of the table after he gently lowers Ester into her chair. Her breaths are labored and quavering. Her skin seems as thin as paper, with every vein etched in blue across her face, neck, and hands. Always frail, Ester's shoulders now hunch toward her sunken chest.

Her deterioration has quickened in the weeks since her collapse. How much longer will she be with us? I can't imagine Granda without Granma, but it appears inevitable. Although, as my ma always said, "No one gets far thinking they ken the mind of God." Ester's a strong woman. She could outlive us all.

A rattling cough rumbles in her chest as if in response to my hopeful thought, dashing it away like a feather on the wind. It sounds like her breaths scrape over sand on the way out of her throat. Granda leans close to her and whispers, but she shakes her head. Sighing, he dabs the corners of her mouth with a white cloth. Deep crevasses crease his brow when he glances down at the napkin. Are those smears of blood? He folds it quickly before I can see it.

If the earth opened and swallowed the cabin whole, I wouldn't be a bit surprised. My whole world is crumbling around me—again.

What have I done, Lord, to deserve another round of torment and loss? Isn't losing everything that mattered to me once enough for You?

The others wander in, all except Buck, and take their places, but the conversations, usually lively and boisterous, remain muted, like the whispers shared at a visitation.

"Ian got off without a hitch." Uncle Chris glances apologetically at his daughter.

Silence.

"The winter wheat's looking good." Uncle Liam shovels a forkful of eggs into his mouth.

Granda grunts his acknowledgement.

Silence.

"I thought we'd have a ham this Christmas." Aunt Julianna's lighthearted attempt at excitement thuds in the room like someone dropped a heavy bag of wheat on the table.

Silence.

Granma coughs again, a harsh retch that won't stop. Granda stands, fussing over her, trying to get her to drink water, and finally carrying her from the table and up the stairs, leaving her meal untouched. The rasping sounds echo down the stairwell until Granda's footfalls creak above us and their door shuts.

Then, silence.

"May I be excused?"

Uncle Liam nods, so I pick up my half-empty plate and dash from this funereal chamber, through the kitchen, where I drop my dish on the counter and race out the door. I stop on the path between the big house and the barn to inhale a deep breath of fresh air and bask in the warming sun, but deep in my bones, a deathly chill remains.

I take Uncle Chris' suggestion to keep busy, mucking stalls, throwing out hay, splitting firewood, checking fences, filling water troughs, and feeding the pigs. Poor things. If Aunt Julianna has her way, one of them will be on our table before long.

I guess there's no escaping death, no matter how far or how fast I run.

With all the chores I can think of finished, I wander into the back pastures, looking for where Buck's gotten off to, but I can't spot him. So, to soothe my soul, I make my way to where the horses congregate. My favorite, a solid black quarter horse named Raven, nuzzles my hand, looking for food.

"Sorry, girl, I don't have anything for you today." I grab her mane, pull myself up on her bare back, and wrap my arms around her neck. "Let's run, girl. I need to feel free."

In response to my gentle kick, she bolts from the others, galloping at full speed through the tall grass down the mountain toward the falls. Her mane whips against my face, so I sit up, clutching her mane in my hands, and let the wind bathe over me like a cleansing balm.

As we approach the waterfall, a glimmer atop a ripple in the pool catches my eye. I squint to make out what moves the otherwise smooth surface as Buck erupts from underwater, shaking his head and sending a stream of droplets as far as the shore.

"For goodness sake, Buck, what're you doing? The water must be freezing!"

He whips his head around and finds Raven and me peering over the edge of the falls. "It's just what I needed." He waves his hand. "Come on in."

I chuckle. "No thanks. I'd rather not choose pain. I have enough of it already."

"It's refreshing. Helps clear your mind."

I tug Raven's mane and urge her down the path to the edge of the pool. "You missed breakfast. And lunch."

Buck shrugs, then dives down, coming up under the falls. The sheet of water crashes over his head, pounding his shoulders and washing his red hair into his eyes. After letting the water beat him for a minute more, he swims toward me, climbs from the pool, and slips on his clothes without waiting to dry.

"Want a ride back?"

He chews the inside of his cheek, looking around, then scratches his chin. "Hmm. I might stay out here."

I don't blame him, not a lick. The pall over the big house sticks to the skin like a slick of black oil. But Granma and Granda have already lost so much. It seems cruel to abandon them now, when their need is greatest. "Don't you want to spend time with Ester before…"

"Before she dies?" Buck's words slice like a sharp edge, and his bitterness taints the fresh air.

"Yes—before she's gone and you *can't* see her anymore."

"Who wants to sit around watching someone suffer? Watching them waste away before your eyes until they're a shell of themselves?" He tosses his wet curls. "Not me."

The familiar burn Buck always seems to provoke rises in my chest. "Well, maybe it's not about you. Maybe it's about giving her some peace in her final days. Maybe it's about showing love to someone who has sacrificed and given so much for you."

Buck's lips press into a thin slash as his nostrils flare. "I didn't ask for your opinion."

In my mind's eye, I swing my leg over Raven's back, grab Buck by his jacket collar, and drive my shoulder into his chest until he is knee deep in the pool, where I shove him under the water and hold him there until bubbles stop rising. Instead, I pull Raven's mane to turn her around and start back up the path to the top of the falls. "Have it your way."

"Wait up."

I pull to a stop but refuse to look at him.

"I'll take that ride."

"Very well."

Buck pulls himself up behind me. I urge Raven into a slow walk, taking the long way around the mountain so we approach the cabin on the path through the waving winter wheat, as we did the first time we came to the farm, over six long years ago.

Only, it's not the same. Ester's silhouette isn't framed in the doorway, wrapped in her colorful native blanket with her hands clasped at her chest. Mac isn't standing behind her, ever watchful, making sure the blanket doesn't slip off her shoulder.

And the sun's usually brilliant rays appear pallid and dull, covering the scene in a wash of gray, because joy has abandoned this mountain, never to return.

Chapter Twenty-One

February 1914

Thick drapes cover the large picture windows in the main room, the sitting area, and the dining room for the first time since we arrived at the farm. We move through the house like ghosts, using the feeble light of a single candle or feeling our way in the darkness, treading as softly as possible. We barely speak, and then only in whispers, lest we disturb Ester's sleep.

Nowadays, she sleeps most of the time.

I've not laid eyes on Mac or Ester in weeks. Aunt Julianna and Aunt Emma take turns carrying trays for Granda and Granma to their room, but when they come out, little food is eaten, and our aunts look ashen and stricken.

Buck and I aren't allowed inside.

Uncle Liam goes into town at least twice a week to send telegraph updates to his siblings and Ian. He keeps us informed on the messages back from Ian and Uncle Bear.

The news from New Zealand is grim. The nationwide strike is over, but Ian says no one has recovered, food is scarce, and many people have lost everything. Uncle Bear's ongoing payments to the Māori are all that have kept Mani's village from total devastation.

Ian reports other rumblings, too—unrest in-country along with concerns about events happening in central Europe. But he says he is keeping his head down and his wits about him, focusing on rebuilding our station a little at a time.

Every time Uncle Liam reads a new telegram, Claire asks some version of, "When is he coming home?" The answer is always the same: "He doesn't say."

Her pinched brow and pouting lips tell me she grows impatient, so I keep a close eye on her, especially when Buck is around, which is rare these days. He leaves mid-afternoon and spends almost every evening in Morganton or Blue Ridge, coming home in the wee hours to sleep until noon. Then, he eats and is off again. None of the elders ask where he's going or where he's been, and when I ask, all I get is a cryptic "I'm goin' to town."

His face has taken on a sickly pallor. Deep gray smudges encircle his eyes. If I didn't know better, I'd wonder if he was drinking. I'm pretty sure he's gambling at cards since he always seems to have money.

Pa would have his hide if he knew what he was up to.

Katy is the one bright spot in the ever-growing gloom. With Claire always morose and complaining, and Buck always gone, Katy and I have become best friends. Together, we handle the outside chores while Aunt Julianna and Aunt Emma prepare the meals and clean up inside. Then, she and I go on a ride together, or take walks, or sometimes we sit on the front porch steps and share our dreams, our desires, and our sorrow.

But today, the wind howls down the mountain, and the clouds threaten snow, so we drift among the shadows like spirits, invisible to the other living creatures surrounding us, unable to affect our fate.

Uncle Liam finds Katy and me ensconced in the sitting room, reading by a shared candle. "Where's Buck?"

I shrug.

"Go find him."

I close my book slowly. "And where would you suggest I look?"

Liam bends down and sticks a finger close to my face. "Don't give me your attitude right now. I have no patience for either of you and your selfishness." He heaves a trembling sigh. "But Ma is asking after you. So, go find Buck, and you bring him home."

"Yessir." I swallow hard. "I'm sorry, sir."

He nods once, then whispers, "Hurry."

Katy and I grab our coats, dash to the barn, tack up our horses, and ride at our best possible speed, given the snow, to Morganton, hoping we run into Buck somewhere along the way. But no one at the local night spots has seen him in days.

So, we ride on to Blue Ridge, starting with the saloon Ol' Dezzy, the thief who stole my running away money, frequents.

And there we find Buck, sitting at a table in a back room with four rough-looking men, a tumbled pile of coins strewn before him, holding cards in one hand and a glass filled with amber liquid in the other.

I deepen my voice in my best imitation of Pa. "Barclay MacAlister."

His head jerks up, his bleary eyes wide until he sees me. Then, they narrow. "What're you doin' here?"

"What in blazes are *you* doing?" I march to the table and snatch him to his feet by his collar. As I suspected, he wavers on his feet and does little to resist.

I drag him toward the room's entrance and call Katy, still standing in the door of the forbidden establishment. "Order some coffee."

"Wait! My money!" Buck jerks from my grasp, shrugging off his jacket as he lurches to the table. He spreads the jacket on the table and scrapes the coins into the center, then folds the jacket and ties the arms to create a makeshift bundle.

The four men rise slowly from their seats. One of them reaches a hand into his pocket. "Where ya goin' with my money, Buck?"

"It's my money. I won it fair and square." Buck turns his back on the men and stumbles to my side.

"A decent man would give us the chance to recover our losses."

I glance over my shoulder at the four men. "Better let them keep it."

"I won't. It's mine, I tell you."

I lift my hand to the men. "Sorry. He's out." I haul Buck to the counter, where Katy is paying the barkeep for a cup of black coffee. "Keep them coming." I lift the hot cup to his lips.

"Stop it."

"No, *you* stop it." I smack his cheek with my open palm. "Look at you. What would Pa say? What would Ma say?" I lift the cup again, and this time, he drinks.

"Ow."

"Too hot for you? Good. I hope it burns you good and gives you a taste of the hell that's waiting for you."

Buck lays his arm on the bar and flops his head on it. "Leave me be."

"I wish I could. But those men aren't happy with you. We need to get out of here." I thrust the cup against his lips. "Drink up."

A second cup of coffee appears. Buck gulps it down with a shiver. Suddenly, he bolts from the stool and staggers out the door, where he heaves up the coffee and liquor in a steaming pool on the dirt.

I fold my arms, standing over him until he's done retching. "Let's head home."

Buck reaches up for my hand to help him up, but I turn on my heel, take Katy's arm, and walk to our horses.

Buck yells at my receding back. "Why won't you just leave me alone?"

I spin around, march back to him, grab his arm, and yank him to his feet an inch from my nose. The reek off him is nauseating. "Because Granma is asking after you." I grasp his shoulders and give him a hard shake. "She's dying, Buck. Dying. She may die this very night. And by all that is holy, I will not let you disappoint her last request."

This time, Buck drags along behind me, reeling.

"What are you going to say to Granda?" Katy glances over her shoulder at Buck, who is still struggling.

"I hope I don't have to say anything. I hope Granda sees what's happening and brings down the wrath of the Almighty on Buck's sorry, thick skull."

"But we mustn't upset Granma."

"No. You're right." I groan and rub my forehead. "I don't know what else to do except give him coffee to sober him up. I've never been around anything like this before—well, only once, when I was robbed."

"I haven't a clue, either."

Tossing my head, I cut my eyes toward Buck, trying to catch up. "Well, as far as I'm concerned, he deserves to reap the whirlwind. But I won't allow his stupidity to break Ester's heart."

"She would be devastated if she saw him like this."

"I know. Still, Uncle Liam told me to hurry, so I can't figure how to handle it." I raise my brows and study Katy's eyes. "What would you do?"

She lowers her eyes and tugs on one of her braids. Her jaw clenches, and when she lifts her head, her glare is hard as steel. "I would take him straight to Granda. Let him decide."

"Very well."

When we reach the horses. Buck appears a little more stable on his feet but is still sickly-looking.

"Can you ride?"

Buck nods. "I think so."

"You take Raven, then. I'll ride with Katy."

The ride through town in the driving snow is laborious, tense, and stone silent, but thankfully, we don't see hide nor hair of those men. As we reach the edge of town and take the turn up the mountain, a different kind of quiet settles around us. The snow cushions the horses' hooves and caresses the trees with a stillness that seems to absorb all other sounds. An incomprehensible peace buoys me, as if I'm drifting along on a cloud of cotton. Maybe it's the Spirit of the Lord, coming to carry Ester home.

We round a bend in the trail, and a stench, something like spoiled meat, stale cigar smoke, and a sheep's pen after the slaughter, assails my nostrils a second before I see the four men hidden along the edge of the wood. They surround us before we can kick our horses to gallop.

And they have guns.

"We'll take our money now." The man in front of us reaches out his free hand while pointing his rifle at us to make sure we see it.

I hiss between my teeth. "Buck, give them the coins."

The man to my right grabs Katy's arm. Her scream shatters my eardrums and causes our horse to buck, snatching her arm from his grasp. She barely hangs on to me as I pull back the reins, trying to stop the horse from spinning. A loud crack pierces the snow's blanketing silence as the leader fires his weapon.

Buck throws his jacket to the ground with a metallic thump. "There. Take it all."

The man beside Buck sneers. "That ain't good enough." He drags Buck from Raven, jumps down beside him, and clobbers him good. Two of the other men dismount and join in, one of them kicking Buck in the side. The crunch of his ribs under the man's boot is sickening.

"He gave you your money! Let him be."

The leader, still on his horse, snickers as he scoops up the bundle with the end of his rifle. "Interest. Plus, a fee for our trouble." Then he whistles, and the other three men mount quickly and ride off into the darkness of the forest.

I swing my leg over the horse. "I'll ride with Buck. I don't think he can manage it."

"I'll help you get him up."

Between the two of us, we manage to pull Buck onto Raven. I sit behind him, reaching my arms around him to take the reins. "You fool. You're lucky to be alive."

"Are they gone?"

"Yes. Hold on, you'll face the music soon enough."

Buck's moans and whimpers with each hoof beat mar the forest's peace the rest of the way home.

Liam waits for us at the front door as we ride up. "Katy, can you take care of the horses?"

"Yessir."

"I need to have a word with the boys."

"Yessir."

"Head home to your ma when you're done."

When Buck's feet hit the frozen dirt, he stumbles, catches himself on the rail, and pulls himself up to the porch, where Liam stands, arms folded. He sniffs the air, and his face folds into a thunderous scowl. Snatching Buck's arm, he drags him into the house.

I follow slowly, keeping my distance. Liam's berating comes in waves of ominous whispers through clenched teeth. After calling Buck several choice names, he boxes Buck's ears, who starts to cry, prompting Liam to slap them again. "Quiet."

"I'm *sorry*." Buck's wail is pitiable, but I have little sympathy for him. I don't even know who he is anymore.

"*Quiet*. I don't want to hear one word out of you, is that clear?"

Buck nods once, his eyes wide and bright with tears.

"Clean up the blood, change your clothes, wash out your mouth, and try to get rid of that stench. I will come to your room to get you when it's time." Uncle Liam pulls Buck's face close to his. "And you better be on your best behavior when you're with Ma. At least pretend to be a loving, attentive grandson."

A single tear slides down Buck's cheek before he bolts up the stairs and disappears into his room.

Uncle Liam glances my way and shakes his head. "Where did you find him?"

"A saloon in Blue Ridge. Gambling."

"If I tell Pa, he's going to kill him."

"He deserves it."

Liam closes his eyes and sighs. "I never thought I'd see the day someone from this family…"

"I'm sorry we've ruined everything."

His head snaps up, and he looks about to light into me. Then, his expression softens. "Thank you for finding him. Now get yourself cleaned up. You'll be seeing your granma soon."

"Yessir."

As I tread up the stairs, a twisting dread knots my stomach like wash going through a wringer. What will I walk into? I've never been at someone's deathbed before. How will she look? Will there be a smell? What should I say?

When I pass Buck's room, his ragged gasps leak under the door. Good. I hope he's as miserable as a human can be. Serves him right.

I choose my nicest shirt and pants for the visitation. Granma always likes it when we dress up for church, and this feels like going to church to me, like we'll be doing something holy and worshipful. I wish Buck were forbidden to participate because his presence could taint the sacredness of our time with Granma. She's nothing if not discerning, and if she notices Buck's condition—well, I better pray she doesn't.

Sitting on the edge of my bed, I fold my hands but find my heart turning from its focus on Buck to a hard look in the mirror. "Heavenly Father, forgive me. I've been selfish and heartless and angry for so long, I don't know what's happened to who I used to be. Please, Father, make me a better man." Something clenches in my spirit, and new words rise from my chest. "Make me the man you created me to be." Tears brim in my eyes. "I willingly let go of all the hatred and rage I've been carrying around. Please, Lord, change my heart from stone to flesh. Make me a grandson worthy of Ester's legacy."

I close my eyes and imagine seeing Granma, and my heart swells with love and gratitude. "Thank you, Father. And thank you for giving us Ester to love us and teach us and care for us so well." I swallow hard. "If you must take her home to be with you, Lord, I understand. But if she can remain for a while longer and not suffer, I'd love to spend more time with her. I…I haven't done right by her, and I'd like the chance to do better, if it be Your will." I wipe the moisture from my face. "I love you, Lord. And I think I'm ready now."

A few minutes later, Uncle Liam knocks on my door. "Ready?"

"Yessir. I am."

"Come along, then."

Buck stands in Liam's shadow when I open the door, his hair still wet from cleaning up, and his shoulders slumped with shame. The Lord must be answering my prayer, because for once, I'm not moved to anger or disgust, but to understanding. I move to his side and take his hand. "It's OK. I don't want to lose her, either."

A wash of tears floods his red cheeks. "Why does everyone have to leave?"

I squeeze my eyes closed and picture Ian's face, then Ma and Pa. "I don't know, Buck. I surely don't."

Uncle Liam taps gently on Ester and Mac's bedroom door. "May we come in?

Granda murmurs, "Come in."

Liam pushes the door ajar. "Ma, I've brought the boys to see you."

"Ooo." Granma voice sounds like the coo of a dove. "Come closer, boys."

The room is dark, a single candle burning on the table in the corner. Granda sits on the edge of the bed, holding a frail, bony hand. At his feet, his sleeping pallet spreads across the floor at Granma's bedside. His Bible lies open on a chair on the other side of her bed. A chamber pot stands like a strange ornamental decoration beside the chair. A half-full wash basin and several used wash rags hide under the corner table. And on the bed, piles of blankets and quilts create a kind of swaddling cocoon, and amid them all, glowing white like an angel's, Ester's face.

"Granma." The word chokes in my throat. I tiptoe slowly, carefully, to the side of the bed.

"Give me a hug." Her voice sounds thin, overpowered by a crackle like someone crumpling paper. Feeble arms reach out from beneath the mounds of covers.

I lean down but barely pat her arms, as if I might break her.

"Come now, you can do better." And with that, her face breaks into a beaming smile—Ester's smile, one like no other.

I bury my face against her chest, wrap my arms around her neck—and feel the details of her bones, as if her skin has evaporated, leaving only a skeleton. A flash of pain sears my chest.

"I love you." Her whispered words skate atop the searing pain, deepening their sting.

"I love you, too, Granma. So very much."

"I know you do." She strokes my back. "I'm proud of you, Fin." Each word arrives on an exhale, her speech slow and deliberate as if she wants to make sure I can hear and understand her. "Your Ma and Pa would be proud, too. You've become a good man."

A good man. I hope, with the Lord's help, I will become one. But from Ester, a good man is the highest praise.

"You're a gentle soul, like your ma. Don't allow this world to harden your heart. Always walk with the Lord, Fin. Never leave His embrace. And all will be well with you."

"Yes'm. I will. I promise."

"Buck? Is Buck here?"

"I'm here, Granma."

I step back and allow Buck to slide into my place.

"Give me a hug, young man."

"Yes'm."

The moment of truth.

But Ester shows no indication she suspects something is amiss. After a brief embrace, she whispers, "I love you," and Buck responds in kind.

"Buck, I know it's been hard. Losing your family. Leaving your home. Having to come here. But don't let the past turn your fire into hatred and anger. The Good Lord gave you that fire for a reason, just like your pa. Turn your passion toward doing good, as he did."

Granma is so right. Pa had the same fire as Buck. The difference between them is that Pa expressed his passion through helping others, and Buck has allowed his passion to become for himself. Oh, Lord, please help him to hear Granma's words.

"I will, Granma."

"Good. Mac? My love?"

"I'm right here, love."

"I'd like to see Katy and Claire now."

Mac clears his throat. "It's not too much? Should we wait until the morning?"

Ester's lashes flutter. "I don't think I want to wait any longer." Her soft smile brings more light to the room than the candle. "I think I'll have everyone come in now."

"Liam, would you go and fetch your wife and children, and Fin, would you bring Chris, Emma, and Claire?"

"Yessir."

"Hurry along, then."

Uncle Liam and I dash down the stairs. While he turns to head toward his cabin, I race to the barn, mount Raven, and ride down the hill toward the stream and the cabin where Uncle Chris' family lives.

The snow has stopped falling but remains in tall drifts, making for slow going on the steep trail. But something in Ester's voice drives me forward. Is it a sense of the story's completion? Or maybe it was her mention of readiness, from the armor of God.

Chris directs Claire to mount behind me, while he and Emma share one of their horses. We pick our way through the snow, following the trail from memory and frequent use rather than sight.

"Is Granma Ester dying?" Claire's frightened whisper brings a crushing reality to my fears.

"I think so."

"Oh."

Nothing more need be said.

Liam and his family are already at the bedside when I bring Chris and the others into Ester's room. After Ester speaks quietly to each one in turn, the family lines the walls like watchmen awaiting the Lord's return to Zion. Mac slides under the voluminous covers and scoops Ester into his arms. Her head rests gently against his chest.

The candle sends the flickering shadows fleeing to the corners of the room, leaving its circle of light illuminating the two lying in loving embrace. Ester and Mac exchange words I cannot hear until at last, she falls silent. Her breaths begin to shallow, but she doesn't resist or flail about, nor does she cry out in pain or fear. She simply smiles a contented smile, closes her eyes, and drifts away.

Part Three

Age shall not weary nor the years condemn

CHAPTER TWENTY-TWO

August 1914

As it has since Granma's passing six months ago, the big house, empty and cold, perches atop the hill like a silent mausoleum. Like every day, Granda sits as still as a headstone in his overstuffed chair, wrapped in Ester's precious buffalo hide, staring unseeing out the picture window at Ester's favorite vista of blue mountains shrouded in mist, folded one after another to the horizon. In his gnarled hands, he clutches Ester's colorful Lakota blanket to his chest as if he's biding his time until he can return it to her in person.

"Someone's comin'." Buck drops his book on the arm of his chair, walks to the door, and peers through the glass. "It's Uncle Chris, Granda."

Granda gives no indication he heard Buck or cares about our visitor.

In moments, Chris bursts through the door, brushing past Buck, and waves a yellow piece of paper. "We have a telegram from Ian. It isn't good news."

My book slides from my lap as I jump up, grabbing the telegram from Chris' hands. "What is it?"

"Great Britain has declared war on Germany. Ian plans to join the Expeditionary Force."

"The what?"

Uncle Chris sighs and pokes the paper. "Ian is going to fight for New Zealand in the war."

"No."

The three of us whirl to stare at Granda. It's the first word he's spoken in six months.

Slowly, painfully, he pushes himself to stand, supporting himself on the arm of the chair. "No." He growls low in his chest. "I won't have it."

"Granda?"

"No one of *my* kin will fight in a cursed war. Not now. Not ever."

Uncle Chris slides to Granda's side and slips an arm around his waist, holding him upright. "Here, Mac, sit back down."

"Give me that." With surprising quickness, Granda snatches the telegram from my hands and squints at the pale lettering. "'I must fight for the country I call my home. It is my duty.'" The paper flutters to the floor. "I won't allow it, I tell you."

"Mac, it's already done. He joined up the day he sent this telegram." Chris pats Granda's hand. "There's nothing for it, I'm afraid."

Granda shrugs Chris' arms away and shuffles toward me, pointing his crooked finger in my face. "You will go and bring that boy home. Do you hear?"

"Yessir."

Chris drapes his arm across Granda's shoulders. "How's he going to do that, Mac? There's a war going on over there. It isn't safe to travel."

Granda ignores Chris, his fierce gray eyes boring into mine. "Bring him home. Do whatever you must."

"Yessir." I glance at Uncle Chris, begging with my eyes for help.

"I'll go with him, Granda." Buck picks up the discarded telegram. "I'll figure a way to get him out of there and bring him home. I swear it."

Granda's voice, silent for so long, now rattles Ester's porcelain angels on the bookcase shelves. "Ha! You? A wastrel like you would be more hindrance than help." His words split the air like a well-aimed arrow and find their mark. Buck's brow creases, a flush of color rises from his neck to his cheeks, and pain flashes in his eyes for an instant, then they grow cold, and his jaw and back stiffen.

Granda doesn't seem to notice. "Why are you standing around? Get going." He grabs my shoulders. "You *must* get to Ian before he's sent into battle."

He shoves me toward the stairs and shuffles down the hall toward the kitchen, muttering under his breath. "I must speak with Ester.

If anything happens to that boy, it will break her heart. She will never forgive me. Don't you see? War will ruin him. Destroy him."

"Granda?"

He spins and barks, "Get going!"

I droop like a wilting flower, close my eyes, and groan. "What am I supposed to do now?"

Uncle Chris heaves a deep sigh and shakes his head. "I don't know. I haven't even told Emma and Claire yet. I should head home to break the news."

Buck winces. "Poor Claire's gonna be devastated."

"I know." Chris gestures toward the stairs. "Why don't you pack some things so Mac sees you're doing something. And we should get a message to Bear. He can tell you if any ships are sailing to New Zealand. It could be nothing is available, which lets you off the hook."

"OK. Buck and I will go into town and take care of the telegram."

"I'll come back with Emma and Claire later this afternoon, and we'll put our heads together and make a plan."

"Thank you, Uncle Chris."

We bid Chris goodbye and head up the stairs. When we reach the landing, Buck whispers, "Granda's not thinking straight. Did you hear what he said?"

"About speaking with Ester?" Is Granda addled with grief?

"No, about me being a wastrel and a hindrance."

I close my hands into fists. "*I* need your help. I don't know how to do any of this."

"Saint Ian figured it out."

I trail my finger along a rough-hewn board in the hall leading to the bedrooms. "He had Uncle Bear's help."

"We don't matter one spit to Granda. You know that, right?" Buck's chin lowers to his chest. "We're men without a home. Orphans.

We've always been unwanted problems. Like he said, a waste of space. That's all we are to them." He raises his head, his lip curled. "Granda's expecting us to risk our lives to rescue Saint Ian, and all he can do is criticize us." He tosses his red curls. "Why should we suffer when it were Ian who made a rash decision?"

"Come on, Buck. Have a heart. Granda's scared for Ian, and he's grieving and confused. You know what it's like to feel you can't bear one more loss."

Buck tilts his head and lowers his eyes. "I do."

"Granda had a terrible time during the war, and after, so his fear for Ian is understandable. You've heard Uncle Bear and Uncle Chris tell some of those terrible stories."

"Yeah."

"So, be patient. He doesn't mean what he's saying."

Buck sneers. "But you know one thing he believes. Ian is the good one, and you and I are worthless, damaged goods."

I sputter my lips. "I don't believe that."

Buck rolls his eyes. "I'm gonna pack a stupid bag."

"After that, let's ride into town, send the telegram to Uncle Bear, and find out the train schedule to Atlanta, and from Atlanta to San Francisco. Hopefully, that will satisfy Granda." I set my jaw, feigning a determination I don't have.

Buck inhales, his brows raised. "You know this whole thing is doomed from the start."

He's right. Rescuing Ian will be like taking a wild shot in the dark wearing a blindfold. The chance of hitting the target is almost zero.

After throwing a few clothes in a bag, Buck and I ride into town and visit the telegraph office, where we send a message to Uncle Bear asking for his help in securing passage to New Zealand and a place to stay in San Francisco.

Our next stop is the train depot. "We need to go to Atlanta and catch the train to San Francisco. When does the train run next?"

The ticket master squints at a board behind the counter filled with chicken scratch writing. "Train leaves for Atlanta tomorrow morning, 6 am. Train to San Francisco…" He pauses, running his finger down the board. "Three days hence. Leaving at 3 pm."

Buck's brow furrows. "Couldn't we wait three days to leave for Atlanta so we don't have to find a place to spend the night?'

"Yessir, you could do that. Three days from now, you could leave at 6 am for Atlanta, arrive at 10 am, then you'd have time for lunch before catching the 3 pm train to California."

"How much to buy two tickets for both trains?"

"Let's see, that'll be $2 to Atlanta, and $65 each to San Francisco making your total $134."

"*Te hia kore*!"

Buck leans near and whispers in my ear. "It might as well be 1000."

"Granda will give us the money."

"He better."

Buck and I don't speak on the ride home. As promised, Uncle Chris, Aunt Emma, and Claire stop by the big house later in the afternoon. Claire's red-rimmed eyes glow with moisture and fear, making her more beautiful than ever. Buck is quick to comfort her, while I share with Chris what we learned in town. At the end of it, we all agree it's best to leave in three days for San Francisco, relying on Uncle Bear to arrange for passage to New Zealand—if it's still possible.

The next three days pass as slow as tree sap in winter. After six months of sitting, Granda is suddenly as antsy as a squirrel gathering for winter. He paces the downstairs, wrapped in the buffalo hide, muttering to himself and gesturing wildly. At times, he appears to be speaking to someone, but of course, no one else is there in the vacuous cabin besides the two of us.

Several times each day, Granda berates us for waiting. We explain each time about the tickets, but he doesn't seem to hear us. Or if he does, it doesn't stick with him.

He rants on and on about Ian as if he's the perfect child, Ester's favorite, the one who could do no wrong. I ignore him, but after two days of it, Buck's irritation is building toward eruption.

No response arrives from Uncle Bear.

The first pale rays of dawn on the third day find us sitting on a wooden bench at the rear of the train, watching the town disappear behind us as the train rounds a bend and heads through the mountains to Atlanta. As the conductor promised, we reach the station a little after 10, so Buck and I grab a couple of sandwiches from a vendor.

"Do you suppose Uncle Bear will meet us at the station?"

I shrug, my mouth full of ham, cheese, and bread.

Buck slams his fists on his hips, leaning down over me. "You know, this whole thing is stupid. Only a couple of fools would willingly sail into a war zone based on the whims of a doddering old man who talks to his dead wife."

"Don't say that about Granda."

"He's lost his wits."

"Think how we acted when Ma and Pa died. You know firsthand what grief does to a person."

"We should never have come." Buck stalks away and leans against a large marble pillar, gazing out at the tracks.

For four days on the train, Buck and I move past each other like phantoms passing in the night. We do not speak. And when we finally exit the train in San Francisco, we do so separately.

I'm the first to spot Uncle Bear on the platform. He waves and rushes to my side. "It's wonderful to see you. Where's Buck?"

At first, I shrug, then see him approaching over Bear's shoulder. "Oh. There he is."

Uncle Bear turns and claps Buck on the back. "There you are."

With that one gesture, the ice around Buck cracks and falls away, and he wraps Bear in a hug. "It's good of you to meet us."

"Of course!" Bear chuckles, adding me to the hug. "Let's get your luggage. We have a lot to talk about."

Uncle Bear leads us to a black motor car.

"Is this yours?" Buck hoots. "I've never seen one of these!"

"Climb in." He slides our bags into a back compartment, turns the crank handle, and hops behind the wheel. Buck's gales of laughter get swallowed in the wind as we race down cobblestone streets to a tall, brick-front building. "Here's my home."

"Wow. You live in there?"

Bear nods. "Top floor."

His home occupies the entire top floor, featuring broad windows that overlook the bustling downtown area, high ceilings, and a modern kitchen with in-house plumbing. He even has a bathtub in the bathroom.

"This is mighty nice, Uncle Bear."

He gestures toward the oversized couch in the main room. "Come, sit. We must discuss what I've discovered." Then, he grimaces. "How rude of me. Are you hungry? Can I get you something to eat or drink?"

"I'm starving." Buck's eyes ogle at the stacked shelves in the pantry.

"I'm more anxious to hear what you found out."

"Then, I will make you some food and talk about our plans at the same time. How about it?"

Buck rubs his hands together. "Sounds good to me."

"How about clam chowder and corn bread?"

Buck wrinkles his nose. "Clam chowder?"

"Give it a try. I think you'll love it." Bear chuckles at Buck's sideways glance. "OK, here's what I found out so far. No passenger ships are currently entering or departing New Zealand—only cargo ships. So, I secured passage on a cargo ship leaving in two days." He winces a bit and shrugs. "You'll have to work while aboard, but it shouldn't be too hard."

"What kind of work?" Of course, Buck's going to balk.

"Probably cleaning. Moving cargo. Like that."

"Is the passage dangerous?" I don't mind the work; I'm more worried about the ship staying afloat.

"There's some danger, but Australia and New Zealand have just joined the fight, so hopefully their enemies won't have an organized opposition in place yet." He spoons up the soup into bowls, then adds a slice of corn bread on the side. "I also found out the New Zealand troops are departing from Wellington, so that's where you're headed. When you get there, you'll need to find the place where they are assembling and search for Ian. If you don't catch up with him and convince him to leave the army before they depart for Australia to join forces, it will be too late to stop this."

"Wait…what do you mean, too late?" Buck shakes his head. "We're going to get Ian out. To bring him home. I promised Granda."

Uncle Bear's jaw pulses. "That's the other thing I found out. Ian can't abandon the army now without getting in trouble. Legal trouble. So, you'll have to sneak him out of the country without getting caught by the authorities."

An ice-cold hand clutches my chest and squeezes. Buck turns his gaze to meet mine, his eyes burning. "Because Ian decided to sign up, we might end up in jail." He throws up his hands, shoves away from the table, and marches across the apartment to the large bank of windows, his soup left uneaten.

"Specific information was hard to come by, but there are indications the New Zealand force plans to leave for Australia sometime in October. If so, you should have time to find Ian."

My stomach has soured like curdled milk, so I push my chair back and join Buck at the window.

"I'm sorry, boys. This is the best I could do."

Buck folds his arms across his chest. "Does anyone care about us? Or is Ian the only one who counts?" His lip curls. "We're walking into this like lambs to the slaughter."

"Of course you matter. To all of us." Uncle Bear plods to the window, standing behind us with a hand on each shoulder. "I assumed you wouldn't want to leave Ian to suffer through this war alone. Besides, the three of you have gotten into and out of some bad scrapes before, but you've always been there for each other. You're better together, like *The Three Musketeers.*"

I heave a deep, tremorous sigh. "You're right, of course. We would never abandon Ian."

"Speak for yourself." Buck strides to the door, slings it open, and walks out of the apartment.

"Well, that did not go well." Uncle Bear chews his lip. "When did Buck become so hardened?"

"He's been that way for quite a while, but I think Granma getting sick and then dying was the last straw. He's not been the same since." A wistful smile crosses my face. "She had a way with him no one else has. She could always soften him. But all that's gone now." I lift one brow. "Plus, he's angry at Ian for proposing to Claire."

Uncle Bear's head snaps back. "Why would Buck be mad about that?"

"He wants—wanted to marry her, but Ian asked her first."

Bear groans and rolls his eyes. "Few things damage relationships more than jealousy."

"What if he decides not to come with me? What can I do?"

"Nothing." Uncle Bear's chin drops to his chest. "Sometimes people need to work things out for themselves."

"But…"

Bear lifts his hand. "Buck made a promise. We'll have to trust the Lord to convict him to follow through on his word."

"And if he doesn't?"

"Then you have a choice to make." Bear walks to his fancy kitchen and slowly gathers our bowls. I remain at the window, staring at the strange city sprawling across hills and valleys, searching for Buck's red hair in the crowd below and whispering under my breath a prayer that God would bring him home.

Bear finishes cleaning as the encroaching darkness makes it impossible to spot Buck in the diminishing crowd, so we sit in his main room in tense silence, watching the door, waiting and hoping for Buck's return.

"Uncle Bear, may I ask you a question?"

"Certainly."

"Why aren't you married?"

Uncle Bear's wistful smile makes me wonder if I've stepped into something better left alone. "I never met the right girl, I suppose."

"How do you know if she is the right girl?"

He chuckles. "I fear that's a question for someone with more experience. You might ask Liam. Or your Granda. Both found their soul mates." With a slight frown, he tilts his head. "Why do you ask?"

"No reason." I scrub my toe against the gleaming hardwood floor. "What if I don't find anyone? Like you?"

"Oh, I wouldn't worry about that. You're young yet. Pa met Ma when he was much older than you."

I dare not tell him the truth, that I've found the one for me—and she belongs to my little brother.

Late that evening, as Uncle Bear and I sit beneath electric lamps and read, Buck drags through the door and flops down on a chair, sprawling like a hound dog on a front porch step. A sickly, pungent aroma wafts from him.

Uncle Bear folds his arms, his eyes narrowing beneath knit brows. "Well?"

"OK." Buck leans his head back against the cushion. "Let's have it over. When do we leave?" He juts his chin toward me and crooks his brow. "All we have is each other. Right?"

Relief washes over me like a cool rain shower, and for the first time in a long time, Buck returns my beaming smile with a woozy, crooked grin of his own.

"All I have to say is, they better watch out. The MacAlister brothers are comin'."

CHAPTER TWENTY-THREE

September 1914

The crossing is smoother than either of us thought possible. The manual labor proves a blessing, because it makes the time seem to pass quickly. But when we arrive in Wellington, our problems begin.

The city is chockablock with young men, some already in uniform and many more ready to enlist, often with their families or sweethearts in tow, so there are no rooms available for us. The crowds move like a herd of cows during a cattle drive, in a kind of organized chaos, and we're right there among them, pressing against bodies in our push to get to the next place.

We spend a day wandering through the streets, seeking the army camp, but the directions we receive are too vague for us to follow or are simply wrong. Finally, mid-afternoon, we stumble upon a recruitment center. The line is out the door and down the street to the next block, so we take our place at the end for the long wait.

The line moves as slow as a tortoise in summer heat, and it soon becomes clear we aren't going to make it to the front before nightfall, so Buck and I leave the line in search of someplace to make camp. The open spaces near the recruitment office are packed with tents already, so we wander up Mount Victoria until we find a section of dense woods isolated from the crowds where we use our packs as makeshift bedding.

The lights and cookfires of the city below us sparkle through the limbs of the trees like a magical fairy village trying to hide from human eyes. If not for the pressing crowds, this would be a beautiful place.

"I hadn't imagined this many men would enlist for England's war. How are we ever going to find Ian?"

Buck grunts. "Maybe the army camp is more organized, and we can ask someone to take us to him."

"You know, they probably won't let us enter the camp since we aren't soldiers."

"One problem at a time. We must find the camp first." Buck turns his back to me. "Let's get some sleep."

Buck's breaths slow and deepen, but sleep won't come for me. When I try to plot out our next steps, I find nothing but obstacles and impossible hurdles to overcome. If we find the bivouac, how do we sneak in? How can we spirit Ian away in the night from a well-guarded army encampment filled with soldiers? How do we convince Ian to come with us?

My skin tingles like I've been shocked by a cattle prod, so rather than flop around like a fish out of water and disturb Buck's sleep, I creep away to a rocky ledge and look out over the teeming city. Shouts and gales of laughter drift up the mountain. What must all these recruits feel? Frightened? Excited? Proud?

Or are they all little boys playing a game, thinking this will be a grand adventure and not giving a whit for everything they're about to lose or all the people they are going to kill?

I've heard Granda's stories of war since I was fourteen years old—the senseless death, the brutality, the suffering, the anguish of loss—I know too much to believe the recruitment poster's lines about the nobility of service to King and country. Ian heard these same stories. So why did he do this? What could've motivated him to enlist? He has his whole life ahead of him, a life with all he ever wanted—the love of his life, our land, his sheep, his Māori family, all there for the taking.

It's the life I wanted but will never have.

Enough. I stand and brush off my pants as if the dirt will carry my disgusting self-pity away with it. *Be the man your pa taught you to be.* I drag back to our little makeshift camp beneath the sheltering limbs of a gnarled tree, lie down, and squeeze my eyes closed against my destructive thoughts. *Grow up. You're not entitled to anything. Be thankful for all you have.*

But the sick feeling in my stomach won't go away, and the glow of dawn along the horizon finds me wide awake and exhausted.

We collect our belongings and make our way down the mountain back to the recruitment office. The line is already forming. I even recognize some of the young men who were in line near us last night.

"You hold our place in line. I'm going to find us some food." Before I can respond, Buck bolts down the street toward the town center. And by the time he returns with biscuits and hot tea, I'm near the front of the line.

I cram the whole biscuit in my mouth and down the scalding tea as the sergeant looks up from his papers and gestures for us to come forward. Buck trails behind me, still munching, so I suppose he expects me to do the talking.

"Age?"

"Sir?"

"Your age, son. How old are you?"

"Oh. Twenty, sir."

"And your companion?"

"Eighteen."

"Very well. Name?"

"Fin MacAlister."

He scratches my name on the paper before him. "Did you bring your identification? Birth certificate?"

"No, sir. Sir, excuse me. If I may?"

He glances up, his mouth quirked to one side and a single brow raised.

"Sir, I'm looking for my brother. Ian MacAlister. Where might I find him?"

"Son, I've signed in thousands of recruits over this last month. You expect me to remember one individual?"

"No, sir. But I thought you could tell us where the recruits go once they're signed up."

The sergeant leans back in his chair. "Are you here to sign up?"

"No, sir."

His frown deepens. "Why not, young man? You're of age."

Buck steps forward, with crumbs decorating his mouth like a careless five-year-old. "We ain't fightin' in no stinking English war, that's why. We're Americans."

"Then, leave this line at once. You're wasting my time and slowing the process down for others who've been waiting patiently for the opportunity to serve their country."

"Won't you help us? Please, sir? All we need to know is where the soldiers are being housed?"

The sergeant heaves an exasperated sigh. "The soldiers from out of town are billeted at the Awapuni Racecourse. Now, move along."

Buck snorts. "A racecourse? Where is that?"

"Palmerston North. Next?"

I grab Buck's arm. "Come on, Buck. Let's get out of here before they draft us. We can ask around for directions, now that we know where to look."

We scurry from the office onto the main road. "There." Buck points to a hardware shop on the next corner. "They might know."

The owner of the shop, a burly, balding man with a thick, black moustache, hails us as we enter. "How can I help you today?"

"We need to find something called Awapuni. At Palmerston North."

"Aye, lads, that's quite a trek. It'll take you the better part of three days tramping. You'll want to take the train."

"I'm afraid we don't have enough money to buy train tickets."

"Aye, tramping it is then." He walks to his doorway and points up the road. "Walk to the water and follow the coastline heading north. You'll turn inland at Ohau, then you've got a winding trail to Palmerston North." He crosses his arms over his large chest. "You'll need to be asking along the way to make sure you're on the right path. The trail isn't marked."

"Thank you, sir. You've been very helpful."

"Glad to help." He slaps my back. "Going to sign up for the fight, are ye?"

"Um, no, sir. No, we're Americans. We're here looking for our brother."

"He signed up, did he?"

"Yessir."

He shakes his head. "Hmm, that might pose a wee problem. They won't allow just anyone to wander onto their encampment."

"Yessir. We hope to speak to someone in charge. Maybe he'll allow us to see our brother."

"Best of luck to ye, then. I hope you find what you're looking for." The man grasps my hand in his thick, meaty palm.

"Thank you, again, sir."

"Take care along the road, young men."

As we exit the store, Buck groans. "*Three* days?"

"We better get started, then. Where'd you find those biscuits?"

Buck gestures up the road. "It's on the way to the water. They have dried meat, too, and some fresh fruit and vegetables."

"Let's stock up enough for three days. No telling when we'll find another place on the trail."

The little shack offers a surprising number of options to carry while hiking. We both select some things we want, along with a good supply of biscuits and two water containers. The proprietor, a Māori man with a broad smile and broken English, confirms the hardware store owner's directions with a lot of pointing and gestures, and offers a similar warning about the trail. Stuffing our purchases in our packs, we thank the shopkeeper and head toward the silver-blue water glistening in the bright sunlight.

Soon, the trail winds along high bluffs overlooking the shore. Waves pound the black sand, sending plumes of steam through rock formations like the smokestack of a train's steam engine. It's like nothing I've ever seen.

Somehow, being away from the bustle of the town, out in God's magnificent creation, clears my mind. The jumble of responsibilities, worries, and fears smooths out like the sand after the ocean passes over it, and I'm able to lay it all aside and enjoy the journey. Buck also seems enraptured by the views and the huge expanse of crystalline water.

The first night, we camp beside a freshwater creek running through the blackened sand to the ocean, building a fire using driftwood deposited by the tides. I'm so tired, sleep comes quickly.

Buck gets up before me and has a fire going by the time I awaken. "Breakfast is served." He grins and hands me a biscuit. "Our menu today includes…let's see, hmm. Yes. The same thing we had yesterday."

I rub my hands together. "Yummy! Dry biscuits."

Buck tosses me a biscuit. "Want a side of jerky with that?"

"No, thank you, sir. I believe I will save the meat dish for luncheon."

"Suit yourself." Buck shoves a strip of dried meat in his mouth, digs his teeth into it, and yanks.

By the end of the second day, we've made it to Ohau and the turn on the trail that leads to Palmerston North. Another night of heavy sleep and a morning of biscuits drowned in spring water, and we're on the last leg of our journey.

Our pace quickens, and our steps are lighter as we weave through the hilly terrain heading toward the mountains to our north and east. Buck chatters away, excited to see Ian and finish our task, but for me, approaching the army encampment rekindles my worry. What if the commander won't let us speak to Ian? What if Ian refuses to come with us? What will we do then?

Neither of us wants to disappoint Granda, not in his present state. Will Ian feel the same way, or will he claim he's duty-bound to remain and fight?

I don't speak these thoughts aloud to Buck, though—no need to dampen his enthusiasm.

We set a goal of reaching the camp by mid-afternoon, hoping to make our request, speak with Ian, make our plans, and spirit him away after nightfall. By mid-morning, dreary weather flows in from the west, and storm clouds build at our backs. Then, the bottom drops out and slows our pace to a crawl. We can't see beyond the reach of our arms and soon lose the trail altogether.

Buck yells to be heard over the pounding rain. "We better wait out the storm, or we'll get so off course we'll never get there."

"There's no cover here."

Buck holds one hand up to his brows to shield the water from his eyes. "Looks like an outcropping to the right. It might give us some cover."

He and I slog to the cluster of overhanging rocks, and as he predicted, it affords some meager protection from the pelting rain. "We can wait it out here."

By the time the worst of the rain passes, the sky darkens beyond the gray of heavy clouds toward dusk. "We may as well camp here and try again tomorrow."

Buck slams his fist against the ground with a muddy splat. "We're so close. Come on, let's try."

"You were worried about getting lost in the rain. What do you think is going to happen in the darkness?"

Buck groans and sinks against one of the rock faces. "I guess you're right." He eyes his dripping clothes. "But this is going to be one miserable night."

"Yeah."

He tries to wring his clothes with little success, then throws up his hands and lies against his pack with his back to the rocks.

I slide next to him and set myself up the same. "Hey, does this remind you of the time we stayed at Mani's camp, when we ran away from Uncle Bear?"

Buck snickers. "Mani's camp was better."

"We had fun, though, didn't we? Living on our own, hunting and fishing, providing for ourselves."

Buck jabs his elbow in my ribs. "You mean the Māori village providing for us."

I shrug one shoulder. "Yeah, I guess so. Although it seemed like we were on our own, the three of us against the world."

"And each other." Buck laughs. "You remember things a little differently from how I recall them."

I echo his laughter. "I guess I do see those times through rose-colored glasses. It was a grand adventure." My head drops to my chest. "The adventure has gone out of our lives these days. Now, everything is duty and obligation."

"Pa made sure we had lots of wonder and plenty of adventures growing up."

I glance over at Buck, although I'm pretty sure he can't see me in the deepening darkness. "You know, you once quoted Pa to me—about making your own destiny. I thought at the time, you're so much like him." I chuckle. "Granma and Uncle Bear said the same thing. You have Pa's fire." My chin drops to my chest. "I wish I had it, too."

"What're you talking about? You're like Pa in lots of ways. Stubborn, hard-headed…"

"Hey."

"Opinionated, rebellious, always thinking you're better than the rest of us…"

"I do not."

"Smart. Capable. Courageous."

My mouth hangs open a bit. Buck's never said anything resembling this before.

"You're a leader, like Pa. I might have his fire, but you have his presence—his command. People listen to you." He shrugs. "Ian and I would follow you anywhere."

"It sure didn't feel that way sometimes. Most of the time."

"Well, it's true."

The rain pelting the rocks around us roars in my ears. Am I like Pa? I prayed the Lord would help me become more like him, but I never believed He'd be willing or able to pull it off with so little to work with. It was too much to hope for.

"We better get some sleep. Tomorrow's a big day."

Buck's right. We have no idea what we'll face in the morning. All I know is, my brother isn't safe, and it's up to me to bring him home.

CHAPTER TWENTY-FOUR

September 1914

The sun rises in a clear sky, but a heavy gray pall lingers over our makeshift camp. Buck is unnaturally quiet as he tosses me the last of our biscuits. The weight of responsibility for Ian hangs like lead in my chest—and choking down the dry biscuit doesn't help.

We gather our soaked packs and trudge through the matted grass, hoping to rejoin the narrow trail we followed yesterday, but the hard rains have flattened everything, and the trail has disappeared.

Buck kicks some muddy clumps aside with a grunt. "So. No trail."

I shake my head. "We head northeast and hope we don't miss it. Maybe someone along the way will point us in the right direction." I sigh. "If we've not reached the racecourse by noon, we'll know we went too far."

Buck shrugs. "Let's go, then."

We walk with our heads down. My pack rubs against my wet clothes until my back feels on fire, and my soaked shoes scour holes in my feet, but I press on without complaint. An occasional moan from Buck is all that tells me he's suffering, too.

Fortunately, the field we're crossing ends on a wider trail heading in the right direction. With that and the relief of the sun drying our clothes, we pick up the pace. Before the sun reaches it's full height, we crest a rise, and in the valley before us, we see a vast camp teeming with brown-clad men, rows of canvas tents, and countless stacked boxes ready for transport.

"We made it," Buck sighs.

"Let's try to make ourselves presentable before we go in."

Buck gestures down the hill. "There's a lake outside the camp. Probably their water source for so many soldiers."

"Well. We can't do anything about our clothes, but at least we can wash our faces."

We scamper down the hill toward the small lake. Buck lets out a whoop, kicks off his shoes, and steps into the water, where he leans down and scrubs his face and arms.

I study my mud-caked shoes. They're already wet, so I might as well rinse them off. Plowing straight into the water, I splash my face and try to rub as much dirt off as possible.

We inspect each other and agree we're passable.

"Do you have a plan?" Buck asks.

I shrug. "Go to the gate and ask to see Ian?"

"Did you see how many men there are in the camp? No one's gonna know who Ian is."

"Then, we ask to come in and search for him."

"Well, it's better than no plan, I guess." Buck picks up his shoes and slaps them together several times to clean off some of the mud. "Let's go."

As Buck predicted, the guard at the gate doesn't know an Ian MacAlister.

"He's our brother, sir. Can we enter and see if we can find him?"

The guard's expression doesn't change. "Only army personnel allowed."

"Could we speak to a commanding officer?"

"Do you want to enlist?"

"No, sir. We just need to talk with our brother."

The guard stares past us. "No one other than army personnel may enter."

Buck steps out from behind me. "I understand you'll be leaving soon."

The guard doesn't respond.

"Sir, do you have a brother?"

He cuts his eyes toward Buck for a moment but doesn't reply.

"If you have a brother, you know what it would be like if he were leaving for war and you didn't get to say goodbye."

"My brother enlisted with me." He raises a single brow. "Why didn't you enlist with your brother?"

I clear my throat. "We are Americans. My brother lives in New Zealand." I take a step closer to the soldier and hold out my hand. "Fin MacAlister."

He glances at my outstretched hand but doesn't take it.

"We came all the way from America to see Ian before he leaves. Please, sir, isn't there anything you can do?"

The guard moistens his lips. "Look, I can call for a personnel officer to come and speak with you. At least he might know who your brother is and confirm he is here." He shrugs. "Other than that, I can't help you."

Buck's head bobs as his dimpled grin spreads across his face. "That would be wonderful. Thank you."

The guard sighs and rolls his eyes, then picks up the telephone in the guard house to convey our request.

"Wait over there." The soldier gestures for us to move from the gate entrance, which we do, but not out of sight of the gate or the guard.

Buck leans close and whispers in my ear. "What do we do now? Sneak past him?"

I shake my head. "If we get caught, it's prison for us. No, we hope the personnel officer has a heart."

"Doubtful."

Time creeps along slower than a possum, but no one comes. Buck and I find a somewhat dry place to perch, resting our tired legs, but within minutes, Buck's up again, pacing.

"What's taking so long?"

"I'm sure we're low priority."

"Maybe we should've told them we wanted to enlist."

I chuckle. "That would've gotten us in, yeah. Then what?"

"Then, we find Ian and hightail it out of here."

When I don't move or respond, Buck resumes his pacing.

The golden hour before dusk mutes the sky's blue before the gate guard waves us over, then escorts us inside the gate to a tall, thin-lipped soldier. "This is Corporal Taylor. Corporal Taylor, these men are asking to see their brother, who is one of the recruits."

The corporal looks down his nose at our dirty clothes and clicks his tongue against the roof of his mouth. "Civilians are not allowed on the base."

Buck adopts the pleading, doe-eyed expression he'd used with the guard. "We came from America to see him. Ian MacAlister. That's his name. His grandmother died, and he missed the funeral, so we promised his grandfather we would pass on her final message to him in person."

The corporal's sour expression lightens a bit. "I see. Very well. I will see what I can do." He spins smartly and strides away.

"Wait here." The guard returns to his post, leaving us alone inside the entrance with a tempting, wide-open space lying before us.

"Come on," Buck whispers. "Let's go find him."

I shake my head. "We'll never find him. We wait for the corporal to bring him to us." I raise one brow and grin. "We'll make a show of holding our devastated, grieving brother and ask for a little more time and privacy. Then, we run."

"Will Ian play along?"

"I'll figure how to make him cry. One way or another."

Buck gestures toward the setting sun. "It would be nice if all this took place under the cover of darkness."

"Here's hoping."

We have another long wait before Corporal Taylor returns with a skinny boy in an oversized brown uniform behind him, scampering to keep up.

"Ian!" Buck waves his arm above his head.

Ian's mouth drops open, then breaks into a wide smile. He races past the corporal and wraps Buck in his arms. "What are you doing here?"

Buck whispers something I can't understand, and Ian draws back, a crease forming between his brows.

I jump in, grabbing both in my arms, and saying, loudly enough for the corporal to hear, "It's Granma. I'm so sorry. I'm so sorry."

Buck leans his head back and wails. I make some boo-hooing noises, then lean close to Ian's ear and whisper, "Play along. We need to talk."

After staring at us for a moment—which played well in the scenario we were painting, as if he were in shock—then he screws up his face and gasps out a sob.

Buck wipes his eyes and breathes in a shuddering breath as he takes a step toward Corporal Taylor. "Sir, thank you so much for bringing Ian to us. May we have a few moments of privacy…" He strategically chokes on his words. "…so we can grieve together."

"Of course." The corporal walks several steps away and turns his back to us.

"We don't have much time. We're getting you out of here."

"What?" Ian stutters. "N-no. *No.* I'm here by choice."

"Stupid choice." Buck clasps his arm. "We're leaving, and we're taking you with us. Time to go home."

Ian pulls away from our embrace. "No. I'm prepared to do my duty to serve my country."

"Look." Buck's nose almost touches Ian's. "I promised Granda I'd bring you home, who, after all he's been through, doesn't need this new worry. It's driving him crazy. So, you're coming. By force, if necessary."

"I can't. I've enlisted."

"Uncle Bear has a boat waiting for us." I take a firm grip of his other arm. "We can make it if we run *now.*"

"I can't. I'm sorry." Ian jerks his arms from us. "Corporal? Please escort my brothers from the base."

Corporal Taylor blinks several times, then moves quickly to our sides. "Gentlemen?" He gestures toward the gate.

It's too late. We failed.

Ian backs away. As we trudge toward the gate under the corporal's watchful eye, Ian calls to us. "Mani is here."

Buck spins. "Mani?"

"He's in a different battalion, so I never see him, but we enlisted at the same time. He's here, too."

Buck's face reddens, and his shoulders quiver as if he might jump out of his skin. "Did you make him enlist?"

Ian frowns. "Of course not. He wanted to fight. Several Māori men from the village joined up."

"He's too young," Buck growls under his breath. "You know he's imitating Ian. That's why he signed up. How could Ian let him do this?"

Ian lifts his hand slowly. "Goodbye, brothers."

I wave, but I can't say goodbye, knowing it could be the final time I see him. Buck ignores him, although I'm not sure if it's out of fear or anger.

Once we're outside the gate, I throw up my hands. "What are we going to do now?"

"It's over. There's nothing we can do if he won't come. We can't force him."

I plant my hands on my hips, close my eyes, and chew my bottom lip. "I only see one choice."

"Yeah? What's that?"

Slowly, I open my eyes and meet Buck's piercing glare. "If he won't come to us, we have to come to him."

Buck snorts and spits out a wad. "We just tried that one."

"No. I mean, we join him. We enlist."

"What?! No, no, no." Buck paces in a frenzied circle, flattening the grass until it's packed into the mud. His hands flap like seal flippers. "You can't be serious."

"You got a better plan?"

"That's not a plan. It's suicide."

I open my palms before him. "Listen. If we're over there, we can shield Ian from the worst of it. Protect him."

"And get killed in the process. Are you nuts? How does that solve anything?"

"We make sure he comes home like we promised." My throat clenches as the reality of what I'm suggesting sinks in. I close my eyes against the growing terror. "It'll be after the war is over instead of now, but he'll be home and alive. And that's what matters to Granda. You said so yourself."

Buck clenches his fists and storms away, but I remain, standing a few feet from the guardhouse as if at the edge of a great chasm, stretched between two futures like a piece of saltwater taffy. Before Buck reaches the base of the hill, I call, "I'm staying. Whether you do or not."

"Fine." His bark echoes back to me on the early evening breeze.

"Buck?"

He stops and twirls to face me. "What?"

"Please. Picture Ian, alone, running through gunfire and explosions. And little Mani." Here I am, about to choose to walk straight into that nightmarish scene. I shake the horror of it from my mind. "You know how Ian is. It will destroy him." I clasp my hands as if in prayer. "He needs us."

"Uh-uh. Guilt ain't gonna work on me." Buck points an accusing finger. "You all made your beds."

"Very well." So much for following me anywhere. All my energy drains away like someone opened a spigot, leaving me somewhere between resolved and despairing. "Go home to Granda and pass on the message that I will bring Ian home, but you refused to stay and help me."

Nothing. So, I shuffle to the guard. "I changed my mind. I decided I'd like to enlist."

He claps me on the shoulder. "Good man. And your brother?"

I sigh. "No. He's returning to…"

"Wait." Buck's rapid footfalls pound the earth behind me.

I glance over my shoulder. Buck's backpack slams into him with each running step, making him look like a drunken sailor on deck during a storm.

"You comin'?"

He lurches to stop beside me. "Yeah. I'm comin'."

He looks none too happy about it. "What made you change your mind?"

He sneers. "*The Three Musketeers.*"

The guard escorts us to the recruitment office, where Corporal Taylor perches behind a desk stacked with mounds of paper and clipboards with blank forms.

"These two want to enlist," the guard announces.

"Very well. Your brother convinced you to join our cause, then?"

No, my blind obedience to family responsibility convinced me. "Yessir."

"Excellent." He hands me a clipboard, then pulls out another for Buck.

"Sir, will we be assigned to our brother's platoon?:

"Once we get your paperwork done, I'll do my best to see you assigned to your brother's section. His tent has open beds."

"Thank you, sir. We would appreciate that."

The enlistment process is quicker than I expected. Buck is surly throughout his questioning, but he signs the form and accepts the uniform, then the corporal leads us to a large tent housing eight soldiers, Ian among them. His eyes widen as the corporal introduces us to the section and ushers us to two cots near the back of the tent.

Ian trails behind us. "You've enlisted?"

Buck snarls, "How else are we gonna save your behind?"

Ian's melodic laugh fills the tent. "The three of us, together again on a grand adventure." He drapes his arms across our shoulders. "No one can stop us now."

A bullet might.

CHAPTER TWENTY-FIVE

February 1915

The men of the Wellington Battalion pack shoulder to shoulder on the deck of the ship as it pulls away from the harbor, watching the good people of Wellington cheer, wave banners and flags, and sing songs. Why do people cheer when they're sending soldiers to die? I don't understand it.

We are heading to Europe, straight into the teeth of the war. Dread haunts my nights and fatigue my days as we cross the open water. But mid-voyage, we hear a rumor, whispered by the war correspondent traveling with us, a Mister Charles Bean, that our ship is diverting from a European landing.

The officers don't confirm the rumor or explain their rationale for the change in plans. Infantry soldiers are always the last to know.

The long voyage ends at a place called Alexandria, in Egypt, of all places. Does this mean we won't be part of the main attack force? I dare not hope.

Other battalions arrive, and then we all board trains to Zeitoun, a base northeast of Cairo, where we begin training exercises. The Aussies camp at Mena, about 10 km away. They are a cheeky lot, particularly the Light Horse. They seem to think they're superior to all other ground forces.

When we aren't marching across the dunes, which is the extent of our training, our main job is keeping peace in the streets of Cairo. Since the thousands of rowdy soldiers roaming the streets are the main reason they aren't peaceful, it makes for an interesting conundrum. Conflicts and one-upmanship between our boys and the Aussies are constant. Buck has a good time pulling off several pranks that take them down a notch or two.

At long last, a problem not of our own creation happens. Corporal Phillips, our section leader, wakes us in the middle of the night.

The Turks are crossing the desert to try to take the Suez Canal, and we are to stop them.

We take a train to the Suez Canal, where we march out in lines, as we are trained to do, and establish our front in rows. The Turks approach mid-afternoon, attacking in a frontal assault in broad daylight. It proves a foolish strategy. Our boys fight like a well-oiled machine, firing round after round into the Turkish lines on the open field until their soldiers devolve into chaos and flee back into the desert. The whole thing is over in less than ten minutes with no New Zealand casualties. The Turks can't say the same.

Buck and I keep Ian behind us the entire battle.

"Is that all they've got?" Artie, one of our best mates, shakes his fist toward the running soldiers, cackling like a fairytale witch. Artie's slight build and long nose add to the witch-like illusion.

"Watch out for stray bullets there, mate." Will, a tall, muscular young man with blonde curls from the coast, who looks more like a tanned fisherman than a soldier, claps Artie on the back.

Buck joins in their laughter. "If today is any indication, we'll be home by spring."

"I don't know." I heave a deep sigh. "I hope you're right."

Will chuckles. "Fin, the optimist."

"Don't mind him. He's prone to the vapors." Buck fans his face, rolling his eyes back.

I punch his arm. "Stop it."

"Oh, my. The poor dear." Will gestures for his bunkmate, Charlie, and the two of them scoop me up like a sack of wheat.

"Hey. Cut that out." I writhe in their hands until they relent and drop me unceremoniously on the sand.

Jameson, who we call Bulldog because of his squat build, squashed nose, broad forehead, and square jaw with an underbite that makes him appear perpetually pouty, hunches his back and juts his already prominent chin. "Oh, woe is me. We're doomed. It's hopeless."

He shakes his head. "Shark, you truly are a gray cloud on a warm, sunny day."

"Listen. I'm a realist."

Ian chuckles and reaches out to help me up. "Never mind. Let's get back to camp and celebrate our first win."

As usual, when Ian speaks, everyone falls in line and starts for the train. What is it about him that commands such respect? At times, the others treat him with affection like a favored little brother—he is the youngest in our section, after all. But at other times, they respond to him as they would a Brigadier General. No one ever gives Ian a hard time except Buck and me, but the others tease us and each other unmercifully. It's curious.

Except for one company that remains behind, watching for the Turks' return, the rest of us are shuttled back to Cairo. Our quick and decisive victory earns us a modicum of respect among the Aussie soldiers, even the insufferable Light Horse. They join us in a day-long rowdy celebration through the streets.

Early evening finds Ian, Buck, and me climbing the side of one of the pyramids. We choose a perch on a jutting stone overlooking the vast sand sea beyond and set a small fire so we can spend the evening together.

Something about the grandeur of the structure beneath us has us speaking in hushed tones.

"We really showed them, didn't we, Fin?" Ian's big eyes glisten in the firelight.

Buck snorts. "Those Turks don't know what they're doin'. It's like a cat playin' with a mouse. All we gotta do is keep wearing 'em down until they run out of men or get tired of gettin' beat."

"I wish you two wouldn't jinx it." I fold my arms over my knees. "You're going to tempt Satan to prove you wrong."

"Nah." Buck swipes his hand through his hair. "Like I said, we'll have Ian home by spring."

"*Me* home? What do you mean?" His brow creases. "I'm not coming with you back to Georgia. My home is in New Zealand." He blinks rapidly. "I thought…"

"Thought what?"

"I thought—maybe you'd come to New Zealand, too, and build your homes on the station." Ian swallows. "Like we always talked about."

"Not me." Buck lifts his head and stares into the opaque darkness of the desert. "When all this is over, I think I'm headin' to Montana for a spell."

I lay my hand on Ian's arm. "Granda needs our help with the farm. We can't abandon him, not at a time like this."

"I sure could use your help, too."

Buck blows a puff through his nose. "You'll have Claire to help you. It's no different than Pa and Ma when they first came to New Zealand. And they got along fine."

Ian shrugs and studies the dwindling flames. "I was just hoping."

"Maybe one day, Ian." Do I mean what I'm saying?

"Y'all have at it, then." Buck stands and brushes his hands down his pant legs. "I'm not plannin' on settlin' down any time soon."

The wind across the desert picks up, sending swirls of sand against the sides of the pyramid. After several minutes of uncomfortable silence, I push myself to my feet. "We'd better be heading back."

The silence continues until we reach our barracks, where Will, Charlie, Lucas, Bulldog, Declan, who we call Rabbit, and Artie wait for us to go for rations. Our mates are still buzzing from the victory party, so they chatter away, yelling over the noise of Cairo's teeming streets. Buck joins right in with them, but Ian and I remain quiet—and strangely distant.

After their hasty retreat, the Turks establish defensive positions in the Sinai Peninsula, and our job becomes to repel sneak attacks and kill snipers trying to wreak havoc on traffic through the canal.

But we begin to hear whispers of a shift in British strategy. Rumors have it that the British navy, under Winston Churchill's command, attacked a place called the Dardanelles Strait and failed to advance, losing several ships. Soon after, Corporal Phillips calls us to the base for a meeting with our whole company. Captain William Bolton, the B Company commander, stands before the group of 200 men with a large map behind him.

"At first light, we shall proceed to Lemnos Island, specifically Mudros Harbor, to join with the British fleet and our Australian brothers. The naval attack through the Dardanelles Strait has stalled. The plan is now a new operation, and this crucial task has been assigned to the ANZAC." Bolton's face is as stiff as a stone. "Our success is imperative in the war effort. Victory could herald a swift end to this war. I've assured Lieutenant Colonel Malone that we are more than capable of achieving complete success." His dark eyes narrow. "I expect nothing less."

When Captain Bolton finishes his speech, we return to our sections to go over the details of the plan. The boys around me prattle on about the Turks' stupidity and how we'll take them without difficulty, some even wagering on how many days until the battle is won, but a growing sense of dread tightens my stomach.

From the looks of it, we'll be landing on difficult terrain with gun placements and the Turks already well-entrenched. The commanders seem to believe we'll swarm the beaches, take the peninsula, and be on our way to Constantinople in a matter of days.

I'm not so sure.

Three days pass in torrential rain, as we wait to depart for Gallipoli. Our opportunity for surprise is waning by the hour. The Aussies' 3rd Brigade under the command of Ewen Sinclair-Maclagan is scheduled for the first wave, arriving on the beachhead in pre-dawn hours.

We're in the second wave, along with the Australian First Division.

My mates are disappointed, saying most of the fighting will be over by the time we arrive. They don't want to hear my opinion on the matter, but I figure the Turks will be wide awake and firing everything they've got when our group lands. We'll know soon enough.

In the wee morning hours, as soon as the moon sets, the first wave of soldiers boards several British troop carriers. Even though we are many miles from the peninsula, the Aussies board in complete silence. We've all heard the whispers of the Aussie command predicting massive casualties, so the mood is somber and the air metallic with terror and despair.

We must wait for the transport ships to return before we can deploy. The sun brightens the sky by the time we board. So much for the cover of darkness.

The ships carry us to an anchorage well beyond the cove where the first wave now charges up the steep, rugged cliffs. Smoke rises against the blue sky from the distant ridge on the peninsula, confirming my worst fears that the Turks are already engaged and ready to fight us. We climb onto steam-powered landing boats to head for shore. Before we reach the shallows, we transfer into rowboats, a clumsy, cumbersome task that leaves us vulnerable to enemy fire.

We row as hard and fast as we can, as the pelting from the Turks rains down around us. Have the Aussies secured the beach? Have they taken the first ridge? How many men were lost? But when we approach the beachhead, we can't see our Aussie mates. Our transport ships anchored north of their location, at Fisherman's Hut near North Beach, and the heavy smoke blocks our view of the rest of the cove.

I leap from the foundering rowboat into waist-deep water. The boys from our company drop around me like swatted mosquitoes. Buck and Ian jump out behind me. One of them is screaming, a high-pitched wail reminding me of when we stood by Ma and Pa's grave.

"Come on! We gotta get out of here!" I reach to grab Ian's arm, but Buck already has him and is pushing forward, so I plow through the water, ducking my head—although I know it won't make a bit of difference if a bullet has my name on it.

Captain Bolton charges onto the narrow beach, barking orders and waving his arm. "Get off the beach! Get off the beach! To Baby 700. Hurry!"

The water surging onto the shore turns the shingle and pebbles crunching under our feet a deep crimson. Face-down bodies undulate in the waves like flags waving in a breeze. I can't help but step on them as I run across the narrow strip and duck behind a large outcropping of rocks. Buck and Ian tuck in beside me.

Captain Bolton stands a few feet away, bellowing for his men. "B Company! Form up. Get behind the ledge. Come on! This way!"

I glance back to the beach, where bodies are stacked like cord wood. Whatever order existed at the base has degenerated into complete chaos. I don't recognize most of the men whose panicked faces seek shelter behind the ledge. Where are the rest of our section—Bulldog, Rabbit, Charlie, Lucas, Will, Artie, and Corporal Phillips? They were in our boat, but I don't see them anywhere.

Cries and moans from up and down the beach echo off the rock face accompanied by the musical pings of bullets striking stone and the deep booms of large artillery. Geysers of pebbles, coarse sand, and busted bits of shale blossom around us, then catch in the wind to seek our eyes and ears and slide down our shirts.

"Off the beach! Now!" If Bolton could physically carry every man up the side of the cliff, I think he would.

"Our mates! I see them!" *Yes!* I spot Corporal Phillips leading a group of men, including our section, up the side of the craggy cliff face not far from our position.

"Come on," Buck shouts. "Let's take this godforsaken hill."

Ian pokes his head above the edge of our escarpment. He looks like a duck in a shooting gallery at a carnival.

"Get your head down!" I shove his shoulder, forcing him to his knees.

Ian stares at me, blinking. "We need to stop those big guns, or this whole company will die on this beach. If we could find a protected route up this rock face and skirt around behind the gun placements, we could drop grenades…"

"Yeah, and if wishes were horses, beggars would ride." Buck butts Ian with his shoulder. "Do you *want* to die?"

"No, but I don't want our mates to die, either. Look!"

Ian's right. Corporal Phillips and our mates are already pinned down amidst the rocks and scrub brush.

Buck leans closer. "We ought to join our mates—safety in numbers, for them and us."

"The captain's command is to push up the hill. Someone's gotta do it. Might as well be us." I stare back at Ian. "Stay behind me and keep your head down. Do you hear?"

Ian nods once and hoists his rifle.

"Let's go," Buck growls.

Suddenly, my feet won't move, as if they're stuck in plaster. I lean forward, ready to circumnavigate our outcropping, but my body freezes. Bullets chatter against the rocks above our heads.

"Let's *go,*" Buck repeats.

"Give me a second." I close my eyes, whispering an old prayer our ma used to pray over us. "Circle us, O God. Keep hope within, keep despair without. Circle us, O God. Keep peace within, keep turmoil without. Circle us, O God. Keep safety within, keep harm without. Be to me a bright flame before me. Be to me a guiding star above me. Be to me a smooth path below me. Be to me a kind shepherd behind me. Today, tonight, and forever."

My muscles loosen as I speak the old words. I look up at the rugged cliff before us, and a bright beam of sunlight pops from behind a cloud, striking above a natural cut angling up the side. "There. Do you see it?"

Buck grunts, and Ian says, "I see it."

"That's our path. Take a direct line through that scrub brush up to the swale, then follow it up the cliff as far as it goes." I hunch my shoulders, preparing for the barrage of bullets. "Ready?"

"Go!"

I bolt from behind the outcropping. I can hear Ian's footfalls crushing the vegetation behind me. I hope Buck has Ian's back.

The Turks' bullets shred the scraggly bushes around us like tearing newsprint. Only the force of my will keeps me from falling face-down in the brush and crawling back to our nice, safe rocks. But Ian and Buck are counting on me, so I increase my speed. Everything around me slows to a standstill, like I imagine it did when God stopped the sun for Joshua. Maybe He's giving us time to make it to the swale.

"They're followin' us."

"What?"

"Phillips and his group. They're followin' us."

Oh, dear Lord, please don't let them get killed on my account.

From the beach, I hear the captain's baritone screaming, "Attack! Attack!" The battle yells of a hundred men flow in a wave up the cliff face and gather me up to carry me the rest of the way to the swale. When I look down from comparative safety, the men look like a swarm of ants pouring out of a newly disturbed mound. Turkish gunfire intensifies as the men gain ground.

"If we can make the top of this rise, we can take the first ridge. I'm sure of it." Ian's smile beams from his flushed face. "We must keep going."

"It would be wise to wait for the others. Then we can attack as one force."

Ian exhales and cuts his narrowed eyes toward me. "What about those gun placements?"

Buck shakes his head. "We need more men to take them out anyway, Ian. Let's wait for the corporal. Shouldn't he lead the charge?"

Ian huffs. "They wouldn't have gotten this far if Fin didn't find this swale."

I roll my eyes. "I'm just trying to survive."

"But you're the one who saw the cut first. Now everyone is coming. They're following you."

"Well, I want none of it."

Men start pouring into the crevasse, Phillips and our mates among them. The corporal waves and barks, "Keep going!" so I dash up the swale with Ian and Buck following close behind me.

As we near the top of the rise, the swale narrows and shallows out. Continuous fire pours over our heads from the Turkish guns. To take the first hill from the Turks, we'll have to come into the open and into the gunfire. Most or all of us will die.

I squat, and Ian and Buck follow suit. "OK, Ian. I see your point. As soon as we poke our heads up, we're dead."

"So, we circle behind them, like a deer hunt." Ian points. "We stay below the ridge and cut across—there—then sneak up on those gun placements from behind."

Corporal Phillips scrambles up beside us, the creases on his face blackened with dirt and deepened with worry. The rest of his men crouch in a long line down the swale with more on the way. "Good work, boys. As soon as we're all gathered, we'll attack."

"Corporal Phillips, we have a plan." Who knew Ian could be so bold? "If we could get the rest of the men up here…"

"What plan?"

"To take out the gun placements."

The corporal lifts a single brow. "And how will you do that?"

"Sneaking up on them from behind." Ian reviews his plan, and to my surprise, the corporal considers it.

"Just the three of you?"

"Yes, Corporal."

"And what will the rest of us do?"

"When the guns are down, you can attack the Turks and take this hill."

Corporal Phillips quirks his mouth. "It's a suicide mission."

Ian grins. "I don't know, sir. We're pretty sneaky."

"You're volunteering?"

"Yes, Corporal."

After a pause, he sighs. "Very well. We will provide you with some cover fire. The Turks will think they have us pinned."

"Yes, Corporal."

"Give me five minutes."

Phillips, bent at the waist, scurries down the swale, giving orders and organizing the men into shooting lines.

In the meantime, I take out my range finder and scan the cliff above us. Turkish officers collect on the top of the ridge, believing themselves to be out of range of our guns, while the rest of their soldiers fire from rows of trenches dug into the cliff face. It's a Biblical scene.

I gesture for Ian and Buck. "We'll have to go down to go up. Otherwise, they'll shoot us before we can get around the hill." They nod their agreement.

When Phillips returns, we've scoped out a reasonable path through dense scrub brush, moving from outcroppings of rocks to overhanging ledges. If all goes as planned, we'll move without being spotted. The corporal approves, and after a few words of encouragement and a shake of his head, he gives the order to fire, then turns to walk the line behind his men.

The three of us crawl from the edge of the swale down the cliff face to the next overhanging ledge, which we duck beneath. With some cover, we scamper toward the end of the ridge, then use the thick brush to shield us from view from above.

Once we near the ridge's end, the Turkish line is directly to our left, and we've not yet been spotted. So far, so good. But the collection of officers standing atop the ridge poses a problem. Cover on the back of the hill is sparse, so if the Turks happen to glance our way…

"What now?" Buck whispers through clenched teeth.

I chew my bottom lip, scanning the officers with my range finder, then scoping the gun placements. "We can hope they'll stay focused on the front line."

"We could take them out." Buck lifts his rifle, lining up his sights. "It's an easy shot."

Ian moans. "But it gives away our position. And how many could we take out before they shoot us? Five or six? And those guns will still mow down our men."

Killing Turkish officers seems a worthy goal, but Ian's right. It won't help our mates. "There's nothing for it. We'll have to risk being spotted and hope for the best." I grab Ian's arm. "Stay low and behind us."

Ian curls his lip and blows out a breath.

"Let's have it over." Buck crouches low and dashes into the open across the side of the hill, with me following in his steps, and Ian bringing up the rear.

Miraculously, we make it to a cluster of rocks near the first gun placement without a single shot fired in our direction.

When we crouch behind the rocks, I put a finger to my lips and pull out a large knife from my belt. Ian and Buck nod, getting their knives and slipping their rifles over their shoulders.

Once more, I use my range finder to scan the emplacement. Two Turks man these guns, so I gesture for Ian to remain behind the rocks, ignoring his pout, while Buck and I slither on our bellies up the hill to the fortification, hoping the continuous pounding of the guns will cover the noise.

Buck slides over the sandbags into the dug-out hole, but as I follow him, one of the men turns—I suppose my movement caught his eye—and with his eyes widening, he rises to meet the threat. Buck is on him in the blink of an eye, slashing his throat. Before the second man can react, I swipe my knife across his throat, and he slumps against his gun, as a growing pool of blood gathers on the dirt.

Time is against us now. Someone will notice these guns have stopped firing and will investigate. So, we slide back down to Ian's position, scope the next set of guns, and dash across the hill.

This time, there are no rocks to hide us, so we go straight for the Turks manning the guns—four this time. Buck makes quick work of the first soldier, which alerts the other three. My target reacts to our attack without hesitation, grabbing my knife hand and wrestling me to the ground.

I recoil at the stench of his hot breath in my face, kicking his gut, and shoving him off me before he can secure his grip on my throat. I swing my knife, catching him on the arm. He howls, clutching the slash now gushing blood, but leaps on me again, teeth bared.

If I weren't holding my knife in front of me, he'd have me, but when he tackles me to the ground, my knife buries to the hilt in his chest. His eyes flash a moment of terror before they glaze, staring at some distant, unseen point, and he collapses against me, pinning me down. His blood soaks through my uniform, wetting my skin.

I roll his body off to find Ian standing over one dead soldier, wiping his knife against his pants leg, and Buck jabbing his knife into another.

"One more. Let's go." Ian climbs from the bunker.

Seeing a wash of blood on Ian's uniform wrings my stomach. "Are you hurt?"

He glances down. "No, not my blood." He raises a brow as he scans my chest. "You?"

"Not mine."

"Come *on*," Buck hisses.

We scramble over the sandbags and make the final dash to the other side of the hill, the gun with the best vantage point over our mates' position.

A barrage of bullets pings the ground in front of Buck, kicking up dust and small rocks. No need for surprise now, so we unsling our rifles, duck our heads, and run full speed for the final gun. At the edge of the bunker, I spray five quick rounds before leaping into the hole. Buck and Ian jump in beside me as I slam my rifle butt into the head of one soldier, then point my weapon into the chest of another and fire. Ian and Buck have taken out the rest of the soldiers.

"Let's get outta here." Buck scrambles from the bunker but hits the dirt immediately as a rain of bullets flies over his head.

Grabbing one of the big Turkish guns, I swing it toward the ridge where the officers congregate and open fire. The officers dive to the ground and scramble for cover. Punching Ian's arm, I scream, "Go! Get out of here!"

He leaps over the sandbags. As I continue to fire, Buck and he race back the way we came.

From below the ridge, I hear shouts rising. Corporal Phillips must've seen the big gun firing at the officers and called for the attack. Sure enough, moments later, our troops swarm from the swale and race up the cliff face.

Out of the corner of my eye, I spot Ian and Buck turning toward the fray, so I jump from the bunker and sprint to join them.

We race toward the ridge where the officers were perched to find them fleeing up the hill away from our troops. They raise pistols and fire at us, but we return fire, so they scatter, leaving the ridge wide open for our forces. But first, they must make their way through the maze of trenches between the swale and the ridge top.

With their leaders fleeing, the Turkish soldiers begin to pour from their trenches, coming straight for us. All we can do is keep running and fire our rifles. For some unexplainable reason, the troops veer away from our gunfire. It's as if they never expected us to make it this far, and now they don't know what to do, or the loss of their big guns has them spooked.

We arrive at the top of the ridge at the same time as our mates. Ian heads straight for the corporal. "There's nothing to stop us between here and the hilltop."

Without hesitation, Phillips pinwheels his arm. "Keep going! Take that hill!"

So, with the rest of the men, we turn on our heels and race back up the hill. Phillips spreads the line to sweep for our enemy, but the scattered Turkish troops, often hidden in thickets and behind rock outcroppings, take their toll with quick volleys followed by a hasty retreat to a new cover position, while we have little success in thinning their numbers.

These guerrilla tactics are a type of warfare we didn't train for. Our advance slows as our troops and leaders grow more cautious in the face of their ambushes.

Phillips barks his frustration at the men, demanding they keep going, but sections begin to lag as our advance meets heavier resistance. Our troops are disorganized, often leaderless, and soon clusters of our men burrow down on the cliff face while the few of us under Corporal Phillips push forward.

"We're going too slow," Ian grumbles. "We're giving them time to reform and counterattack."

I'm not used to Ian being this aggressive. What's happened to his sweet nature? "We must slow down. We've left more than half of our men on the hillside."

He grunts and pushes ahead of Buck and me. "Come on! We can take this hill."

Buck growls under his breath, "He's gonna get us killed."

"Come on." I jog ahead to catch up to Ian, and after huffing for a moment, Buck follows, but the remainder of the men follow Phillips' lead, progressing slowly if at all.

We come upon a cluster of men behind a tangled brush who jump out with knives and bayonets gleaming in the afternoon sun. Our rifles are useless. The three of us resort to grappling with the Turks, trying to wrench their weapons from them. The one who has me in his grasp babbles some incoherent syllables as he grasps my head in the crook of his elbow and twists. I try to call out, but the bone of his arm presses against my neck and chokes the air from me.

Light fades to gray along the edges of my eyes as the Turk presses his mouth against my ear and snarls, "*Ölmek*." Suddenly, his eyes pop wide, his mouth drops open, and his grip loosens. I shove him off to find Buck's knife protruding from the soldier's back as he collapses to his knees.

Buck yanks his knife out, blade grinding against bone, and pushes the Turk onto his face in the dirt. "Come on." He reaches his hand, which I grab, and he pulls me to my feet. "We need to find Ian."

"What do you mean? You lost him?"

Buck twists his face like a screw. "No." His lower lip puffs out. "Well, sorta. He went on without us."

"Is he bound and determined to get himself killed?" I retrieve my rifle. "Which way?"

Buck gestures up the cliff. "He's determined to take this hill, is what it is."

"And he believes three boys from Georgia can do it?"

"Guess so."

"Come on."

We trudge up the steep incline, checking behind rocks and brambles for lurking enemy soldiers along the way, and soon spot Ian climbing the last few meters to the top.

"Stay low!" I call to him. "We're coming."

I'm relieved when he heeds my instruction and stays just below the rise to wait for us.

Buck and I lie down beside him. "What are you thinking, going off by yourself?" I punch him in the chest.

He shrugs. "You were busy."

I groan. "Ian, please, I'm begging you, stay with us from now on."

His answer is to slip closer to the top of the hill. "Give me your glass."

Instead, I crawl up beside him and pull out my range finder to scan the area beyond the rise. Movement to the left catches my eye, but when I lift my head to check, a bullet whizzes by my ear.

I flatten myself against the rocky ground. "The Turks are reforming."

"I knew it." Ian pounds the dirt. "We could still take the hill if the rest of them would hurry."

I scan down the hill to check on the status of our men, only to find them scattered to the four winds up and down the cliff face, useless.

Buck shields his eyes and surveys the scene. "Can you get Corporal Phillips' attention?"

"That's the problem." Ian's teeth grind. "There's no communication between the different sections or the commanders on the beach. Everyone is following their unit leaders instead of following the captain's orders."

"Not much we can do about it," Buck mutters.

I turn to scan the Turkish position again. "Yes. They are forming up for a counterattack. And we are sitting ducks."

"This is ridiculous." Ian stands to his feet. Immediately, bullets pelt the hilltop, but he ignores them, marching down the hill.

We have no choice but to follow.

Someone stands and waves his arm over his head, calling to us. "It's Will." I point him out to the others.

"Maybe he knows where to find Captain Bolton."

We run in Will's direction, keeping an eye on the surrounding bushes, and find him, along with the rest of our section and Corporal Phillips, dug into the side of the cliff.

"What do you see?" the corporal hisses as we slip in beside them.

"The Turks are readying for a counterattack." I point toward their position. "They have already reformed. I thought I saw some of the officers organizing them."

Phillips winces. "That's bad news. We aren't organized for it."

"Where is Captain Bolton?" Ian's question carries an edge to it. If the corporal were to notice, he might take umbrage.

But instead, Phillips' head drops to his chest. "I don't know. He was leading a large unit up the hill the last time I saw him." He sighs. "I hope he hasn't fallen."

The corporal's despondence is unnerving. "Corporal Phillips, can you rally the men to prepare for the attack?"

"I can try." He pulls his whistle from beneath his shirt, stands, and blows several short bursts. "To the hilltop! Move! Move! Move!"

I hear the word passing from cluster to cluster, and some of the groups closest to our position creep from their hiding places to start the march up the hill.

Corporal Phillips gets more strident. "New Zealanders! You will take this hill!"

Ian, Buck, and I stand beside the corporal, waving our arms and calling to our mates. "Forward! Forward! Take the hill!"

Soon, the cliff face is crawling with our men, who begin to congregate together as they make their way to the top.

At that moment, an ominous drumbeat sounds from beyond the hilltop. Minutes later, a horde of Turkish soldiers crest the hill, running straight for us, screaming with ungodly rage.

CHAPTER TWENTY-SIX

April 1915

Our men freeze. Corporal Phillips blows his whistle with renewed vigor as he races up the hill, firing his weapon at the Turkish flood. Ian, Buck, and I follow.

The Turks have the high ground now, and our chance to take this hill dashes away with the sweeping enemy soldiers. A handful of our mates run up beside us, but not enough to meet the attack. The only thing that keeps us from being mowed down like winter wheat is the difficult terrain, which hinders the Turks as much as it does us.

Then, Colonel Phillips falls. Ian rushes to his side and kneels beside him, clamping his hands down on the blossoming pool of crimson on his chest, but Buck grabs his arm, drags him to his feet, and shoves him down the hill.

"Get out of here!"

With Ian hopefully out of harm's way, I turn to face the threat and run headlong into the butt of a gun. My knees collapse, and I tumble through a cluster of brambles, rolling down the hill until my shoulder crunches into a boulder. The Turk is on me in a flash.

Ignoring the pain, I use my rifle to fend off his flailing fists, but he manages to land a blow against my ribs. A sharp crack tells me his strike did some damage.

With renewed fury, I swing my rifle across his face, shattering his cheekbone. He falls back with a howl, far enough so I can turn my rifle around and fire a shot. At such close quarters, he is blown back several meters.

Only then do I become aware of the chaos surrounding me: men grappling and pounding each other; sparks from the muzzles leaving the fetid smell of burning gunpowder lingering in the air; terrorized screams of the dying rising into heaven like anguished pleas; and blood, so much blood, and dead bodies everywhere I look.

Those troops not already engaged with the Turks flee down the hill, many jumping into the vacated trenches left by our enemy. Others run for the swale.

Where is Buck?

I whip my head around, searching up the hill, but I can't find him in the chaos, so I run toward where I saw him last, firing at every Turkish soldier I see—hitting many of them.

Still no sign of Buck or Ian.

With the corporal gone and our men dropping like ripe apples in late October, folks appear to be losing the stomach for the fight. More of those still standing fly toward the swale, but I push against the tide, searching for my brothers. If they're dead, I refuse to leave their bodies moldering on this godforsaken land.

A hand grabs my leg from beneath a tangle of thorns. I swing my rifle, ready to fire, but find familiar, large, round eyes staring up at me through the brush.

"Ian!" I drop to my knees. "Are you wounded?"

"Where's Buck?"

"I don't know. I can't find him."

"Go." Ian waves his fingers. "Get him."

"Are you hurt?"

"Not too bad." He groans. "Go. Hurry!"

My chest rips in two. Do I carry Ian down or find Buck and bring him back? After a second's pause, I shake my head. "Buck can take care of himself." I sling my rifle over my shoulder, praying the Turks won't notice us in the brush, grasp Ian under his arms, and lift him, cradling him in my arms like a bairn. Running at an angle down the hill at my best speed, I search for the path we took to the gun placements, away from the heart of the battle.

Taking the long way around the hill has me arriving at the swale after most of our soldiers. A few strays, still trying to get through the Turks, the injured, and the dead are all that are left on the hill above.

Will and Artie race up to greet us as I gently lay Ian against the side of the crevasse, slapping my back and patting Ian's head.

I bend over Ian, searching for his wound, but blood covers so much of his uniform, so I can't tell what of it belongs to him. "Where were you hit?"

"The others?" Ian asks.

Will's face falls. "Charlie. And Lucas…"

Ian groans. "No…I'm so sorry, Will."

"Bulldog is injured, but not bad. I doubt he'll be sent to the ship." Artie offers a half-hearted grin. "The rest of us made it back relatively unscathed."

Ian's bloody brow furrows. "What about Buck?"

"I haven't seen him." Will frowns. "You weren't with him on the hill?"

"I was but lost him." I press my hand against Ian's chest. "*Where* were you hit?"

Ian's expression sours. "In my calf. I think it was a ricochet, though, because it's not too bad."

Will gestures to Artie. "Let's carry Ian to the medical tent so Shark can look for Buck." He glances at me. "We'll make sure he's well cared for."

"Thanks, mate." I stand, brushing my hands against my pants. "Knowing Buck, he's found some trouble to get into."

Artie chuckles. "Likely so."

Will and Artie pick Ian up using a two-handed seat and head down the path toward the beach.

I walk up and down the swale, asking after Buck, but no one has seen him, and the sun is sinking in the west. If I can't find him before dark…

What if he's up on the slope like so many, lying in a pool of blood, dying—or dead?

I refuse to believe it. Buck is too stubborn to let some Turk get the best of him.

Then, where is he?

Maybe Will and Artie will see him in the medical tent.

What began as a rumbling concern has spiraled into a tornado of raw panic. Using my range finder, I risk sticking my head above the edge of the crevasse to scan the rocky ground between our position and the Turkish line. What I see stops my heart cold in my chest.

The battlefield is littered with piles of bodies from both sides. Many are tangled in a perpetual war dance, breathing their last in each other's grappling arms. Others lie with blank, open eyes and missing limbs or bloodied chests on the chewed-up ground. It's the stuff of nightmares.

But I don't see any sign of Buck's distinctive red hair. As the light fades, I give up my search and begin to pray.

Soon after, Will and Artie return, along with Rabbit, Bulldog, and Ian, whose leg is bandaged. He walks with a limp but otherwise seems to be in good spirits. Bulldog's round head is wrapped in white cloth, covering a blow to his head.

"Did anyone see Buck?"

Ian frowns. "No. He's not back yet?"

I shake my head.

All five turn their faces toward the hill, but no one says a word, as if talking about what we fear will speak it into existence.

Word comes down the line, orders from Captain Bolton to dig trenches. We build a small fire for light and start carving into the side of the swale, using the dirt and rock to create a fortification we can defend and take shots at the enemy. It's difficult work, particularly in the dark, but I'm grateful for it. Digging takes my mind off Buck.

We continue to hear occasional rifle fire from the enemy lines, but I can't imagine its purpose. We're out of their range, and no one is risking climbing out of the swale to retrieve our dead—not that I can see anyway.

As we dig, Will shares memories of his best mate, Charlie. Then, Bulldog and Artie tell stories of some of their escapades with Lucas in

Cairo. Ian extols Corporal Phillips' bravery and leadership. His voice cracks, and I think he might be crying, but I can't tell for certain in the dark.

"We can't even give them a proper burial." Will slams his shovel against the growing wall of our trench. "They're left out there to rot."

"It isn't right," Ian murmurs.

A disembodied voice chimes in from the darkness beyond our fire's little circle of light. "Don't worry. I paid those *koretake* mongrels back for killing our mates."

Buck!

He steps into the light, his teeth gleaming white from his mud-smeared face. I'm on him in an instant, wrapping him in my arms. "I was worried sick! Where've you been?"

Buck chuckles. "Don't be such a *māmā,* Fin."

Ian grabs Buck, as our other mates cluster around him, slapping his back and shaking his hand.

"When I saw we were gettin' overrun, no chance we could hold the ground, I circled back behind their lines." He elbows Ian and grins at me. "Same as when we took out the big guns."

I stare at Buck. "That was you we heard shooting?"

Buck smirks and nods. "Hide, fire, and run. Like Granda's stories of fighting a whole Union company when they tried to slaughter the buffalo herd."

"Good chap!" Will shakes his hand again.

But I punch him in the side. "Idiot! What if you were captured?"

He shrugs again. "I wasn't."

"They're going to give you a medal." Artie beams a big smile and wags a finger in Buck's face. "Maybe even a promotion."

Buck wrinkles his nose. "Nah, I don't want no promotion. All I wanted was payback. For Charlie and Lucas and the others. And Corporal Phillips."

Without another word, of one accord, we stand in a circle around the fire, arms entwined. Ian begins to sing, hushed and slow, "Abide with me; fast falls the eventide; the darkness deepens; Lord, with me abide; when other helpers fail and comforts flee, help of the helpless, oh, abide with me."

One by one, we join him. "Swift to its close ebbs out life's little day; Earth's joys grow dim, its glories pass away; change and decay in all around I see—O Thou who changest not, abide with me."

By the time we reach the end, men are singing with us up and down the line. "Where is death's sting? Where, grave, thy victory? I triumph still, if Thou abide with me."

We stand watch, solitary and silent, through the night. None of us sleep, and fatigue, along with hunger and thirst, begins taking a toll.

A runner arrives well before dawn, bidding us to follow him to Captain Bolton's command post. Buck twists his mouth.

"Are we in trouble?"

But the soldier offers no reply.

We sprint down the swale to the end, where a temporary shelter has been erected inside a dugout in the wall of the crevasse. The captain sits inside with two other officers. He looks up when the runner announces us.

"Very well. Come in, privates. Pull up a rock. We have more than enough around here."

We perch along the wall, waiting as the captain finishes his discussion with the lieutenants. When they are dismissed, Bolton places his hands, palms down, on his small table.

"Well, now. I would like to discuss your incursion behind enemy lines with you. What did you observe?"

"They have gun emplacements all up and down the line as far as I could see." Buck glances at the hand-sketched map hanging on the wall of the cave.

"The Turks seem somewhat cavalier about their defense." Ian folds his arms. "They were standing around without any lookouts and seemed unprepared. I don't think it crossed their mind we'd be so bold."

"And they would've been right, except for the three of you." Bolton stands and holds out his hand toward Buck. "I understand you had a busy night."

"Yessir." Buck takes his hand.

"A successful one?"

"The Turks don't think so."

The captain grins and gestures to Ian and me. "Are the two of you crack shots as well?"

"Yessir!" Ian straightens, his eyes gleaming in the dank cave.

"You are now our official sniper unit." Bolton sits back down behind his table. "If the Turks are as lazy and unprepared as you say, you could do some real damage."

"Yessir."

"Your platoon needs a new corporal."

A pained expression crosses Ian's face as his head drops to his chest. "Yessir."

"Phillips was a good man." Bolton's jaw pulses under his skin. "How does Corporal MacAlister sound?"

We stare in silence at the captain for several seconds, then Buck finally speaks up. "Which MacAlister, sir?"

Captain Bolton chuckles. "Right." He swipes his hand across his forehead. "It's been a long twenty-four hours." He looks straight at Buck. "Buck, right?"

"Yessir."

"How does Corporal *Buck* MacAlister sound to you?"

But Buck winces. "Not too good, Captain. My apologies, but I'm no leader."

"That's not what I observe."

Buck shrugs. "Ask my brothers. They'll tell you."

"Buck will make a fine corporal, sir." Ian's chest puffs out like a proud *māmā*. "The men in our platoon respect him. They'll follow him."

"Then, it's decided." Bolton reaches behind him and fishes a corporal's insignia from a bag, two downturned chevrons. "Add those to your sleeve, Corporal."

Buck wilts under the captain's gaze, reluctantly taking the stripes.

After a few minutes of discussion on the deployment of Bolton's new sniper unit and a review of his orders for our platoon, he dismisses us. "Let's see how much damage you can do, soldiers."

"Yes, Captain."

Ian punches Buck in the arm as we exit the cave. "*Corporal.* Isn't that something?"

I can't help but tease him. "Granda would be *so* proud."

But Buck frowns, shaking his head. "Granda would be furious. He hates everything about war and armies and killin'. That's why he sent us to bring Ian home." His shoulders slump. "Now, I'm bound to stay because I have others depending on me."

Ian lifts a brow. "That's always been the case, Buck. You just haven't been paying attention."

"Well, I want none of it."

After tolerating Buck's moody silence for a few minutes, I've had enough. "Look, at least we get to fight this war on our terms. Our way. It'll be like hunting deer."

"*The Three Musketeers,* like Uncle Bear said." Ian bounces next to Buck, tugging on his arm. "It'll be great."

But Buck's surly sneer tells me he's not to be persuaded.

As we near what remains of our section, Ian dashes forward to share the news, to a lot of hooting and hollering. Buck's reddened cheeks bring on more grief from our mates.

"Do we call you Corporal Buck or Buck Corporal?" Artie guffaws.

Bulldog bends at the waist, laughing. "They're dredging the bottom of the barrel for certain."

"In other news." I heft my rifle. "*Corporal* Buck, Ian, and I have been designated as the sniper unit for our platoon.

Will's eyes widen. "Wow. That's a dangerous assignment."

"I'd rather be moving than sitting here in the mud waiting to be picked off like ducks on a pond." Buck grabs his rifle. "We're to head out as soon as I relay the captain's orders."

Rabbit pinches the bridge of his nose. "Is it another attack?"

"Yes. At dawn, you're to take the high ground." Buck's mouth twists. "While we take out as many of the officers as we can."

Will shakes his head. "You be careful. I hear the Turks don't take prisoners."

"They have to catch us first."

The three of us move down the line, passing on the orders about the dawn attack, when shouts rise from beyond the ridge. Deep, resonant booms vibrate the ground, rattling loose rocks from the edge of the swale, followed by a piercing whistle seconds before artillery shells explode above us, raining shrapnel down on our heads. I slam myself against the wall of the swale and curl into a ball, clutching my helmet. Screams of anguish echo up and down the line.

Round after round light the sky, from our forward position all the way to the beach. It's as if God opened the heavens and poured all His wrath down upon us in the form of metallic rain. Dirt pelts my face, filling my mouth and choking my throat with dust that tastes of burnt powder and sulfur.

The barrages come in uneven rhythm, with pauses just long enough for me to think perhaps it has ended. Then, the next scream through the sky, nearer, louder, and another terrible blast. Each detonation pounds against my ribs. Some men press their hands over their ears, but the booming shudders inside my head and chest, inescapable.

The barrage lasts until the first faint edge of light colors the horizon, then everything falls deadly silent.

Seconds later, guttural howls like the call of wolf packs on the hunt reverberate from the ridge.

I peek over the edge of the swale. Shadows move in the half-light, weaving like spectres through the scrub as they pour down the hill.

Buck, crouching beside me, also raises his head, peering over the rim. "Here they come." He leaps to the top of the swale. "Attack! Attack!" He waves his rifle over his head. "Attack!"

He dashes up the hill toward the ridge, a lone soldier against thousands. Ian and I follow on his heels. Behind us, men pour over the top of the swale to meet the oncoming enemy. Their muzzles spit flame into the morning haze in reply to the Turks' continuous stream of bullets. To our left and right, soldiers fall to the ground, screaming in agony.

From their superior position on the higher ground, the Turks ravage our lines. Many men turn and run back toward the swale, only to be shot in the back. Others dash for boulders or scraggly bushes to hide behind. We've no choice but to dive into a thicket and try to fire from there.

A shout rises from our left flank. "They're breaking through!"

And the Turks are on us.

No use hiding now.

I leap from the thicket and slam a Turk in the nose with the butt of my rifle. He drops in a heap. The soldier behind him points his gun at my chest, but before he can fire, I swing my rifle and whack the side of his head.

I'm vaguely aware of Buck's raging scream, which brings me some comfort. At least one of my two brothers is still alive.

A Turk on my left tackles me around the waist, and we fly past our former hiding place, rolling down the hillside, clutched in each other's arms. I manage to land a blow, but when we stop rolling, he's atop me. I squirm, using my legs to try to dislodge him, but he starts pummeling my face—left, right, left—until my head swims and my vision grays along the edges.

Suddenly, his eyes widen, and he slumps to my chest. Above me, Buck holds out his hand. "Come on."

"Thanks." I struggle to my feet, my vision still blurred.

"Let's go." He races left, taking a route parallel to the swale. Ian follows behind him, so I do my best to follow, dodging bodies and bushes as I try to keep up.

Buck holds his knife in one hand and his rifle in the other, swiping anything he can hit with the knife and slamming heads and bodies with the end of his gun, but allowing nothing to veer him off his goal. Ian has managed to attach his bayonet, which he uses to skewer enemy soldiers.

I fire my last round into an oncoming Turk, the recoil jolting my shoulder, then I lower my head and barrel through the enemy like a battering ram. The battle line dissolves into chaos, with bodies grappling, the crack of rifles, and the savage, sickening sound of steel entering flesh. The sky colors soft pink as if a pale reflection of the bloody slaughter below.

From a distance, somewhere behind us beyond the ridge, a bugle calls, and the Turks fall back, dragging their wounded.

Are they retreating?

"Hurry!" Buck lowers his head and presses ever forward toward the left flank. "They're gonna fold us up like wet paper."

"But they're retreating," Ian cries.

"No, they're not. Wait for it."

And with that, the shattering booms, piercing whistles, and mid-air explosions start again. Our soldiers who are able scamper back to the swale, hugging its walls, while our wounded lie in the open, looking face-up into the barrage like beached whales. Buck, Ian, and I dive into a cluster of rocks that offers some protection from the onslaught of shrapnel falling around us. The lead balls ping off the stone above us, rolling into piles at our feet.

"As soon as this volley stops, we must get to the left flank and help them hold. If the Turks break through…" Buck presses his lips together until they are bloodless, as if to prohibit the prophecy from leaving his mouth.

"They'll drive us into the sea," I finish for him.

Buck nods once.

Time's passage weighs on my chest as if its hands clutch me like a child's doll and squeeze until I can't breathe. When at long last the barrage falls silent, Buck bolts from the rock formation, ripping across the hill with no regard for the things in his path, including the dead.

Ian and I do our best to keep up but fall further behind the longer we run. The left flank, where the swale is most shallow, offers little to no protection and is the most vulnerable position on the line, which the Turks are clever enough to know. Buck's right. If the end of the line falls, the Turks will come at us from the front and sweep over us from the end, and all will be lost.

"Who's in command?" I can hear Buck's shout as he races up to the beleaguered soldiers.

A quaking private, his hand fumbling with the bolt of his rifle, stutters, "N…n…no one."

"Our lieutenant was taken out by artillery fire," another said.

"Very well." Buck grabs the arm of the second soldier. "Spread the word up the line. We must hold at all costs. Tell everyone to regroup here and prepare for a counterattack. We're gonna retake the ground we've lost, then we're gonna hold it. Got it?"

"Yes, Corporal."

Ian and I help the young private share the orders, and before the next artillery barrage, Buck has them organized into fighting lines, with one group of soldiers tasked with digging along the end of the swale to make a deeper trench.

Then, hell's fire comes upon us from above, and we all dive for whatever meager cover we can find. And when the barrage ends, the pit of hell opens, and a fresh horde of demon soldiers sweeps toward us with their teeth bared, spitting fire and cursing us in their strange tongue.

And we meet them head-on, with Buck leading the way.

Chapter Twenty-seven

April 1915

Acrid smoke drifts across the ridges, hanging low and burning in my throat. Hundreds of Turks lie scattered in the scrub side by side with our soldiers, their uniforms indistinguishable in the haze.

We haven't yielded, though God only knows how we manage to hold this small stretch of earth.

Sometime during the attack, more New Zealand soldiers arrived, fresh from the boat, and their numbers helped us hold the flank. Then, the Royal British Navy bombarded the ridgeline with their big guns, causing the Turks to withdraw for a time.

By midday, the merciless sun beats on our heads until sweat runs in rivers from beneath my helmet into my eyes. My face burns as red hot as a farrier's fire. My tongue swells and sticks to the roof of my mouth, and my lips crack until they bleed. The water we brought ashore is long gone, and the new arrivals are even worse equipped than we are, having rushed to join the battle as soon as they landed. The cove behind us is a death trap under the pummeling of the Turks' heavy guns, so a trip to the beach for water feels like a gambler's throw of the dice. No one volunteers for it.

The air quivers with the roar of the naval guns thundering from the sea, their shells screaming over our heads to smash the ridges where the enemy gathers, and from the Turkish guns pounding out position, their shrapnel bursting all around us, cracking open rocks, shredding plants, and shooting plumes of dust and smoke in the air, tinged red with blood.

I've fired my rifle so much it's hot to the touch, and the bolt grinds with grit, making it difficult to eject spent cartridges or load a new one, so I attach my bayonet and pull out my trench knife, readying for the inevitable attack.

When the naval guns stop, the Turks press forward, spits of fire from their rifles snapping from behind every bush, rock, and fold of ground. They seem to have an endless supply of bodies to throw at us. The shadows of their commanders flicker along the ridge above us.

"We gotta get to those officers." Buck groans through clenched teeth. "The captain expected us to have taken care of them by now."

"We had no choice," Ian whispers. "The men were leaderless. They needed you."

"Tonight. Once the fighting slows down, we circle behind them and take them down."

"I need more ammunition." I nudge Buck with the butt of my gun. "And maybe a new rifle. This one's giving me fits."

"Mine, too." Ian grunts. "We also need sleep. It's been over 58 hours since we slept. We're going to go mad if we don't get some rest."

Buck snorts, shooting a sideways glance at us under lifted brow before returning his attention to the Turkish line. "There won't be any sleeping anytime soon. The Turks will see to that."

"They have to sleep sometime."

But Buck spits and shakes his head. "We'll go tonight."

"Very well." Bending at the waist, I wander down the line, asking after ammunition and weapons, but no one has any to spare. When I near the right flank, I finally find a lieutenant who has brought a cache of guns and ammunition up from the beachhead.

"Captain Bolton ordered three of us to circle behind enemy lines and snipe the Turkish officers, but we need ammunition and rifles. Do you have three rifles to spare? And some ammunition?"

"Soldier, no one has anything to spare. But if Captain Bolton ordered you on this suicide mission, I suppose I must allow you to have your supplies."

"Thank you, sir."

He collects new rifles and three hundred rounds. I stuff the ammunition in my belt pouches and pockets, sling the rifles on my back, thank the lieutenant again, and dart back up the swale to my waiting brothers.

As the sun sinks out of sight, the cliff falls strangely quiet, save for the low moans that drift up from the gullies where the wounded still lie. The light slants red across the slope, as if the earth bleeds in compassion for the piles of bodies strewn across the hill.

I lean hard on my rifle, using it to support my weight, but my blistered hands and trembling shoulders make it difficult. My knees threaten to collapse from weariness as I stare into the darkening haze.

Buck's lips move, but he doesn't make a sound, as though he's lost in another world. Either that, or he's speaking to me, but my ears have gone deaf from the constant booming of the big guns.

Stretcher-bearers move up and down the swale like shadows among the small fires dotting the hillside, bent under their burdens. Some try to dart onto the open space between the lines to collect the wounded still crying out for help, but when they do, the ridgeline crackles with rifle fire, their barrels flashing like fireflies, and they're forced to dive back into the swale.

Darkness deepens but brings with it no rest. The smallest sound sets everyone on edge. The scrape of a boot, the rustle of brush, the clatter of a falling rock, could be the enemy creeping closer. Some men fire at those phantoms, which only stretches our nerves tighter. The stench of blood and decay hangs heavy, thickening the night air, pressing into my nose until I must pull my bandana over my face to keep from retching.

Buck juts his chin toward the end of the swale. "Let's go."

We slip from the dugout like wraiths, moving slowly, hugging the shadowed ground. Every step feels like it echoes through the gullies, though the crackle of rifle fire helps cover the scrape of our boots against the rocky ground. My pulse drums in my ears, louder than the gunfire, but I keep my breathing even.

We're counting on the darkness to hide us as we circle wide across the open hillside. The moon is a thin sliver, veiled in drifting cloud, providing enough light to show the edges of rock and shadows beneath the scrub, and the humped curves of dead bodies littering the slope. I step over a sprawled Turk, his eyes gleaming in the moonlight, then catch sight of one of our men lying face-down, hand stretched toward his rifle. Ian stops beside me, bending over the soldier, but I hiss each step a silent prayer that our presence will not be betrayed, until we reach some tumbled rocks above the enemy's command post.

Ian and I seek a perch among the rocks looking down on the slope interlaced with Turkish trenches, while Buck scans the area for a second position to dart to after we fire our first shots. When he returns, he gestures the direction for us to move, then settles beside me, his rifle at the ready. I cradle my weapon as if it were an extension of my flesh, lifting the scope to my eye and following the shapes below. The Turkish officers, restless in the dark, mutter amongst themselves. Easy marks from here. Ian exhales a shuddering breath, so I reach over and squeeze his arm.

Buck takes the first shot, the flash splitting the night and blinding me for a second. The echo reverberates across the ridge in a wave. One of the officers jerks, stumbles, and crumples in the dust. The enemy camp erupts, men scattering to the four winds, shouting as panic spreads.

I fire next, as calm as if I were back home stalking a deer in the woods. I blow a slow breath, work the bolt, and fire again. Then, Ian fires his shot, and Buck hisses, "Go."

We move as one, without hesitation, wordless, following Buck's lead to our new hide. As I slide into place, Ian ratchets his bolt and fires again. His target clutches his chest and drops to the ground. I check my sights for the next target, watching the chaos envelop the ridge, while Buck scans through his sights for our next hideout.

There. Based on the markings and decorations on his coat, he must be a high-ranking officer. Taking careful aim, I fire, but the man turns at the same moment I pull the trigger, and my shot misses wide. Quickly, I slide the bolt in place, reacquire my target, and fire again, this time striking his shoulder. I watch him through my sights as he clutches his arm, and blood soaks the front of his uniform. Then, he turns his gaze, and I swear, he looks right at me. His eyes harden as he stares, almost as if he can see through the rocks into my soul.

Buck lifts his gun, but I press the end of his rifle down and whisper, "They see us."

"Move." Buck sprints from the hide, and Ian and I follow behind him, this time ducking low as Turkish rifles fire in our direction. With each shot we take, as each muzzle flash paints our location, our risk of discovery grows. Sooner or later, the Turks will bring hellfire down upon us. But none of us seems ready to run for it—not yet.

Our new hide is some distance from our original cluster of rocks, but it offers less cover, which means we can take only one shot before having to move again. Buck doesn't have time to scout our next position, so we scamper into a nearby gulley and wait, hoping the Turks are too unsettled to send men into an unknown force, the invisible death from above.

Their shouts, which sounded like panic before, now sound like barked orders. "We have to get out of here," Buck mutters.

I grunt my agreement. "Where to?"

"I say we circle further around. Throw them off our scent."

Ian cranes his neck to check the officers' movements. "They're organizing to come find us. It's now or never."

"Down behind the ridge?"

Buck nods, and with a deep breath, he explodes from our cover to race down the hill into pitch darkness.

I leap after him, taking several choppy steps before my toe catches on a jutting crag, and I pitch face-first, rolling down the hill like a driftwood tossed into a rushing stream. My rifle gouges my back as the rocky terrain eats chunks out of my flesh. I flail my arms, seeking purchase in the scrub brush, but the relentless slope pulls stronger than my grasp.

The world passes in a blur, the hillside hammering against me as I tumble end over end. My teeth clack together, jolting my jaw. My breath rips from my lungs in ragged gasps. Grit fills my nose, making it impossible to breathe. Suddenly, my shoulder slams into something solid, and I spin sideways, skidding hard across the scree, until there is nothing but air beneath half of my body.

I kick against the air like a swimmer heading for shore. Loose pebbles rattle into the void, which yawns like a black abyss below me. I splay my fingers wide and claw the earth, my nails biting into gravel, but my momentum wrenches me forward, and I slide farther over the lip. For one breathless instant, I hang there, half in the world of the living and half ready to join my fellow soldiers in the afterlife.

The depth beyond swallows the echoes of my pounding heart slamming against my ribs, every beat louder in my ears than the gunfire above. And there my body stops, sprawled crooked on the brink, the darkness pressing close as if eager to claim me.

A rain of pebbles peppers my face as footfalls half-pound, half-slide down the hill toward me. *Turkish troops?*

"Are you hurt?" Ian's frantic cry is a little too high-pitched and loud for my liking.

"Shhh. You'll bring the whole bloody army down on us."

When I open my eyes, Buck stands over me, his hands planted on his hips. "Well, that was fun." He reaches his hand down. "Here. We'd better get going." He pulls me away from the edge and helps me to my feet.

I brush clouds of dirt from my uniform. "Where to?"

Buck points to a narrow fissure running parallel to the ridgeline. "If you're up to it, we climb up to that crevice and follow it around to the other end of the ridge. It should provide good cover, at least until daylight."

"So, we're done?"

Buck's mouth twists. "Not done. Relocating." He brushes his hands together, adding to my billowing dust. "I think we've overstayed our welcome on the left side. Time to take out some officers on the right."

"Maybe we should head back." Ian takes my elbow as I try the first few tentative steps.

"Truth is, from where we are now, this is the safest route back to our line." Buck's teeth shimmer as the fingernail moon slips from behind a cloud. "Might as well take out a few more on the way."

"I can make it." I limp up the hill, slipping once, but Ian is right there to grab my arm. It's slow going, but we finally reach Buck's crevice and make our way across the face of the mountain until we reach the far end of the ridge. Then we make the long, slow climb until we find a new place to perch.

This time, we decide to spread out, hoping to confuse the Turks. Leaving Ian and Buck in their respective hides, I wedge between two stones, pressed against the face of the ridge with my rifle balanced on a cut in the rock. The Turkish line stretches below me, a restless scatter of figures in the pale moonlight. Officers drift among the trenches, pacing, waving their arms, and scanning the far rocks where our shots once rang out.

A rifle cracks, and one shadow folds without a sound. I check my sights, draw in a slow, deep breath, and squeeze. Another figure arches his back, then collapses like a split sack of grain.

One after another, men drop in the dust, until I lose count of how many we've hit. It's a grim harvest at each pull of the trigger.

Fingers stab upward. Someone spotted our muzzle flashes. In an instant, rifles swing toward us, and the hillside is alive with gunfire. A bullet whines past my ear to clip the stone, stinging my cheek with hot grit.

"Down!" I hiss, though my brothers aren't close enough to hear. I press flat, hugging the rock, as a hail of bullets rakes against my stones. Sparks shower my helmet. As the Turks pause to reload, I slide on my belly back down the face of the mountain, scraping against the rocks and thickets with my rifle clutched to my chest.

The Turks fire blindly into the dark, peppering the end of the ridge in a wide scatter of shot. My heart thrashes like a trapped animal, but I force myself to move slowly so as not to give away my position.

The ridge falls behind me. I crawl into a dry gulch to wait for my brothers. At long last, Ian tumbles down the hill, half crawling and half sliding, his eyes wide, white circles as though he's clawed his way out of a grave. I give a quick whistle, and with a sigh of relief, Ian crawls to my hole and collapses in the dirt, his chest heaving.

Buck is slow to leave his hide, and when he does, he's running full out. "They're coming!" Behind him, a growing roar floods down the hill in a wave.

Ian and I jump up, and the three of us race at our best speed around the end of the ridge, cross the no man's land between the two lines, and spill back into our swale.

For the time being, we've cheated death again.

Chapter Twenty-eight

May 1915

By the end of the first week, it's apparent that our goal of taking the heights and then marching on to Constantinople is not going to happen, at least not anytime soon. The commanders have us digging deeper trenches, piling sandbags, and stringing wire whenever the Turks pause their relentless assaults, which lets us know we're in for a long haul.

The heat during the day takes a terrible toll on us, but even worse is what it does to the corpses rotting a few yards from us. Biting flies swarm around the bodies and soon find their way into our newly dug trenches, where they torture us day and night. Between the flies and the stench, it's an unbearable misery.

Beyond that, casualties continue to mount, with our wounded stacked down on the beach like cord wood, and the medical staff unable to keep up. We can still hear the cries of injured soldiers from both camps who are stuck between the lines, where no one can reach them. I've never felt such an intense sense of powerlessness and shame in my life.

Unlike our troops, the Turks seem buoyed by their success. They've held the high ground and prevented any advance, and their attacks have decimated our numbers. Thankfully, more reinforcements arrived today. But the horror of what they're walking into is sinking in, and their morale is deflating faster than a punctured balloon.

After our two losses on the first day, our section has miraculously remained intact. Along the line, we're now considered the "old ones" because we survived the initial push. There are few enough of us old ones left.

Buck, Ian, and I are gearing up to go out for our nightly sniping raid when a fresh onslaught of shells explodes over our heads.

"Here they come!" Buck swings his rifle to rest between two sandbags, but after a glance through his sights, he looks over his shoulder at us, his eyes rimmed in red. "The whole Turk army's comin' over that hill."

I stand there with my mouth hanging open like an overheated cow while Ian leaps into position beside Buck. When it finally hits me, and I come back to my senses, I call up and down the line for our mates to hold this line at all costs, then I join Buck and Ian.

As the Turkish soldiers come into range, we let loose an unending barrage of fire. As one man stops to reload, the next man steps up in his place. We fight like a machine with interlocking gears, decimating the Turkish lines as they roll toward us in waves. Bodies pile ever higher, with each new wave having to climb over their fallen comrades before they can push forward.

It's a bloody disaster for both sides, but the Turks took the worst of it. When they finally withdraw, they've lost thousands of men and gained nothing.

It's the closest thing to a victory we've had since we arrived on this God-forsaken peninsula.

Rumors circulate of a massive counteroffensive, a combined Allied assault to take Krithia. The navy is supposed to prepare the way for our troops with a massive bombardment, but the orders come down to attack, and the promised bombardment never materializes. Under Bolton's command, our company races up the hill to occupy the main force of the Turkish army while the Aussies, English, and French launch attacks toward Achi Baba.

Much like the phantom naval assault, the English fail to muster their attack until the Aussies are already engaged and suffering massive casualties, and the French are repulsed within the first few minutes of their uncoordinated attack. The assault is a complete failure. As we retreat to our trenches, the word filters down the line. 6500 casualties.

So many lost due to a lack of planning and coordination. And there's not one thing we can do about it.

After the battle for Krithia, our situation worsens. The biting flies carry disease to more than half of our troops. Will and Bulldog fall ill. Rabbit is seriously wounded by sniper fire and gets sent to the hospital ship. One of the British battleships sinks in the bay, hit by Ottoman torpedoes. A heavy sense of futility hangs over us all.

Then, the Turks launch another massive assault against our lines. Wave upon wave of enemy troops crash against our battlements, like a drumbeat that won't stop pounding. Somehow, we manage to hold our ground as the number of enemy casualties grows in heaping mounds on the open ground before our trenches. The muddy morass of that open space has become a soup of rotting corpses and blood, with fresh bodies piled on top, pressed deeper into the muck by the boots of the next wave of enemy forces. The surreal tableau gives the whole affair a sense of unreality, as if I'm in a nightmare that won't allow me to awaken.

As night falls, the Turks retreat to the high ground, having lost tens of thousands of their fighting force in a failed attempt to drive us into the sea. The stalemate is complete.

The next day, the Turkish commander sends a message to the ANZAC commander, requesting a temporary truce to bury the mass of bodies lying in the sun, decomposing. He promptly denies their request. Four days of unbearable misery pass, with a new round of black flies and escalating incidences of disease. The stench seeps into my clothes, my food, and my water, and starts consuming my thoughts as if the smell of death has become part of who I am. Finally, on the fifth morning after the battle, the general relents.

For the first time since the landing, no crack of rifle fire rings in our ears, no mortar bursts rain death on our heads, and no shells scream overhead. The stillness is the strangest thing—not peace exactly, but more like a collective holding of breaths.

Buck peers over our sandbags. "White flags. Looks like they mean to honor the truce."

Orders came quickly, along with shovels, stretchers, and white armbands. Buck and I climb out first, followed by our mates, drifting onto the open space one by one, so as not to spook the men across the field. At my first step onto the field, my boots sink into churned earth and are soon caked with rotting flesh and red with blood.

The Turks come out, too, moving slowly, ever watchful. They look haggard, which I'm sure we do as well, with their cheeks sunken and faces smeared with grime. Many of them wear blood-soaked bandages on different parts of their bodies.

One boy who looks to be Ian's age gives me a nod of gratitude as he walks by me. I nod back. It's strange, that little moment of civility in the middle of such savagery and carnage.

He and I work side by side in silence, digging a long canal in which to throw the bodies. Buck and Ian act as stretcher bearers, carrying bodies to pile into the newly dug trenches. I try not to look at the dead boys' faces.

Then, an Aussie nearby offers a cigarette to a Turk, and the man grins, tucking it behind his ear. Several other men follow suit, and soon, other items like coins, buttons, and insignia from our uniforms begin to change hands. The young Turk beside me pulls a blood-stained black and white photo from his tunic and thrusts it toward me. The faded image of a lovely, dark-haired young girl stares back at me, her black eyes staring through me, accusing me of crimes against humanity. I can't argue with her.

"Girlfriend? Wife?"

The young man takes the image back and gestures toward my pocket.

"Me? Oh. No." I shake my head. "I'm not married."

He gestures again, but I have no pictures to share, so I take out a coin and hand it to him. He takes it with a gleeful grin, holding it up to the sun to see it shimmer. Again, my sense of reality shakes as if I've bumped into a concrete wall.

We spend the remainder of the day digging beside each other. We compare blistered hands and commiserate through moans about our aching backs. But as we lower one final body into the burial canal, he glances at me. "New day…fight."

What do I say? My throat tightens. I feel a strange kinship to this young man. He could be my brother if we lived in another place and time. He and Ian could be best friends. But I don't even know his name.

I press my hand against my chest. "Fin. My name is Fin." I open my palm toward him. "Your name?"

He pauses for a moment, I suppose trying to figure out my clumsy gestures, then his eyes brighten. "Mehmet oğlu Hasan."

"Mehmet oh-loo Hasan?"

The young man chuckles at my attempt to mimic his language. He lays his hand on his chest, imitating my gesture. "Hasan."

I nod. "Hasan." I stick out my battered hand. "Nice to meet you."

He takes my hand and gives it a strong shake. "Fin. Good meet."

By late afternoon, refilled canals line the slope, marked by stones. A bugle call blasts away the quiet, sharp and final.

Hasan and I drop our shovels. He grasps my hands in his. "Fin."

"Hasan."

His dark eyes rim with tears as he shakes my hand one final time, then turns and walks slowly back up the hill. As they reach their encampment, the Turks pull down their white flags and drop them in the mud.

I crouch low against the sandbagged wall. The boy with the dark eyes disappears over the top of the ridge. Tomorrow, like he said, we'll fight. All I can do is pray we don't meet each other again on the battlefield.

The stalemate is as entrenched as the troops on both sides of this war. We try again to capture Acbi Baba and even gain a few hundred yards of ground but don't break through. Those yards cost us dearly. Artie and Bulldog, newly recovered from his illness, are both shot and killed, along with over 6000 other soldiers. Turkish losses are even more severe.

Moving forward into their trenches reveals some additional horrors. Some of their dead have been pressed into the floor of their dugouts rather than moved and buried, leaving a sickening, spongy morass for us to walk on. We thought the biting flies were bad in our trenches, but here, the flies fill every space, crawling up our noses and into our ears and eyes, gnawing on our flesh like a smorgasbord. I'd almost rather give back the ground than continue to live here, but we endure it. We don't have a choice.

Death becoming our constant companion makes it difficult for us to mourn our dear friends, but when darkness falls, we carry them behind the lines, beyond our old swale, and dig graves for them. Buck builds a small fire, then we lower their bodies into the graves and shovel the dirt over them.

Ian places his hand on his heart. "You should be going home, not lying here. It's not fair, and it's not right. But you died as soldiers, side-by-side with your mates, protecting their backs and standing strong. That's something no one can ever take away."

Buck swipes his hand across his brow. "Artie, man, you could always make me laugh. I'm gonna miss you. And Bulldog, you gave your mates grief with the best of 'em. Who's gonna spar with me now?" Shaking his head and glaring around the circle, he growls. "It's a cryin' shame, that's what it is. Why? Someone tell me why? They died for what? A worthless patch of mud?"

"They died for honor. And for their country," Ian murmurs.

Buck spits on the ground, and striding away, he throws one last comment over his shoulder. "That's what I think of their country."

No one speaks for a long time, until a ragged, wet cough rips through Will's throat. Swallowing hard, he clears his throat. "Brothers." Suddenly, he bends at the waist, coughing violently. When he finally lifts his head, his cheeks and eyes glow red in the firelight. "You gave everything. We'll hold the line, I swear it. And I promise, we'll never forget you."

"Will, come and sit." I take his elbow and guide him to a flat-topped rock. "You should go back to the med tent."

"They sent me here because there's no room. Too…" He coughs again, his voice catching on his words. "Too many wounded."

"You don't sound good."

Will crooks his brow. "Don't feel good, either."

"Rest a minute, then we'll head back."

Ian's gaze drifts toward the sea. "There's just the four of us left." He lowers his head and closes his eyes. "Do you think I'll ever see my Claire again?"

"Sure, you will." To my shame, my chest clenches in pain at the thought. "You'll be home before you know it."

"That's what Artie and Jameson thought. And Charlie and Lucas and Declan." Ian gestures toward the graves. "Look at them now."

After a few minutes of rest, I help Will to his feet, drape his arm across my shoulder, and half-carry him back to our trench. Ian follows well behind us, his feet dragging through the mud. But as Will and I reach the edge of the bunker, a barrage of shots rings out from the ridge, one of them narrowly missing us.

"Here they come again!" Buck cries.

"Ian!" I push Will into the trench and turn to look for Ian. He's nowhere to be seen.

I race back toward the swale, ducking my head and running in zig-zags to dodge the hail of bullets. The swale lies in deep shadow, our small fire too far to offer any light, so I jump down and run straight into Ian, cowering against the wall.

"You scared the pee out of me!" I snatch his arm, but he pulls back, covering his head with his arms, his forehead pressed against the packed earth.

"Ian?"

A sob hitches his shoulders.

"Ian, what's wrong?"

High-pitched keening pierces the night. I wrap my arms around him and clutch his back against my chest. "I'm here. You're OK. I'm right here."

He glances back, his eyes wild. "I can't do it anymore."

I squeeze tighter. "I know. I know." Stroking his ragged curls, I whisper in his ear. "No one should have to endure such horrors. It's unthinkable."

"I can't."

"I know." Gently, I turn him to face me. "You've been so strong, holding everyone together through the worst times. You need to have a good cry." I cup his chin. "Go ahead. Let it out."

As bullets and mortars fly over our heads, my brother, wrapped in my arms, chokes out gut-wrenching sobs and wails like a lone wolf who lost his mate. And I weep silently with him.

CHAPTER TWENTY-NINE

August 1915

The futility of our situation has sunk into our bones. Other than a failed British advance and some sniping and pot shots from both sides, nothing is happening. No movement, no apparent plan, no supplies or ammunition, no relief from the oppressive heat.

Then, word of a massive offensive push comes down from command. We are to attack and hold Chunuk Bair. Simultaneously, the Aussies are to take Lone Pine, as the Light Horse attack the Nek and fresh British troops land at Suvla Bay, pushing inland to meet at one central point and finally take the high ground.

Captain Bolton briefs us on our task, but he is uncharacteristically *kiriweti* as he outlines the plan.

Buck leans close to my ear. "What's wrong with the Captain?"

"No idea."

"We'll be getting reinforcements from the Māori contingent," Captain Bolton continues. "Additional ammunition will arrive with them." The corners of his mouth turn down. "Remember, all we are to do is take Chunuk Bair and hold it. That's it." With a final grunt, he strides down the trench. Buck follows him, so Ian and I trail after Buck.

"Captain?"

Bolton doesn't stop—once again, not his usual attitude toward his men—but spits an irritated, "What is it, Corporal?" over his shoulder.

"Captain, what are you not telling us?"

That brings Bolton to a stop. He turns slowly, his eyes closed and brow deeply furrowed.

"Sir?"

"We're a feint."

"A what?"

"A feint. A distraction. We are to occupy the enemy while the British advance, then scamper back to our little caves to wait out the rest of the assault." He snorts. "They don't need to hold Chunuk Bair."

"I don't understand." Buck shifts his feet in the muck. "Are you saying the Brits are using us to cover their advance?"

Bolton grits his teeth and continues his march down the trench. "That's what command says. That's not what I say."

"Sir?"

Bolton whips around. "We'll take that ground, and we'll keep advancing. The British can catch up to us, if they can." As he strides away, he mutters under his breath, "My men will not be spent as ploys to further British glory."

Buck looks at me, raising a single brow. "Well, that's new."

Ian sighs, his voice a barely audible rasp. "He's tired of incompetence costing New Zealand lives."

I grasp Ian's arm. "Did you hear him? The Māori contingent is joining us. That means…"

Ian lifts his head, his eyes brightening for the first time since his breakdown during the Turkish offensive. "Mani will be with them."

I grin and nod. "Mani."

Buck claps Ian's back. "With the four of us together again, the Turks don't stand a chance."

We share a refreshing laugh before returning to our position on the line. Will is excited to hear about our friend. "When the Māori arrive, you'll have to find him and bring him here."

Before long, a line of troops marches single-file in swooping curves up the cliff face like ants following a scent trail. Buck races down the trench toward the command post to greet them and find Mani, and when he returns, his face beams as he calls out, "Found him!"

Ian and I rush Mani and almost tackle him to the ground. Mani's long, dark curls and lilting laughter haven't changed a lick. But his skin has darkened, and he looks dangerously thin.

"Happy to see sons of Mister Clay."

Ian drapes his arm across Mani's shoulders. "What have you been doing this whole time? Sunning on the beach?"

"No sun. Digging."

"Digging?"

Mani bobs his head. "Digging lots."

You haven't been eating. That's for sure and certain."

Mani chuckles at my dig and pinches my side. "You miss some meals."

"We all have," Ian sighs.

"Let's get you set up," Buck says, dragging Mani to our dugout. Will, this is Mani, the friend we told you about."

"It's very nice to meet you. I only wish it were under better circumstances."

"Happy to meet friend of my good friends."

Buck and Will set a fire for the night, while Mani and I talk about his Māori unit. "No fighting. Only digging."

"Strange. The Māori are good fighters."

Mani cocks his head. "Not trusting, I think."

"Why, for goodness sake?"

Mani points to his chocolate-colored arm. "Not different in army from home."

I roll my eyes but can't disagree with him. "Well, you'll be fighting this night."

Mani lays his rifle across his lap, his expression flat and inscrutable.

Ian brushes mud from his hands. "I'm going to the command center for ammunition."

"Need any help?" Buck asks.

"No, I got it."

Will holds up a hand. "I'll go with you. It is better if we don't travel alone. Plus, with two of us, they may give us more pouches."

"We can hope."

By the time Will and Ian return, Bolton has issued his final orders.

"We leave before the dawn." I take my portion of the ammunition, a paltry amount for such a major offensive, and stuff them in my belt pouches. "Better get some sleep while we can."

We settle down against the trench wall, the dank mud seeping into our clothes. But none of us got any sleep.

The night is so black, I can barely see our mates sitting beside me when Bolton calls for the march. As we line up to exit the trenches, the only sounds are the rustle of uniforms against skin and the occasional muffled ring of a rifle slapping against something metal or a boot scraping against rock.

The climb up the steep slope is nightmarish in the pitch black. No one can afford to get left behind, so the pace is achingly slow. Still, some of the men get lost on the trail, and others must double back for them. The stench of death clings to our clothes and snakes up our nostrils as we move through areas contested over the last few weeks.

The last few hundred yards, we crawl on our bellies through the bones, and by dawn's break, we cling by our fingernails and the dug-in tips of our boots to the edge of the steep slope of Chunuk Bair. My heart hammers in my chest as sweat pours down my face and drips from my armpits.

"Fin." Mani inches up beside me, his voice a low moan like a whisper of wind. His dark eyes catch mine, a spark of fire in the thick darkness. "Almost there, brother."

I nod, though my legs are as heavy as carved stone.

A quick whistle blows at first light. The Māori *haka* rises behind me, deep and fierce, rolling up the hill like thunder. Mani takes up the chant, and his powerful bellow lifts me and drives me forward. As if driven by a whip, we surge over the crest.

For a moment, the whole peninsula opens before me. The Dardanelles lies like a ribbon of silver in the distance. As I stand on the heights, for one breath, victory seems possible.

The brief pause lengthens. Perhaps the Turks, daunted by the Māori *haka,* hesitate to attack us. Then, suddenly, their shells rip through the scrub around us. Men to my left and right drop like rag dolls as the air fills with the crack of Mauser fire from the slopes below. I hug the earth, trying to scrape a shallow indentation into the rocky ground with my bayonet and bare hands.

Mani crouches beside me, his shoulder pressed against mine. "We hold. Whatever comes."

His words vibrate in my ears, reminding me of Ma humming her favorite hymn as she tucked me in for bed. I start humming his words, repeating them like an incantation. "Whatever comes. We hold. Whatever comes."

The counterattacks come in waves of Turks pouring up the slopes, shouting, with their rifles blazing. I cut one down, then reload and fire again. Māori howl their *haka* into the smoke-filled air, stomping the ground and roaring like a hundred lions. Mani, his voice ragged, bellows a challenge with every word.

Hours blur. The sun climbs higher, scorching my neck. I'm running low on ammunition already, and my water can is empty. Still, we hold. Whatever comes.

As men fall, others step forward to fill the gap. Several of Mani's Māori brothers cluster around me now, coming up to take the place of the white men who scorned them. Their rifle shots find a home in many Turks. And we hold.

At dusk, the crest of the mountain glows crimson red in the setting sun, and shadows stretch long across the ridge as the Turks retreat down toward the valley. Chunuk Bair is ours. Mani grips my arm. His face is streaked with dirt and blood, but his eyes glow with pride. "We won."

I want to argue, to tell him the Turks will be back—they always come back—but the words stick in my throat in the face of his joy. Instead, I grasp his hand, hard, and nod.

The ground is captured at a massive price. The ridgeline groans with the voices of the wounded, both Turks and New Zealanders, but at the end of the day, we still hold the line. And beside me, for now at least, Ian, Buck, and Mani still stand.

Captain Bolton, crouching low, treads down the line, whispering instructions to dig in for the night, rest while we can, and prepare to continue the push in the morning.

"How do they expect us to keep fighting without ammunition?" Will takes his frustration out on the rocky earth, scratching out the beginnings of a shallow trench.

"I guess we'll be using our teeth and fingernails," Buck quips.

He's not wrong.

The night stretches before us like an endless tunnel with no light in sight. Smoke thickens the air, making it difficult to breathe and worsening my burning thirst. Despite our exhaustion, no one in my group sleeps.

And the promised Australian forces taking Lone Pine and the Nek to complete our front line, and the guaranteed British armies charging to relieve us from Suvla Bay? They never come.

At the first rays of light, dulled to a hazy smear on the horizon, Turkish war cries rise over the ridge, and they come at us again, surging up the slope and overrunning our position. My half-scratched trench is useless, so I leap up and swing my rifle as a club, left, right, and left again, then whip it around and stab my bayonet into a Turk's stomach.

Then, Captain Bolton, with his bayonet raised in the air like a sword, calling for the charge, takes a shot to the head. His bush hat flies off. His eyes widen in a now all too familiar look of surprise as his knees buckle beneath him, and he crumples to the dust.

"Nooo!" The scream erupts from my gut like a geyser from a hot spring.

The battlefield descends into absolute chaos.

Mani, one of the few of us with some ammunition, fires into the face of the Turk who shot Bolton, who is standing an arm's length from me. Another Turk, screaming his rage, races toward Mani, his knife raised to strike. Mani stumbles back as the Turk swings. The knife grazes Mani's chest, blood blossoming and spreading quickly on his tunic. Lowering my head, I ram my shoulder into the avenging Turk's side, and we tumble together down the slope. When we stop rolling, I'm kneeling over him, with him on his back.

As I whip my knife from its sheath, his eyes dart and tremble in fear, and in that moment, I recognize him—the young, curly-haired boy who showed me the picture of his sweetheart. Hasan.

I freeze, my knife dangling near his throat. Recognition widens his eyes farther, then he grins. It's so surreal and disorienting, I flop backwards, and he scrambles away from me like a scurrying crab. We stare at each other, mirroring each other's shocked expression, as the battle blurs around us.

He raises his hand in greeting. Slowly, I respond in kind. Then, we both push to our feet, our eyes locked, his reflecting deep mistrust, tinged with fear and sadness. Abruptly, he spins and races back up the slope to the heart of the battle. I follow a step behind him, but I'm met before I reach the crest by two charging Turks. One takes my knife in his throat, and the other wrestles me to the ground. After taking several punches, I grab a rock and slam it into the side of his skull, and he slumps on top of me, unconscious.

I shove the man off me and scramble to my feet just as Will crests the hill, racing toward me.

"Fin! Fin!" Before he reaches me, the crack of a shot rips the air. Will's flies forward as if propelled by an ocean wave, landing face down on the earth.

My eyes cut up the hill to find the rifleman and come to rest on Hasan, who gawks at me for a moment, then swings his rifle toward me. My skull vibrates with an uncontrollable wail coming from my body as my consciousness steps aside, an interested observer watching my arms drive my bayonet through Hasan's stomach and out his back. Again, I thrust, pull back, thrust until Hasan is skewered on the steel blade like a pig over a spit.

As he slides off the blade, I drop my rifle and catch him, lowering him gently to the dirt. His mouth opens and closes, so I lean down, my ears touching his lips, wet and warm against my skin. He mutters a phrase I don't understand. Then, his eyes shift to the sky, and his body grows still.

Something inside me breaks.

"Fin!" Ian's hand clamps down on my shoulder. "Fin! Are you injured?"

I look down at my hands, smeared and dripping with blood. No wonder he thinks I'm hurt. My head shakes, no.

"Get up! We must get out of here."

Will, the last of our friends, lies unmoving beside me. Hasan, the boy with the lovely girlfriend or wife waiting for him at home, lies across my legs, dead.

"Fin!!!" Ian pulls my arm. "Come on!"

As sluggish as a bug in pine sap, I struggle to my feet and stumble behind Ian to the crest. The ridge is alive with screaming men running aimlessly, continuous rifle fire, and billowing smoke from burning brush dotting the hillside. Another wave of Turkish soldiers crests the hill behind us, and the few men left standing, including Buck, Mani, and Ian dragging me behind him, gallop down the slope to dive into our trench and comparative safety. Chunuk Bair, ours for one single day, slips from our grasp, and all we carry away with us is the weight of the dead.

The slope is carpeted with piles of wounded and dead. A steady stream of stragglers flows into the trench, as my brothers race to tend the wounded, including our Māori friend. The smoke, the fire, the cheering Turks all crowd my mind like the hum of a million bees, but the only things I see are Will's eyes as he falls and Hasan's dark eyes trailing up to the sky before going blank.

And it's all my fault.

CHAPTER THIRTY

December 1915

The four months following Chunuk Bair rush over me in a blur of heavy rains, freezing temperatures, and sickness. Most of our meager supplies sink in the harbor or in the waist-deep mud. Sections of the hillside wash out, carrying moldering corpses with it, both the buried and the unburied, and leveling our trenches along the way.

Despite the horrors of the scene surrounding me, it's my nightmares that harass me in my sleep and assault me in my waking hours, although I'm never quite sure whether I'm awake or asleep at any given moment. With minimal fighting taking place due to the inexorable foul weather, I'm left with nothing but time and my assailing thoughts for company.

What if I had killed Hasan when I first had the chance? Would Will be alive today? Why didn't I call out to Will to turn back? Would Will still be alive? If I had reached Will in time to prevent the fatal shot, would Hasan be alive, too?

What if Hasan had killed me? He, Will, and Mani would've all been safe.

Everyone would be better off if I'd died.

Truth be told, I'm as good as dead anyway.

The orders come down in whispers, passed along the line as if the wind itself might carry the words to the Turks. Tonight's the night. After months of blood, fire, and death. we are to slip away like shadows.

That will not be a problem for me.

One of the Aussie soldiers came up with the idea of rigging several rifles to keep firing all along the line, so the Turks won't notice us retreating. At least, that's the hope. So, Buck positions rifles among the rocks, using a clever assemblage of dripping water, a balanced tin cup, and a string tied to the trigger of the rifle. When the water fills the cup, it tips, pulling the string and firing the rifle. To complete the deception, we set fires along the line and leave them to smolder, aiding the illusion of life. What a fitting thing, leaving ghosts behind to fight for us.

We wrap our boots in sacks to muffle our steps. The wall of the swale, once teeming with men, stands at attention beside us, like a ghostly commander supervising our formation, as the remnant of soldiers shuffles into single-file lines to leave.

As the sporadic rifle fire begins, we start our silent march. I trail along behind Buck and Ian, with Mani following behind me. We are so quiet, I can hear his slow, steady breaths like the whisper of a gentle breeze. Words are dangerous, threatening to shatter the fragile quiet that holds the night together, so we communicate with hand signals.

As we file through the trenches ever downward toward the beach, I bear the weight of every mate who will never leave these ridges—Will, Artie, Charlie, Lucas, Bulldog, Rabbit, Malone, and too many others to name.

And Hasan, whose life ended before it began, like so many of the boys on both sides of this fight.

Each step away from the cursed swale stings like a betrayal, as if I'm abandoning them all.

At the cove, the sea spreads before me, black and silent, the edge of the shore filled with rows of boats waiting for us, rocking gently in the lapping water. My movements are clumsy with fatigue and grief as I climb into a boat. Several boys around me scan the hillside, their eyes white orbs in the darkness, but I don't fear being discovered by the Turks. If they shoot me, they'll be doing me a favor.

The oars dip without making a sound and pull us slowly away from the shingle and the cliffs. Away from the graveyard.

I look back once. The heights loom above like stone sentinels, blocking the stars, leaving our fires dotting the hillside as the only sources of light. In the distance, I can barely hear the periodic crack of the rifles that cover our exit.

Beside me, Mani rests his head against the gunwale, his eyes closed. Ian crouches in the stern, his uncovered head hanging down between his knees. Buck sits tall on the edge of the bow. A sputtered fit of hysterical laughter escapes my lips as I picture him as the carving of a mermaid on the front of a pirate ship, like in the books we read as children.

"Shh." The stern eyes of the lieutenant chasten me, so I bite my tongue and lower my head.

The British ship sent to carry us away materializes out of the shadows. One by one, we climb up the cargo net to the deck. I don't turn back toward the peninsula. I've had quite enough of it. Instead, I turn my face into the wind. The salt-tainted air stings my skin, and for the first time in months, I breathe in something besides gunpowder and decay.

Gallipoli lies behind us. But it will never truly let me go.

After a brief stop in Mudros, we steam back to Egypt to spend January through March training in the desert near the Suez Canal and reorganizing into a new infantry brigade with fresh troops to replace our losses. I refuse to learn the names of these new, rosy-faced boys, still bearing the bright look of someone used to life on a New Zealand farm, excited about the adventure of the upcoming deployment in France. I don't bother to set them straight. They'll learn soon enough.

The desert sun in Egypt is merciless, but I hardly notice. As I plod through the motions of the useless training exercises, my restless thoughts refuse to relent. Will, lying in the dirt with the back of his uniform soaked in blood. Hasan sliding off my bayonet, his breath hot against my ear.

Hasan. His name is carved into my skin, the letters pressing deeper every night until I think they might pierce my heart. The bayonet that robbed his life now rips open my chest, spills my guts on the ground, and leaves my soul in tatters. Instinctively, I clutch my stomach to hold it together.

Will calls and waves, reaching as if he needs something from me, but he never asks. Hasan stares at me like he's still waiting for an answer I don't have.

So, I do the only thing I know to do. I push harder. I fire my rifle until blood blisters pop on my trigger finger. I polish my gun until the steel shines like gold. I march until my legs ache. I keep my kit neat, my boots tight, my buttons squared. Maybe if I hold to the rules and follow the routine, I can keep the cracks from showing.

Ian notices. He always does. Sometimes he puts a hand on my shoulder, as if to anchor me. I try to pretend it's enough, but he knows the truth. I can tell. No amount of training will scrub Hasan's blood from my hands, or drive Will's call from my nightmares.

Fin! Fin!

Once again, I bolt up from my cot, screaming. "Go back! Go back!"

Ian is beside me in a flash, stroking my arm. "Will?"

I sink back onto the thin mattress. "Yeah."

His eyes close, but he says nothing more, sitting with me until I finally drift back to sleep, only to awaken again to the sound of my screams.

Sadly, Mani is sent back to the Māori Pioneer Battalion, relegated to digging trenches and building communication stations. I'm envious.

Buck is given another promotion, to Sergeant, and put in charge of a small unit of snipers. Of course, Ian and I are drafted into his unit. I spend the remainder of my days in Egypt alone, shooting at distant stones and tufts of brush until they are obliterated.

April finds us sailing to France. Our division is stationed in the north near Armentières, where we continue training. The commanders believe the new recruits need the time to acclimate to trench warfare. After each day of training, my brothers spend the evenings telling them the realities. Truth be told, nothing will prepare them for what's coming, so I spend my evenings sitting in solitude by the barracks window, searching the stars. For what, I don't know.

On July 1, we're finally deployed to the Somme. At first, we fight in skirmishes where we exchange fire and raid trenches, but the main bulk of the force is farther south, so we're the lucky ones. So far.

Then, our luck runs out. They move us near Fleurs-Courcelette for a major offensive push. The barrage begins before dawn, a rolling, deafening thunder that floods my mind, even banishing thoughts of Will and Hasan. As we crouch in the trench, bayonets fixed, the pebbles around our feet dance and the walls tremble as though the world might split open and consume us. I find Ian's eyes in the dim light, focused and steady, and my galloping heart slows.

The whistle shrieks the command, and we climb, line after line pouring over the edge of the trench. Ahead of us, the creeping barrage of artillery marches like a wall of fire, tearing into the German line. We push up close behind the artillery, hoping the guns will offer some semblance of a shield, but men up and down the line still fall as machine guns spit from nests the shells miss.

The ground is pocked with craters from weeks of shelling, so the men hauling the artillery struggle to gain ground, often getting stuck in the pits' mud. I force my legs to keep moving as the ground heaves and quakes beneath me, every crater an open mouth seeking to swallow me whole.

Suddenly, a strange churning roar overshadows the artillery's booms as one of those new beasts they call a tank lumbers past us, gears groaning against the sucking mud. Smoke pours from its ribs as it crawls straight over barbed wire and through trenches as though they aren't there. For a moment, the German fire falters at the sight of the massive thing.

The morning air thickens with smoke until the tank becomes a monstrous shadow against a yellowing sky. Suddenly, someone screams, "Gas! Gas! Gas!"

In training, they told us to keep the mask always hanging on our chests, but I hate the thing, nothing more than a clumsy sack with two round glass eyes and a rubber tube ending in a filter tin that rattles when I run. It smells of rubber and sweat, and the straps bite into the back of my head, so I leave it stowed away in my kitbag.

The officers said if we aren't masked in under six seconds, we'll be corpses. Six seconds. I paw through my bag, pull out the bundle, tear open the flap, and sling the thing over my head, holding my breath against the invisible poison already in the air. Chlorine gas will sear my lungs if I give in and inhale. Phosgene is worse. Around me, men who had dumped their masks to lighten their load start to claw at their throats, coughing up green froth. I fumble with the straps as the mask's bug eyes fog over, blinding me to the creeping yellow-green ghost swirling around me, seeking to turn my lungs into fire.

For several moments, our line disintegrates, some men dashing back toward our trenches to flee the silent killer, others falling to the earth to find some sweet, clean air. I can't find Ian anywhere. But Buck and a few other sergeants pound up and down the line, yelling for us to get up and move, move, move.

Slowly, the line reforms, pressing forward in the wake of the tank and artillery. Step by agonizing step, we push toward Flers, or whatever's left of it, since it's been under continuous shelling for weeks.

German soldiers pour from their dugouts, wild-eyed and bellowing their rage, but they're disorganized, some fighting and some fleeing as our rifle fire cuts through them. I lift my rifle to fire, but I can't make myself pull the trigger. Unbidden images of Will, Bolton, and our other friends collapsing in the dirt with blood pouring from their bullet wounds choke my breath. The thought of recreating those scenes on a different battlefield forces hot, bitter fluid into my throat. Paralyzed, I can only stare at the grotesque scene as it unfolds.

"Fin! Come on!" Buck pauses as he runs by me, shoving me forward. "What are you doing? Move!" His voice sounds like he's speaking through gravel as his mask muffles his commands.

I stare at him through the haze of my glass eyes. How can I explain that I can't?

A German soldier rushes Buck, babbling and swinging his knife. Buck spins and thrusts his bayonet into the young man's stomach. As Buck pulls the steel blade out, blood spurts onto his rifle, and Hasan's stricken expression replaces the German soldier's face. I stagger back, my hands flailing to brush away the image.

Buck glares at me and screams, "Move!" then disappears into the fog.

My mates fight on, bayonets and bullets piercing flesh, and rifle butts cracking bones. I'm finally able to force my feet to move, but my hands still refuse to pull the trigger. Some sniper I make.

By midday, we reach the village and drive the Germans out. I've not fired a single shot.

Flers, no longer a village, only splintered beams, heaps of brick and shattered concrete, and the blackened shells of what were once houses, an empty, silent ghost town.

The price for the village is scattered on the field behind us. Friends lie twisted in the mud, their limbs cranked at impossible angles or missing altogether, and their faces distorted by agony or shock. Two kilometers of dirt in exchange for thousands of lives.

Cries for stretcher-bearers cut through the dense smoke. As I stand in the ruins of what used to be someone's home, wooden planks still smoldering at my feet, the weight of all the death, from Gallipoli to the Somme, crushes me until I collapse on the shattered floor, heaving out bile and bitter tears. When nothing more comes up, I throw my head back and howl until my voice dies in my throat. When I can't scream anymore, gut-wrenching sobs bend me in half. And when my sobs dry up, I pound the charred boards until my fists drip blood.

Is this what victory feels like?

Chapter Thirty-One

September 1916

The next morning, rain begins to fall, turning the whole area into a giant mudhole. The mud coats our boots as we slog north of Flers to establish a new line and prepare to push onward to Grease Trench, Switch Line, and Gird Trench, the German stronghold.

Except for the cliffs, it's just like Gallipoli—take a meter of mud, lose it, gain a German trench, lose it—a pointless exercise of innocent men sacrificed for vanity and power.

Bodies are left strewn and unburied in the field, and I can still hear the pitiful cries of the uncollected wounded. To venture into no man's land is a certain death sentence, so after the first few failed attempts, no one else tries.

Gas alarms sound the same when a morning mist rolls in and when phosgene gas threatens to fill my lungs with fluid until I drown, so all day, I remain in a constant state of panic, whether it's called for or not. Rats feed on the corpses they find under the village wreckage, and when I sit still too long, they try to nibble on me. I carve the earth with a pick and entrenching tool until my hands blister and nails split open.

I've had a belly full of all of it.

The darkness brings new horrors. Although a faint glow tints the sky from fires still burning in the ruins, it's not enough to reveal the shadows of German soldiers sneaking up on our position, so sleep is impossible unless we want to wake to our throats being slit.

As we settle into the knee-deep mud lining the trench, a major counterattack lights the sky with artillery shells shrieking overhead, thudding into the muck, and exploding in columns of mud and flame. The trench shudders with each hit. I press myself against the wall and clap my hands over my ears against the constant roar.

My world shrinks to two circles of fogged glass and the rasp of my breathing through the filter. I sense Ian against the trench wall beside me, but I can't see him for my mask. I don't speak to him, not that we could hear each other anyway. What is there to say?

We hold the line that night, if holding means shivering in the muck, half-buried, waiting for the next shell to hit. Victory? If so, victory tastes of ashes.

After Flers, the days blur into a single, ugly tapestry of fire, mud, fear, and blood. Morning. Evening. What difference does it make when the sky is perpetually grey and raining death? Buck, Ian, and I huddle in a captured German trench, which is nothing more than a shattered, half-collapsed ditch filling with water faster than we can bail. Every push forward means climbing out into no man's land, wading through muck and barbed wire, and clawing our way into another length of trench a few steps ahead. If we make it that far. The air stinks of wet clay, mold, and dead bodies.

Ian rubs his hands together, trying in vain to warm them. "So here we are again, sitting in a German hole, waiting to be blown to pieces."

Buck gives a crooked grin, though his eyes appear distant and hollow. "Better their hole than ours. At least they did the digging for us this time."

I try to force a chuckle, but it sticks in my throat. Something I've been pondering sits heavy in my chest, and my attempt to join in with their weak attempts at humor opens my mouth, so the thought pours out, unbidden. "What have we kept of ourselves?"

Ian pulls his greatcoat tighter, staring at the floor. Buck lights a cigarette, the flare brief and piercing in the gloom, then cuts his eyes toward me. "Leave it to Fin to kill the mood."

"I'm serious. After all this is over, what will be left of us?"

"I know what I'll do when we get home. First thing, I'm building a fire so hot it'll chase the cold out of my bones for good. And I'll roast me a lamb, real lamb, with rosemary." Buck smacks his lips.

Ian chuckles low. "I'll settle for a bed that isn't crawling with lice."

"Or Germans," Buck mutters.

I lean my head against the wall of the trench, the mud seeping through my hair and down the back of my neck. "I'll settle for making it home at all."

The silence that follows is a jarring statement, saying the odds are against us. But none of us dares to say it out loud.

A few minutes later, Ian's quiet voice weaves around us, almost melodic, like a whisper of grace. "The Lord is my strength and my shield; my heart trusted in him, and I am helped: therefore my heart greatly rejoiceth; and with my song will I praise him."

Buck sputters, then belts out a harsh guffaw. "Helped?" He tosses his cigarette in the mud. A finger of smoke drifts up, curling around his leg. "If this is His help, I'd hate to see His punishment."

"Buck…"

"No." Buck grinds his boot heel into the stub of his cigarette. "Don't talk to me about God. If there is a God, He's a cruel, vindictive, and hateful monster." Buck waves his arm. "What kind of God would allow—this?" Shaking his head, he spits to the side. "No, thank you. I want nothing to do with such a God."

Ian's face sags. "Don't talk like that. You'll break Granma's heart."

Buck's eyes turn hard as steel. "Granma is dead." He twirls and stalks away, disappearing around a curve in the trench.

Ian's chin falls to his chest, a brief whimper escaping his lips.

"He has a point." I rest my hand gently on Ian's arm. "It's hard to see any purpose to all of this."

"Granma always said God never promised life would be easy, but He promised He'd be with us through it all."

"I don't see evidence of God's presence anywhere."

"Then you're not looking." He places his hand on top of mine. "The three of us are still here, together, against all the odds."

"What about all those who aren't here? Will. Artie. Bulldog." Hasan. "Where was God for them? Does God not love them?"

Ian sighs. "Of course He does."

"Then why didn't He 'shield' them? They died for nothing." My words spit from my mouth and burn like lye in my ears, setting fire to my heart.

Ian wilts beneath their sting, closing his eyes as if to bar their entrance. "You don't know that."

"I do, in fact." I turn my head to glance over the lip of the trench. "If I make it out of here, God and I are going to have a reckoning."

Ian takes a slow, deep breath, then blows it out through his lips. "Don't let this war steal everything from you, Fin. Hold onto what you know, or it will consume you and leave nothing but bitterness and rage."

After a moment of heavy silence, I lift my head and face Ian. "What are you holding onto?"

"The certainty of God's love. The hope of coming home. Claire." Again, he closes his eyes. "I want to return to her the same man she fell in love with, not some ghost of myself, empty and cold, devoid of love."

"I don't have a Claire."

He grasps my arms, squeezing tight. "But one day, you will. And you'll want to be the kind of man she will love with all her heart, like my Claire."

A brief flash of Claire in Buck's arms sours my stomach. Poor Ian. He's so innocent and naïve, even now. "I just don't have your faith."

"You could. And it would give you the strength you need to get through this." Ian's eyes glisten in the dim firelight. "I love you, Fin. I don't want to lose you, too."

"I'm still here." But the expression on Ian's face says otherwise.

There's nothing left to say, so we settle in to try and get a little rest, maybe even catch a few winks. The night drags on, our fire dwindling. Out of the fog, Buck reappears, crouching low. He grins, his teeth flashing in the dim glow. "Wanna have some fun?"

I roll my eyes. "What harebrained scheme have you cooked up this time?"

"Bring your knives. Leave the rest." Without another word, he melts back into the mist.

Ian stirs. Sliding his kit aside and leaning his rifle against the trench wall, he buckles his knife to his belt.

"You're not going with him, are you?"

He looks down at me, his face a quiet lake. "If he goes alone, he won't come back. You know it's true."

Blast it all. If Ian follows, I must, too. I grab my knife, stow my rifle, and trail him through the winding trench until we find Buck perched at the end.

He points into the dark and whispers, "German line. A hundred meters."

My jaw drops. "You've lost your mind."

Buck mimes walking fingers, then draws his thumb across his throat.

"To their trench?" My words come out as a breath.

He chops the air—one, two, three. Each of us takes a man. Silent kills. Then move on.

Ian nods, already drawing his blade.

I hiss, "And when they spot us?"

"Run fast." Buck's grin is wolfish.

"That's no plan."

"Three Musketeers," Ian murmurs.

Buck grasps Ian's shoulder. "Ready?" And before I can argue, he scurries onto no man's land, crouching low.

No choice. Ian and I follow, moving like wraiths through the shadows. Somehow, we reach the German trench without being spotted. Slipping over the wall, we creep forward. Four soldiers huddle around a tin-can fire up ahead, their helmets low.

Buck signals: he'll take the two on the right, we handle the rest.

We move as one, just like when hunting back home. Our mud-coated boots slip soundlessly along the boards. In a breath, Buck charges. Our blades flash in the fire's light. My knife opens one throat. Ian drives his point under another chin. Buck dispatches his men, though the first one slumps against his comrade, alerting him. A wet gurgle ends the alarm before it begins.

Buck props the corpses against the wall, then peeks around the corner. He signals six ahead.

I shake my head fiercely. Too many.

Buck ignores me, swooping in, with his blade swinging left and right. Ian dives in after him. Growling, I follow, stabbing wildly, finding ribs and slicing tendons until their hot blood slicks my hands.

One German shrieks, "*Hilfe! Hilfe!*" Ian's knife silences him, but the cry hangs in the air, assuring our doom.

"Go! Now!" I hiss.

A soldier grapples me from behind, raising his knife to strike, but Buck buries his blade in the man's chest, wrenching him off me and finishing him off. Ian cuts the last throat, then we bolt, vaulting the trench wall and sprinting onto open ground.

Shouts erupt behind us. Rifle cracks reverberate through the air. A bullet smacks the mud at my feet, spraying a sheet of filthy water into my eyes. Blind, I double over, running until my lungs burn.

Our trench comes to life, with friendly rifles spitting staccato fire into the dark. I risk a glance back. No pursuers, only shouts of chaos from the German line.

We tumble headlong into our trench, our chests heaving and clothes covered with blood. The coppery smell follows us in a wave as we make our way back to our positions, amid the congratulations and cheers of our mates.

Without speaking, we settle down on wet blankets to try and get some sleep before the sunrise, but before we can catch our breath, Captain Riddell storms toward us, his greatcoat flapping. His jaw is set in stone.

"What in God's name was that?" His voice lashes me sharper than a whip.

At first, no one answers. Then, Buck grins, his bloody knife dangling loose in his hand. "Pretty good, eh?"

Ian straightens, silent and still. I keep my eyes on the mud.

"You three," the Captain growls. "You have just endangered every man in this sector. Do you understand that? An unsanctioned raid in the middle of the night? You kill a handful of enemy soldiers, and what do we get in return? Artillery. Retaliation. A barrage that buries good men." He steps closer, his nose almost touching Buck's. "Do you think this is some kind of game?"

"Ten. Ten soldiers." Buck's grin fades but not entirely. "We got them so they can't get us."

"Silence!" the Captain barks. "You are not American cowboys on the frontier. You're soldiers in His Majesty's army, and you'll follow orders or hang for treason."

The silence stretches on, thick as the fog. My stomach sinks. He's right. Every word is right.

But then the Captain's gaze shifts and softens a little. His voice drops low. "Still, God help me, there's courage in what you did. Even if it was reckless." He lets the words hang, then straightens and brushes them away. "Clean yourselves up. And if I hear of anything like this again, you'll be on burial detail for a month."

When he stalks off, Buck is the first to break the silence. "See? He liked it. He'd do the same if he weren't tied down by command."

Ian frowns. "Don't twist his words. He admired the courage, not the act. There's a difference."

"What difference?" Buck blows a loud breath through his lips. "Courage is courage. Kill them before they kill us. That's the only rule worth keeping."

Ian shakes his head, his eyes narrowing. "That wasn't courage, Buck. It was pride. There's a difference between fighting for survival and hunting men like beasts."

"It weren't pride! I was only…"

Their voices grind against each other like steel on steel. I can't stand one more second of it.

"You're both wrong. It was madness." I swallow hard, the words lodged for a moment in my throat. "We weren't soldiers tonight. We were butchers."

Buck turns away, his jaw tight, while Ian studies me with those wide, pitying eyes. His look cuts deeper than any German knife.

And in that silence, the rift opens wider between us. Buck chasing glory—or death. Not sure which one. Ian clinging to his faith and naïve hope. And me, left stuck in the mud with the blood of boys on my hands.

Chapter Thirty-Two

June 1917

Before September ends, our division rotates off the line to Armentières, replaced by recruits fresh from training, poor souls. Captain Riddell tells us a major offensive is in the works, and we're to play a key role. I don't relish the thought of another frontal assault, but it's better than sitting in the same stinking mud until my flesh rots.

Training is relentless, carrying on day and night for weeks. We drill coordinated maneuvers with British, Irish, and Australian forces, pushing until every soldier moves as one and every step is perfect. The Māori dug replica German trenches for our rehearsals, making this round of training disturbingly real. Sadly, the Māori Pioneer Battalion rotated out before we returned, so we missed Mani. Seeing him would have done us all good. As it is, Buck and I barely speak, and Ian wears the worry of it on his face like a permanent shadow.

The three of us crouch in the half-finished trench, the smell of damp wood and freshly turned earth thick in the air. A whistle shrills, and the line of men surges forward, their boots pounding over duckboards. I heave myself up and follow, my rifle digging into my shoulder and my breath coming in gasps as we run the timed drill.

"Keep your bloody spacing, Fin!" Buck bellows from two men down. "You're bunched too tight!"

I grit my teeth, forcing my feet wider, though the urge is to press in close, Safety in numbers. "You worry about yourself," but my throat is too tight to shout, so he doesn't hear.

By the time we throw ourselves down in the replica trench, with mud smeared on our faces and uniforms, Buck is grinning, cocky as ever. "That's how it's done. Clean sweep. Quick and dirty."

I brush a wad of muck from my rifle. "You think the Germans are going to wait for us to line up proper before he fires his machine guns?"

Buck's grin falls, his jaw tightening. Ian, crouched between us, sets a steadying hand on my shoulder. "Fin, he's only trying to keep us alive. Discipline produces success."

I swing my head toward Ian, heat flaring in my chest. "Discipline didn't save Will. And it won't save us either."

For a moment, I cringe, regretting my harsh words, but Ian's face remains calm, though his eyes are heavy with sorrow. "Maybe not." He lowers his eyes. "But faith will."

Buck rolls his eyes, reaching for his canteen. "Here we go again."

But I can't look away from Ian. Somehow, in the middle of all the blood and death, he believes that God still sees us. And though I want to dismiss it, the part of me that lies awake at night replaying Hasan's dying gasp aches for the faith that carries him.

Our billet is a drafty wooden barn on the edge of town, filled with the smell of hay, wet wool, and leather. We huddle close to a sputtering fire, our conversations drowned out by the rain beating against the tin roof. Boots and tunics hang from makeshift lines, dripping mud onto the straw.

Buck leans against a post, chewing on a crust of bread. "I'll tell you what keeps a man alive," he shouts, gesturing with the bread. "Not prayers. It's keeping your head down and your eyes sharp. Courage and grit, that's all."

I hunch on my kitbag, turning my mess tin over in my hands, watching the light flicker on the roughhewn walls. The faces of the dead float around me in the smoke, demanding answers, but I have none to give.

Ian shifts closer, his face pale in the glow. "I don't pretend it makes sense. But I know this. God hasn't abandoned us. Every shell that doesn't find me, every morning I wake, that's His grace. And when the worst comes, even then…" He pauses, raising his eyes to the pitched ceiling. "Even then, He'll carry me through. Death doesn't get the last word."

Buck snorts. "Easy to say now, with a roof over our heads. Let's see you preach it when the shells are falling."

Ian's gaze doesn't waver. "I'll say it then. too."

For a long time, we don't speak. The rain drums the rhythm of a dirge, I trace the rim of the tin with my thumb, and my chest tightens with the flood of memories.

I want to believe Ian. Lord, I want to. But all I can see are the faces of the dead.

Finally, Buck tosses the last of his bread aside, sighing. "Well, if faith keeps you steady, Ian, then hang onto it. Just don't expect me to start praying."

Ian smiles faintly, though sadness lingers in his eyes. "I won't force it on you, but I'll keep praying for both of you. Always."

I don't answer. I can't. But when the fire flickers low and the three of us lie back on makeshift pallets of straw, I whisper into the dark, hoping my words make it through the storm, though I'm not sure if I mean it as a curse or a plea: *God, don't leave us here.*

We've been waiting forever, packed tight, chest to back, shoulder to shoulder in the forward trenches. The air hangs thick around us, smelling of cow dung, body odor, and fear. Officers speak in clipped whispers. Engineers and Māori diggers disappear for hours underground. Ian prays more often than usual. Buck, always restless, cracks jokes that ring hollow.

At 3:10 in the morning, the world splits open.

The ground beneath us heaves like waves in a storm. A deafening roar swallows every other sound, booming louder than heaven's thunder at the coming of the Lord, until the bones in my chest vibrate and my ears bleed. The ridge before us erupts in a column of flame and smoke, as geysers of earth launch skyward, blotting out the stars, and the entire ridge collapses into a vast, gaping hole where the German line was dug in, waiting for our advance.

The blast knocks us back and would've brought me to my knees had I not been pressed on every side. Dirt rains down in great clods, pelting us, but we've no way to duck and nowhere to move.

Then, an eerie silence descends, as if the whole world is stunned and paralyzed by the shock of it.

When a whistle shrills, we rise as a single mass, moving forward through the thick haze, rifles in hand. The land ahead is no longer a ridge or trenches. It's—gone. The entire German front line has vanished, consumed by the earth, just as the ground swallowed Korah and his followers for rebelling against Moses. We pass by what remains, nothing but twisted wire, splintered timbers, bodies flung like rag dolls, and the vast hole created by our buried mines.

Buck whoops, charging ahead with his knife in his teeth and his bayonet poised. Ian follows behind Buck, his lips moving in what looks like a silent prayer, and his eyes fixed on the strewn bodies as we creep forward like a spreading fire. I stumble along beside Ian, choking on the dust, my ears ringing, and every nerve in my body screaming.

Messines looms ahead, half-hidden in smoke. The few German survivors form the explosion scramble up from crater or out from under the rubble, their faces white as chalk. Some fire wildly, and others throw down their weapons and flee.

Ian fires precise, measured shots, each squeeze of his trigger an act of duty that wounds his soul. Buck leaps headlong into the crater, wrestling a soldier to the ground in a frenzy of shouts and fists, then taking on another.

A boy barely as old as Hasan staggers from the wreckage a half meter in front of me. His helmet is gone, and his face is cut and bloodied. He looks straight through me with eyes wide and rimmed in white. My hands shake on my rifle. He could be Will or Hasan or one of the many hundreds of ghosts I've created since Gallipoli.

The boy raises his hands, muttering something I can't understand.

"Fin!" Ian's voice snaps me to the present moment. His hand shoves me to the ground just as a shot pops off.

The shot came from the boy, who had pulled a pistol from his belt unseen by my eyes. Ian drops him with a single round to his chest.

The boy falls, his mouth open in a silent cry, smoke curling from the end of the pistol still clutched in his hand.

I gawk at Ian who touches my shoulder. "Don't carry this one, brother."

But I know I will, like I carry the others in my nightmares and my waking torment.

Slowly, we press forward into Messines, facing a German resistance that has little hope of success. Truth is, most of their resistance is buried beneath tons of dirt and ash in a crater we exploded into existence from beneath the earth. My mates say it's a great victory. But for me, it's another slaughter, adding thousands onto the pile of bodies already crushing me.

The guns fall silent at last, though their echoes are etched into my bones and ringing in my ears. Messines Ridge is ours. The officers call it a triumph, a model of precise planning, coordination, and execution. They don't mention the torn flesh, the splintered trees, the fractured earth, or the faces of boys on both sides blank with shock as they bleed out in the mud. Every time someone slaps me on the shoulder, congratulating our victory, I feel nauseous. What type of victory leaves the ground carpeted in corpses?

In a few days, we will rotate to the rear lines, once again relieved by green recruits. But for now, I trudge beside my brothers with my eyes down, counting boots instead of seeing faces. Then, a booming laugh rolls over me from a work detail of the Pioneer Battalion, busy digging the trenches for the new front line. It's Mani, broader now, his shoulders corded from months of digging, but his grin hasn't changed a lick since the days we played together back home.

"Fin!" He drops his shovel, brushing dirt from his hands, and drags me into an embrace so tight it nearly knocks the wind out of me. "Ian! Buck!" Ian's face beams like sunlight breaking through dense clouds, and even Buck's sour sneer eases for a moment.

He falls into step with us, showing us the trenches his men are carving across the sodden fields. "We dig and build so you mates can fight." His broad smile shows his teeth, bright against his dark skin. "You see? We dig great big tunnel and make big boom. That was Māori." His chest puffs up. "Keep my friends alive." He elbows me and winks.

"Not all of them." A moan rumbles in my chest.

"Hey, we made it, didn't we?" Buck slaps Mani on the back. "Thanks, brother."

Mani's eyes soften as he studies me. "Seen too much already, brother. No let it eat you."

I want to argue, to tell him that the blood will never wash off my hands, but Mani wraps his arm around my shoulders and drags me into the rhythms of his laughter. For a few hours, with just the four of us around a fire, sharing memories from our youth in New Zealand and stories of our time apart, I almost believe him.

But far too soon, we're pulled away, marching off to training grounds where officers bark at us through endless drills. We charge at dummy pillboxes, dive into replica trenches, and fit our masks until the reek of rubber chokes us. They say this is preparation for another push, this time through the Ypres salient in Belgium. The men whisper the name of the place like a curse: Passchendaele.

By September, we're back near the front. The ground is already turning to soup beneath our boots from the constant shells falling day and night, gouging craters that fill with water until men literally drown in them. And then there are the rumors of how impregnable the defenses are, and how many divisions before us have broken against their strong German wall.

Watching Ian's peaceful grace, Mani's pride at his contribution and lack of complaint despite his bleeding hands and stooped back, and even Buck's determination and force of will, I try to hold onto their strength, but the truth drags me into an abyss as large and black as the crater on the ridge. As horrific as Messines was, it isn't the end. It is only the beginning.

CHAPTER THIRTY-THREE

October 1917

The rain never stops. By the time October comes, the land has become a swamp. Old trenches collapse into piles of unburied bodies and mud. Duckboards, once used to navigate the soaked ground, float by us on seas of muck. Horses, men, and machinery alike sink into the mire. Each step is a battle. Boots cling to the mud like the earth is determined to drag us under.

We move out at dawn, slogging toward Gravenstafel Spur. Mani marches with us this time, his shovel slung over his back beside his rifle. "No point digging trenches when ground no hold."

"So, you're going to fight, Mani?"

"Yes. All Māori fight." He's seen the horrors of this war firsthand, yet he appears to be facing battle with a confident resolve. I can't help but be impressed. Mani glances my way, his gentle, knowing smile providing a tether I didn't know I needed.

As at Messines, the artillery and tanks roll out ahead of us. But this time, the weather conditions defeat the best laid plans. Tank engines drown in water-filled bomb craters. Artillery bogs down, holding up our line, so the barrage fails to put a dent in German defenses. Every time the whistles blow, we stumble forward, only to be swallowed in an ocean of mud where the German machine guns can cut wide swathes through our lines. Men fall and vanish into the sludge, their hands clawing for help before the swamp closes over them.

Out of desperation, I mumble, "Dear Lord, please don't let me drown in the mud." But I hold little hope my childish begging is heard in the heavens.

Because the mud is so deep and thick, we can't see where the Germans have spread barbed wire across our path. Each tentative step holds the risk of being snared, and everyone who gets caught in the wire hangs there for target practice for the Germans, their bodies spasming with each bullet. Easy pickin's.

Another whistle blows, so we press forward, only to overtake the mired artillery, leaving us laid bare for the slaughter. Our own artillery shells start landing on our line, killing more than the enemy's bullets, and the line disintegrates into chaos.

Then, a yellow-orange fog drifts across the battlefield, and the cry of alarm rings out. "Gas! Gas! Gas!"

I don my mask while slogging through the mud toward the German lines, figuring I'm safer there than where our line is stalled since our artillery isn't coming close to reaching the Germans. The pungent stench of mustard gas tastes bitter in my mouth. Buck appears beside me, bellowing as he plunges into a German trench, his face reddening as the mustard gas does its work. I whip my head around, trying to find Ian, but I can't see beyond the reach of my bayonet.

The mud seems to roll beneath my feet. My ears ring and my chest aches with constant vibration from the cacophony of agonized screams, booming explosions, and the stuttering roar of machine guns. It engulfs me until my thoughts scatter like ashes in the wind, and all I can think is *run, run, run,* but I don't know where.

Then, Buck appears out of the fog, his face battered and bloodied, waving his arm. "This way! Attack! Attack!"

A few men draw toward his call. He waves his arm and cries, "Follow me! Forward!"

He takes off, his arm still in the air, continuing his cry. I turn to follow him.

Suddenly, everything screeches to a stop, except for a single, buzzing sound followed by a strange pop, like someone slurping the last drop of a cup of cocoa, and something biting my leg. A screaming pain blossoms, radiating up to my chest as I teeter and fall face-first into the mud.

This is it.

Seconds pass, or maybe minutes. A hand pulls at my arm and slowly flips me onto my back. Ian looms above me. "Fin! Are you hit?"

I don't know. My mouth works but nothing comes out.

He paws over my chest, looking for blood or wounds, working his way down, but when he gets to my legs, his mouth gapes and his eyes widen. "Oh, Fin."

"What?" The word mires in my mouth like the tanks in the mud, sounding more like mush than a word.

"We must get out of here."

Somehow, Ian lifts me to my feet. The pain doubles me over, but Ian sweeps me up and over his shoulder. As he spins away from the German line, a second popping sound hits like a slap, and Ian jerks beneath me. Then a third pop, a final twitch, and Ian collapses to his knees.

"No! No! *No!* Ian!" I slide from his arms and grab his shoulders. "Ian!"

His brow furrows, his lips parting slightly as though the words he wanted to say slipped from his grasp. His eyes shift to stare at some distant point on the far horizon, taking on a dreamy cast.

Oh, God, what do I do? "Buck! Buck!"

Ian closes his mouth, and a half-smile graces the corners. "It's warm," he whispers.

"No, Ian. Stay with me." Ever so gently, I lower him to the ground.

His eyes shift again, looking through me. "Fin."

"I'm here."

"Promise me."

"You can't die. I won't let you." I press my hands into the blood pouring from the two wounds in his chest.

"Promise me you will take care of Claire."

"You're gonna take care of her yourself. You'll get married and have babies…"

"Promise me."

I stare at my baby brother, the best man I've ever known, and shame rips through me like a scythe. If he dies instead of me because he tried to save me…

"Fin, promise me."

My heart sinks into a pit in my gut, and lies there, burning and writhing. "I promise." The hardest words I've ever spoken.

"And promise me…" Ian gasps in a ragged breath. "Promise you won't give up on God."

"I promise."

Another gasp, shorter this time. "This…isn't." Air wheezes through his throat, seeking entry, failing. "…your…fault."

His eyes lift, seeing past the mustard gas, smoke, and black rain clouds to gaze longingly into the heavens. "I see."

His mouth goes slack.

I lean my head back and wail, a rough-edged, gritty howl ending in a sharp, sucking hiss as I run out of breath. I clutch my brother to my chest, bellowing louder until my chest heaves, and I take a shuddering gulp of the rancid air, then sob in jagged bursts as pain claws the inside of my chest and tears stream through the mud covering my face. I rock him like a bairn, as if I could press him back into his body or force him to awaken. Nothing.

A shriek shatters the darkness. Buck races to us, sliding through the mud to skid to a stop beside Ian, grabbing him from my arms. He shakes Ian's limp body. "Ian!"

Buck shoves his ear against Ian's nose, then against his chest, before he sits on his haunches, staring at our brother. Horror blanches his face beneath the scalding burns from the mustard gas and rims his eyes in white. "Not Ian."

"He tried to save me." It's all I can muster as an explanation.

"Not *Ian.*" Buck launches skyward with an explosive roar, his feet churning up the mud as he races toward the German line, his eyes wild with rage. As he disappears into the clouds of mustard gas, the last thing

I see is him firing into the face of a German soldier at point-blank range. I still hear his screams long after he's out of sight.

I lie in the muddy soup of no man's land, holding Ian—I don't know how long—as the Germans advance and our troops retreat around us. Perhaps we're invisible because we're coated with mud, or maybe we both appear dead upon a cursory glance, but no one bothers to check on us. No one offers help.

As darkness advances across the sky, a large figure, shrouded in shadow, pauses to stand over us. He doesn't speak, so I can't tell if he's German or one of our allies, and at this point, I'm beyond caring. A quick gasp of air breaks the heavy silence, and his hand flies to his mouth.

"Fin?"

My head weighs a thousand kilograms, but I do my best to lift my eyes and see the face of my savior.

His strong arms scoop me up as if I weigh no more than a wee bird and tosses me over his shoulders so I'm draped around his neck, then he cradles Ian gently in his arms. His voice is low as he whispers, "I carry you home."

"Mani?"

He grunts, then slogs through the mud, but he doesn't speak again until we reach the Regimental Aid Post, just beyond the front line, squatting in the side of a half-collapsed trench. The sandbagged entrance opens onto a low, dank chamber dug into the chalk and mud. The air inside is stifling, thick with the smell of copper, iodine, and vague whiffs of ether. Lanterns burn low, casting long shadows over the hunched forms of doctors tending men sprawled on stretchers, some groaning and writhing in pain, and others deathly still.

A stretcher-bearer shuffles toward Mani, his voice low but hurried.

"One dead. One wounded," Mani mutters. The stretcher bearer takes Ian from Mani's arms, then Mani lowers me onto an empty cot.

Buckets overflow with bloody bandages, but they don't manage to keep the blood from splattering over the floor and walls. Beside me, a medical officer works on a soldier whose open chest is black with blood, his hands sewing in a weary, almost futile rhythm until he heaves a deep sigh, wipes his brow, and gestures for a stretcher-bearer to take him away.

This place is more of a holding pen than a hospital, where they patch up what they can or tag the body either for transport to the rear or burial.

Ian. His toe will be tagged for burial. *I'll never see him again.* I struggle to raise myself from the filthy cot, but Mani presses me down. "No get up, Fin. Bad shape. Very much bad."

In the weak light of the lanterns, I can finally see his face, streaked with mud and a wash of flowing tears. His black curls are matted with blood. "Are you hurt? Your head."

Mani blinks, then waves a hand in dismissal when the doctor tries to check him. He points to my leg. "Must hurry. Save leg."

Save my leg?

The doctor cuts my uniform pants open, chewing his lip at what he finds. "I doubt we can save the leg. Infection is already setting in."

"You won't cut off my leg. *No*, sir."

The doctor wilts under my glare. "Son, if you won't let me cut off your leg, which is your greatest chance for survival, we'll use this new Thomas splint and hope for the best. But if we don't get that infection cleaned out, you'll die without an amputation."

"Then, clean it. Because you are not taking my leg. I'd rather die."

He prods the open wound with his fingers, and a scream escapes my lips. As a gray haze passes over my eyes, the last thing I hear is, "The bone is shattered."

I awaken under bright lights on a bed with white sheets and a nurse dressed in white fussing over a tube hanging from a pole, carrying liquid into my arm.

"Where's Mani?" My mouth feels full of cotton, and my tongue is swollen, so I don't know if she understands me. "Mani?"

"Lie still, now. You've had a bad go of it."

My leg. With the thimbleful of strength I have, I snatch the sheet off, then breathe a deep sigh. A traction apparatus holds up a thick, white cast covering my leg. They didn't cut it off.

"Thank the Lord."

The nurse raises her brows. "You're lucky." She fusses a moment more with the tubing, then struts to a bed on the other side of the room, where a soldier lies, his eyes covered in bandages and his skin mottled with blisters. Mustard gas.

"Where am I?" I call after the nurse.

"Ypres."

"How long have I been out?"

But the nurse strides away without answering.

Over the next few days, I learn that after the RAP, I was taken to the Casualty Clearing Station near Ypres, where the doctors gave me blood, debrided the wound, removed the bullet, and put my leg in a cast. Apparently, Mani was by my side the whole time, refusing to let them cut off my leg. They tell me that when the doctor finally agreed, Mani passed out from his head wound and was taken for immediate surgery.

"Where did they take him? Did he make it?"

No one seems to know.

With nothing else to do but lie in this bed and wait for the bone to heal, I'm constantly tortured by Ian's death, from accusations, guilt, and regret to the unbearable, wrenching grief. I relive that day at Passchendaele repeatedly, searching for a way out of it, for something—anything I could've done differently that would've saved him.

If I hadn't been confused and scared, running willy-nilly, but had been strong like Ian, maybe he'd still be alive. If I hadn't followed Buck, fool that he was that day, then I might not have been shot, and Ian wouldn't have tried to carry me off the line. If I had been more forceful with him and made him retreat with the others, he'd be with us still. Oh, why didn't I make him put me down? I didn't even try to tell him no.

And once he was shot, I flailed around like a sheep stuck in barbed wire, doing nothing while he bled to death. Buck would've done something. He would've known what to do.

He should've been there. Why wasn't he there? Why didn't he come when I called him?

Where is he?

After weeks in traction, they approve me walking with crutches. My muscles scream at me, and I lose my breath after a few steps, but I press forward, wandering the grounds around the field hospital, searching in the various tents for Mani. It takes several days, but at last, I find him in a partially bombed chalet, now converted into a recovery center.

The place has a kind of smell that never seems to wash away, even when the nurses fling the windows wide to let the sea air in, the reek of decaying flesh, urine, and vomit. I hobble on my crutches between rows of iron beds, looking for soldiers I recognize, until a familiar face catches my eye near the end of the second row.

Mani.

His head is wrapped in layers of white bandages, leaving his dark hair sticking out at odd angles. One eye is swollen, and that whole side of his face glows a greenish-purple. He's propped up against a thin pillow, his eyes closed, and his large, calloused hands crossed over his chest.

"Mani?" My voice cracks.

He looks up slowly, like he's dragging himself from a deep sleep. But when his eyes find mine, they light up, not with joy but with weary relief. "Fin."

I cross the few steps to his bed, my leg screaming with every movement, and grip the rail. Up close, he looks even worse. His skin has a washed-out pallor beneath the deep bronze, but the vaguely distant look in his eyes is what takes my breath away, like he's gone somewhere else.

"You saved me." The words tumble out. "You carried Ian and me when you were injured yourself."

Mani's lips press tightly together. His words are halting and sluggish, almost as if he's bewildered. "Ian is gone."

The truth spoken aloud by my friend cuts through me like shrapnel. I swallow hard, my knuckles white on the bedframe. "You should've saved yourself. You nearly died, Mani."

His gaze locks onto mine, steady despite the fog over his eyes. "You are my…brothers. Not…leaving you."

I shake my head, tears blurring the ward. "I've gone over and over it, the moment Ian fell. The sound of the bullets hitting him." I close my eyes against the vision. "The way I couldn't—" My voice breaks, and I press my fist against my mouth to keep from sobbing aloud. "I should've…I should've…"

Mani drags his hand to lay over mine. His arms are terribly weak, but he manages to keep his hand from trembling. "Do not. Do not carry…blame. Ian was…who he was. This…you know."

I bow my head, shoulders shaking.

"Be *kaha*," Mani whispers. "For him…for me."

I gaze down upon him, so thin, bandaged, bruised, pale, but still unbroken, and my shame deepens, my weakness exposed. Here he is, comforting and encouraging me while he lingers near the edge of death.

I shouldn't be here, bothering him, asking him to carry me. Again.

"I'm sorry, Mani." I shake the remnants of tears from my eyes. "I'm so sorry."

"You…did nothing…to Mani." Mani's lips curve in the faintest ghost of a smile. "I…love you…brother."

"And I love you." I lower my head. "We lost so much that day."

"True." He breathes out a shuddering sigh. "Also true…we are still here." He closes his eyes and drifts away to that space between life and death.

Since that's all I have, it will have to be enough for now.

PART FOUR

A richer dust concealed

CHAPTER THIRTY-FOUR

January 1918

"The doctors approved my discharge from service. I'm cleared to leave the hospital." I lounge on the end of Mani's bed, with my cast stretched out under the next cot and my crutches propped against the rail. Mani remains bedridden, and although the doctors aren't sure what is causing his paralysis, they say they are still hopeful he will make a full recovery.

"Much…good news."

I pout my lips with a frown. "I don't want to leave you."

He blinks, and as he often does, stares into someplace beyond my vision. After a few moments, he shifts his eyes and offers a half-smile. "Mani…goes home. Soon."

But which home does he mean?

"Fin…no worry. Mani *kaha.*"

"Stronger than anyone I know." I swallow my tears, wanting Mani to believe that I, too, am *kaha.*

"No say…*haere rā.* Say *kia ora.*"

I clasp his hand to my chest. "*Kia ora,* my brother. Promise me you will fight to get better."

"Promise…come home…visit Mani."

"I promise." Now, my tears flow, unbidden. "I love you, brother."

"*Kia ora, kauaemua. Aroha ana ahau ki a ko.*"

After our tearful goodbye, I make my way to the command post, housed in a bombed-out structure on the outskirts of Ypres.

I'm sent to Major General Russell, the New Zealand division commander, for my formal discharge and transport orders from Belgium. But when I'm announced, the commander's face turns red with fury.

"MacAlister. You are one of Sergeant Buck MacAlister's brothers, is that correct?"

"Yessir." Oh, Lord, what did he do now?

The commander lowers his eyes. "I'm sorry for your loss, son. I've heard nothing but good things about your brother, Ian. He is a genuine hero."

I bite the inside of my lip and swallow down the lump building in my throat. "Yessir, he is. He saved my life."

"And the lives of many others, I understand. I'm sure he will receive a posthumous commendation." He clears his throat. "Now, about your other brother."

"Yessir?"

"Do you have any idea where he might be?"

My eyebrows bunch for a moment. "I assume, still on the front lines, sir." I tilt my head with a frown. "Is he not?"

"No one has seen him since the first battle at Passchendaele. He is AWOL."

My throat clenches shut. He must've been captured—or killed. "The last time I saw him, it was on the battlefield. He was charging toward the German lines." I gulp down the choking squeeze. "Do you think he was…captured?" The Germans are not known for favorable treatment of prisoners of war.

"No, we do not. Several men report seeing him running across the open field and into a thick wood, *away* from the battle." Russell's eyes narrow. "I know he is your brother, but you have an obligation to report his location so he may be properly disciplined."

"I don't know where he is, sir." I hand him a bundle of documents, signed by my doctors, attesting to the severity of my wound, which, even without paper, is obvious enough. "I haven't heard from him."

Russell sits with a thump, signs my discharge, and shoves the papers into my hands. When I don't leave right away, he looks up through his thick brows. "Now what do you want?"

"I'm hoping after transport to England that I may be allowed to return to America instead of New Zealand. My home before I joined was in America, and I'd like to return home. If that is acceptable."

He waves his fingers in dismissal. "Very well. See the sergeant. He will draw up the orders. But you'll need to find your own passage to America, which might prove quite difficult at this time." His gray eyes glint as he stares into mine. "If you hear from your brother, you are to contact me at once." He sits back, his eyes narrowing again. "See if you can convince him to turn himself in. It would go well for him to do so."

I know what "go well" means—a court-martial and life imprisonment, which I suppose is better than a firing squad. "Yessir."

What would possess Buck to run like that? He seemed to enjoy the war—almost.

They billet me with other wounded scheduled for medical discharge for a few days before we board a hospital ship and cross the channel to England. There, I'm housed until it's time to take off my cast and given physiotherapy to help recover some use of my leg.

At first, I can't put any weight on it at all. But gradually, my muscles rebuild until my leg can support my weight. Soon, I'm walking with a cane, but the reconstruction aides tell me I will have a limp for the rest of my life.

I've never felt so alone.

Ian is dead. Buck is missing. Mani is far from himself. And who do I have to go home to? Granma is gone. Granda has lost his mind. I've never been fond of Uncle Liam, Aunt Julianna, or Samuel, who was more Buck's pal, and Uncle Chris' boys, Tom and Mac, never had anything to do with me. Which leaves Katy. And Claire.

Claire, whom Ian asked me to care for in his stead. But how can I? He asked me, not knowing I've loved her since we first came to the farm. Would he have been so quick to ask me to look out for her if he knew I harbored anger and envy toward him, and had contemplated trying to woo her myself?

Trying to arrange passage on one of the few steamships risking the trip across the Atlantic, what with German U-boats patrolling the waters, is a bigger challenge than I thought. Tickets are scarce, but my army pension check makes it possible, and after several days of walking London streets during the day and hiding in shelters with strangers to escape the Zeppelin bombings at night, I finally secure a lower berth on a Cunard ship, the *Mauretania.* Twelve days later, after taking a circuitous route to avoid the U-boats, the ship arrives in Manhattan.

America is now part of this war, so as a wounded soldier in uniform, although a foreign one, I receive a warm, hospitable welcome. Strangers come up to me on the street and ask me about the war—where I fought, how many Germans I killed, how was I wounded, what was it like on the Somme. I offer as few details as possible without being rude. When they discover I fought in the doomed Gallipoli campaign, their interest peaks even more. It's driving me up the wall, but still, I hesitate to board the train for Atlanta.

What kind of greeting will I receive there? Do they know Ian is dead? What have they heard about Buck?

Will Granda blame me for all of it?

How I wish I could take a different train, one heading west to San Francisco for a visit with Uncle Bear. But first, my obligation is to Granda, and to Claire. I must tell them how Ian died a hero and take responsibility for my failure to bring him home. So, I made my way midtown to Seventh Avenue, prepared to face the music.

The train shudders and groans as it pulls away from the great cavern of Pennsylvania Station, steam hissing into the night air. I sink into the heavy leather seat, the compartment smelling of polished brass, and the lingering scent of tobacco. The steady thrum of the wheels over the rails is almost soothing, though I still jump at every sharp clack when the train passes over a gap in the rail where two sections connect—too close to the sound of gunfire.

Through the smudged glass of the window, the sprawl of New York City flickers by in a blur of gas lamps, tenements, and smoking factory stacks. Before long, the city gives way to darkened fields and isolated farmhouses, their windows glowing faintly like watchfires in the night. How many of those homes await their loved ones coming home from Europe? How many will never see their sons again?

By morning, the train rumbles into Washington, D.C. Porters in crisp uniforms hurry down the platform, calling out destinations and hoisting trunks as new passengers board. I step off to stretch my stiff leg, then reboard and settle in for the long haul as the train swings south through Virginia, with its green countryside of wide, rolling fields.

Granda fought on these fields, so many years ago. I've heard the stories a hundred times, about the horrors of the Wilderness, the battle for Richmond, and how he got his nickname. He first met Granma when he convalesced at their home, and he saved her life and her entire family from the fires when Richmond burned.

As the hours drag on, I doze, lulled by the rhythmic sway of the cars and the low murmur of fellow travelers, but my peace is short-lived as a dream startles me awake with a yelp. By that time, the light is fading from the sky, and the aroma of roast beef and potatoes drifts through the corridors.

The further south we travel, the warmer the air becomes, even this deep in winter. Pines replace oaks, red clay replaces loam, and the accents of new passengers thicken into the familiar drawl of the South. I press my forehead against the cool glass, watching the small towns slip past, marveling at how similar they are to the small towns of France and Belgium. Only these towns aren't filled with bombed-out buildings and craters from artillery shells.

By the second morning, the tracks curve into Atlanta. The city's red-brick warehouses rise on the horizon as the train pulls into the station, bustling with soldiers, farmers, and factory workers. As the train squeals to a halt, I clutch my small kitbag to my chest. Have I left one war to walk into another? My chest tightens with stirrings of a familiar feeling—anticipation mixed with terror and exhaustion.

I clomp down the narrow metal steps and make my way through the depot to purchase my ticket for the final stretch to Blue Ridge. The L&N train doesn't leave for a couple of hours, so I wander down Forsyth Street in search of a meal, or at least some coffee.

I limp into a soda shop and sit on a stool covered in red leather, order a ham and cheese sandwich, and try to imagine the farm without Ian and Buck. The echoing loneliness returns, squelching my appetite, so after a couple of bites, I thank the young waitress.

"What's the matter, hon? You didn't like the sandwich?"

"It's very good. I guess I'm not that hungry after all."

She beams a smile. "Let me wrap that up for you, then. You can finish it later." While she wraps the sandwich in wax paper and stuffs it into a paper bag, I take a final sip of my soda.

"Thank you, ma'am."

She chuckles, bowing slightly at the waist. "Why, you're most welcome, kind sir."

I open my mouth to ask her name, but before I humiliate myself, I clamp my teeth together, spin around, and limp out as quickly as I can manage.

When I return to the station, families gather in clusters, greeting new arrivals or sending sons off to war with tearful goodbyes, but I sit apart, the weight of emptiness pressing inside me until I swear my chest might burst. When at last my train is called, I board the train, a cloud of dread hanging cold around me, mixed with the sting of grief and longing. The whistle's shrill cry urges me onward toward what remains of home.

The train hisses as it rolls into the station, a plume of steam rising from the engine, with the brakes squealing and smoke rolling over the platform. My heart pounds as hard as it did under shellfire. Through the grimy window, I catch the first glimpse of home in three and a half years. The ridge line rises, blue-gray against the winter sky, their familiar outlines etched deep in my memory.

The conductor's call echoes down the car: "Blue Ridge! Blue Ridge station!"

I shoulder my kitbag. My leg protests the movement, but I bite my lip and ignore it, stepping down onto the wooden platform with a sharp breath. The air smells clean and pine-scented, quite a change from the Somme or the cliffs of Gallipoli, but the smoke from the locomotive curls like battlefield haze, and I have to steady myself against the railing until the world rights again.

I limp down Main Street to the end of the block, then left to the livery stables, owned by Mr. Callahan, a friend of my Granda. His weathered face breaks into a grin. "Well, I'll be. Thought I'd never see the day. Welcome home, Fin."

"Hello, Mr. Callahan."

"I bet yer folk be 'bout to bust to see ye."

I manage a nod, but my chest clenches, choking my words.

Callahan smiles gently. "What can I do fer ye, Fin?"

."I wonder if I could borrow a horse." I lift my cane. "I'm not sure I can make the walk anymore."

Mr. Callahan shakes his head, wagging a finger. "Come with me."

I follow him into the stables, where he tacks up a horse and hitches him to a wagon. "Ye ain't ridin' a horse up the mountain on that gimp leg, not as long as I'm a-breathin'. I'd be proud to take ye home myself." He takes my kitbag and tosses it into the back, then gives me a hand up.

I climb awkwardly into the wagon, the boards creaking under my weight. As the old horse plods from the stables, I sit back and enjoy the familiar rhythm of the wheels running over the ruts and ridges as we follow the winding path up the mountainside.

Following the kindness of the young waitress, Mr. Callahan's unexpected warmth and generosity open a small crack in my steel-hard armor, and for the first time since my journey home began, I let myself breathe deeply. The farm lies ahead, and yes, so do all my ghosts. I'm just not sure what will greet me first.

As we cross the boundary of our land, mist coats my eyes, as thick as the fog settling into the valley between the mountains. I'm home. For so long, I was certain I'd never see it again; yet, here I am.

Only I never expected to arrive alone.

Mr. Callahan brings the horse and wagon to a stop by the front porch, helps me down, grabs my bag, and carries it to the door. "I'll be a-goin' now. Don't want to intrude on your homecomin'."

"You're welcome to stay and visit with Granda. I know he'd love to see you." And I'd love the distraction.

But Callahan shakes his head. "Hope to see ye around town." With that, he mounts the wagon and snaps the reins.

"Thank you, Mr. Callahan."

He tips his hat as he rolls away. "Welcome home."

He rides away, leaving me standing by the front door. The farm seems unnaturally quiet. No young boys tumbling down the hill, roughhousing. No little girls giggling, their curls bouncing in the breeze as they chase the chickens. I don't even hear any cows lowing in the fields. Is anyone home?

My curiosity overcomes my fear enough to lift my hand, but before I can knock, the wooden door swings open and Katy peers around the edge. For a moment, we stare at each other, then her eyes pop, and she squeals with delight, shoving her fist in her mouth.

"It's you! I can't believe it!"

I can't help but grin at her exuberance. Shrugging, I lift my palms. "It's me."

She screams again, leaping onto my chest, her arms clutching my neck in a viselike grip. Releasing my cane handle to catch her, I stagger back and almost fall down the steps.

"Whoa! Be careful. I don't want to drop you."

"It's wonderful to see you. Oh, I've missed you so much." She squeezes me in a hug, laying her head on my chest.

"I've missed you, too."

She grabs my arm. "Come in! Granda is going to be thrilled."

Will he? Or will my news sour everything?

Katy yanks my arm, but I hold up my hand. "Wait, let me get my bag." I sling my kitbag over my shoulder and grab my cane as she drags me into the foyer and down the hall to the sitting room, where Granda sits in his big chair, looking out the window at the mountains, much as when I left him.

"Granda, look who's home!"

His head turns, and to my surprise, he smiles, his eyes gleaming with tears. "Findlay! My boy!" A single sob escapes his lips as he pushes himself to standing and shuffles over to me, his arms open wide. I fall into his strong embrace, relief flooding over me.

"Granda." It's all I can muster through the choking in my throat.

He holds me, his swollen, misshapen hands clutching my jacket as if I might disappear if he were to let me go. As his tears drip down my neck, something releases in me, a dam I've had in place since we left for Gallipoli—no, since Ma and Pa died, and my sorrow rolls through me unhindered in wave after wave of anguish.

"I'm so sorry, Granda. I'm so sorry. It's all my fault." My chest heaves, straining to gulp air through my closed throat. "I'm so, so sorry."

Granda's mutterings in my ear don't make sense to me. I squirm in his grip, but he won't let me go.

"I couldn't. I couldn't bring him home."

"I know, son. I know."

"I failed you. I failed *him*." A low moan swells in my gut, rising until it becomes a shriek. "Ian's dead!"

"I know, son. They sent a letter stating that Ian was a war hero who had saved many lives." As his words catch in his throat, Granda releases me. "War hero. Is there such a thing?" He paces back toward his chair. "But you didn't fail him. Or me. It's the war that is to blame." Granda grinds his teeth, spitting his words through a clenched jaw and lifting his fist. "War is evil, a pestilence against humanity that destroys lives and murders our children." He swipes the fist across his cheek and closes his eyes. "'The Lord trieth the righteous: but the wicked and him that loveth violence his soul hateth.' I take comfort in the fact that the Good Lord hates the violence of war as much as I do."

"We should never have gone."

Granda raises a single brow and dips his chin in agreement. "But Ian was bound and determined to defend his country, and nothing any of us could say was going to dissuade him." He closes his eyes again. "For someone so gentle, he was as hard-headed as his granma."

Shaking his head, Granda gestures for me to sit in the chair beside him. As I hobble over, he winces, his eyes focused on my cane. "Now, I have something I need to say to you." He clears his throat. "I apologize. I was wrong for sending you to collect Ian. I showed little regard for you by expecting you to do the impossible and sending you into harm's way to do it." He breathes a deep sigh. "I'm thankful I was allowed by the Good Lord the chance to say how sorry I am."

"No, Granda, I was…"

He raises his hand. "My only explanation is that I was not in my right mind at the time, but that doesn't excuse it. Can you ever forgive me?"

"Of course, Granda. There's nothing to forgive."

"Oh, but there is. So much." He bows his head slightly, still meeting my eyes. "Thank you."

"Will you forgive me, Granda? For my failure to protect Ian?"

"If I could, I would release you from your guilt. But I'm afraid that is between you and the Lord. For what it's worth, I hold nothing against you."

"Good, that's all settled." Katy plops down on the settee. "We need to catch you up on everything. Tom, Mac, and my Samuel…"

I sit forward on my chair, my breath shortening. "Where are they?"

"They are overseas. Fighting for America."

"No," I groan, wringing my hands.

Granda turns his head to gaze out the window and beyond, to the rolling curves of the mountains, his face etched with lines of pain.

"Granda tried to stop them, but they are as stubborn as Ian and insisted on going."

"Claire?"

"She is in mourning, devastated by Ian's loss and her brothers' leaving."

"This cursed war will consume us all," Granda grouses. "But one day, wars will be no more. As the Psalmist says, 'He maketh wars to cease unto the end of the earth; he breaketh the bow, and cutteth the spear in sunder; he burneth the chariot in the fire.'"

"Where is she?"

"Her cabin. We've been staying here to help out Granda, since all the men are gone. But she went home to be with her parents when we got the letter."

I gape at Katy. "You've been running the farm by yourself?"

"Not all by myself. Liam and Chris have helped."

I lean against the back of my chair. "Well, I'm here now. You're not alone anymore."

Katy reaches across the low table between us and grasps my hands. "Neither are you."

My unbidden tears well again. My homecoming is nothing like I imagined. Where I anticipated rejection, blame, and anger, I've received nothing but love and support.

"So, what's the news of Buck? Where is he?"

They don't know? I lick my lips before answering. "I'm not sure. The commander told me he was seen running into the woods from the battlefield. But that is so unlike Buck, I don't believe it. I can't. He was always running *into* the battle."

Granda sits forward, his elbows on his knees. "They are saying he ran away? A deserter?"

"Yes, Granda. And they are looking for him."

Granda strokes his chin. "When was this?" he whispers.

"Supposedly, the night Ian died."

Granda slumps back into his chair, his forehead and jaw working furiously. A hush falls over the room as Katy and I wait for his reaction.

Finally, he rises and wanders to the shelf where Ester's porcelain angels remain, standing guard over our home. He fingers the wings of one of her favorites. "Sometimes, the death of someone you love deeply kills a big part of you."

I limp to his side, straining to hear his words. Katy comes to stand beside me.

"I've died many times over in this life. My pa, shot before my eyes. My ma and my sweet sisters, murdered by Yankee soldiers for sport. My Lakota wife, Wiwílamni Kalúsya, my Flowing Spring, killed because Union soldiers came looking for me. Our son, Súnkawakan Sápä, and our unborn bairn, mercilessly slaughtered. Mato Waäylo and Hanhepi Wi Nagi, my Lakota brother and sister. Martin, my dear friend. Ester's mother, Mary. My son, your pa." He sighs. "And now my sweet Ester and Ian."

He turns to face Katy and me. "I know what that feeling is like. You're lost in a wilderness no one can reach. Pain takes form and shape, like a dark creature tearing at your insides, ripping your heart open, and spilling your blood and guts onto the ground." Granda crosses his arms and bends over them. "You fold in on yourself like a crumpled piece of paper because the hole in you is so vast, you can't contain it. It threatens to eat you alive." He straightens. "It consumed me, on more than one occasion."

I recognize that feeling, too. "Granda, you think that's what happened to Buck?"

"Buck would've felt responsible, like you. But Buck doesn't weep, he rages. And rage destroys." Granda shakes his head. "I fear Buck is lost in the wilderness, sucked into the hole left by Ian's loss."

"What do we do?" Katy's eyes plead with Granda for an answer.

Granda pauses, looking to the ceiling. Finally, he lowers his eyes and exhales. "All we can do is wait and hope. And pray."

CHAPTER THIRTY-FIVE

March 1918

I awaken to the dwindling echoes of screams vibrating the wooden beams over my head. A moment later, I realize I'm the one yelling, but I can't figure out where I am. My nightshirt and linens drip with sweat, and as I try to pull the soaked neckline away from my skin, my hands tremor like an old man's.

Suddenly, the door swings open and Granda rushes in. "Are you well? What's wrong?"

That's right. I'm home. I mop my brow with the cuff of my sleeve. "I'm sorry, Granda. I didn't mean to wake you."

"You're white as a sheet, son."

"I guess it must've been a bad dream."

Granda shuffles over and sits on the side of my bed. "A memory from the war?"

I pout my lips and shrug. "I don't know. I don't remember." Heat floods my neck and rises into my cheeks. "Did I say anything?"

Granda's face relaxes. "A lot of yelling. Stop. Go back. Move. Watch out. Things like that. Some names, too."

I wilt back against the moist pillow. "Ugh."

"You've had these nightmares before?"

I nod. " I thought they'd get better once I go home, but if anything, they're getting worse."

"Tell me about the worst of it."

Biting my lip, I shake my head. "No offense, Granda, but I don't want to talk about it."

He folds his hands across his lap. "What if not talking about it means the nightmares keep on coming?"

Slouching further into the coverlet, I groan. "What good would it do? Talking about it doesn't change anything."

"I thought so, too. Until my sweet Ester made me share with her." The edges of his mouth lift as his eyes drift to the window. "She chased me down and wouldn't take no for an answer. But once I started talking, the floodgates opened." He tilts his head and glances at me. "I felt much better after. Cleansed somehow."

A sick wave rolls over me as flashes of dead faces race through my mind. "I don't think anything is going to clean me."

Granda stills himself, and it soon becomes obvious he isn't going to leave me alone. "Well, I think I'll go back to sleep."

He nods.

"I'm well, Granda. You can go to bed."

"Mmm-hmm."

I flop on my side, turning away from him and pulling the coverlet over my ear, but sleep won't come. Minutes creep past, my discomfort rising with each tick of the clock.

Stubborn old goat. Why doesn't he leave?

He clears his throat. "I've never told you this, but I had a dear friend during the war. Will was his name. Will Hatcher."

My breath hitches, and my blood runs cold.

"Will and I were in the same division, the 11th Georgia, so we made it through many battles together, along with another friend, Josiah." He pauses, taking a deep breath before continuing. "During one of the battles, Will was fighting a Yank hand-to-hand when another Yank took aim at Josiah. I saw it all, but I couldn't make myself pull the trigger on my gun. I froze, and both of my friends were almost killed because of it. Had Will not killed that Yank and saved Josiah, his blood would've been on my hands." He sighs. "Later, Will gets bayonet stabbed right next to me. He died in my arms. I couldn't save him. Then, Josiah was wounded and left a cripple. I couldn't save him, either."

I roll over and sit up, crossing my legs beneath me. "I'm sorry, Granda."

"War puts men in the position of betraying their values or betraying their friends. You're damned either way."

"I suppose that's so."

Granda leans toward me. "Son, whatever happened over there, I promise you I've done worse. When Will got killed, I lost my mind. The boy who couldn't pull the trigger became a cold-blooded killer." He lowers his eyes, leaning his elbows on his knees. "I'm ashamed of what I became. But Ester helped me to remember who I was before the war took it away from me."

"How?"

A soft, wistful smile blooms on his face as he looks toward the window again. "She saw me. She called me by my true name. She knew me through God's eyes, not through the tainting of what I'd done." He sighs deeply. "She helped me to see myself through God's eyes again."

Gnawing my bottom lip, I slump against the pillow. "That's what I'm afraid of."

"What's that?"

"How God sees me now."

Granda leans forward and takes my hand in both of his. "God sees the heart He created before you were a bairn in your ma's womb. He knows the great love you have inside you, the kindness of your heart, your thoughtfulness, and your maturity. He sees the way you stepped up to care for your brothers. Ester always said you were like a cornerstone of your family, a foundation for your brothers, and strength for those around you."

I bark out a laugh. "I'm anything but strong. Buck is the strong one."

Granda lifts his brows. "And that's why you are here, helping me, and supporting Katy and Claire, and Buck is AWOL, running away from himself and his responsibilities." He shakes his head. "My Ester was always right about people. Always."

"Granma doesn't know what I did over there."

"Oh, I imagine she does. I'm thinking heaven is a place where all is revealed because it's a place of light." He smiles. "And for sure and certain, the Lord knows, and He loves you just the same."

The memories press into my throat, squeezing unwanted tears into my eyes. How could God love me now? I betrayed my friends. I failed my brothers. I killed and caused the deaths of those I cared for by my actions.

"*War* betrayed you. *War* failed you and your brothers. *War* killed your friends and your enemies."

Did I speak aloud? My tears start to flow freely.

"Tell me the stories, son." He squeezes my hand. "Let them go."

A sob escapes my lips. "I have a Will, too." Then, the stories of Hasan and Will, and the real story of Ian's death rush from me in a tidal wave of shame and agonizing pain. Granda sits as still as the lake in the morning mist, listening but saying nothing as I pour it all out in a gush of blubbering words and gasping cries.

When I'm spent, he wraps his strong arms around me. "The Lord forgives you, Fin. Now, you must forgive yourself."

Ian's words return to me like an echo drifting on the wind. *Promise you won't give up on God.*

I promise.

Granda holds me close as I cry myself to sleep.

Light flickers behind my eyelids, and when I flutter them open, the world gleams soft white through the window. A dusting of late snow has covered the mountain overnight, making the evergreens shimmer and the mountain's crest glow in the sun.

I hobble to the glass and raise the window, sticking my head out to inhale the fresh, cold air, then exhaling the bitter sting of last night's tears. The new lightness in my chest reflects the bright radiance of the day. Granda was right, confession is good for the soul.

I shrug on my clothes and clomp downstairs to find Katy and Granda have already broken their fast.

Katy quirks her mouth, shaking her head. "Good morning, sleepyhead. You almost missed breakfast."

"There are biscuits and bacon for you in the kitchen." Granda studies my face. "How are you feeling?"

"I'm well, thank you, Granda." My face relaxes as I meet his gaze. "Thank you very much."

He purses his lips and nods. "Good." Gesturing toward the kitchen, he pushes his chair back from the table. "Go on, get your biscuits. We have work to do."

"Yessir."

For some reason, the biscuits taste richer, the honey sweeter, and the bacon more savory than I can recall. While overseas, I forgot that eating was more than sustenance for survival. Nothing we had over there was worth tasting anyway. But this morning, joy returns to my mouth.

Katy dons her jacket and shoves a knit cap over her braids. "Better bundle up. It's chilly out there."

Katy convinces Granda to stay inside in the warmth—not a difficult task—while I grab an old coat of Granda's from the coat closet and my cane before heading out to feed and water the horses and pasture the cows. Katy takes care of the hens and hogs. Then, at her insistence, we climb to the top of the hill to build a snowman, the last one of the year.

Because the snow is powdery and thin, Katy must roll the balls up and down the slope to collect enough. I'm mostly useless, but at least I'm able to help her stack the finished balls. Still, our snowman is small and a little pathetic, but we have fun anyway. Then, she hits me in the back with a snowball.

"Hey! That's not fair!" I wave my cane. "How am I supposed to get you back?"

Katy throws her head back and laughs. "Spoil sport. Come on then." We make our way down the hill to the pasture, where she instructs me to set up a fort behind a bale of hay and pile an arsenal of snowballs. She does the same behind a nearby bale.

After several minutes, she calls, "Ready?"

"Are you? You better be."

"I'm ready!"

And it's an all-out war until we're too wet and too cold to keep going.

After we change out of our wet clothes, we sit by the fire in the sitting room. The warmth and gentle crackle of the flames licking the logs lulls me close to dozing off until Katy startles me awake.

"When will you go see Claire?"

I blink several times. Is there an accusation in her tone? "I don't know."

"You know she wants to see you. To hear about Ian."

I nod, my chin slumped on my chest. "I don't know if I can talk about it with her."

Katy sits forward. "You must. She is torturing herself because she doesn't know, imagining horrible scenes and a long, drawn-out, painful death.

"Oh."

"You can't avoid her forever."

"I know."

Katy harumphs, folding her arms and staring into the fire.

"I'm doing the best I can." Ian's pleading voice whispers again in my head. *Promise me you will take care of Claire.* So far, I've done nothing to fulfill my oath.

"I'll go with you. We can go down after lunch."

How can I explain to Katy—or Claire—the crippling guilt of knowing Ian died trying to save me? Claire will never forgive me.

Have you learned nothing?

I startle, glancing around the room before realizing the words came from inside my mind. They weren't cruel, more curious than harsh.

Would you set yourself up as a greater judge than I? Or would you make Claire your judge rather than trusting my judgment?

What is going on? Am I losing my wits?

I have forgiven you. Now, you must forgive yourself.

Granda's words, but spoken from…from the One who forgave me? "Lord?"

Katy glances at me, her brows lifted.

Do you trust me?

Heat flushes my face, but it's not from the fire. My heart aches in my chest. "I want to."

"Good. We'll go together." Katy grasps my hand. "It will be good for both of you."

Do you trust me?

The voice is infuriatingly insistent. "I don't know how."

Katy frowns. "I'm sure stories of the war are difficult to share, especially to those of us who've never seen one. And Ian's story will be the most difficult of all because he's your brother, and Claire was to be your sister-in-law." Katy's fingers touch my chin and turn my face toward her. "Tell her the truth, Fin. We'll be there to support her through it."

I am the way.

"I need Your help."

Katy smiles gently. "I'll be with you."

I am with you.

I murmur, "Thank You."

Uncle Chris and Aunt Emma greet me with warm hugs and expressions of gratitude for my safe return.

"May we speak with Claire?" Katy asks.

"Of course, dear. She is in her room." Emma tilts her head, her lips pursed. "Be gentle with her, Fin. She is having a rough go."

"Yes, ma'am." How can I be gentle when what she wants to hear is so horrific? *Lord, I need Your help.*

I am with you.

Katy leads me to Claire's room, a small log-walled addition that Uncle Chris built for her onto the original cabin. She is curled up under a mound of covers, her face hidden from us. I try desperately to tread quietly and fail miserably.

"Claire, it's me, Katy."

The covers rustle a bit as Claire moans, a hollow, distant sound echoing from beneath the heap.

"Fin is here, too."

"Fin?" Slowly, her blankets slip back, and Claire sits up. Her hair is unwashed and uncombed, her clothes are wrinkled from lying in bed for who knows how long, and her face is mottled from crying. "Fin." She lifts her arms, so I limp to her bed and sit on the edge so I can embrace her lightly. She clings to my neck as if she's drowning, and I'm her one hope for shore.

"I'm so sorry, Claire." It's the only thing I can think of to say.

She starts to weep, her fresh tears wetting the front of my shirt. "Oh, Fin. Ian is gone." A sob escapes her lips. "Whoever will marry me now? I waited for him, and now I'm too old. No one will ever want me."

I've wanted you since the first time I met you. "I…I…Katy said you wanted to hear how Ian died."

She snuffles, smearing her fist across her nose. Her chest heaves in a staccato rhythm, reminding me of machine gun fire. "Yes, of course. I do." Her eyes bulge. "Was he in a lot of pain?"

"Some, I think. I'm not sure." I take her hand. "All he talked about was you."

The fingers of her other hand tap her lips like she's playing piano keys. "He did? He spoke of me?"

"Yes. He wanted to make sure you were well cared for."

This news brings on a new round of heaving sobs.

I close my eyes. "And right before he died, he looked into the sky, and he said, 'I see.' I believe he saw the Lord coming to take him home." My chest swells with a hope I haven't felt since Ma and Pa died in the fire. "He had such a look of peace on his face that I'm sure of it."

"But he spoke only of me before then?"

"Yes, he spoke lovingly of you."

Katy sits on the other side of Claire's bed and rubs her back. "You see? You were expecting a story of great suffering, but it's really a love story."

Claire squeezes her hands together at her throat. "His last thought was of me." She flutters her lashes and looks toward the ceiling. "Oh, Ian. I will love you always."

CHAPTER THIRTY-SIX

May 1918

"The spring planting's done, Granda." Katy, Claire, and I stomp the dirt from our shoes before entering the house, as Ester would've wanted. I use my cane to knock the dirt off the shoe on my gimp leg.

Granda calls from the dining room. "Come. I've made something special for you. A reward for a job well done."

Katy's eyes light up. "Ooo, I wonder what the surprise is."

We tread down the hall beneath the stairs to find Granda standing at the end of the table, a glorious buttermilk pie in the center, and Ester's best dessert plates arrayed on doilies with napkins and silver forks beside them.

"Granda! You must've worked on that pie for hours!" Claire clasps her hands at her throat. "You know how much I love Ester's buttermilk pie. Thank you, Granda. What a special treat!"

Katy beams. "It's beautiful, Granda, just like Granma Ester's pies."

"I didn't know you could cook." I slump into the closest chair and reach for the knife.

"Uh-uh. You go and wash up first." Granda folds his arms. "We are still civilized in this family."

"Yessir."

After we wash, Granda has us stand around the table holding hands. Katy stands on one side of me, Claire on the other, but it's the gentle touch of Claire's delicate fingers that sends a shiver to my toes.

"Lord, we come to You with our thanks, for the bountiful harvest You will provide, for strong arms with which to complete our labor, and for the joy of being together. We pray as always for those who are not with us and ask Your protection over them, wherever they may be." Granda pauses, then heaves a tremulous sigh. "Amen."

"Amen and pass the pie." I meant to lighten the mood but had the opposite effect. Granda's prayer and my poor imitation of Buck's joviality cast a longer shadow over the table than the setting sun's rays outside the picture window.

Katy cuts our slices, and we eat in silence, a state that has become more usual than not in the last couple of months.

Katy shovels in her last forkful, moans in delight, then grins. "You know, Granma would be furious, Granda. You're ruining our supper."

"It's a special occasion. She'll understand."

He still speaks of Ester as if she were with us. I suppose for him, she still is. But for me, this table's many empty chairs remind me of how much we've lost as a family. I remember when I first arrived at the cabin, the table felt daunting, noisy, and too crowded for my liking, but now, I miss the chatter. I even miss Buck's elbows over my plate when he spreads out to enjoy his meal.

Will I ever see him again?

Katy pushes away from the table. "I best be heading home." She winks at Granda. "I won't tell Ma that you fed me dessert."

He smiles, a rare enough occurrence. "I would appreciate it."

Katy laughs, bids us farewell, and dashes out the door.

"I'm going to clean up." Granda sighs. "Spending time together was nice, wasn't it?"

"It was, Granda." Claire gets up and gives him a quick neck squeeze. "Thank you so much for the lovely pie."

"I'll help you with the dishes." I grab Katy's plate and stack it on top of Claire's and mine.

"There isn't much to do." Granda takes the stack of plates. "You must see Claire home. It will be dark before long."

A queasy feeling rumbles in my stomach, churning the pie. "Yessir."

Claire hooks my elbow with a coy smile. "Come along, then."

We're forced to plod along because of my leg, but Claire spins and flutters around me, chattering about the lovely weather, the flowers, the songbirds, the buttermilk pie, anything to fill my empty silence. The girl ties my tongue, for sure and certain, and I already don't talk much, not since the war. So, she fills the air with her lilting voice and the scent of rose petals and violets. I inhale it all in, savoring each moment.

"We need to find Katy a beau. She's convinced she's going to be an old maid, but I won't have it." Claire twirls to face me, walking backwards up the hill past the barn. "I keep telling her, if she will take a little care of her appearance and dress in something besides those old dungarees and her brother's shirts, she would snare a man in no time." She rolls her eyes and spins away, flouncing her skirt. "But she says if they don't like her for who she is, she doesn't want them anyway."

"Uh-huh."

"So, you must find someone who'll love a tomboy."

I shrug. "I'm sure Katy can find her own husband."

"What about one of those boys who served with you in the war?"

I stutter my steps, almost falling over a clod of clay.

"Well, what about them?"

"They're dead."

To my surprise, she puckers her lips. "Not all of them, surely."

"Yes. All of them."

She huffs a sigh. "Oh." Waving her arms, she skips ahead of me. "Well, you'll think of something." As she reaches the bend in the path at the ridge's crest, she turns and calls, "Hurry! Come and see!"

Hurrying for me means severe pain, but I won't disappoint Claire, so I hobble and hop, mainly on one foot, up to the ridge and around the bend, grunting with each step.

The vista opens on a magnificent rose and coral sunset over the blue mountains, bathed in white mist.

"Isn't it lovely?" Claire leans her back against my chest and nestles her head beneath my chin.

Gently, tentatively, I lift my arm and wrap it around her waist. She doesn't balk. "Lovely."

She raises her eyes, glittering in the waning sunlight. "Are you speaking of the sunset?" Dimples crease her cheeks.

"Yeah…" I'm balancing on one foot, dizzy from breathing the heady closeness of her, my head spinning, and before I can catch them, the words leak out in a whisper. "And you."

A knife blade gouges my chest, coating my throat and insides with acidic slime. *What am I doing?* Claire is Ian's girl. He's gone less than seven months, and here I am with my arm around her. Some brother I am.

I can't do this. I promised to protect her, not take advantage of her. My arm drops, a hanging dead weight at my side.

She turns her face to the sunset, tossing her hair, which makes the flowery scent of her envelop me even more. "Oh." She flips her hair again. "Are you saying you think I'm beautiful?"

"Um…."

"Say it, then."

I groan. "You're beautiful."

She spins and shoves me, almost pushing me over. "You can do better than that, surely." Her giggles trail behind her as she scampers down the hill toward her family's cabin.

"Wait!" It's much harder to do my little gallop steps going downhill, and I almost trip over my own feet twice before I catch up to her, where I find her bent at the waist, with her hands on her knees.

"Are you hurt?" I rush to her side, grabbing her shoulder.

She raises her head, her laughter bubbling up and overflowing. "Just my pride." She brushes leaves from the front of her skirt. "I took a tumble, but I'm not injured."

"You should be more careful."

In one gliding move, she presses against my chest, her face turning up to mine, her eyes hooded and a bewitching smile gracing her lips. "You're worried about me."

"Of course, I am. You were to be my sister."

Claire takes a sharp step back with a huff. "Is that how you think of me?"

"Well, yeah…" *God help me, no.*

She sticks her nose in the air and tosses her curls. "Very well. Forget it." With a flourish, she stalks down the path.

"Claire…"

"*Forget* it. I can walk myself home. *Brother.*" With that, she disappears into the darkening forest.

"Claire, wait." Nothing. "I'm sorry."

Her voice, low and silky, flows from the darkness. "Are you truly sorry?"

I heave a deep sigh. "Yes, I'm sorry. I never meant to hurt you."

"Then, prove it."

I pause a moment, my mind filled to bursting with desire and shame, warring for dominance until desire wins, and I race to her as fast as my bum leg can carry me, wrapping her in my arms and caressing her exquisite hair, allowing her scent to burrow deep into my soul.

"Kiss me."

Her whisper startles me from my trance, and the knife twists, dredging up the burning guilt, but her full, parted lips are almost touching mine, and the aroma of roses clouds my thoughts, and to my shame, I press closer until the sweet, moist taste of her fills my mouth.

She moans, causing me to press in deeper. A strange, intoxicating warmth spreads through me, sending my head spinning and my heart racing.

No. Stop. Before it's too late.

I pull back, but Claire presses closer, reaching her hand behind my head and pulling my mouth to hers, and I'm lost, adrift in the tingling shiver down my spine, the trembling of my limbs, and the burning in my chest. I want to consume all of her, to press her close until the softness of her skin melds into me.

Then, she pushes me back with a tremulous breath. "Let a girl breathe."

"Oh. Sorry. I…"

She runs her finger along my cheek. "Don't apologize."

"I didn't mean…"

Her soft laughter rings in my ears, stirring the flame inside me again. "It felt like you meant it."

"No, I…I mean…I didn't hurt you, did I?"

She shakes her head, no, then tugs on my chin and whispers, "Kiss me again."

I do. God, forgive me.

Some time passes, too long but not enough to suit me, and Claire finally places her hand on my chest. "I really need to get home. Mother will be worried."

A worm of desperate desire writhes in my gut, but I agree. We follow the path, now in pitch darkness, until we see the soft glow of light from the cabin's windows.

"When will I see you again?" The worm inside me is developing claws.

Claire makes my knees wobble with her sly grin. "You want to see me again?"

"Yes."

"Soon?"

"Yes. When?"

She shrugs, tossing a curl from her face. "I'm not sure." She touches my neck near my shirt collar. "Maybe tomorrow. Maybe not."

A hunger like none I've felt gnaws through me, and heat rises into my cheeks. "You don't want to see me?"

She tilts her head, her lips parting ever so slightly. "You'll have to wait and see." She skips up the steps, stopping at the cabin door when I call her.

"Claire."

"Hmm?"

"I love you."

She throws her head back and laughs. For a moment, I wonder if she's laughing at me, but then she lowers her eyes, wide and glistening in the dim light from the window, and says, "I know." With that, she snatches the door open and disappears.

The ache begins immediately. The closest thing I've experienced to this intense a need was at Gallipoli, when our food supplies drowned in the torrential rains, and we were left starving for days.

This is worse.

The next morning, I busy myself with chores, and when I return from the barn, Claire is waiting for me on the porch, rocking in Ester's old chair but with a sour look on her face.

"You shouldn't keep a girl waiting." She folds her arms across her chest and taps her foot.

"I'm sorry. I didn't know…"

"I told you I might be coming today." Claire sniffs, tossing her head.

"You also said maybe not." I fold my arms across my chest in reply.

"Well, then, if you'd rather I go home…"

"No!" The bark came out louder than I intended.

She raises her brows, waiting for me to continue.

"I'm glad you're here. I didn't know for certain when to expect you, or I would've been waiting for you." I try to moisten my lips, but my tongue is parched, scraping over my lips like sandpaper.

"Very well." Claire pats her lap as if I'm a wayward child come home. "I forgive you." She stands and rubs her hands together. "So, what shall we do today?"

"What do you want to do?"

Her sideways glance and cheeky grin tell me what she has in mind. I'm happy to accommodate her. "Why don't we make a picnic lunch? We would ride to the waterfall, and maybe even have a swim. It's a warm day."

"I don't have a bathing suit."

"Well, we could ride to your cabin first so you could get one." I shrug. "It's not too far out of the way."

"Or?"

What is she up to? "Or…maybe you don't want to swim?"

She giggles. "Or…?" She skips down the steps, kisses my cheek, and whispers, "What about nude bathing?"

I gasp, taking a step backwards. "I would never dishonor you in such a way.":

She frowns, pouting her lips. "Very well, spoil sport. I will get my suit, if I must."

"Your mother would skin me alive if I let you swim…in that way." I glance toward the front door of the big house. "And so would Granda."

Claire's disappointment evaporates in a blink. "I have something I want to talk with you about."

"I'm listening."

"No, not here. On the picnic."

"Oh. Very well." A buzz of agitation stirs in my stomach, souring my breakfast. What now?

We go to the kitchen, stopping to inform Granda of our planned outing before making up a basket of fruit, cheese, cider, and bread. I tack up two horses, and we ride to Claire's cabin, where she retrieves her suit, then it's a wild gallop across the fields to the waterfall.

I've almost forgotten about her enigmatic statement when she sits on the blanket, reaches across the spread of food to take my hand, and clears her throat. "Here goes." She takes a deep breath. "You said you love me. Was that a heat-of-the-moment declaration, or do you mean it?"

I try to swallow down the lump in my throat, to no avail. "Claire, I…"

"Tell me the truth. I don't have time to waste."

Time to waste? What is she talking about?

I lower my eyes as heat rises in my neck, making my cheeks burn. How do I explain my feelings for her? When I look up again, her crestfallen expression tells me she believes my hesitation is proof I didn't mean it. I must say something, and fast. "I do love you, Claire. I have loved you since the first day I met you." I swallow again as her eyes brighten. "I also spoke rashly; as you say, in the heat of the moment. I'm struggling with my feelings because of Ian."

Her head jerks back. "Ian? Why?"

"You are his one great love. You were engaged to marry him, and he's my brother. It feels like a betrayal." There, I've said it aloud. Now, there's no going back.

Her face falls flat, her eyes lifeless. "Ian's dead, Fin. How is it a betrayal?"

"He loved you so much. It's as if we are cheating on him."

"He's dead."

"I know."

Claire stands up and wanders to the edge of the lake at the base of the falls. She wraps her arms around herself as if she's protecting herself from the cold.

I get up and move beside her. "I do love you, Claire. More than I've ever loved anyone."

"But you won't marry me because your dead brother, who abandoned me, wanted to?"

My mind spins, trying to make sense of what she's saying. Marriage? Abandoned? "Ian didn't abandon you, not by choice."

"Of course, he did. He chose his 'cause' over me, and left me as an unmarried woman, not a widow exactly, but like one, too old for anyone to want." She glares across the expanse of water. "And now, you're going to abandon me, too."

"No! I will never abandon you. I promised Ian I would look after you."

Her eyes brighten as she whips her head around and clasps my hands. "So, you'll marry me?"

My mouth opens and closes, then opens again. What do I do? What *can* I do? Do I betray my brother by marrying his true love, or do I betray my promise to him by leaving her alone for the rest of her life? Either way, guilt will gouge out my heart and ravage it until its last drops of blood are gone.

She beams her beautiful smile, and my resolve melts. "Of course, I'll marry you."

A sharp intake of breath whistles in her throat, followed by a flood of tears from a deep well of pain, grief, and longing. Tears sting my eyes as well, but for a completely different reason. She collapses into my arms, and we stand in that tight embrace by the edge of the water until the last of her tears are spent.

At long last, we return to our meal. As I spread some jam on a piece of bread and hand it to Claire, I clear my throat and murmur, "I have one request."

"You do?" She flutters her lashes, her eyes darting away. "What is it?"

"If you don't mind, may we please wait a decent amount of time before we announce our betrothal? I would feel better if, through our actions, we didn't disgrace Ian." I hold my breath while she rolls her lips behind her teeth and studies her bread.

Finally, she asks, "What is a decent amount of time?"

"One year? I believe that is an acceptable length of time for mourning."

She chews her lower lip, closing her eyes. After several moments, she looks at me with a stilted smile and nods. "Very well. One year." She reaches out her hand. "We will wed in October."

I take her hand and lift her delicate fingers to my lips. "October." With an impulsive yank, I pull her across the blanket, scattering our food, but I don't care. All I want is to taste her sweet breath and feel her warm body against mine. Claire, beautiful Claire, is going to be my wife. "I love you, Claire."

"I know."

CHAPTER THIRTY-SEVEN

September 1918

Katy bursts through the front door, waving a yellow slip of paper. "Granda! Granda!"

My throat closes as we hurry into the foyer. Deep lines crisscross Granda's brow. "What's happened?"

"It's Samuel and Mac. They're coming home!"

The constriction in my throat tightens. "Are they wounded?"

"It doesn't say. I don't think so."

Granda gathers Katy in his arms. "When will they arrive?"

"The telegram says they must first go to Camp Gordon for processing, and from there, they will come here. It could be as soon as a few weeks. But…" Katy clasps her hands together as if in prayer. "They are out of harm's way at last."

"An answered prayer," Granda breathes.

"Pa and Ma are so relieved. Ma is beside herself." She gives Granda's cheek a quick peck. "I must go tell Claire and the rest of the family." Katy spins to bolt out the door.

I reach for her elbow. "Wait! I want to go with you."

"Come, then."

I grab my cane and a light jacket, and together we head down the path to Uncle Chris' cabin with the news.

"Anything in the telegram about Tom?" I ask.

"Nothing, but I don't think Tom was at the front like Samuel and Mac." Katy taps her lip, her eyes angled up toward the sky. "I believe Pa said they placed Tom in some kind of logistical or organizational position behind the lines."

"That's good." Although I'm aware that behind the lines in France and Belgium doesn't mean safety, I don't voice my concern with Katy. No news is still good news during a war.

After Katy reads the telegram, Chris hugs her tightly, tears rimming his eyes, while Claire squeals in delight. Emma stands beyond the tumult with her eyes closed and her face lifted toward the ceiling.

"It will still be a few weeks until we see them, but they'll be nearby and safe before long."

"Nothing on Tom?" Chris asks.

"Nothing."

"We will give praises and thanksgiving for the miraculous return of our two boys, and we will lift our prayers for Tom's safe return." Emma's prim smile and quiet manner hide any concern for Tom she might be having.

Claire, who has been bounding around the room, leaps onto me, her arms around my neck and her legs circling my waist. "Isn't it wonderful news?"

A thrill jangles my spine at her touch. "Yes, it is."

She kisses my cheek and whispers in my ear, "We'll have some good news of our own to share by the time they arrive, won't we?"

"Yes."

The month passes quickly, filled with the harvest and preparations for Mac and Samuel's homecoming. Everyone pitches in, and somehow, all three fields are gathered, all the food is preserved, two rooms, one in each of the outlying cabins, are prepared, and a huge welcome-home party is planned for mid-October.

On October 12th, we receive a telegram from Mac, nailing down October 17th as their arrival on the afternoon train, and requesting pick-up in Blue Ridge. Chris volunteers to take his wagon down the mountain to get them, so the rest of us pitch in to prepare the cabin and set up the meal. Katy hangs a Welcome Home banner on the front porch. Claire collects a few mums from the garden, along with asters, goldenrod, and witch hazel from the fields, to make a lovely golden bouquet for the dining table. Julianna and Emma take control of the kitchen, while Liam brings them supplies from storage, and Granda and I set the table with Ester's finest tableware.

The cabin hums with chatter, laughter, and even a few brief harsh words as we all try to make everything perfect.

"Here they come!" Katy calls when she spots the wagon cresting the first rise, and we all rush to the front porch. Julianna still wears her apron with flour smeared on her face, and Liam holds a bundle of firewood he was collecting before Katy's call rang out.

"Mac!" Claire cries, jumping up and down on the top step, waving.

Katy squeals. "I see my Samuel!"

I squint to make out Chris' face, for if something were wrong, his face would show it, but they are still too far away.

Claire tugs on my arm. "Why don't they hurry?"

I pat her hand, but my eyes are fixed on the approaching wagon and its occupants.

Finally, Chris pulls the horses to a stop near the base of the stairs. Katy and Claire race down to Samuel and Mac, embracing them before they've even climbed from the wagon. Samuel manages to hop down and sweeps Katy high into the air. Her laughter rings out, bright and innocent, and for a moment, it feels like the war has been forgotten.

Then, Mac steps down, and I'm stopped cold. He moves slowly, with one hand gripping the wagon's edge for balance. When he falls into Claire's eager arms, he winces. His ashen skin and sunken eyes are shadowed with a grayish pallor that looks strange on a young man.

Everyone crowds around, their joy still bubbling over, unaware of the chill creeping in.

Julianna's flour-coated face is streaked with her tears. "We have a meal prepared for you. All of your favorites."

When Emma caresses Mac's cheek, her expression falters. Her hand finds his forehead, and the last drops of her joy fade away. "You're burning up."

"I don't feel well." He groans.

"It started on the train." Samuel's smile fades. "He complained of a headache, and it kept getting worse. Then, he said he was freezing."

Emma's tone sharpens to a mother's command. "The meal will have to wait. Fin, fetch cold water and cloths. Quickly."

The laughter dies in the air. I sprint to the well, draw up a bucket of cold water, and carry it inside. In the sitting room, Mac lies on the settee wrapped in a blanket, his body shivering.

"Quickly now. Wet the cloths." Emma pulls the blanket back despite Mac's protest. Claire mops his brow as Emma presses wet cloths beneath his arms and against his chest.

"He's hot as fire," Claire whispers. "The water isn't helping."

"Husband, fetch the doc…." Emma's voice breaks. Chris bolts for the door, his boots pounding down the steps.

"I've never seen anything come on so quickly, or so violently." Julianna wrings her hands. "What could it be?"

Liam places his arm around Samuel's shoulder. "At Camp Gordon, were any other soldiers sick?"

Samuel hesitates. "Not that I recall. But they would've been kept in the infirmary, not in the barracks."

"If this is catching, we need to get the girls out of here." Liam takes Granda's arm. "You, too, Pa."

Claire shakes her head, her eyes flashing fire. "I'm not leaving my brother."

Seeing Mac's misery and the anguish in Claire's eyes, I take her hand gently. "Come, Claire. Listen to Uncle Liam."

"He needs me."

"Let me care for him. Come, now." Pulling her to her feet, I take her place at Mac's side, dripping cool water on his head. Touching his skin is like putting my hand on Granma's stove.

"Girls." Granda's authoritative voice brooks no argument. Claire and Katy follow him from the sitting room, dragging their feet, their wide eyes fixed on Mac the whole way.

Emma looks up, her eyes wet brimming with tears. "His fever isn't coming down. What do I do?"

"We might have to put him in a cold bath." Julianna swallows hard.

Liam frowns. "Wouldn't that make it worse?"

"If we don't bring the fever down," Julianna whispers, "he may not survive the night."

Emma closes her eyes, mouthing a private prayer as she replaces the rags. Julianna strokes her shoulder. "The doctor will be here soon."

Mac wheezes in a ragged breath, then his body jerks with a harsh cough that rips through the quiet. The dry, rasping hack becomes a racking, violent fit, bending Mac at the waist and turning his face purplish red. When the cough subsides, he gasps for air, his breath shallow and strangled.

Emma tries to give him a sip of water, provoking another long coughing fit that ends with Mac falling back against the pillows and screaming, "Gas! Gas! Gas!"

"He believes he's at the front." Samuel sits on the settee and cradles Mac's head in his lap. "We're home now. You're safe."

"Sniper! In the window!" Mac thrusts his arm in the air.

Samuel clasps Mac's flailing hand tightly. "I'm here."

The room falls quiet.

After what feels like hours, Chris returns with the doctor, who takes one look and pales. "He's just home from Camp Gordon?"

"Yes." Emma's reply is barely a whisper.

The doctor sets his bag down. "There's talk of another outbreak, the influenza from the spring. But this…" He touches Mac's burning forehead. "This is worse."

He reads the thermometer, his face tightening. "One hundred and six. We must cool him now."

He pulls a bottle labeled *Rubbing Alcohol* from his bag. "Strip him down and bathe him with this." He shoves two white tablets between Mac's lips. "If it climbs any higher, he could seize."

Samuel and I strip Mac's limp body, while Julianna and Emma begin the alcohol bath. We work in silence. The air in the room grows thick with pungent fumes, and I become aware I'm holding my breath, not against the sharp smell of alcohol but out of fear.

Then, without warning, Mac's back arches. His body jerks violently, his arms and legs flailing. Emma screams his name. The doctor flips him onto his side, but the convulsions continue, rattling the settee and shaking us all.

Emma's hands hover helplessly above her son, trembling as if mirroring his movements, as she cries out to the only name that might help us. "*Jesus.*"

Finally, the fit slows, and Mac's body relaxes. The doctor shines a light in Mac's eyes and listens to his chest, then straightens. "I need to speak to the family."

Liam collects Granda and the girls as the rest of us wander in a daze to the main room.

Once we're all gathered, the doctor clears his throat. "I'm afraid I will have to quarantine you all. The Spanish flu is extremely virulent, and you have all been exposed." He raises his brows. "Most of you will likely fall ill within the next day or two, although segregating the sick and limiting contact could help slow the spread."

Granda steps forward, his voice steady. "Then we will all remain in the main house. That way, we can care for one another. Upstairs will serve as our sick room. Those still well will remain on the first floor." He closes his eyes. "Two of us will tend the sick, but the rest will stay downstairs."

The doctor nods his approval of Granda's plan. "Feed them clear broth and water as often as they'll take it. I'll return tomorrow with more supplies. We'll know more then."

Julianna clutches her blouse at the throat. "Doctor, is it worse for some of us than others?"

He hesitates. "In the spring wave, younger adults were hit hardest. I assume this will be the same. But no one is immune."

"I rarely catch whatever's going around, so I'll handle caring for the sick." Chris shifts his weight. "Besides, I rode with Mac sitting next to me all the way from town. If I'm going to get it, I'm already exposed."

"Shouldn't a woman be upstairs caring for the sick as well?" Emma's voice wavers, her eyes pleading.

Granda shakes his head. "We need Julianna and you cooking, washing, and keeping the rest of us alive. You'll leave food and water at the top of the stairs. Chris and I will manage."

"No, Pa! It should be me." Liam folds his arms, his face reddening. "It's more dangerous for him, isn't it, Doc?"

The doctor gives a small shrug. "Actually, the elderly fared better than younger adults."

Granda lifts his hand to quiet Liam. "I need you on the farm. The work won't wait because we're sick. The cows, the horses, and the rest of the harvest all need tending. Fin and Samuel will help."

Katy plants her hands on her hips. "What about us? We're not helpless."

"You'll help your ma and aunt or your uncle, whoever needs you more," Granda says firmly. "But you will not go upstairs. Is that understood?"

"Yessir."

The doctor speaks softly during the pause in the discussion. "Try to limit contact even among yourselves. The flu spreads before symptoms show." His gaze sweeps the room. "Some of you may already have it."

A hush falls. The clock's ticks reverberate in the air. Everyone's eyes move from one to another, their faces pale and eyes wide with fear.

Granda breaks the tense silence. "How long?"

"Twenty-four to forty-eight hours." The doctor turns to Samuel. "You rode in with Mac?"

"Yessir."

"Do you have a headache?"

Samuel shakes his head. "No, sir."

"Scratchy throat?"

Samuel swallows, hesitating. "Maybe a little."

The doctor's mouth presses to a thin slash. "Then, you'll likely show symptoms first, if you have it."

Granda's jaw stiffens as he lowers his eyes. "Samuel, stay apart until morning. We'll see how you fare."

"It's for the best, son." Chris lays a hand on his son's shoulder.

"Pray for strength." Doc closes his bag. "You'll need it."

As he strides out the door, no one speaks. The fire crackles and pops in the grate, echoing the ticking of the clock as we wait for morning and whatever arrives with it.

CHAPTER THIRTY-EIGHT

October 1918

Chris disappears upstairs, carrying Mac cradled in his arms, while Julianna fumigates the sitting room and Emma wipes everything down with carbolic acid. We set up sleeping pallets for everyone except Samuel, who takes the couch in the main room.

No one mentions the celebration dinner.

Dusk colors the horizon, bringing a slight chill to the air. The ceiling boards creak above us, telling us Chris and Granda are ministering to Mac. Is he having another seizure? Has his fever broken? Not knowing is even worse than watching him suffer.

"We all should catch some sleep while we can." Liam kneels on his pallet, pulling back the blanket. "We don't know what tomorrow holds."

Opening the door to the kitchen, Emma tips her head. "You go ahead. I'm going to make some broth." Her voice trembles. "In case Mac wants some."

My heart wrenches in my chest. "Mac'll pull through, Aunt Emma. He's strong."

As the door closes behind Emma, her words echo from the hallway. "'The Lord is my strength and my shield; my heart trusted in him, and I am helped: therefore my heart greatly rejoiceth; and with my song will I praise him.'"

My blood freezes and drains from my face.

These were Granma's words when her heart failed her.

These were Ian's words when our plight at the Somme looked hopeless.

Both are gone now. The best of us, taken. Are these words the harbinger of doom yet again?

Please, Lord, not again.

I dash out the front door, ignoring the searing pain in my leg, and stumble down the steps, across the field, and up the hill, gasping in lungfuls of the cooling air. How do I pray? My chest burns like my cramping leg, raging against the failures of God's providence. *Who will you steal from us this time? Mac? Samuel?*

Claire?

A glimmer of fear tweaks my throat. Challenging Almighty God might not be a good idea. But my anger overcomes my sense, and as I reach the ridgeline, I lift my fist, shaking it at the darkened sky. "Curse You! You already have Granma Ester and Ian. What more do You want from us?"

Do you trust me?

"Not if You take another one of us, no."

'Ye shall not tempt the Lord your God.'

"So, if You must have another, take me."

Silence

"Or have I not been through enough? How much more will You demand from me?"

Everything.

"Then take me! I'm right here!" The words spit from my tongue like acid.

I want your heart.

My leg gives way, and I collapse in a heap on the mountaintop, curl into a ball, and sob. Gut-wrenching tears give way to guttural screams as naked as my grief until my throat fails me.

I don't know how long I lie there in the dew-coated grass, but when I finally drag myself to my feet, lights glow in the first-floor windows of the big house.

Has something happened?

I half-gallop, half-roll down the hill to the cabin, clambering up the steps and bursting in the door to find Julianna, Liam, and Katy huddling around Samuel.

"What happened?"

Katy's stricken eyes find mine. "Samuel has a fever."

That's what I get for praying.

The whites of Samuel's eyes glisten in the dim candlelight as his eyes dart from Liam to Julianna to Katy. "Am I going to die?" A tremor rolls through his words.

"Let's get you upstairs." Uncle Liam, as always, so business-like, wraps Samuel in a blanket. "Can you walk?"

"Yessir, I think so."

With Julianna on one side and Liam on the other, Samuel disappears up the stairs, as Katy falls into my arms, weeping.

What can I say to her? I have no comfort to offer, so I hold her against my chest.

Uncle Liam appears on the landing. "Julianna refuses to leave Samuel's side. You will need to help Emma take care of food preparation in the morning while I tend the animals." He rubs his hands together. "Better get some sleep. You're going to need it."

"How is Mac?"

Liam's brow creases as he lowers his eyes, but he doesn't answer.

He doesn't need to.

Katy and I wander to our palettes where Claire lies sleeping, but it's futile. Sleep won't come for us.

Before the sun rises, Liam shrugs on his coat and heads for the barn, and Emma, Claire, and Katy start their work in the kitchen. At Emma's direction, I collect eggs and bring in milk, water, and wood for the stove. Once breakfast is prepared, I limp to the top of the stairs with trays of eggs and biscuits for Granda, Uncle Chris, and Aunt Julianna, and bowls of broth for Mac and Samuel. The minty coolness of camphor mixes with the pungent aroma of alcohol, urine, and the sickly-sweet smell of raw meat, reminding me of my time in the hospital.

Chris meets me at the top of the stairs, his eyes puffy and bleary from lack of sleep. "Thank you."

"How is Samuel?"

"His fever seems stable for now." Chris turns toward a rasping, wet cough coming from the first bedroom. "Mac is having trouble breathing. We tried sitting him up in the bed, but it didn't help much."

"Nothing is helping?"

He chews his lower lip, rubbing his hand across his hair. "I've never seen anything like it. He has all the look of someone drowning. Blue lips. Purple blotches on his face." He closes his eyes, his mouth twisting against a stab of pain. "He's coughing up blood."

A heavy pause lingers between us before I can find words. "Do you need anything?"

He shrugs. "Nothing is working." His jaw stiffens, pulsing below his ears. "This sickness is pure evil, I swear it." Taking the trays, he shuffles back to the bedroom. When the door opens, I catch a glimpse of Mac sitting against a pile of pillows, his hair dripping wet, his face the color of a cloudy sky at dusk, and his eyes rolling back in his head while Granda swabs his neck with a wet cloth.

Any thin strand of hope I had left disintegrates into dust.

Emma, Katy, and Claire bombard me with questions as I drag myself into the dining room to join them for the meal, so I relay Chris' information, sparing them the detailed description of what I witnessed.

Liam soon joins us from outside, slumping into his usual chair while Emma prepares his plate. Seeing us pick at our food, Liam grumbles, "Y'all had better eat. You need to keep up your strength." He snatches up his fork and wolfs down his eggs, but none of us follow his example.

The hours seep past like rain runoff thick with mud. I try not to, but I'm compelled to keep checking Claire for any signs of the flu starting to ravage her. I'm haunted by my imagining of her with blue lips and a purple face, gasping out her last breath, but so far, she seems well.

When I carry lunch up to Uncle Chris, his haggard, forlorn expression tells me things have worsened. I almost hate to ask after them, but it seems uncaring not to. "How are they?"

"Samuel's fever is spiking. We need more supplies."

"The doctor said he would return today. I'll make sure he leaves more." Fear twists its tendrils around the base of my spine. "What about Mac?"

Uncle Chris simply shakes his head.

A wild voice screams, the words unintelligible. From another room, a hacking cough rips through the air. Without another word, Chris takes my tray, jutting his chin toward the messy breakfast tray dropped haphazardly on the hall's side table. As I lift the old tray, I see that almost none of the food has been touched.

As promised, the doctor returns in the gray hush of afternoon, his horse lathered and his eyes weary. He carries a leather satchel weighted down with bottles of rubbing alcohol, bandages, and small brown vials. The sharp scent of disinfectant trails behind him as he steps through the door. When he hears of Samuel's condition, he wastes no time with greetings, mounting the stairs two at a time. We gather at the bottom, a silent cluster of pale, lined faces, watching his shadow disappear around the landing and listening to the soft thud of his steps above, each one echoing like a heartbeat.

We've a long wait before we hear his footsteps descending again. The creak of each step tightens my stomach. When he finally appears, his face tells us what we fear before his words confirm it. The lines around his mouth deepen, and his eyes carry that hollow look I recognize in those who bear bad news.

He sets his satchel on the table with a dull thump and wipes his brow with a handkerchief. No one speaks.

"I've done what I can." He uses his handkerchief to rub his glasses. "The fever's holding high for both young men. Mac's lungs are beginning to fill."

Emma presses a hand to her mouth. "Is he—"

The doctor shakes his head before she can finish. "He's still fighting, but it's a hard battle. Once this flu takes hold, it doesn't let go." He sighs and looks around at us, as if weighing how much truth we can bear. "You'll need to be prepared for others here to fall ill soon."

Liam nods, his square jaw set. "We'll manage. What do we need to do?"

"Keep them cool. Sips of water if they're able. When their breathing worsens, prop him up so they can draw air more easily." The doctor hesitates, then lowers his voice. "And pray. There's nothing else medicine can do."

He gathers his things, his hands moving slowly now, as if reluctant to leave. "I'll return before... " He doesn't finish the sentence.

As he steps back out into the afternoon's cloud-covered gloom, no one moves. The house feels small now, and the air thick as though the sickness hangs around us, waiting to pounce.

Katy is the first to fall. Not long after, Chris brings word that Julianna has taken to her bed. As darkness presses against the windows, swallowing what light remains, Claire clutches her head and groans, and a ravenous dread digs its claws into me, squeezing and ripping until I'm nothing but a tattered scrap, flapping helplessly in an unforgiving, icy wind.

Liam joins Granda and Chris on sickbed duty upstairs, leaving Emma and me to hold the fort, Emma handling the inside duties and me the outside. It seems pointless to keep isolating us from the others since we've all been exposed now, but Granda insists.

Emma stands rooted at the base of the stairs, gripping the banister until her knuckles are white, and watching the ceiling like she expects it to cave in or for the Lord Himself to come through it. She whispers, "Please, Lord. Please, Lord," until her dry throat gives out: Her face looks carved from stone, but her hands betray her with their trembling, twisting, and clutching at the air. When Claire's first cough rings in the stairwell, something tears loose in her, making her sway like a tree struck by lightning that refuses to fall.

"I should be up there." Her tortured voice cracks at each word. "My children need me."

"Granda and Uncle Chris won't allow it."

"Julianna went up to care for Samuel." Emma buries her trembling hands in her skirts. "Why can't I see my children, too?"

"And Aunt Julianna is sick now." I touch her elbow in a feeble attempt to offer comfort. "Come, Aunt Emma. You need your rest."

Her blank eyes stare at the ceiling, straining as if by the force of her will she could levitate to the sickroom. Her breathing shallows to a pant, then stops. She lowers her head, pinches her lips together, and inhales deeply. "I will prepare for the evening meal."

"Why don't you make sandwiches? They are simple to eat, and they'll last if the caregivers are too busy to eat them right away." I glance up the stairs. "Plus, they haven't really been eating anything I've taken up."

"Very well." She takes one step toward the kitchen but freezes when another ragged cough sounds in the hall. When the cough subsides, she takes another deep breath. "And broth for the sick."

I'm alone in the quiet now, but it's anything but peaceful. It's the quiet of labored breathing, urgent whispers, and restless nightmares. Every random sound, like the creak of bedsprings and hurried footfalls, pulls me up short. *Is someone coming to tell me it's over?*

I collect water for the night to refill the basins upstairs, and when I bring the fresh water to the kitchen, Emma sits huddled in the corner in a tight ball with her tears streaming onto her skirts. I set the basin down softly, afraid any noise might shatter her. She glances up for a moment, her eyes red-rimmed and vacant, then returns to her curled up position. I want to say something, anything to reassure her, but my throat closes around the words.

Exiting as quickly as my leg will allow, I lean against the hallway wall, my hands shaking. Wind outside hammers against the shutters, heralding an approaching storm that mirrors the torment inside me.

It's wrong that I'm still standing.; wrong that my breaths are steady when they strain, and my lungs pull in clean air while they choke and drown. I press my palm to my forehead, half hoping to feel the heat rise so I can be one of them instead of the one left watching, but it feels cool to the touch.

Why me? Is it because I asked you to take me instead? Is this my punishment? To be the one left alive?

Silence.

When Aunt Emma calls, I carry the trays up the stairs, but no one meets me to collect them. I leave the sandwiches on the hall table, collect the luncheon trays, and return them to the kitchen. Aunt Emma has retired to the sitting room, so I retreat to the main room, stretching out on the floor before the cold, empty hearth.

I lie awake, listening to the wind howl, the rain beat against the cabin's logs, and the muffled cries from above. The house moans with them. I pray as I heard Aunt Emma pray, repeating, "Please, Jesus," but the words fall flat against the ceiling, swallowed by the silence that answers my pleas.

Sometime during the worst of the storm, I must've fallen asleep, because I wake to Uncle Chris shaking my shoulder. In the thick darkness, I can't make out his expression.

"Fin. Fin, wake up."

My eyes snap open, heart hammering, as my worst fears tumble through my thoughts like falling leaves caught in a cold wind. "What is it?"

"Come with me."

I scramble to my feet and follow him to the stairs, where Emma stands waiting, her face lined with anguish, her eyes red and swollen, and her hands twisting the fabric of her skirts. She doesn't speak or acknowledge our presence.

Chris leads us down the hall to the bedroom. The air is thick with the heat radiating from Mac's body and the rank smell of sickness. Mac lies still on the bed. His face is ghostly pale, and his lips and fingertips are a startling blue. Granda kneels beside him, whispering prayers that drift between hope and pleading. His weathered hands tremble against the damp sheets.

For a moment, all sound fades but the rasp of Mac's shallow, uneven breaths fighting to find some way in or out. Aunt Emma moves to his side and sinks onto the mattress, gathering his limp hand in hers.

"Stay with me, my son," she murmurs. "Please stay."

Mac's eyelids flutter, and a faint smile flickers across his mouth, gone almost before it can be seen. A gurgling sound, wet and ragged, rises to his throat.

Is he trying to cough or speak?

Emma presses her ear to his lips, but his breath turns clipped and jagged, and when she dabs a cloth to his mouth, it comes away streaked with red.

"Not yet. Jesus…" Her voice cracks. "Jesus, please, not yet."

Granda bows his head, the cadence of his prayer falling silent. Chris grips the bedpost with white knuckles, while I stand frozen in the doorway, holding my breath.

Then, one long, low, ragged sigh, and the air leaves Mac's chest, never to return.

For a heartbeat, no one speaks. Only the storm outside howls in anguish to acknowledge the loss.

Then, Emma's body crumples forward over her son's chest, her cries drowning out the storm. Chris, his face ashen, steps to her side, but she shoves him away, clutching Mac's hand as though she can hold him in this world.

Granda's eyes close. Moving his lips silently, he reaches to pull the blanket up to Mac's chin. "He's at peace." I barely hear him over the wind and Emma's cries.

Granda rises slowly, laying a hand on Emma's shoulder, but she doesn't stir. Her head rests on Mac's chest, with her fingers tangled in his shirt. Chris kneels beside her, murmuring words I can't make out. And there they remain. It's as if this tableau is frozen in time, marking an end to the lives we've known. I stand beyond the scene as witness but not a part, an outsider encroaching on something sacred, meant only for real family.

A pinch of guilt twists my gut. I've never been close to Mac. When I was younger, I felt ignored by him, so as an adult, I never responded to his attempts to reach out to me, choosing a comfortable reliance on Buck and Ian over a connection with Mac or Tom. Now, that opportunity has passed. Forever.

I can only imagine the pain Aunt Emma, Uncle Chris, and Granda feel, but I don't feel it.

I don't belong here.

Stumbling from the room, I close the door and lean against the wall in the hallway. I can still hear Emma's cries, the low, broken sound that twists knots in my stomach, and I can still see Granda, murmuring hoarse prayers rising toward a Heaven that feels impossibly far away.

Claire.

She will be devastated. She idolizes her brothers, especially Mac. It isn't my place to tell her the news, but at least I can be there for her when Emma and Chris let her know Mac's gone.

As quietly as possible, I pad down the hall and open the door to Claire's sickroom. "Claire?"

Her eyes flutter open, unfocused and glazed with fever, but then a faint smile touches her dry lips. "Fin," she whispers, her voice like breaking glass.

I move to her side, taking her hot, damp hand. Her pulse flutters beneath my fingers.

"I'm here. You rest now."

Her gaze drifts toward the window, where the dim light of candles reflects from the mist-coated glass. "It's so quiet."

I swallow hard. The silence stretches, humming between us. Finally, I nod once. "Yes."

Her breath catches, a small, broken sound trembling in the air. She turns her face toward the wall. "Mac's dead, isn't he?"

"Yes."

Her shoulders curl toward her chest as she folds in on herself with a rasping sob, her grief too deep for words.

I reach out, brushing a strand of hair from her cheek. "He's not hurting anymore." The words squeak out, sounding hollow to my ears. "He's at peace now."

A tear traces a line down her temple to her ear. "Where is Mama?"

"She's with him. She hasn't left his side."

Claire's eyes close again. "Will she come to me before I die?"

"Don't talk like that!" My words are sharper than I mean them to be. My throat tightens. "You're going to get better, you hear me?"

Her lips twitch. "You don't know that."

I press her hand to my chest. "I believe it."

She doesn't answer. Her breathing, shallow and uneven, catches in her throat and deteriorates into a rattling cough that shakes her body in spasms, continuing in wet, gurgling waves until it seems her lungs might come gushing out of her mouth. I hold her hand, listening to the rain starting again, steady and relentless.

After brief moments of ragged, shallow breathing, another cough, deeper this time, flecks her lips with red. She sags back onto the pillows, exhausted. "It hurts."

I lean my forehead against the mattress, fighting to hold back the swirling tide rising in my chest. "I know. I know. Just keep breathing. Please."

Her eyelids droop again, and the world narrows to the sound of her uneven breaths and the patter of rain against the window.

Uncle Chris slides into the room, his steps heavy with weariness and grief. Moving slowly to her bedside, he touches her cheek.

"She's holding on," he whispers. "That's something."

I nod, unable to speak. But as her breathing slows, I can't help the thought that slips, unbidden and terrible, through the cracks in my faith.

God has abandoned this family.

Is it because of the things I did in the war? Have I not paid enough of a price, losing Will, Hasan, and Ian? Must you destroy everyone I know and love?

Her breaths continue to shallow, and the pauses between them grow long enough to steal the air from my lungs. I dip a cloth into the basin beside the bed and press it on her forehead. Her head burns ever hotter.

Down the hall, the low murmur of voices drones in rhythm with the rain. Granda prays an uninterrupted stream of Scripture. Uncle Liam gives quiet encouragement to Julianna and Katy. Aunt Emma moans, punctuated with guttural sobs.

Claire stirs, a soft sound like the call of a mourning dove escaping her lips. "Fin?"

"I'm here."

She opens her eyes a fingernail's width. They roll back in her head, showing the bloodshot whites "I dreamed… I saw a light. Mac was in it. He looked like a bright morning."

I can't speak. I hold her hand tighter, afraid that if I let go, she'll drift toward that light and never return.

Then, slow footsteps thump in the hall. The door opens, and a sliver of lamplight falls across the bed. Emma stands in the doorway, slightly bent at the waist with her arms folded across it as if trying to hold herself together. Her cheeks and around her eyes are hollowed out and gray. Her skirts are wrinkled, and strands of her hair have slipped loose from their pins. She looks older, not by years but by lifetimes.

"Aunt Emma." I jump to my feet.

She doesn't answer but crosses the room on unsteady feet. Uncle Chris greets her, laying a hand on her arm, but she brushes past him and sinks into the chair beside Claire's bed.

"Oh, my sweet girl," she breathes, her voice breaking. Her hand trembles as she touches Claire's cheek.

Claire flutters her eyes open again. Recognition flickers across her face. "Mama?"

Emma nods, choking back a sob. "I'm here. I'm right here."

Would you steal two children from her? Are you that cruel?

Don't make Claire pay for my sins.

For a long moment, the room falls deathly silent, then Emma starts to hum soft, broken fragments of lullabies from Claire's childhood.

I can't bear it, the sight of a mother whose heart has already been ripped and laid bare once today, now bracing for it to shatter again. I turn away, striding toward the door.

Behind me, Emma's whisper drifts through the still air. "Lord, please don't take her, too."

She's still praying, amid her terrible grief?

How can you ignore such deep faith?

The clock downstairs strikes the half hour. I bow my head, my teeth grinding as I start praying with her, though the words seem empty, and the silence that follows is heavy and cold.

Then, Ian's voice echoes in my ears, as if he were standing in the room with us. *Promise you will not give up on God.*

And the faint echo of my reply, *I promise.*

CHAPTER THIRTY-NINE

October 1918

Leaving Claire and her family to their mourning, I cross the hallway and tap gently on the door to the room where Katy, Aunt Julianna, and Samuel lie.

Liam responds. "Come."

I slip through the door, taking in the scene. Liam sits beside Julianna's bed, holding her hand and with his other hand, dousing rags in water to wipe her face, neck, and chest. Julianna's thin, cotton dressing gown is drenched with sweat and clinging to her body. Her chestnut hair, always pinned up in a neat bun, spreads in a pool of waves around her head like a dark halo. Her face is as white as her gown, and her sunken eyes are rimmed in red. Like Claire, her breaths come thick with fluid, ragged, and shallow, and her coughs return with each exhale, deep and rasping.

Her other arm stretches to the bed beside hers, her thin fingers weaving a web through Samuel's fingers and kneading his palm. His cheeks glow red with fever.

And beyond Samuel, Katy lies on a pallet of thick blankets. Her wild eyes meet mine and grow wider as she strains to sit up, reaching her hands toward me. She babbles a few incomprehensible words, then screams, "Ian! Watch out!" before slumping back onto the blankets.

"Uncle Liam?" When he glances up for a moment, I motion for him to come.

He closes his eyes, drops the cloth in the basin, and scrapes the chair across the wood floor as he stands. "What is it?"

Again, I motion for him to step outside. Furrows deepen around his eyes as he pinches his lips, but he sighs and strides out the door. I close it softly behind us.

"Uncle Liam, I wanted to let you know…"

"What? What is it?"

"Mac has passed away."

All his irritation and impatience melts away in an instant. His shoulders sag as tears well in his eyes. "Very well." He glances behind him at the bedroom door. "You were wise to tell me beyond their hearing. I don't need them getting upset right now."

"I thought it would be better to let you decide."

"We will wait to tell them until they are well." With that, Liam stalks back into the room, shutting the door in my face.

I drag myself down the stairs. The whole house seems to groan as I push out the front door and into the cold night, gasping as rain pelts my face. I sink to my knees in the mud, pressing my palms to my eyes until all I see is red.

Please spare my loved ones. No one deserves such torture as this illness brings.

Silence.

So, I keep repeating my prayers, naming each person in turn, hoping that if I follow the example of the widow who wouldn't leave the judge alone, the Lord might finally relent and give me what I ask, if for no other reason than to make me go away.

After a while, the rain thins to mist. I remain outside until my breath steadies, and numbness takes hold of my body and mind. By then, dawn bleeds over the mountains in a thin, gray fog that spills across the cabin. No one else is available to do the morning chores, so I trudge through the mud to the barn to care for the animals. Then, I collect the milk, water, and firewood to take to the kitchen. I remove my muddy shoes before entering, out of respect for Grandma Ester, and close the door behind me.

The thick, humid air carries a rancid smell mixed with alcohol, liniments, lye, burning coals, and rotting food left untended in the kitchen. My stomach turns, and spit fills the back of my mouth. Somehow, being out in the fresh, washed air deceived me into a sense of finality, as if the new dawn meant the nightmare had come to an end.

"Fin."

The flat, hollow sound of Uncle Liam's voice freezes my heart.

"Katy is asking for you."

No, the nightmare isn't over. It's just begun.

I follow Liam on the long walk to Katy's sickroom as if I'm on a death march. Liam busies himself with Aunt Julianna while I kneel beside Katy's palette.

"I'm here."

She raises her brows to force her eyes to open. Purple smudges surround her red-tinged eyes, and matching purple blotches color her cheeks. "Fin."

"Hi, lazy bones. I just had to do the chores all by myself."

She blinks slowly. "Where are Buck and Ian?"

I pause, swallowing down the lump rising in my throat. "You know them. They're off doing whatever they want while I'm left holding the bag."

She presses her limp hand against my chest as if trying to mock punch me. "You be nice to your brothers."

"I will try. For you."

"When is Samuel coming home?"

"He's home, Katy. Remember?"

"We must have a grand celebration when they come home. With cakes and pies."

"Of course, we must have cakes and pies."

Her eyes roll toward the window. "It's so dark tonight."

I cut my eyes to the window where the sun's rays filter through the rain coating the glass, spraying light across the wall. "You don't see the sunlight?"

"There aren't any stars tonight."

"No. It rained all night."

"You're all wet."

I chuckle. "That's what happens when you sit out in the rain."

"Mmm." She closes her eyes, and they linger until I think she's drifted off to sleep. Then, she sighs.

"It's warm."

It's warm. My throat squeezes shut until my breaths sound like Katy's. *Ian said the same thing before he died. And it's anything but warm in this room.*

"Uncle Liam?"

"Yes?"

"Could you come and check on Katy?"

Liam rushes to my side. "What is it?"

"I don't know, maybe nothing. Can you check her?"

He presses his hand against her head and then her belly. "She's burning up." He dashes to the dressing table and brings back two cloths drenched in alcohol. "Here. On her forehead."

I spread the cloth over her forehead, allowing the liquid to drip down her neck, while Liam wipes down her chest and stomach. The fumes sting my eyes. Following Liam's example, I turn the cloth over and mop her brow and the back of her neck, but her skin continues to burn as hot as a flame.

"It isn't working."

"Katy? What's happening?" Aunt Julianna tries to sit up but falls back immediately, holding her head and moaning.

"Lie down, dear. I'm taking care of her." But Liam's grim expression and frantic movements give the lie to his words.

Katy's breathing becomes more coarse, and within minutes, her lips and fingernails take on a blue-gray cast, an all-too-familiar turn.

"The doc said sit her up to help her breathe more easily."

Liam nods. Propping pillows behind her, he slides her up onto them, but her face pales almost instantly, and she flails her arms in protest, sliding back down into a curled-up position where her breaths shallow to a quick wheeze followed by a wet gurgle.

"Samuel? When is my Samuel coming?" she cries.

Liam tries to hold Katy, but she arches her back and shoves him away, pounding on his chest with surprising strength and calling for Samuel again.

Samuel's eyes flutter, but he doesn't or can't respond.

I try to help Liam hold Katy up, receiving a punch in the nose for my efforts. Her head rolls on her neck as if her muscles have turned to jelly, then she collapses, unconscious.

Time slows and stretches, one minute seeming to take an hour and the next hour passing in a blur. Liam and I battle Katy's fever like we're facing demon armies, combining prayer with washing her body in alcohol and pounding her back to loosen the congestion. As the sun dips below the window's ledge, Liam grabs her shoulder and shakes her limp body.

"You will not die! Do you hear me, Katrina Marie? You are not to leave your mother."

Julianna cries out, clutching at the air as if something unseen floats above her that she wants to grab and hold. "Liam, the baby is crying!"

Liam rushes to Julianna's side, soothing her with assurances and asking her to pray with him, but she doesn't seem to hear him, responding instead to something we can't see or hear.

I continue my frantic bathing, murmuring a constant stream in Katy's ear. "You are my best friend. I love you like a sister. I don't want to be in a world without you in it. Please fight. Don't give in. Stay with me. I need you. I love you."

As night rolls over the cabin, her face starts to darken. Her breath becomes more sporadic. A thin thread of blood leaks from the edge of her mouth.

I've seen it all before.

"Katy." I shake her gently. "Katy, look! The stars are out."

Her ragged breath hitches in her throat. I pretend that means she hears me. "The breeze is chasing the clouds away, and the stars are shining bright, just for you, sweet girl. Just for you. Do you see them?"

I pry my eyes away from Katy to glance toward the other two beds where Liam is ministering to his wife and son. "Uncle Liam. You might want to come."

He strokes Julianna's hair, then strides to Katy's side.

"Look, Katy. Your pa is here."

Liam takes her hand gently. "I love you, Katy-did. I love you." His chin drops to his chest, and for the first time in my life, I see Uncle Liam's strength crumble. His shoulders shake, his chest heaves, and tears stream down his tortured face. "Oh, my Katy. My girl."

"Katy!" Julianna cries out.

Liam closes his eyes, turns his head away, and shuffles back to his wife.

"Let's watch the stars together. How about that? We can count them and see what shapes we can make out of them. Hey, look at that! Those stars look like a lion. What do you see?"

I wait for the hitch in her breath, but this time, it doesn't come.

"Katy?"

My vision swims, the weight of the pain pressing against my ribs and squeezing the air from my lungs. Somewhere deep inside, something breaks, and years of throbbing, stinging grief gush from my mouth in a ragged, continuous scream.

When the well of agony finally runs out, I bury my face in Katy's long, red curls, still wet and smelling of alcohol. My body trembles, but my heart doesn't have the fight left to contain my tears, and my legs don't have the strength to move from her side. Liam doesn't speak. The only sounds are Liam's muffled cries and the faint ticking of the clock at the foot of the stairs.

I don't know how much time has passed when I hear a strong knock at the front door. I'm aware of Granda's heavy footfalls in the hall and on the stairs. A few minutes later, our door cracks, and the doctor steps in, pausing in the doorway when he sees our tear-stained faces.

After a few moments, he tiptoes to Katy's palette and touches her neck. His eyes close as he lowers his head, then spins and performs a similar check on Samuel and Aunt Julianna.

"Samuel appears to be turning a corner. His fever has broken. If the congestion clears in the next day or two, he should be out of the woods."

Liam nods, but the good news doesn't change his distressed, sorrowful expression. "What about Julianna?"

The doctor shakes his head. "We don't know yet. Tomorrow will tell the tale." He places a hand on Liam's shoulder. "I am sorry for your loss."

Liam's "thank you" sounds more like a groan than words.

The doctor clears his throat and straightens his back. "You will need to bury them as quickly as possible. Their bodies can still spread the disease."

Bury them? How can we possibly have a funeral with everyone sick?

As if reading my mind, the doctor continues. "You can have a memorial service later, once the danger has passed, but for now, get the bodies in the ground." He winces, closing his eyes again. "I'm truly sorry. But the disease is spreading in town, and we must do all we can to stem the tide."

"We'll take care of…things." Liam crosses to the door as if to hurry the doctor out.

"What about Claire?" The question leaps from my mouth before fully forming in my mind.

"I'm going to check on her now."

When the door closes behind the doctor, Liam stands for a long while, his hand still resting on the doorframe, shoulders bowed beneath a weight too heavy to bear. His eyes are red but dry, and he carries the look of someone who's run out of tears but not grief.

"Fin." His voice is low and hoarse. "We need to move her."

I stare at him, not understanding.

"Katy. We can't leave her here." He swallows hard. "We'll… we'll put her in Mac's room for now, until I can dig their graves."

His words crash over me like waves of thunder. *Dig their graves? What is he talking about?*

My throat tightens. She looks so small there on the palette of thick blankets. *She's only sleeping.* Her hair spills across the pillow, the once vibrant red dull now against the bluish gray of her skin. *She's only sleeping.*

"Fin." Liam's voice cracks this time.

No. You can't take her.

Liam bends down to gather her up in those blankets.

"No!" I shove Liam's hands away. "I'll do it."

My hands shake as I slide them beneath the blankets, careful to be as gentle as I can, as though she might feel me lifting her. Her body is as light as a bundle of fresh linens taken down off the line. I can't help but think of all the times we raced across the pasture, chasing the wind through the fluttering wash after Ester hung it out to dry, her laughter ringing through the air and echoing off the trees. And now this stillness, this awful forever silence.

Liam bends to help, but I shake my head. "I have her." Fresh tears spring to my eyes. The boards creak under my feet as I carry her through the hall. When I reach Mac's room, I can't bear to look at him.

The two beds stand side by side, one waiting for my Katy. A knife twists inside me, sharp and unbearable. *I can't do this.*

Liam stands beside me for a moment, his head bowed, then he reaches out, takes her in his arms, kisses her face, and lays her on the bed, drawing the sheet up over her face. His fingers linger on the edge of the fabric before falling away.

"God forgive us," he whispers.

I grip the bedpost to steady myself. My chest is hollow, like all the air's been sucked from my lungs. "How… how are we supposed to do this?"

Liam doesn't answer right away. His jaw pulses beneath his skin, and when he finally speaks, his words are as thin as his breath. "We must keep going. That's all there is left."

The wind outside picks up, rattling the shutters. Somewhere down the hall, another wet, ragged cough reminds me that the sickness isn’t done yet.

Liam straightens, his eyes glazing. “I’ll need to start digging before the cold makes the ground harder.”

“You haven’t slept in two days.”

“Neither have you.” He manages the faintest ghost of a smile. “But we can’t wait, Fin. You heard the doctor.”

He turns and leaves before I can argue, the door closing quietly behind him.

I sink to my knees between the two beds. For a long time, I stare at the shape of Katy beneath the sheets, willing her to move, to sit up, to take a breath. I try to pray, but all that comes out is a broken whisper.

“Please… no more.”

CHAPTER FORTY

October 1918

The first light of a gray dawn streaks through the window, thin and cold. I must've fallen asleep sitting with my head on Katy's bed and slept through the afternoon and overnight. My neck aches, and my hands are stiff from clutching the covers during my long sleep.

I hear movement downstairs, someone's boots scraping, a chair sliding, and the back door opening. I push myself slowly to my feet against my body's creaking protests and go to the window. Outside, Liam's walking across the yard, spade in hand, his breath billowing white in the early morning air.

Time to be a man. I hurry downstairs, pull on my coat, and step outside. The air bites my face and hands, burning my lungs on the first breath. Frost glitters on the grass like tiny shards of glass. The world feels—wrong. Even with the clouds, the day is too bright, and the air too fresh. And the birds are singing. A seed of anger blossoms in my stomach, burning its way into my chest. *Don't they know what's happening?*

Liam glances back when he hears my boots crunch across the yard, but he doesn't speak. His eyes are rimmed red and circled in gray, and his face is drawn tight. I pick up another spade leaning against the barn, then hurry to catch up to him.

"Ground's like a stone," he mutters.

We walk in silence to the graveyard behind the barn atop the hill where Liam started digging yesterday while I slept. He points to a second site adjacent to the one he started and gestures for me to begin. When I drive the blade down, the earth resists, stiff and unyielding as if refusing to accept the precious planting, but I keep at it, matching Liam's steady rhythm. The sound of the shovels scraping the earth fills the silent space between us.

After a long while, Liam stops, leaning on the handle. Sweat pops out on his forehead. "Two graves." He stares into the shallow pit. "Side by side."

His words empty me. For the first time, their deaths are real. I can't speak, so I shove the spade into the ground, allowing my anger to be the fuel.

We dig until our arms shake and our blistered palms bleed. By the time the holes are deep enough, the clouds have scattered, and the sun is throwing long shadows across the field.

Then, Granda steps around the barn, walking slowly up the hill, supporting Emma on one side, while Chris holds her elbow on the other. Emma looks smaller somehow, as if her heart has shrunken and her body has shriveled to match it. Her steps falter, but Chris catches her arm and steadies her on her feet.

When they reach the graves, Emma looks down, her pale lips trembling. "Side by side," she whispers, echoing Liam's words. She drops to her knees and covers her face with her hands.

Liam brings Mac, and I carry Katy. The sheets rustle in the breeze as we lower them slowly into the holes in the earth. It all feels too final, two white-shrouded bundles with mounds of dirt behind their heads, ready to cover them up forever.

Emma lifts her hands. "Lord." The word chokes in her throat. "Take care of my baby."

Chris kneels beside her on the hard ground. Liam stands by the dirt mounds, leaning on his shovel, his eyes staring at some distant point on the horizon. Granda bows his head. Moving his lips in silent prayer.

But my hands hang useless at my sides. I have nothing left to pray. The cold has found its way into my bones and frozen my heart.

After several minutes of tense stillness, Granda says the Lord's Prayer, his voice cracking every few words. Then Liam scoops up a shovelful of dirt and, after a brief pause, throws it into Mac's grave. I take up my shovel and mirror his movements, shoveling dirt onto my best friend, like the betrayer I am. Each clump of dirt thuds when it hits their bodies, as if beating for their silent hearts. Chris and Emma's weeping provides the background rhythm, ebbing and flowing with each new shovelful.

We set two simple, wooden crosses at the head of the graves until we can do better. Emma stays there long after the rest of us turn toward the house, with her hands resting on Mac's fresh mound of dirt. Her skirts and face are covered with mud as she rocks gently, whispering his name like a lullaby left unfinished.

I glance back only once, but the sight burns into my mind.

The air in the house remains stale with sickness and heavy with sorrow. I slump at the kitchen table and press my cheek to the rough wood amid the half-empty bowls and untouched plates from the last endless days. My body is stiff and cold.

From upstairs, I hear a long cough, although not the deep, racking kind that took Mac and Katy. This one sounds wet and weak, like wind ruffling the water on the lake or passing through rain-drenched leaves. Then, the house falls quiet again.

I wander into the sitting room to find Granda in his rocker by the window, with a blanket draped over his knees. He stares out the window, his eyes wide open, but I don't think he's seeing anything outside.

"Granda?"

He finally responds, his voice gravelly and low. "I thought burying my wife was the hardest thing I'd ever have to do." He pauses, his throat working and jaw pulsing. "I was wrong."

There's nothing to say that wouldn't sound as hollow and empty as I feel, so I nod, rubbing the heel of my hand against my eye.

When a knock rattles the door, the sound makes me flinch. For a moment, I can't bring myself to move, afraid of what new blow might come. But when Granda shifts as if to rise, I lift my hand to stay him and limp to the door.

The doctor stands, hat in hand, holding his leather bag. His face looks older than it did two days ago, drawn, and the kind of tired that comes from seeing too much death.

"I came as soon as I could," he says quietly as he enters the sitting room. "The situation in town's worsening. Half the families have someone sick. The church has been turned into a hospital."

Granda nods, then glances at the doctor with a raised brow. "We buried them yesterday."

"I'm sorry." The doc's gaze drifts past me to the stairs. "How are the others?"

Granda turns his head back to the window. "Claire's holding on. Her fever broke sometime before dawn."

The doctor exhales, the first sound of relief I've heard in days. "That's a mercy. Keep her warm, and make sure she drinks plenty of water. If she can keep water down, she may recover." He glances around the dim room. "And the others?"

"Samuel's fever broke, too. Julianna's still bad off."

The doc nods, then squares his shoulders. "I can do no more for you, so I won't be back unless you call for me. I'm overwhelmed with patients, I'm afraid." He lowers his voice. "This version is worse than spring. The depot became a breeding ground with people from the city and soldiers coming through. The young ones are dying so fast." His eyes flick to me, and he swallows hard. "You take care of yourself, son. This thing's not done with us yet."

He leaves a small bundle of supplies on the table, then straightens his coat and steps out into the cold. Through the window, I watch him mount and ride the trail toward the road, his figure disappearing into the late afternoon mist.

The silence closes in again. Somewhere upstairs, a floorboard creaks, and I hear Emma's soft voice humming a hymn, the same one she used to sing when her children were afraid of storms. So, she's with Claire now. Claire will be happy about that.

Did anyone tell Claire about Katy?

Granda has dozed off, so I creep to the stairs and climb as quietly as my leg will allow, then down the hall to tap on Claire's door.

I barely hear Emma's reply. "Come."

As I enter, Claire stirs. Her lips move in a soundless effort to speak. I lean closer, catching one word: “Cold.”

I pull the blanket higher around her shoulders and take her hand. No longer burning, it’s cool and clammy, which is a good sign, the doctor said.

“Fin?” Her voice is hoarse and thin.

“I’m here.”

Her eyelids flutter open. For a moment, I see confusion flicker there, then recognition. And something else. Grief. She knows.

“Katy?” she whispers.

I swallow hard, searching for the right words, but they don’t come. All I can manage is a shake of my head.

Her face folds in wrinkles of anguish, tears streaming silently. I reach for a cloth to wipe them, but she turns her face toward the wall, so I hold her hand until her shoulders stop shaking, and she fades into exhausted sleep.

The last rays of the setting sun spill through the window and across the floorboard. Downstairs, I hear the clink of a pot and the low rumble of Granda’s voice. Claire stirs, her lashes fluttering. “Is it morning?”

“No, dear,” I whisper. “It’s almost evening.”

A faint smile touches her lips. “Then maybe…I made it through. Maybe we all will.”

I want to believe that the return of the sunlight through the clouds means something, that it’s not just the sun but a promise of better days, and a hope for the passing of the angel of death.

Outside, a whippoorwill calls from the woods. One tentative, shrill whistle, but enough to make me wonder if the world hasn’t ended after all. Maybe all we can do now is live one day at a time, until the world remembers how to be warm again.

Over the next several days, Claire grows a bit stronger, though her voice is still a hoarse whisper, and her steps falter if she tries to stand. Each morning, I bring her water steeped with tea and honey, coaxing her to drink, and each evening, I sit by her bed, reading from the worn Bible Ester always kept on her nightstand.

She listens with her eyes closed, her lips moving silently with the words. When I pause, she opens her eyes. "It sounds different now."

"How so?"

"I don't know." She tilts her head. "Maybe because I was so close to death. Maybe because Mac came to me in the light and spoke to me when he died." She shrugs. "Maybe because now, I believe it." Her eyes narrow. "Even though you don't."

I look down, embarrassed by the truth of her words. I've tried praying, but every time I start, all that comes is anger and a hollow ache in the hole that Katy left in my heart.

"I've been so selfish. I treated Katy horribly." Her lashes flutter, blinking away her tears. "And now, it's too late to make it up to her."

"What are you talking about? You and Katy were fast friends."

If eyes had a voice, hers would be groaning with anguish. "I made a point to brag to her about how all the boys wanted me, and how pretty they all thought I was, when I knew she felt embarrassed about no one pursuing her and sad about her looks. Keeping her down made me feel…powerful? Important?" Her head slumps. "I don't know."

"Katy loved you."

"I know. She loved me because that's who she was. Just like Ian." Her fingers pick at the quilt covering her legs. "That's not all. I toyed with Buck and Ian's affections to set them against each other, hoping they'd fight over me." She makes a retching sound in her throat. "I can't believe how awful I've been." She pauses, cutting her eyes toward me. "If I could've gotten away with it, I would have made it a three-way fight, but you'd have nothing to do with me."

"I always loved you, but you were Ian's girl."

She half-sneers. "Until Buck was around anyway."

"Ian never knew."

Her eyes fill with moisture. "I didn't deserve him." She lifts her head. "But I want to live the rest of my life in a way he would be proud of."

"He thought you hung the moon." I offer her a gentle smile, softening my eyes. "You could do no wrong."

"He was a wonderful man." Claire shifts on her pillow, watching me. "So are you. But now, you're lost."

I open my mouth to protest, but my words fail, so I study the wood grain of the floor.

"Fin, what happened to you over there?"

I want to explain, to tell her how many people I've killed; how I befriended a stranger who was my enemy, only to kill him; how another dear friend died because of me; how my Māori brother, Mani, almost died trying to save my life; how it's my fault Ian died; how I betrayed both of my promises to him. I want to tell her how I betrayed Katy, too, by dumping her in the cold, hard ground and shoveling dirt over her. But the confessions won't come.

Instead, I whisper, "I don't know how to do this."

Claire's hand, thin and frail, reaches across the quilt to find mine. Her touch is cool but sure. "You don't have to do it alone. We'll learn together."

For a moment, everything else fades. There's only her hand, her eyes, and the smallest glow of warmth, more than I've felt in days.

When her breathing slows again, I pull the blanket higher around her shoulders. She drifts off, the soft, steady rhythm of her breathing returning after so many fearful days praying for the next breath to come.

I stay there as the sunlight retreats across the floor like the brush of a kiss, pondering how a fragile miracle can fit in the space of a single breath or the touch of a hand.

I realize I'm smiling for the first time since the sickness came. It feels strange, almost foreign, but I allow it to stay.

Claire is alive. And for now, that's enough.

CHAPTER FORTY-ONE

November 1918

Word reaches us that a peace treaty has been signed in France. The war in Europe is finally over, but our celebration consists of praying and tears, for we also receive a telegram informing us that Tom is hospitalized in France with the Spanish flu.

Emma retreats to the kitchen table, remaining there long after sunset, with a single lamp burning beside her. Her hands rest in her lap, as still as Katy's hands after she passed. Her Bible lies open before her, the pages rippled from tears, but she's not reading. She doesn't look up when I step into the room.

"Claire's asking for you."

Her eyes move, but she looks through me. She's lost in some far-off place that I can't see. "I can't," she whispers.

I pull out a chair and sit across from her. "She needs you. She's worried about Tom."

"I *can't*," she repeats, her voice splintering with the final word. Tears rim her eyes. "I've prayed, Fin. Every hour, every day, all night I've prayed, and He's taken them anyway." The lamp flickers, throwing shadows dancing across her face in a macabre mockery of her grief. "Mac…Katy…now Tom."

"He didn't take Claire. And we don't know about Tom yet. Don't give up hope."

She presses a fist to her mouth, choking back a sob. "He allowed them to suffer. He let them die. And for what? Some warped attempt to teach me a lesson? As payment for a sin I committed? Or was it simply cruelty?"

I open my mouth to speak, but she lifts her hand, not in anger but with terrible weariness. "Don't tell me it's His will. Don't dare say it."

Her familiar words, spoken in my heart more times than I can count, hit me hard. I stare at this woman who sits hollow-eyed before the same book she once clung to as if it were life itself. *What can I say to her? I've asked the same questions, and I have no answers.*

Finally, she murmurs to herself, "If accepting this is faith, I don't know how to hold onto it anymore."

I reach across the table, resting my hand over hers. Her skin is cold. "Talk to Claire, Aunt Emma. She has found something…wonderful. Let her hold faith for you for now."

Her shoulders sag as if not believing is as heavy as her grief.

The lamp sputters, and in the dim light, I see tears trace down her cheeks, falling onto the open Bible and blurring the words. I stay with her until her breathing steadies. Finally, she spreads her open palms on the table in something that looks like surrender. Then, she closes the Bible, stands up, brushes the front of her skirt, and wanders into the hall like a ghost of the person she once was.

In a moment, I follow her and watch from the hallway as she treads slowly up the stairs, hopefully to Claire's room. Then, I join Granda, who sits in his usual spot, staring out the sitting room window.

I've often wanted to ask him what he's looking for, but I don't want to stir his grief, so I curl up in the opposite chair, and we sit together in silence for several minutes.

"What's on your mind, son?"

I startle at his sudden question, then suck in a deep breath. "I'm worried about Aunt Emma. Because of her losses, she's doubting her faith."

Granda cuts his eyes toward me and lifts a brow. "Is it her doubt you're asking me about, or your own?"

Wincing, I lean my head against the chair's pillowed arm. I've never been able to hide anything from the man. "Both, I guess."

Granda turns away from the window, leaning forward with his fingers laced and his elbows on his knees. "I'm acquainted with loss and what it can do to someone's beliefs. You know the stories. We've talked about them before."

"I remember."

"Ester pulled me out of a very dark place." He covers his face with his gnarled hands. "I wanted to die rather than face life without my Lakota family. To my shame. But Ester reached deep into my heart and found me."

"You told me."

He sits up, straight and tall in his chair. "What I didn't tell you was, when Ester's love shattered the hard covering over my heart, I heard the Lord's voice." He squeezes his eyes tight. "I'll never forget His words. He said, '*You are my precious son. Accept my love, and the love now beside you, and let it bring healing to your wounded heart.*' Can you imagine?" His voice catches as his eyes fill. "He called me His precious son." He folds his hands as if in prayer. "Since that day, I've never doubted His existence again."

"Even when Ester died?"

"Even then." He chuckles. "Oh, I've been angry with Him. I've questioned His reasoning, challenged His decisions, and raged against His choices." His smile crinkles the corners of his eyes. "But I know He is real, and I know He loves me. Despite what the circumstances may say."

My simmering rage boils, the heat within me rising. "But how can you believe killing Katy is love? Or Mac? What about the hundreds of people dying in town?"

Granda pinches the skin on his arm. "This mortal flesh must die because of man's failures, not God's. We will all face death because of sin. It's only a matter of when."

"You're saying Katy died because of her sin?" I throw up my hand. "That's ridiculous. Katy didn't sin."

"Of course she did. We all do. But no, her sin didn't bring the illness upon her. The sin that infests this world like a disease, which has tainted everything since the fall, brought all illnesses and death with it." Granda reaches toward me, as if beckoning me. "Don't you see, Fin?

Katy, Mac, and Ester are still alive. Only their bodies died. And they had to die, to free them from the prison of their flesh. You must die, too, to receive your freedom. As must I."

"But why did they have to go first?"

Pain creases his brow. "I wish it had been me. It is hardest for those left behind." His steel gray eyes bore into mine. "But would you wish to bring them back from their freedom and joy to relieve your suffering?"

I've never thought about it that way. "But Aunt Emma made a good point. If death is God's will, then He is cruel."

Granda's face sags, making his jowls hang loose below his chin. "Dear, sweet Emma." He shakes his head. "No, death was *never* God's will."

"Isn't everything that happens God's will?"

His head tilts back, and his belly quivers with laughter. "Hardly. Remember, Jesus tells us to *pray* for God's will to be done. You've seen war, son. Would you call that nightmare God's will?"

I chew on my lower lip, my head spinning.

"Here's what I've come to understand." He lifts one finger. "God despises death. It is an offense to His being. That's why He had to take it on and overcome it Himself."

"Jesus on the cross."

"Correct." He lifts a second finger. "Now, because of Jesus, death is defeated, and God's beloved children are saved from its clutches through the resurrection." Granda offers me an encouraging smile. "God didn't kill Katy or Mac. He saved them. Do you see how everything works together?"

I study my hands for several minutes before replying. "You've given me a lot to think about, Granda."

"One more thing." He leans forward and takes my hands. "You don't have to wait until you get to heaven to know God. He wants to know you now." Granda's soothing smile warms my heart like a fire on a frigid day. "He has known suffering. He knows what it's like to lose someone you love. Talk with Him. Listen for His words in your heart. He is still speaking."

Granda's right. I've heard His voice, challenging me to forgive myself and promising to be with me. *Why can't I hold on to that belief, the way Granda has?*

A knock on the door jolts me from my reverie.

"Go, see who it is, son." Granda leans back in his chair and turns to the window.

I pad to the door and pull it open. A man, elderly by the look of his slumped back, dressed in an oversized black coat, brown wool pants, worn army boots, and a wide-brimmed felt hat pulled low on his head, stands with his back to me.

"May I help you, sir?"

Slowly, the man turns. I blink, then close my eyes and shake my head. When I open them, an icy breath washes over my skin, sending a chill up my back. I open my mouth, only to close it again, any words I can muster lodging in my throat. Finally, a single letter squeaks through. "B…"

"Brother." His voice is thin and ragged as a torn veil.

"B…Buck?"

His drawn face is covered in red scars. His hair hangs in long, dull, stringy strands, sticking out from under his hat. The coat swallows his emaciated frame. I barely recognize him.

But it is him.

He lowers his eyes, studying my shoes. "I'm home."

He sounds like wood scraping over gravel, but I can still hear hints of the old Buck.

"Buck." Something swells like a wave in my chest, breaking through the rusty, iron-hard coating and exploding from me. "Buck!" I wrap my arms around him and lift him in the air, spinning in a circle on the porch. He weighs about as much as a child.

Buck groans as I squeeze him tighter. "Whoa. Don't break any bones."

"I can't believe it! Come in! Come in! Granda will be so excited."

"I doubt that."

I chuckle, remembering my own homecoming. "You'll see. Come on inside!"

"It would help if you put me down."

I guffaw, but instead of putting him down, I spin him again, squeezing even tighter.

Finally, he gasps, "Enough already."

So, I put him down but leave my arm around his shoulders. I'm not sure if I'm trying to protect him because he seems so fragile or keep him from leaving, but I can't make myself let him go. "I've missed you. Where in God's name have you been?"

"That's a long answer, and I'd rather only have to share it once."

I nod. "Fair enough." I usher him into the sitting room, pushing him in front of me like a child presented before company. "Granda. You have a visitor."

"Who is it?" He swings his chair around. When his eyes land on Buck, they widen, and his mouth hangs slack. "Buck? Son, is that you?"

Buck removes his hat. "Yessir." He won't meet Granda's eyes, staring instead at his feet. I can feel Buck trembling through my arm, still firmly on his back.

Granda pushes himself from the chair, beckoning with both hands. "Come here to me, boy."

Slowly, Buck takes a step forward, but Granda rushes to meet him, enveloping him in a huge bear hug.

Suddenly, Buck crumples from Granda's arms and falls to his knees, bending his forehead to touch the wooden planks. "Please…forgive me."

The plaintive wail wrenches my heart. I place a hand on his shuddering shoulders, kneeling beside him.

Stiffly, Granda goes down on one knee before Buck, puts a finger beneath his chin, and lifts his head. "Look at me, son."

Buck's eyes dart like a cornered cat's but finally come to rest on Granda's face. "I'm so sorry."

His voice sounds like Buck at twelve, apologizing to Pa after his death. A vision of Buck at Pa's grave swirls before me, making my breath whistle through my teeth.

"Whatever it is, you are long forgiven. We're just glad you've come home." Granda cradles Buck's head in his arms, holding him steady while thousands of days' worth of tears flow.

Buck's tears seem endless. Even Granda's arthritic knees won't make him let go of Buck, and I might never take my hands off him again.

Finally, through snuffles, Buck asks, "Where are the others?"

My heart stops in my chest. Buck doesn't know. About any of it. I glance at Granda, hoping he'll be the one to break the horrible news, but he lifts his brow and nods for me to tell him.

I heave a huge sigh. "We had the Spanish flu go through here. Mac, Samuel, Katy, Claire, and Aunt Julianna all caught it. Tom also caught it while in France. He's in the hospital still. Samuel and Claire are both recovering nicely.

Buck exhales the breath he's been holding since I said Spanish flu.

"Aunt Julianna's cough won't go away, and she feels weak a lot of the time, but she has improved some in the last two weeks." I pause, dread hanging heavy in my chest. "But Mac…and Katy…didn't make it."

"Mac and Katy are dead?"

Talking about it pokes at the hole in my chest, stirring up the flames of anger. "Yes."

Buck's eyes glaze, his stare fixed.

"Uncle Liam, Uncle Chris, and I have been working like mad to catch up on the workload on all three farms. Aunt Emma is having a difficult go of it, of course, as is Aunt Julianna."

"Katy," Buck moans, clutching his stomach. "May I see Claire?"

"Of course." Granda frowns, pursing his lips. "This is your home. Your family."

Buck's breath hitches, and his tears flow again, quietly this time.

"I say, if Julianna and Emma are up to it, we should have a welcome home dinner. A feast!" Granda, his knees creaking, pushes himself to his feet. "I'll go ask them and start the preparations." He extends his hand down to Buck. "Come with me. You can stop in and see Claire."

"I'll go, too." A tendril of fear snakes through my stomach at the thought of Buck with Claire. *What kind of brother am I? Jealous as a schoolboy without any cause. Assuming Buck would betray me when he just came home.* Bitter shame sends a flush of red up my neck and into my cheeks.

Buck hesitates for a few seconds, then takes Granda's hand and walks behind him up the stairs. The first stop is to see Julianna and Samuel. Samuel is ecstatic to see Buck, clapping his back and making a fuss over him. Aunt Julianna also seems pleased, although her reaction is quite subdued. Both say they feel well enough to come down for a celebratory meal.

Through all this, Buck remains reserved and distant, with his eyes firmly glued to the floor.

Then, we tap on Claire's door. I'm thankful to see Aunt Emma sitting at Claire's bedside, holding her daughter's hands.

Claire gawks at first, then squeals with delight, her hands flying to cover her mouth. "Oh, my sweet Lord! It's you!"

All of Buck's movements to that point have been slow and deliberate, almost belabored. But in a split second, he launches across the floor, wrapping Claire in his arms.

And the tendril grows some leaves as it winds its way and squeezes my heart.

Claire kisses his scruffy cheek. "Eww, you need a good bathing." She wrinkles her nose.

Only Claire could get away with such a comment without offending, but Buck laughs it off with a nod of agreement.

"We wanted to have a welcome home dinner, if you two think you're up to it," Granda explains.

"What a grand idea!" Claire glances at her mother. "Mama, what do you think?"

Emma's blank stare never alters. "Whatever you want, dear."

Claire claps her hands. "Wonderful! Granda, will you kill the fatted calf for our prodigal?"

He chuckles. "I'll cook meat with the meal, for sure and certain. Will that do?"

"Perfect." Claire's laughter makes the windowpanes sing. "I'm so glad you're home, Buck. It's been a long time since we've had anything to celebrate."

Buck stubs the toe of his well-worn boot against the wood floor, his eyes darting back and forth again, and the scars on his face turn into bright red blotches. "You don't have to make no fuss on my account," he murmurs.

"Of course, it's on your account!" Granda scrubs his hand on Buck's head, causing Buck to wince. "We love you, Buck."

Claire nods, her curls bobbing around her face. "We all do."

The vine squeezes tighter.

"Very well. A dinner it is. And I'm off to make it." He takes my elbow. "Fin, would you run and tell Liam and Chris the great news. Tell them to finish up the work for today, because we're having a fine dinner tonight."

"Yessir." *And leave Buck and Claire alone in her bedroom?*

What kind of brother am I?

CHAPTER FORTY-TWO

November 1918

The long table gleams under the soft candlelight and groans under the weight of the heaping platters of roast beef, potatoes, corn, snap beans, and corn bread steaming from end to end. It all looks like something from another life, one untouched by fever and death.

Granda makes Buck sit at the head of the table, with Claire to his right, and Granda to his left. Buck's oversized coat drapes over his chair, revealing just how emaciated he really is. He has washed his face, but the washing makes the red blotches on his face look scalded. Everyone keeps staring at him, but I keep a watchful eye on Claire.

Aunt Emma sits at the far corner of the table, her fork untouched, staring at her plate with her lips moving in soundless prayer. Aunt Julianna sits across from her, coughing into her handkerchief. Samuel sits between Uncle Liam and Julianna, while Uncle Chris sits next to Emma and beside Claire, which leaves me sitting alone at the far end of the table. Some things never change.

Claire giggles at something Buck says, and her soft, musical laughter cuts straight through me. Her blonde curls catch the candlelight when she leans close to him, her easy, unguarded smile forcing bitter bile in my throat.

Granda clears his throat, pushes back his chair, and rises. The conversation quiets.

"It's such a joy…" His words catch, so he swallows and clears his throat again. "A joy to have my family together again."

A searing pain stabs my chest. *Not the whole family. Never again.*

"The shadow of death has walked through our doors, and we've lost pieces of ourselves that can never be replaced. But tonight…" He places a hand on Buck's shoulder. "Tonight, we remember that God giveth as well as taketh away. He brought our boy home to us."

The others clap. Claire squeezes Buck in a quick hug. His shoulders hunch as he shifts in his seat.

Granda waits for the noise to die down, then stands a bit straighter. "Buck, you stood in the trenches, lived through hell itself, and came through the fire. For that, we thank God."

Aunt Emma groans, but Granda doesn't seem to hear it. His voice swells with pride. "When I think of what our boys have endured and what wonderful men they've become, I know the Lord has truly blessed this household."

Emma gasps out a strained squeal, scrapes her chair back so quickly it tips over, and dashes for the stairs. After a moment, Aunt Julianna drops her napkin on her plate and follows behind her. Everyone else freezes.

The stifling air, thick with the presence of those who didn't make it through the fire, who will never again sit at this table, clogs my chest until I can't breathe.

Buck wilts beneath Granda's words, his jaw tightening as his eyes lower. He snatches up his cup to drink it down, then with a strange quirk of his mouth, lifts it in the air. "To home."

Everyone else murmurs, "To home," but their voices are flat, as lifeless as the empty chairs.

Buck's eyes drift to Claire again.

Claire's fingers brush against Buck's hand, and a hot, stinging pain twists in my stomach. *I'm imagining it. She's only grateful to have him home. It's not the old feelings I see in her gaze.* But I'm not convinced.

Granda's voice trembles. "I know we've lost so much, but we're not lost. As long as we are together, we're not lost."

A hush follows, broken only by the faint sound of Aunt Emma's weeping. The silence stretches too long for comfort, and folks start getting restless. I'm vibrating like a struck piano string.

When I can't stand it anymore, I call out, "Buck." In the hushed room, the sound is overloud and abrasive, so I take a breath and try again. "You said you'd share where you've been all this time. How about it?"

Buck breathes a heavy sigh. "Where do I start?"

"What happened after Passchendaele?"

Buck grimaces but nods once. With his chin buried on his chest and his voice droning in monotone, he describes the rest of the battle after Ian was killed and I was shot.

"Soldiers were dying all around me, but I kept a-goin', jumping in trenches and killin' Germans hand-to-hand. Then, the gas got so thick, I couldn't see my hands in front of my face. I didn't know where I was or who was around me." He pauses, examining his hands. "I started shootin' willy-nilly. I didn't know what else to do."

Gently, Granda places his open palm on Buck's wringing hands. "What happened then?"

"Everyone were screaming in agony from the gas. Some of our men started dropping, dead in the mud." He glances at me for a second before putting his head down again. "Some new kind of gas that gets in your blood or something. Worse than mustard gas."

Claire's fingers touch her lips. "How horrible."

"That's what happened to your face?" Uncle Chris asks.

Buck nods once, touching one of the red scars with a finger. "Anyway, I started shootin' wild like I said, killin' anything that moved. And before I knew it, I had killed three of our men." A sharp intake of his breath punctuated his confession.

"Oh, Buck…" Tears rim in Claire's eyes.

That explains a lot. He couldn't face what his wild impulsiveness had done. "So, you ran."

His eyes dart to mine for a second, then drop again. "Yeah. I ran."

"How in heaven's name did you get away?" Uncle Chris shakes his head. "Behind German lines, and everywhere you turn, someone is trying to kill you."

Buck closes his eyes, his voice fading. "Honestly, I don't know."

We wait for several breathless moments as Buck's jaw works and throat bobs, then he blinks several times. "Somehow, I made it to the coast, and I found a skiff." He cuts his eyes toward Granda. "I stole it."

Granda folds his hands. "Go on."

"It was night, and I was lucky. I made it across to England without being spotted." He squirms in his seat. "I stole some clothes and threw away my uniform, except my boots, then I went lookin' for work on the docks."

The words begin pouring out of him, as if he can't get rid of them fast enough. "After I made a little money, I took a train from London to Glasgow and then to Perth, then I walked the highlands to Aberfeldy, where Ma was born." His eyes glisten in the candlelight. "I don't know why. I just wanted to see it."

"Did you meet anyone from her family?" It would be wonderful to have another family, someone connected to Ma. I'd go visit them today if I could.

But Buck shakes his head. "I kept to myself. Worked a bit on some farms for food."

"And you were there this whole time?"

"No, I left after a while, worked on the docks again, and found a boat sailing to the Caribbean. So, I worked in exchange for passage."

"The Caribbean. Where Pa was?"

He nods, chewing on the corner of his lip. "I fell in with some…men, and we sailed, um, carrying goods out of South America."

Granda leans forward in his chair. "You mean illegal smuggling."

Buck groans. "Yessir."

"And were you caught?"

"Yessir. I spent some time in a Mexican jail cell." Buck's eyes dart from Granda to Claire. I suppose he's checking their reaction. Granda's face is impassive, but Claire still has tears in her eyes. "Then, I found I could play cards and make good money, so I did that in Mexico for a spell."

I can imagine the scene. Drinking, smoking, gambling. Granma Ester will be turning in her grave. "Then what?"

Buck's reddened face turns a deeper, almost purplish color. It's eerily similar to Mac's face right before the end. A feeling of dread gnaws at me. *What horror is he going to share now?*

"Things were going well. I had money, a place to live, everything." His face puckers like someone eating a lime. "Then, someone accused me of cheatin'. He came at me, and I shot him."

Granda raises his brows. "You killed a man? Over cards?"

Buck doesn't answer. "I had to get out of there quick. So, I stole a horse, rode out, and made my way through Texas to Montana, where I worked ranchin' for a spell. But the ranchers fell on hard times, and the snows about did us all in. So…" He shrugs. "I came home."

Except for Claire's snuffles, silence descends on the room like a heavy, black shroud. Then, Liam stands, brushing his hands together. "I'm going to check on Julianna." He stalks, stiff-backed, from the room.

"Wow," Samuel exclaims. "You had you some adventures."

Buck shrinks further down in his chair. "I wouldn't call it that."

"No, I wouldn't call it that either," Granda says through clenched teeth.

Buck heaves a trembling sigh. "If you want me to leave…"

Granda slams his hands on the table, causing the silverware to rattle. "Nonsense. You are not to suggest that. Never again, do you hear?" Granda smooths a wrinkle from Ester's fine linen tablecloth. "We are your family. This is your home and always will be."

Claire whispers, "'For this my son was dead, and is alive again; he was lost, and is found.'"

Buck crosses his arms over his middle and folds in half, sobbing. Granda presses his arms around his heaving shoulders while Claire caresses his brow, murmuring, "There, there. It's all going to work out."

I don't share Claire's compassion. Buck's bringing a world of trouble with him, possibly down on our heads, too, and he doesn't seem to care. "Who all is looking for you?"

Buck smears his fist across his nose. "Everyone."

Granda glances at me with a frown. "You'll be safe here. No one knows where you are, and we'll make sure it stays that way."

Buck's sobs start anew. "I'm so sorry, Granda. I don't know what happened. I…"

"We will sort things out. For now, you need to bathe. And throw away those clothes. Fin, do you have something Buck could wear?"

"Yessir, I can find something."

"Very well. Then, we'll all get a good night's sleep and come together again in the morning." Granda pats Buck's back. "Things will look brighter in the light of day."

"I will heat some water for him." After one final caress, Claire waltzes from the room toward the kitchen.

"Come along, Buck." I push away from the table. "Granda, leave the dishes. When I finish with Buck, I'll come back down and clean them."

"Thank you, Fin. I must admit to being a bit tired. It's been quite a day."

Buck trails behind me to my room, where I paw through my clothes to find something on the smallish side. But everything I hold up swallows him.

"What about Ian's clothes? Do you think you could wear them?"

Buck's mouth falls open. "You kept Ian's clothes?"

I press my lips together, trying to slow my breaths. "No one wanted to throw them away, so we put them in a box in the chest."

What used to be Ian's room is now Claire's, so I tread into Claire's room to get the box. As I leave, she's coming down the hall to get Buck for his bath. "Oh! You're taking Ian's clothes?"

I shrug. "My clothes are all too big. I thought he might wear Ian's."

Her delicate brow creases. "I don't know how I feel about that."

"I know." I set the box down and take her hands. "If you want, I will return the box, and Buck can make do with what I have."

"No, I'm being silly." She rolls her delicate fingers in a wave. "Take them. Someone should get some use out of them." Instead of going to my room, she turns into hers. "Tell Buck his bath is ready in the kitchen."

My hand lingers on hers. "Good night, Claire."

Without looking at me, she says an emotionless, "Good night," and disappears through her door.

Has Buck's return cast a shadow over the magic of our love? Does she regret her choice to marry me?

The questions plague me as I clean the dishes, waiting for Buck to finish his washing and slip into Ian's clothes. Then we tiptoe back upstairs.

"I'd like to thank Claire and tell her good night," Buck whispers as we pass her door.

"She's asleep." My answer is unintentionally short.

"I don't think so. I hear her moving around."

"Do whatever you want. You usually do." I sigh, walking on to my door.

"Fin, are you angry I came back?"

Buck's plaintive question softens the ragged edges of my heart. Closing my eyes, I groan. "No, of course not. You're my brother. And I missed you."

"You've just seemed—different."

"Yeah?" My irritation swells again. "Well, I have a story, too, you know."

Buck's brow furrows. "Tell me."

"It's a story for another day." I waggle my hand. "Come on and leave Claire be. You can thank her tomorrow."

I spread a pallet of clean blankets on the floor beneath the window. "You take my bed. I've slept on pallets for the better part of a month now, so I'm used to it, and who knows what you've had to sleep on."

"I couldn't..."

"Enjoy the soft bed. We'll figure out arrangements tomorrow."

Buck shrugs and climbs onto the bed, as I lie on my pallet and bundle the covers around me, staring out the window, finding shapes in the stars and thinking of Claire. Buck's breathing slows and deepens, and soon I drift off, but I awaken to the click of my door closing.

I shoot up to check Buck's bed, and sure enough, he's gone. So, I tiptoe to the door and peek out in time to see Claire's door swinging shut.

That rascal! Nothing ever changes with him.

Hugging the wall to avoid the creaking boards, I slip down the hall and stand outside Claire's door. Luckily, it didn't shut completely, so through the sliver of an opening, I can hear their interaction. Buck is in mid-sentence.

"...for your kindness toward me."

So, he's thanking her. *Fine.*

"Of course. You're like a brother to me."

Buck's footfalls shuffle across the wood planks. "A brother?"

A long pause hangs in the air between them.

"I...I was hoping...well, with Ian gone..."

"Buck..."

"I wanted you..."

"Buck, stop. There's something I must tell you."

"Don't say anything more. I don't care about anything else. I love you, Claire. I've always loved you."

I'm a split second away from barging into the room when Claire yells, "Stop it!" Then, "No!"

What did he just do? He'd better not try anything or I'll...

"I...I don't understand. Don't you remember? We kissed..."

"I'm not the same person now." Claire pauses. "I was horrible. Horrible to Ian, horrible to you, horrible to everyone. I craved attention, and I didn't care who was hurt in the process. But now, I see it for what it was, and I will not go back. I cannot."

"What are you talking about? You weren't horrible."

"I was. Selfish and cruel."

"How can you say that? I love you, Claire. And you love me."

"No, I didn't love you. I didn't even love Ian. I only loved myself." Another pause lingers like a breath. "I don't think you loved me, either, or you wouldn't have willingly encouraged my affections, knowing I was to marry Ian."

"I do love you," he wails. If he isn't careful, he'll wake the whole house, and there'll be Granda to deal with.

"Buck, I love the Lord above all. And I'm in love with Fin."

"Fin?" Buck practically spits my name.

"We are to be married."

"I don't see no engagement ring."

"We are waiting for news about Tom, and for the heaviness of our grief to lighten before we announce our engagement."

"Then, it's not too late."

"Take your hands off me!"

Once again, it takes all my restraint to keep from barreling in to rescue Claire, but her voice, clear and calm, pulls me up short. "It isn't appropriate for you to be in my bedroom. I must ask you to leave. We can discuss it tomorrow in the light of day."

Simmering rage wars with pride, fogging my vision as I creep back to my room and slip under my blanket. Claire has shown herself to be faithful, proving the truth of her pledge to me and the genuineness of her change of heart. But Buck has proven the opposite. He can't be trusted, and nothing has changed.

Buck doesn't return to our room. It's probably for the best, because I don't trust myself to deal with him tonight without pounding him.

But tomorrow, Buck and I will have a conversation and straighten out all this mess—one way or another.

CHAPTER FORTY-THREE

November 1918

The morning brings me a calmer head, but Buck is nowhere to be found. Claire doesn't mention anything about her confrontation during breakfast, so I don't bring it up either, figuring we'll talk about it privately, but her tremulous hands and pale countenance tell me she's shaken by Buck's actions, whatever they were.

As has been usual since the flu devastated our family, the conversation is muted or nonexistent, until Liam growls, "Where's Buck? He could at least help with chores."

Granda's eyes narrow. "Son, show some mercy. Buck has suffered greatly."

Liam snorts. "Mainly by his own hand."

"But not only." Granda tilts his head. "You could do with a dose of compassion. Best not forget you'll account for your own sins before you judge Buck so harshly."

Liam slams his palms on the table and pushes himself to his feet. "If I had done any one of the things Buck's done, you would've thrown me out on my ear." Grabbing a biscuit, he stalks toward the kitchen, calling over his shoulder. "Fin, I'll be in the barn. Join me when you're finished."

The quiet stillness is now replaced by heavy tension, with all eyes on their plates and no one speaking for the rest of the meal. The morning chores proceed as normal with everyone pitching in as they are able, but when lunchtime arrives, still no Buck.

Granda takes me aside after the meal. "Fin, do you know where Buck went?"

"No, sir. I don't."

"Did something happen between you two last night?"

I grind my teeth before answering. "You might want to ask Claire. Buck snuck out of our room last night and went to Claire's room, and I heard some yelling." I lower my eyes. "He never came back after that."

"Do you think he ran away?"

I wish. I shrug, ashamed of my thoughts.

"Are any of the horses missing?"

"No, sir."

Granda sighs. "Strange." After a moment, he takes my arm. "Would you go to town and see if you can find him?"

It's the last thing in the world I want to do, but I won't disappoint Granda. "Yessir."

"Thank you, son. I'm worried."

A sudden, unexpected wave of fear flushes my face. It hasn't crossed my mind that Buck might be so distraught at Claire's rejection, he might harm himself. Until now. "Don't worry, Granda. I'll find him."

"Good man."

I shrug on my coat, tack up my horse, and ride into town, starting with the place I'm certain he'd go. But the saloon is almost empty at this hour, and no one has seen a man matching Buck's description. With no better ideas, I wander up and down the streets, then ride on to Morganton. No sign of him there, either. He wouldn't have tried to walk to Murphy. Surely not.

Think. Where would Buck go?

Back in New Zealand, I'd know exactly where to look. The little camp Mani built for us had been the perfect hiding place. But here? Buck never had a reason to hide, not like this.

Returning to Blue Ridge, I check the saloon again, then the hotel, hoping he might've taken a room for the night. No such luck. I'm about to give up when the hotel clerk asks, "Can you describe him?"

"He's thin, almost gaunt, with red scars on his face and long reddish hair. He's wearing canvas pants, a white shirt, and a black coat."

The clerk's brow lifts. "I saw a vagrant in the alley behind the hotel. He was sleeping back there when I came in this morning. Tried to roust him, but he was drunk and dead to the world. Might've been your man."

"Can you show me?"

He leads me around the building, wrinkling his nose as he gestures toward the narrow alley. "Back there. Among the trash cans."

"Thank you."

His footsteps fade, leaving me alone in the dark, dank passage squeezed between two tall brick buildings. Sludge trickles down the center, carving a jagged gulley. Toppled trash heaps sprawl from both sides, making the way nearly impassable. The alley dead-ends at a wooden fence crowned with looping wire.

It's a miracle the clerk saw anyone at all.

Just past the hotel's service door, beyond a mound of refuse lies what looks at first like a pile of filthy rags. A sharp twinge hits my chest. It's Buck, or at least his long black coat, rumpled over a shape beneath it. Two empty whiskey bottles lie beside him.

I crouch and lift the coat. Buck's mouth hangs open, a string of vomit trailing from the corner of his lips, down his cheek, and into his hair. I swallow hard and turn my face away, forcing back the surge in my throat. He reeks of sickness and cheap liquor.

After catching my breath, I shake his shoulder. "Buck. Buck, wake up."

Nothing.

I pound on the hotel's service door. A kitchen worker cracks it open, his eyes darting left and right.

"Any chance you've got a bucket of water?"

He glances over his shoulder, then stares at me with a lifted brow. "What for?"

"To wake up a drunk."

He snorts, rolling his eyes. "Have mercy. Come on, then." He hands me a wash bucket and points to a sink. "Fill it yourself. And bring my bucket back."

"I will. Thank you."

I twist the lever. Water flows instantly. What a luxury! Then, I haul the full bucket outside and dump the whole thing on Buck's head.

He sputters with a strangled squawk, scrambling up on all fours, his eyes wild and bloodshot. When recognition dawns, he collapses, curling into a ball. "Leave me be." His voice is hoarse, from sleeping outside, drinking, crying, or who knows what.

"You're going to clean yourself up. Then we're going home, and you're apologizing to Granda for scaring him half to death."

"Go away." Buck claws toward one of the bottles.

I kick it out of reach. "I'm not going anywhere. Get up."

He curls tighter. So, I haul him up by the shoulder and under the arm. He stands for a heartbeat, swaying, before doubling over and vomiting again.

I wait, jaw tight. "Are you done?"

He lifts his head, stumbles, and takes a wild swing at me, missing by a mile, spinning off balance, and crashing to the ground.

Buck lies there, half-curled in the mud and vomit, keening like a wounded animal. The fight has drained out of him, replaced by a shivering silence. I stand over him, my breath coming in sharp, quick beats, but my anger cools by degrees into something heavier. Fear, maybe. Or grief. Hard to tell them apart these days.

"Buck," I whisper. "I'm not leaving you here."

He doesn't answer, but lies there, his wet, stringy hair plastered to his skull and his chest heaving.

I reach down again. "Come on. I can't carry you like Mani did. My leg won't hold. But if you try to stand, I'll get you home."

For a long moment, he doesn't move. Then, with a low groan, he rolls onto his hands and knees. His arms tremble beneath his weight. He looks up at me through filthy strands of hair, with his eyes unfocused and the stench of alcohol billowing off him.

"I can't."

"You can. I'm right here."

After another beat, he lifts his hand tentatively, almost as if he expects me to pull away. Once again, I slide my arm under his and pull him up. He wobbles but remains on his feet this time.

"That's it," I murmur. "Just lean on me."

I pound on the service entrance, and the same waiter sticks his head out, frowning. "Here's your bucket. Thanks."

"Uh-huh."

Keeping Buck half-hidden behind me, I press my hand against the door. "Any chance we could wash up and dry off?"

His face sours. "This is a respectable establishment."

"I know, sir. It won't take a second. If we could borrow a towel, we can use the kitchen's sink." I lean toward him and whisper, "No one ever needs to know. It would be a great help to me." I stick my hand in my pocket and pull out some coins.

His eyes roll, but he opens the door and gestures with his head for us to enter. When Buck walks in, he takes a step back. "Hurry up. You're going to get me fired." He shoves a pristine white towel in my hands as I deposit my coins in his.

"Yessir."

I hold Buck's head under the running water, hoping the cold will sober him up, then rub the mud and vomit off him and dry his face and hair. "Rinse your mouth out."

Buck cups some water into his mouth, swishes it around, then spits it out. He sticks his head under the faucet again, gulping in water like a horse after a long gallop. When he stops to take a breath, he staggers back and slumps against the wall.

Disgusted, I dry his face and hair again. When I hand the waiter the filthy towel, he shoves us out the door, slamming it against my back.

We take a few slow steps toward the street. Buck is dead weight most of the way, but at least he moves his feet, even though it's mostly by dragging.

Buck shivers violently in the cooling air. "I need to get you inside somewhere to dry off." But where could we go that would allow us in?

He slurs, "Why'd you come?"

"Because you're my brother." I sneer. "And Granda asked me to."

I can feel the rhythm of his breathing against my chest, short, quick, and ragged.

"Fin…" His voice breaks on my name. "I made a big mess of everything."

I squeeze his arm. "You haven't made a mess you can't clean up. But you must come clean. What happened?"

He stumbles, catches himself, then blurts, "I went to Claire."

"I know."

He stops in his tracks. "You do?"

I nod once. "What did you do?"

He squeezes his eyes shut. "I don't…" He swallows, voice shaking. "I said things I shouldn't have. I tried to…to kiss her. Then I…" He buries his face in his hands. "I just want her to love me."

"You forced your attentions on her?" For a moment, I can't breathe. He nods once. Then something happens I thought never would. I soften.

"Buck…why?"

He wipes his nose on his sleeve like a child. "Because everything's wrong. Ian's dead, Katie's dead, Mac's dead, you almost died. It felt like…if only I could make someone—anyone—want me, love me, maybe life would be worth living again." He gasps, shoves his fist in his mouth, and sobs, his body collapsing against me.

My anger evaporates.

"Your life is worth something." I take his shoulders firmly in my hands. "It's not Claire or me or Ian or anyone else who makes you worth something. You're worth something because…you are." *Lord, please give me the words.* "Because God says you are. Because He made you to be who you are."

His chin trembles as he presses a palm to his forehead above his eye. "I'm so sorry. I'm so sorry, Fin. I shouldn't have gone to her. I should never have done what I done. I hate myself for it."

I grip the back of his neck, pulling his forehead to mine the way Ian used to do with us both. "I forgive you. Do you hear?"

His sobs grow louder as he shakes his head.

"Listen to me." I lock my eyes with his. "I forgive you."

After a few moments, his head bobs.

"And you're coming home."

He nods again, his shoulders shaking.

When we resume walking, he leans against me, but he's not as unsteady. Maybe he finally let go.

When I see the small diner on the corner of the next street, I decide to risk it. A long counter extends the length of the space, with leather-covered stools bolted to the floor in front of it, and three wooden booths, two on one end and one on the other. Three people occupy stools. I opt for the single booth, slipping Buck into the seat facing away from the door. He shrinks into the seat and slips to the far end beside the fogged window.

The sole waitress, a pretty young woman with strawberry blonde curls pinned up under a stiff white cap, steps from behind the counter, holding a notepad. But when she sees, or maybe smells, Buck, she thrusts her nose in the air. "We don't sell alcohol here."

"Yes, ma'am, I know." Remembering our times eating out with Uncle Bear, I offer her a big smile and ask, "What's the special this evening?" I check her nametag, as Bear used to do. "Meg."

Her eyes narrow. "We have beef stew tonight."

"That's perfect. May we have two orders of the beef stew?"

She plants her hand on her hip. "Look, we don't want any trouble here."

I smile again. "We won't be any trouble."

"You have money to pay?"

"Yes, ma'am."

She tosses her head and turns toward the counter. "Two specials."

"Meg? Could we have a coffee, too?"

Without answering, she grabs a white porcelain cup and fills it from the decanter behind the counter, then marches back to our booth and slams it down in front of Buck, sloshing coffee on the table. "Anything else?"

"No, thank you."

She glares at Buck. "Does it talk?"

I can't help but chuckle. "Well, you're a bold one, aren't you?"

She curls her lip. "I don't have any use for drunkards."

"And I don't have any use for surly waitresses." I lift one brow. "Best not judge someone without knowing their story."

Meg spins on her heel with a huff and strides back to her other customers.

Once she's gone, Buck takes his cup with trembling hands. "I guess I deserve that."

"Don't pay her no mind." Clasping my hands on the table, I lean forward. "The war mixed up your thinking, that's all. It did me, too. I was so ashamed of all I'd done during the war. I felt dirty, like I could never be clean again, and I thought God hated me. All I wanted to do was disappear."

Buck's eyes study the swirling black liquid. "Yeah?"

"Yeah. I was so filled with rage that I hurt everyone around me." A pang of guilt and grief pierces my heart as I remember how I treated sweet Katie. And now she's gone. "But Katie and Granda helped me through it." I reach across the table and take his hand. "Granda can help you, too. He understands, more than you know."

Buck shakes his head. "Don't know that anything's gonna help me."

Meg, who has snuck up behind us, slips two plates of stew on the table between us. Then, she leans down, close to Buck's ear, and whispers, "It's never too late to make a change."

Buck's eyes widen as his cheeks color, and he turns to look at Meg for the first time. A half-smile quirks the corner of her mouth. "Enjoy your meal."

"Thanks," Buck mumbles.

Meg throws her head back and laughs. "It speaks!"

Buck ducks his head, grinning despite his embarrassment. And for the first time since the war ended, I feel the faintest flicker of hope that Buck and I might recover some part of what we used to be.

I keep a steadying grip on Buck the whole way home. As he climbs down from my horse, he loses his footing and stumbles, but at least he's not staggering drunk anymore. Meg's beef stew and coffee saw to that. But he still carries that haunted, hollow look of someone scraped out, like something darker than whiskey is eating him up on the inside.

Granda sits in his chair as always, a blanket over his knees and his Bible open in his lap. When he lifts his head and spots Buck beside me, something flashes across his face, a mixture of pain, fear, and a kind of exhausted relief all tangled up in one.

"Lord have mercy," he breathes, barely loud enough to hear.

Buck stops, his hands twitching at his sides. "Granda." His eyes remain glued to the floor.

"Come here, son." Granda's soft, gentle voice soothes like a warm fire on a November night.. "Come and sit with me."

Buck swallows hard, then steps forward like he's walking toward the gallows. "I come to say…I'm sorry. His voice cracks. "For runnin' off. For the drinkin'. For…everything. All of it." He takes a trembling breath. "I'm sorry I scared you." Buck wilts beneath his heavy black coat, shrinking into the fabric under an invisible weight. "I ain't never been so ashamed."

Granda closes his Bible and sets it aside. "Shame's a heavy load."

Buck's shoulders shiver as if something's run up his spine.

"Are you planning on carrying that load forever?"

"I…" Buck shuffles his mud-encrusted boots. "I don't know. I don't want to." His face twists like a wrung-out old rag. "I don't know how to get rid of it."

Granda reaches his gnarled old hand and pats the chair across from him. "Have a seat, son."

Buck shuffles to the chair and slumps into it.

"No matter what you've done, you can't out-sin God's love." His voice softens more. "The Lord doesn't love you because you've been good. He loves you because He's good."

A broken laugh and a sob slip from Buck. "You don't know what I done."

"Doesn't matter. Sin is sin, and we all have the disease."

"I don't deserve love."

"None of us do. That's the point."

My eyes sting as I blink back tears. The air around me grows still.

Granda turns his head to gaze at the mountains. "Look out that picture window. Do you see how the sky spreads before you, beyond what the eye can see? How the mountains stretch, row after row, until they disappear into the mist?"

Buck mumbles, "Yessir, I see."

"Yet, how much of God's infinite creation can you see from here?"

Buck shrugs. "Not much, I guess."

Granda nods. "Barely a glimpse. Now, imagine all the knowledge and wisdom of God from the creation of the world until the end of time. But you can only see this tiny square of it."

Buck's brow furrows. "I don't understand."

A brief, wan smile crosses Granda's face. "My point exactly." He gazes at the distant mountains again. "Do you know why I sit here all the time, looking out this window?"

"No, sir."

"To remind myself that God is God, and I am not. To show me, time and time again, how little I truly see and know." He lowers his head and closes his eyes. "All my many years—all my experiences—yet still, I know nothing." He glances at Buck. "It shows me how much I need God."

Buck gazes out the window for a few moments, then nods once.

Granda takes Buck's hand and squeezes it. "I know what war does to a man. It's unnatural, having to kill another human being because someone in some distant government room decides you must. It steals a man's humanity and consumes his soul." He studies Buck's face for a moment. "But God knows you. Not this broken, shameful man, but the man He created, the man you were before war destroyed everything good in you." He leans close. "He can resurrect that man, if you allow it."

"He should just kill me and be done with it." Buck turns his face away and buries it in the crook of his arm.

Granda sits bolt upright, his eyes flashing. "Don't you speak like that, not with the losses this family has suffered."

Buck shrinks deeper into the cushions. "I'm sorry."

Granda's shoulders sag. "I'm sorry, too, son. I don't need to be heaping more shame on top of you. I've felt the way you do right now. I begged God to kill me." He chuckles. "He came right close to doing it, too. But your Granma Ester reached out her hand in love and brought me back into His loving arms. I've been there ever since." Granda's eyes blink rapidly. "It's the only thing that got me through Ester's…"

He still can't say the words.

For the first time, Buck raises his eyes, concern creasing their corners. "Granda?"

"I miss your Granma." Granda's wistful smile pains me more than his brief tears. "But we're talking about you right now. And you've got someone else who needs to hear from you, I believe."

"Yessir."

"Fin, would you ask Claire to join us, if she's up to it?"

"Yessir." I scamper up the steps, two at a time, and knock lightly on Claire's bedroom door.

"Yes?"

"It's me. Granda is asking if you're well enough to join us downstairs." I pause for a moment, debating whether I should tell her or let her find out when she comes down. "Um…Buck's home."

"Very well. I will come down in a minute."

"I'll wait for you."

A few minutes later, Claire steps from her room, dressed in something besides a nightgown and bathrobe for the first time since her illness. Her forest-green wool skirt, beige ruffled blouse, and crocheted white sweater draped around her shoulders accentuate her beauty. She's bundled her golden curls in a loose bun on top of her head as if purposefully presenting modesty.

I take her elbow. The floorboards groan under our steps, and I imagine Buck wincing at each creak. When Claire sees Buck sitting with Granda, her face freezes for a heartbeat, but she doesn't look afraid, and she doesn't step back.

Buck stands as she enters the sitting room. "Claire…" He gasps for several breaths before he can go on. "I'm sorry. For what I said. For what I tried. It was disrespectful and unforgivable, to you and Fin. And to myself. I was wrong. I ain't askin' for anythin'. I just needed to tell you how sorry I am."

Claire stands very still, studying his face as if she's trying to see past the filth and pain to find the man. Then, she steps to his side and lays a gentle hand on his arm.

"I know pain can make a person do things they regret. But you came home. And you're trying. That matters." Her voice doesn't waver. "I forgive you."

Buck's head drops, his shoulders shaking. "I messed up everything."

"Yes, you did," Claire says, not harsh but truthful. "So did I. But it's not too late for us. We'll all get through this. As a family. Together."

Buck nods once, slowly as if uncertain, but genuinely.

"Come." Granda gestures for us to gather around his chair. "Let's pray together."

We arrange ourselves in a semicircle around his chair, holding hands as Granda leads us in heartfelt prayers for forgiveness, compassion, and restoration.

Outside, the cold November wind rattles the shutters. But here in the sitting room, something akin to peace settles over us, something like mercy, or the first bit of healing, or the faint, fragile hope that maybe this is the beginning of putting our lives back together.

CHAPTER FORTY-FOUR

December 1918

A knock on the door comes during breakfast, sharp as a hammer on cold steel. We all freeze, the kind of paralysis that comes from months of telegrams bearing bad news. Granda reaches the door before any of us can move to find a young telegraph boy standing on the porch, cap in hand, breath fogging in the December air.

"Telegram for the MacAlisters."

My chest tightens, shortening my breath, as Granda takes the yellow paper. He unfolds it slowly, and his eyes move once, then twice over the page. When my chest aches to the point of bursting, he lifts his eyes and stares at us, each in turn.

"What now?" Liam barks.

Claire speaks more gently. "What is it, Granda?"

"It's Tom," he whispers. "Tom's coming home." Suddenly, Granda laughs, a sound so warm, bright, and full it scatters the darkness from every corner of the house. Claire gasps, grabs my arm, and mouths, "Tom!" Her squeal weaves with Granda's laughter to form a beautiful symphony of joy.

Emma drops her wooden spoon and covers her mouth, then falls to her knees, covering her face with her hands. Her body jerks with silent weeping.

Julianna gives a soft, tremulous smile as she slips into the nearest chair. Liam walks up behind her, laying his beefy hand on her shoulder.

It's as if the last piece of a puzzle has fallen into place. All the tension drains from my shoulders, caught in the wave of relief.

"We'll have a celebration! A big, wonderful celebration in gratitude for his return to us." Granda claps his hands like a youth.

Buck glances at me, then whispers in my ear. "Since we're havin' a big gathering and all, do you think he'll mind if I bring Meg?"

"I don't see why not. Why don't you ask him?"

Buck's cheeks turn rosy-red, his eyes glistening. "I really like her."

I chuckle and elbow his ribs. "She's a firecracker, that's for sure and certain. She can keep you on your toes, I'll wager."

"What are you two whispering about?" Claire whispers.

"Buck wants to invite Meg to Christmas dinner."

Claire raises a brow. "Who is Meg?"

"The waitress he met at the diner. *That* night." I grin, hiding my mouth behind my hand to whisper in her ear. "He's been spending a lot of afternoons in town. Drinking coffee." I give an exaggerated wink.

Claire giggles. "I can't wait to meet her. Is she nice?"

Buck rubs the back of his neck. "Nice might not be the word for it."

Claire folds her arms with a devious grin. "Buck, are you bringing home trouble?"

"Probably," he mutters. "But she's the good kind of trouble."

"I know!" Granda bellows. "By heaven, we'll have Christmas! A genuine, old-fashioned MacAlister Christmas! The first real one since the war began!"

Emma's head jerks up like she's been sucker punched, leaving her hands lying open, suspended in mid-air. "What?"

Granda doesn't seem to hear her. "That's it! Christmas! It's the perfect way to celebrate Tom's homecoming." He rubs his hands together. "We have a lot of preparations to tend to and not a lot of time. We'll need a tree, of course, and…"

"Will we share presents?" Samuel asks.

"Of course, we'll have presents. And a big Christmas dinner, just like old times."

Emma leaps up with a shriek and rushes from the dining room into the kitchen.

"Honestly, Mac." Julianna stands, slamming her fists on her hips. "Do you ever think before you speak?" She bustles off after Emma.

"Hon?" Liam rushes to catch Julianna.

Everyone stares at the empty doorway, then at each other. Granda blinks, fingering the tablecloth before wandering into the sitting room, crestfallen.

Claire follows him, and Buck and I trail after Claire. "I think it's a wonderful idea, Granda. It will help soothe the grieving."

"I don't understand." He glances up, catching my eye. "What did I do wrong?"

"I believe Aunt Emma isn't quite ready for a celebration that's just like old times." I wince at Granda's incredulous expression.

"But her son is coming home!" Granda paces in front of the fireplace, his hands grasping the air, as if looking for something to hold onto.

"I know. And her other son is in the ground."

"Fin," Claire whispers, frowning. "Be kind."

"Julianna didn't seem to mind the idea, and she lost her daughter. That is, until Emma up and ran off." Granda pouts his lips. "I lost my wife, too, and I still want to celebrate Tom's homecoming."

"I need to find Pa and tell him the wonderful news. He'll be so relieved. Then, he and I will talk to Mother." Claire smiles gently. "Don't worry, Granda. We'll have your Christmas." Claire snakes her arm through mine. "When we come back, we'll make plans. I'm sure it will be lovely."

But Granda huffs and slumps into his chair, staring out the window, the joy sucked out of him like water down a drain.

I lean close to Buck and whisper, "Stay with Granda. Let him talk about his Christmas plans while we're gone. That might cheer him up. Oh, and you can ask him about Meg, too."

Buck nods and slides into the chair next to Granda, joining his study of the far mountains hiding in the mist.

As we walk together toward the barn, Claire is unusually quiet. "Is something bothering you, my love?"

"I'm worried for my mama. And my pa. Mama has hardly said two words since Mac died, and Pa—well, I'm sure you've noticed, he's not been at the big house since Buck came home. He says he's taking care of chores, but I think mostly he's sitting alone in the dark in that little cabin. And Mama and Pa have barely spoken to each other since the night Mac died."

"I didn't know."

"I need to do something, but I don't know what would help them."

I gnaw on the inside of my cheek. "Aunt Emma was questioning her faith the night we heard Tom was sick. If she's lost the one thing that always held her up…"

"I know. That's why I'm worried."

We don't find Uncle Chris in the barn, so we saddle our horses in heavy silence, then ride the trail down the hill to their cabin. As Claire expected, we discover him sitting alone in the darkened room.

"Pa?"

He lifts his head slowly. His reddened, swollen eyes appear dazed. "Claire. You're feeling better?"

"Yes, Pa. And I bring good news."

"Oh?"

"Tom is coming home."

Uncle Chris blinks several times, then he sits forward. "He's coming home?"

"Yes, Pa. He's recovered and is on his way back to us."

Chris' eyes close as he breathes out a deep sigh. "Oh, thank God." He reaches for Claire with open arms, and she falls into them. "Thank God."

After a few minutes, Claire raises her head from his chest. "Pa, Mama is really upset. I'm worried about her."

"Upset? About Tom? What in the world?"

Claire shakes her head. "No, at Granda. He wants to have a big Christmas to celebrate Tom's homecoming. He said some things that upset her, like he wants it to be like old times."

Chris sighs again. "I guess I better go see to her."

Claire places her hand on Uncle Chris' chest. "Pa, is everything well with the two of you?"

Chris spins away from Claire, his head dropping to his chest. "I can't reach her. She's fallen into a dark place, but she won't let anyone bring her light. It's as if she resents the living."

Claire steps forward and caresses her pa's back. "Perhaps we could try together?"

"Very well. We can try." Uncle Chris, always an encouraging presence in the family, lifts vacant, lifeless eyes to his daughter. "But don't hold out much hope, or you'll be disappointed."

She hooks his arm. "Come, Pa. I put my hope in the Lord. He can do anything."

On the ride up the hill, Claire chatters about Granda's Christmas plans and Buck's new sweetheart, probably to fill the emptiness surrounding Uncle Chris. Once we reach the cabin, the two of them disappear upstairs to find Aunt Emma, and I return to the sitting room where Granda sits, alone.

"Where did Buck go?"

Granda turns from the window, a sly grin crossing his face. "Rode off to collect his new friend. He asked if she could be a part of our Christmas celebration." He tilts his head. "And I, of course, said yes. Told him to bring her around so all of us could meet her."

"And you're happy for her to join the family gathering?"

Granda chuckles. "My first big Christmas was with your Granma Ester, her mother, Mary, and her sisters. They took me in out of the cold and made me a part of their family." He pushes himself out of his chair and drapes his arm across my shoulders. "Christmas is the time for gathering in all the strays and making them feel at home. Meg will be more than welcome."

The following morning, the house buzzes with more life than I've seen since before we left for the war.

"Well now," Granda says for the fourth time since breakfast, "we'll make this a Christmas worth remembering." He says it with such conviction that I begin to believe it's possible. Everyone responds to his declaration except Emma, who stares out the window as if she expects Tom to ride up at any moment. Julianna watches her with quiet worry, although Chris and Claire report she agreed to participate in the Christmas celebration, for Tom's sake.

Granda spreads his hands. "Everyone. We've got a lot of work ahead of us. Tom deserves a homecoming fit for a king, or at least for a MacAlister."

Claire giggles softly. "Where do you want us to start?"

"With food." Aunt Julianna answers before Granda can. "Real food. I'll need flour, sugar if we can find it, and boys, I need you to select a hog for slaughter. We can have pork tenderloin and ribs for the next few days, and a nice ham for the Christmas meal." She keeps muttering ingredients as she walks toward the kitchen, drying her hands on her apron.

"Oh, boy! Pork sausage and bacon for breakfast." Buck's eyes gleam as he rubs his hands together.

I volunteer to ride into town for provisions. Buck tags along, announcing he has "business of his own," which I suspect has less to do with errands and more to do with Meg.

Sure enough, when we pull our wagon up to the diner, we find Meg wiping down the counter, her reddish-gold hair pulled into a messy knot, with her sleeves rolled up past her elbows. She looks up at Buck with a wicked half-smile that somehow manages to look both unimpressed and intrigued.

"You again?" She sneers. "I ought to start charging you rent."

Buck grins and elbows me in the ribs. "Isn't she great?" He saunters to the counter and plops on a stool. "Where were you yesterday?"

"And how is that your business?"

"I came to tell you we're fixin' to get ready for Christmas. My cousin, Tom, is comin' home. The whole family's celebratin'."

"Whoopee for you."

"We want to invite you to come."

Meg pauses, softening. "You're inviting me to your family's Christmas?"

"To all of it. I was hopin' you'd come meet the family today and maybe help with the decoratin'."

"Huh." Meg, usually so self-possessed, looks stunned.

"When do you get off work?"

She blinks as if still trying to figure out what's going on. "Oh. After the lunch crowd is done eating."

Buck jumps down from his stool, slapping his hand on the counter. "Great! We'll stop back by after we get all the supplies, and you can ride with us to our cabin."

Before she can say no, he grabs my arm and drags me from the diner.

Later, after we've loaded all the supplies into the wagon, we return to the diner to find Meg standing outside the door, her arms folded around her big coat, shivering. "Took you long enough. It's freezing out here."

"Sorry." Buck hops down and helps her into the wagon, although I doubt she's the type to need help, then he snuggles up close beside her. "Here, I'll keep you warm."

She rolls her eyes, then flutters her hand like a fan in front of her face. "Such a gentleman, sacrificing for little ol' me."

Buck seems to enjoy her teasing, so I join in with his laughter.

When we arrive, Buck races into the house to call everyone while I help Meg from the wagon. Granda, Liam, Julianna, Samuel, Claire, Chris, and even Emma come to the porch to greet Buck's new friend.

"Everyone, this is Meg. Meg, this is…everyone." Buck's cheeks color as he waits for their reception.

"Welcome." Claire trips down the steps and embraces Meg, who accepts the hug with startled eyes and parted lips. Claire guides her up the steps to receive hugs and handshakes from the rest of the family.

Granda is in rare form. "So, what in the world do you see in this scallywag?" He slaps Buck on the back, who grimaces and shrugs Granda's hand off his shoulders.

"A free meal, obviously," Meg replies, not missing a beat.

Granda throws his head back, guffawing.

Then, Meg pokes Buck in the ribs with what appears to be genuine affection, and my heart melts. *Lord, is she the one? Have you brought Buck the one woman who can set him on the straight path and keep him there?*

"Come on, let's get you out of the cold." Buck bustles Meg into the house. The rest follow, except Claire, who offers to help me unload the supplies.

Our first task is choosing a tree. Granda insists it must be tall, and "Big enough to hold all our hopes." So, Buck, Meg, Claire, and I ride out, then tramp deep into the woods to find the perfect one, with full, deep green branches stretching wide, taller than any of us. It takes most of the afternoon to find one that satisfies Buck. He and I cut it down while Claire oohs and aahs, and Meg stands back with her arms crossed.

"That thing's as big as a house."

"That's the point," Buck fires back.

"How are you getting it to the wagon, much less back up that hill?"

I size up the prone tree. "Meg might have a point. Will it fit in the back of the wagon?"

"We'll tie it in and make it work."

Then, we set out to collect pine and cedar branches for greening the house, which the girls carry back to the wagon.

Hauling it all home is quite the spectacle. Buck and I half-carry and half-drag the tree back to the wagon, then we are forced to walk home, with three of us holding the tree steady in the wagon while Claire leads the horse, who nearly stumbles twice.

Meg chuckles. "It's not going to have any needles on it by the time we get back."

Buck snorts. "More room for decorations."

Meg is different from anyone Buck's ever taken an interest in. She's as sharp-tongued as he is, quick-witted and prone to judge, but warm underneath her tough surface. When she and Buck start bickering over the best way to haul the bundle of pine branches, I catch Claire's eye. She grins, and I can't help laughing. He's met his match for sure and certain.

It takes Liam and Chris to help us drag it inside while Buck and I try to press the limbs close to the trunk. Meg and Claire have a good laugh as Liam steers Buck and me straight into the wall before squeezing the tree into the main room.

"Y'all are sure this tree's not too big?" Meg repeats.

"It'll fit." Buck beams with confidence.

"It won't," I whisper to Claire.

It doesn't.

When we try to prop it up, the top of the tree bends against the ceiling. So, Buck and I set about trimming enough off the bottom to make it fit—barely—and stand it up again.

Meg smirks but doesn't say, "I told you so."

"We can use the extra branches on the mantle." Buck puffs out his chest. "It'll look perfect."

Julianna pops some corn for us to string with cranberries, and Granda hauls out some old, handmade ornaments from the attic. "Ester made these for our first Christmas tree in this house." He smiles wistfully. "She has a knack for making beautiful things."

"They're lovely, Granda." Claire paws through the box, pulling out painted ornaments in various shapes and sizes.

I grab the paper and ribbons from our haul from town, then the four of us sit by the fire to make more decorations, because Granda wants the tree "full to the brim." Claire and I string the corn and berries side-by-side, while Meg cuts paper and ribbon, her tongue sticking out from the corner of her mouth. Buck says he's supervising, but he's really watching her.

Once everything is ready, the whole family, except Julianna, who is working in the kitchen, and Emma, who is nowhere to be seen, helps drape the decorations on the tree. Granda positions the candles, then Buck offers to place Ester's star of Bethlehem on top.

"What are you going to do, climb up the branches?" Meg quips, but Buck has other plans.

"Uncle Chris, can I climb on your shoulders?"

"Sure thing, Buck. Hop on."

Meg giggles at his first awkward attempt to climb on Chris' back. "Don't fall."

"Don't you worry your pretty little head about it," Buck snipes back.

"Flattery won't make you any taller." We all have a good laugh at Buck's expense. Meg always seems to get the last word, but Buck doesn't seem to mind at all.

With the star successfully placed, all that's left is greening the cabin with pine boughs, holly, and branches of cedar. Buck even sneaks some mistletoe in the middle of the doorway.

After we finish, Meg wipes sweat from her brow. "You folks sure do work hard."

Claire smiles. "We've been out of practice. But it sure feels good."

Meg rubs her arms. "Feels itchy to me, all those needles poking me." She grins, and I can't help laughing.

We gather around the tree, shimmering in the candlelight, simple but beautiful. Granda swallows, moisture filling his eyes.

"Granda?" Claire strokes his arm.

"It looks like Christmas," he says, his voice breaking.

My throat starts to ache as tears threaten to well up from a deep place of grief and joy. "It looks like hope."

Aunt Julianna puts out a light spread, and everyone makes a plate to bring back to the main room. No one wants to abandon the Christmas tree. Still, Emma remains upstairs, despite both Claire and Uncle Chris trying to coax her to come down.

"She's just not ready yet." Claire fingers her bread. "I don't know if she'll ever be."

When our plates are empty, Uncle Chris rises and stretches his back. "I believe I will take Emma home. Claire, will you come, too? I think it might help her for you to be with us."

"Of course, Pa. I'll come."

"I better get Meg home." The fact that Buck doesn't move is not lost on me.

"Do you want company?"

Buck shoots daggers at me with his eyes. "No," he growls. "Thanks."

Granda clears his throat. Buck glances his way, sees Granda's raised brows, and sags. "Uh. Yeah. Thanks, Fin."

So, Uncle Chris collects Emma, and Claire and her parents leave in one direction while Buck, Meg, and I head in the other, towards town.

On the way, I find out that Meg lives in a small room above the diner. "I like it," she says. "I'm never late for work, and when I'm done, all I have to do is climb the stairs, and I'm home. Plus, I have a tiny balcony where I can watch the sunrise."

"Did you grow up in Blue Ridge?"

"Near here."

"Oh!" I lean forward to catch her eye. "Is your family still nearby?"

Her face becomes stone-hard and cold. "My parents died when I was young. My grandmother took me in, but she died when I was fourteen. I've been on my own since."

"I'm so sorry." I examine my hands clasped in my lap. "Our Ma and Pa died, too."

"Buck told me."

I grimace. "We know how unbearable it is to lose your parents. But then you were left all alone when your grandmother died. That must've been horrible."

"I cried for weeks. Then I bucked up, and I haven't cried a single tear since then. Probably won't ever again." She quirks her mouth. "What good do tears do? They don't change anything."

"Buck and I barely made it through. How did you ever survive on your own?'

She shrugs. "Wasn't easy." After a moment, she adds, "Mister Wilkins, my grandmother's preacher, who also owns the diner, has been very kind. He gave me a job and a place to live. So, I managed."

Buck jumps in, topping her last line. "Will you decorate for Christmas?"

Meg chuckles. "Why? I just decorated a tree that's big enough for three houses."

"Did you have a nice time?" Buck's hushed question, so nervous and hopeful, earns him a warm smile and a quick peck on the cheek from Meg.

"It was wonderful. Thank you for inviting me."

"And you'll come back? For Christmas?"

Meg offers a wistful smile. "I wouldn't miss it. I haven't experienced anything like that in a long, long time."

Buck walks her up the stairs to her loft, lingering a long time at the top of the stairs. But I can't fault him. He's clearly smitten, and if it were Claire, I'd be doing the exact same thing.

Our work the next day starts at first light. Uncle Liam, Buck, Samuel, Uncle Chris, and I choose the biggest, fattest hog for slaughter and spend the rest of the day stunning, bleeding, scalding, scraping, eviscerating, and butchering the animal, separating the different cuts for curing and smoking. For Buck, we prepare some blood sausage and render the lard for cracklings to use in the cornbread. Then, we take the fresh tenderloins and ribs to Julianna for dinner preparation.

While we are butchering the hog, Aunt Julianna and Granda are busy scrubbing the cabin floor to ceiling, including the windows, doors, and banister. Every time I bring in some meat, I can hear Granda humming "O Come, O Come, Emmanuel" or "Silent Night."

Emma and Claire join us mid-morning. Claire offers to clean the good china and polish Ester's silver, which Granda gratefully accepts.

Emma floats like a ghost through the rooms but doesn't participate in anything, disappearing whenever someone comes into a room that she's in. I never see her enter the front room.

By nightfall, everyone is exhausted. Emma and Chris leave for home, but this time, Claire stays. Again, Julianna puts out a platter of food, and we take our plates to sit around the Christmas tree.

Claire nestles next to me, the warmth of her body and the fire making my face burn. Before long, her breathing deepens and slows, and her head slides onto my chest. I wrap my arms around her, cradling her against me.

One by one, the others excuse themselves and head for bed, but Claire and I remain by the dying fire.

And I'm happier than I remember being in my whole life.

CHAPTER FORTY-FIVE

December 1918

Granda bursts through the front door, waving a yellow slip of paper. "Guess what I found out in town?" He waits a few moments as everyone gathers for the news. "Guess!"

Claire jumps up and down. "What is it? Don't keep us waiting."

A clamor swells through the hall. Emma, standing in the hall doorway, freezes. Her hand goes to the frame, bracing herself for some unseen catastrophe.

"Today!" Granda bellows. "Tom will be home today!"

"Whoop!" Buck cries. "Just in time for Christmas Eve!"

"It's perfect." Claire squeals. "What time?"

"He'll be here on the afternoon train."

Claire whips her head around. "We need to be there to meet him."

"We can't all go," Buck complains. "I was going to pick up Meg anyway. I'll get him."

"No way I'm missing seeing him get off the train." Claire tosses her hair over her shoulder. "So, I'm coming, too."

"If Claire's going, I'm going." I lock arms with her, securing my spot.

"You can't possibly think Emma and I aren't going to meet our boy at the train." Uncle Chris' icy stare has Buck studying his feet.

"Like I said, we can't all go." Buck digs a toe into a knot in the wood floor.

"Well, then, we'll have to take two wagons." Granda shrugs his shoulders.

Liam folds his arms and frowns. "Julianna has all the cooking still to do. I suppose she, Samuel, and I will have to stay back and finish the preparations."

"Aw, Pa!" Samuel groused.

"Very well." Granda rubs his hands together. "Tom is on the way home on Christmas Eve. What could be a more wonderful gift? We are truly blessed."

I catch a glimpse of the pained expression on Emma's face before she wipes her hands on her apron and disappears into the kitchen. Julianna follows behind her.

I tilt my head and wink at Buck. "The four of us can all fit in one wagon. It makes for a cozier ride."

By midafternoon, the seven of us, including Meg, are standing on the platform near the tracks, watching the long curve that leads to town. Smoke puffs in the distance as a long, low whistle sounds.

Claire slips her hand into mine.

Finally, the train inches into the station and grinds to a stop in a billow of steam. The doors slide open, pouring out holiday travelers.

Then, we see him, and my throat tightens.

He's painfully thin, his bones visible beneath his collared shirt. His jacket, two sizes too big, hangs on him like a sack. His skin is pale, with a yellow tinge.

"Tom," I breathe.

Emma's hands cover her mouth as tears spring into her eyes. Chris gathers her in his arms as if sensing she might collapse. Granda belts out a hearty laugh, waving his hand.

Tom smiles and lifts his hand weakly, but it's enough to break the spell. Screaming his name, Claire dashes to the foot of the metal stairs, her hands stretched out to him. Buck and I follow, and standing on either side, we help him down the steps. Claire wraps him in a hug and squeezes him so hard, I fear she might break him. Buck grabs his bag, and arm in arm, we escort him onto the platform, where he is bombarded with hearty greetings, hands pounding on his back, warm hugs, and Emma clutching him to her breast and refusing to let go.

We introduce him to Meg, then help him to the wagon, where he sits with Uncle Chris on one side and Aunt Emma on the other while Granda drives the horse.

Claire's chatter fills the air on the journey home, barely leaving space for more than one or two words from anyone else.

When we crest the last hill on the approach to the cabin, Granda's wagon stops, so Buck pulls our wagon abreast of theirs to see why.

Tom is weeping.

"It's so beautiful." He chokes the words out between hitches in his breath. "The Christmas greens draped over the porch and door, the candles lighting every window. I can even see the tree through the front window." He clutches his throat. "I never thought I would see it again."

Granda straightens his back, his face glowing as if he has one of those candles lit inside him.

Emma lets out a sound that isn't quite a sob or a laugh. For a moment, silence crashes over us. Then, a moment later, she envelops Tom in her arms. "Oh, my boy. My dear, sweet boy. You're home now. All is well. All is well."

The collective sigh of relief wafts the remnants of tension from the air.

When we reach the cabin, Tom swings his legs over the edge of the wagon and lands on wobbling legs, but Aunt Emma reaches him as he slips. Her arms wrap tightly around him, holding him up.

"Ma," he whispers. His voice is paper-thin.

Aunt Emma cradles his face between her hands and kisses his cheeks, his forehead, and his hair. Tears run freely down her face, but she's laughing as she murmurs, "My boy, my boy, my boy."

My throat tightens again. The rest of us hang back, allowing Emma time and space to absorb the reality of Tom's presence.

When Emma finally turns toward us, she's radiant. Her grief isn't gone. I can still see it in the lines around her mouth and on her forehead, in the strain of each breath, and in the curve of her back. But something in her heart has broken open, like a seed whose husk cracks when enough water and warmth reach it, and allows the first green shoots to emerge.

"Bring him inside," she orders, dabbing her cheeks with her apron. "He's half-frozen. And he's skin and bones. What did those army folks feed you, anyway? I'm going to hurry up this dinner. The boy needs to eat."

Granda chuckles. "There's our Emma."

Inside, Tom is carried to the main room, sitting in front of the fire and beside the tree where everyone can fuss over him. Claire piles blankets on him. Emma brings him broth, biscuits, and jam to tide him over. Laughter sings through the rooms as it used to, before the war.

Aunt Emma keeps touching Tom, brushing his hair from his eyes, asking for the twentieth time if he's warm enough, fed enough, and comfortable enough. In the fire's warmth, Tom's face begins to show some color, and his movements become soft and gentle instead of brittle and weak.

As the sun reaches the distant mountains' rise, Tom drifts off to sleep, his face peaceful at last.

Claire snuggles beside me on the chair. "Thank you, Fin," she whispers.

"For what?"

"For helping to hold us together through the worst times."

I swallow hard, unsure what to say.

She buries her head into my chest, murmuring, "I love you."

I press my lips against her glowing hair and whisper, "I love you, Claire."

Around us, the house glows with warm candlelight and the smell of pine and cinnamon. Outside, winter still presses against the windows, but inside, the spring rebirth has already begun.

Later that night, we gather around the long table. Julianna brings out Ester's finest china, the delicate white and gold plates we haven't used since Ian left for the war. The candles and decorations make the table glow like something from a fairy tale. I can't imagine kings and queens having a more beautiful spread.

The table is laden with baked ham glazed with sorghum syrup and seasoned with cloves and cinnamon, fresh sausages smelling of sage, mashed potatoes with butter, sweet potatoes, collard greens, creamed corn, pickled cabbage, snap beans, pickled peaches, and of course, Buck's crackling corn bread. Then, for dessert, Emma brings out apple pie, pumpkin pie, and gingerbread cake.

Granda relinquishes his usual seat, allowing Tom to take the place of honor at the head of the table. Then, we bow our heads as Granda prays.

"Lord, thank You for Christmas and what it represents for us: the gift of Your Son. Thank You for bringing our Tom home. And even when everything seems dark, remind us You are the light of the world."

Julianna squeezes Emma's hand, but Emma's eyes remain fixed on Tom, swimming with tears.

Platters pass from person to person, except Tom. Aunt Emma heaps his plate with mounds of food from every dish until he lifts his hands, chuckling. "Ma, if I ate all that, I'd explode."

Emma wrinkles her nose and waves her fingers toward his plate. "Nonsense. You must make up for lost meals."

Laughter rings out around the table as Claire spoons more food onto his heaping dish, and Tom throws his head back, holding his stomach and yelling, "No more! No more!".

When everyone has eaten more than their fill, Granda stands and lifts his glass. "I would like to thank Julianna and Emma for preparing this most exceptional meal, and the rest of you for helping with the tree, the decorations, and the cleaning and preparations." He winks. "You, too, Meg."

She gives him a broad grin and a mock salute as everyone clinks their glasses.

"Now, I feel we must honor those who are not with us in body but who are certainly with us in spirit. The Lakota believe the spirits of our loved ones remain with us for some time after their death, and their spirits guard over us, helping us, holding us accountable to living better lives, and encouraging us until it is time for them to return to the Great Spirit." He lowers his eyes. "So, I am quite sure our loved ones are here tonight. I believe they brought Tom home. I believe they restored Buck to us. And I believe they are already helping us grow into better men and women." He raises his eyes and his glass. "Here's to Ian."

"To Ian," we murmur.

"To Mac."

"Mac."

"To Katie."

"Katie."

Granda sighs. "And here's to my Ester, my love, who spent her life inspiring me to be a better man just by being herself. To Ester…" Granda's voice cracks. He blinks back tears and swallows. "She lives now in the bosom of her beloved Savior and wouldn't have it any other way."

It's the first time Granda has acknowledged Ester's passing.

I lift my glass higher. "Ester was like a beautiful ribbon. From the look of it, you think it's delicate and fragile, but it's strong, binding this family together. To Ester, the heart of our family."

"To Ester."

"To Ester."

We clink our glasses around the table, lighter and slower this time, but with heartfelt love and appreciation for the people they were and what they meant to us.

After the meal, we gather around the tree to sing carols. Aunt Julianna leads us, singing softly at first, *Away in a Manger*, then *O Come All Ye Faithful.* When we break out in *Joy to the World*, everyone sings at the top of their lungs. Then, we close with *Silent Night*, our voices weaving together in beautiful harmony, joining with the candles' glow and the fire's warmth to create the perfect, peaceful finish to our caroling.

Then, it's time to exchange gifts. They are mainly simple, handmade things like a knitted scarf and cap for Claire, a carved wooden cross for Emma, and a set of embroidered napkins for Julianna. Buck gives Meg a pocketknife.

She flips it open. "Useful."

Buck sinks into the floor until Meg beams a grin.

"I love useful! Thank you!"

"You're welcome." Buck's hands are trembling.

Boy, he's got it bad.

Granda gives Uncle Liam a set of screwdrivers and Uncle Chris a new saw. He gifts Samuel, Buck, and me new shoes.

My heart swells, and tears moisten my eyes when I open Granda's gift. I remember how I clung to my shoes from my former life as if they were my only connection to Ma and Pa, and how Ester helped me to release my grip and move forward into my new life. Now, these shoes have become a symbol for leaving the war behind and moving forward into my new life with Claire. I slip them on immediately.

"My turn." I reach into the branches and pull out a small box. "Claire?"

"Ooo, is that for me?" She claps her hands and bounces like a child.

I kneel in front of her, slowly opening the box. "Will you marry me?"

A quick gasp, and her hands flutter to her face. "Oh! Oh, my! Yes! Yes, of course. Oh, yes!"

The room erupts in cheers and shouts of congratulations.

Claire leans against me, her hand warm in mine. I take the ring out and slip it on her finger.

"The center stone…" She holds her hand up to a candle, moving it back and forth to catch the light in the jewel. "Is it…?"

"Yes. I hope it's acceptable. Granda told me you kept Ian's ring in your bedside drawer, so…I took it and had them use that stone as the centerpiece for this ring." I close my eyes and moisten my lips. "I didn't ask you because I wanted it to be a surprise. But if you would prefer, the jeweler can restore Ian's ring easily, and he agreed to do it free of charge if that's what you want. Then, you can pick out another stone for this ring."

Claire continues to stare at the ring, but I can't read her reaction. Is she in awe or stunned at my invasion of her privacy?

"I thought, since Ian asked me to look after you, it might be meaningful to have his ring be a part of ours." *What is she thinking?*

"It's…" Her voice quavers, "Perfect."

In that moment, I remember how to breathe.

She nestles against my chest. "You finished the story for Ian. Everything is now complete."

"Will we have a spring wedding?" Emma asks.

I lift Claire's chin to look into her moist eyes. "What would you want, my love?"

"Spring sounds nice. A fresh start, a new life."

A new start, like my new shoes. "Then, spring it is."

Buck coughs, then stands. "I like the idea of a spring wedding, too." He takes Meg's hands. "What do you think?"

Meg tilts her head, lifting one brow. "About their wedding? Sure, spring sounds very nice. Lots of flowers."

Buck grins, a wide, toothy, beaming smile from ear to ear. "No. Yours."

Meg's mouth gapes as Buck drops to one knee. "I don't have a ring for you yet, but I don't want to wait another second to ask you. Will you marry me?"

Someone gasps. Granda exclaims, "Oh, my! Two at once?"

Meg stares at Buck as if he has antlers coming out of his head. *Oh, no. Is she going to turn him down? Buck may not recover from that.*

"I love you, Meg. I've loved you since I first laid eyes on you. I've loved you since I saw that first smile." He brings her hands to his mouth, kissing them gently. "Meg, will you marry me?"

Meg drops her hands to her side. "Are you out of your mind? You've only known me…what, a month?" She flops back in her chair. "Married? Don't you think we should date first?"

"We can date. But I'm scared someone else is gonna come along and poach you, and I don't think I could bear it." Buck takes her hands again, squeezing them in his fists. "Please, Meg. You are everything I've ever wanted in a wife. You're strong. You're adventurous. You're passionate. You're beautiful. You're smart. You have a good heart." Buck smiles, his warmth toward her emanating from him in waves. "You are everything."

Meg's eyelids flutter. "You'll give a girl a big head."

"It's all true. And I don't want to lose you."

She breathes a heavy sigh. "It doesn't seem right. It's like we're doing things backwards."

Buck's laughter fills the room. "Darlin', would we do it any other way?"

Meg scowls at him for a second, planting her hands on her hips. "I'll not marry a drunkard or ne'er-do-well."

"Of course not."

"So, there'll be no more drinking and no more gambling." Meg lifts a single brow. "I mean it."

I stare, amazed, as my fiery brother ducks his head. "Yes'm."

Slowly, her scowl turns into a smirk.

"Come on. What do you say?"

The whole room holds its collective breath as we wait for Meg's reply. She studies her hands for a moment, closes her eyes, bites her lower lip, then gazes down at Buck, kneeling before her with his wide eyes pleading.

Her face softens as the corners of her mouth turn up a bit. "Spring sounds nice, I guess." She shrugs one shoulder.

Buck whoops, leaping to his feet, then snatches her up in a bear hug, lifts her high above his head, and twirls her around in circles. She breaks into laughter, so infectious that all of us begin laughing, clapping, whooping, and cheering.

Buck finally sets her down with one final squeeze and a long, deep kiss. When he releases her, she steps back, dabs the corners of her eyes, and grumbles, "Blasted candle smoke got in my eyes."

EPILOGUE

"An April double wedding on the hillside among the flowers." Claire twirls a golden curl and squeals. "I'm so excited. I can braid flowers into my hair. It's going to be beautiful."

"Unless it rains," Buck mutters under his breath.

Claire pokes Buck in the side. "That's why we aren't having it in May."

"I want Pastor Wilkins to officiate the service." Meg puckers her mouth. "That won't be a problem, will it?"

"Oh, no, Pastor Wilkins will be wonderful." Claire flutters to her armoire and pulls out a long box containing a white dress, carefully covered in tissue paper. "This is my mother's wedding dress. She promised to add some lace on the bodice and around the neck for me." Holding the dress up to her chest, Claire preens before her small mirror. "What will you be wearing, Meg?"

"I don't know." Meg's eyes drop. I'll bet she doesn't own a dress other than the black skirt she wears to serve. "I'll figure something."

Buck almost snarls at Claire, then caresses Meg's arm. "It don't matter to me what you wear. You're beautiful in anything."

Claire's brow creases. "I'm afraid I might've been insensitive." She grimaces with a listless chuckle. "Old habits die hard, I'm afraid. I'm sorry, Meg."

"You didn't do anything wrong." Meg tosses her head. "Why say you're sorry?"

"Would you like to borrow a dress? I'm sure I have something…"

Meg scoffs. "I couldn't squeeze one arm into a dress that fits you."

"What about Julianna's wedding dress? You and she are similar in height."

"I'll make my own."

Claire's eyes widen. "Would you allow me to help you?"

Claire's eyes plead, but Meg remains determined, her lip curled. "I can do it."

"I know you can." Claire deflates. "I was only offering to help you so it would go faster. After all, it's only a few weeks away."

A quick tap on the door breaks the tension. "May I come in?"

"Yes, Mama."

Aunt Emma slips her head around the door frame. "Making plans?"

"Yes, ma'am."

Emma steps into her daughter's bedroom. "Have you talked about where you will be living once you're wed?"

"Yes'm." Buck scuffs his toe against the wood. "I thought about going back to New Zealand and running Pa's farm…"

I top his line before he can talk himself into a fatal mistake. "But he's a deserter in the army's eyes, and if he goes home, he'll be court martialed, maybe executed."

"There's that." Buck sighs. "Mainly, it's because Meg really wants to be around family, and we're the only family she's got." He grasps Meg's hand. "She helped me remember how lucky I am to have such a wonderful family."

"How sweet, Meg." Emma grasps Meg's hands. "We're so glad you are looking forward to joining us."

"Thank you," she whispers.

"So, we talked about giving the land to Mani." I swallow the tears that threaten to well up and burn my throat. "He saved my life more than once. And now that the Māori can legally own land, it feels like everything is finally coming full circle."

"What do you mean?"

"Pa and Ma fought for the Māori's rights and died because of it." My jaw locks, grinding my teeth together. "If we give the land to Mani, we deprive the men who killed our parents of the land, and we help the Māori in the process. Two birds with one stone."

"I see."

"So, I don't know where we'll live." Buck swallows hard. "Yet."

"And I suppose Claire and I will continue to live in the big cabin, at least for now. To help out Granda."

Aunt Emma clears her throat. "Well, your Uncle Liam and Aunt Julianna have some thoughts on this. Would you join us downstairs to discuss it?"

"Yes, ma'am."

We follow Emma to the sitting room, where everyone is gathered in a circle around Granda's chair. Liam stands as we enter. "Ah, the happy couples. Come and join us."

The four of us take places on the floor among the scattered dining chairs, brought in so everyone has a place to sit.

Granda clears his throat. "We have some things to discuss." He glances sadly toward Samuel. "Bear has reached out to Samuel, offering him a job in his business. Samuel has decided to accept. He will be returning with Bear to San Francisco after the wedding."

My head whips around to stare at Aunt Julianna, whose moist, reddened eyes I missed when I first walked in the room.

Liam reaches over to pat Julianna's hand. "That leaves us alone in…" Liam's voice cracks. He blinks a few times before continuing. Now, Julianna grips Liam's hand as he continues. "Alone in a cabin too big for our needs." He sighs. "So. We want to offer it to Fin and Claire as their new home."

Claire gasps. My mouth hangs open, staring first at Liam and Julianna, then at Emma. With Claire leaving home and Tom returning to university, Chris and Emma will be alone as well.

Everything is changing again.

"Where will you live?" Buck asks.

Julianna smiles. "We'd like to move into the big house with Mac. He says that suits him just fine."

"We can help out on the farm, keep things going around here," Liam adds.

My brows knit together. "Claire and I planned on helping Granda out still."

Granda smiles warmly. "I thought you would probably say that. But you're just starting. You need your privacy, and your own space to raise your children." He leans forward, stomping his foot. "And I'm expecting some great-grandchildren to come along as soon as possible."

"But what about Buck? He needs a place, too." I glance to check Buck's reaction.

"We'll be fine. We can always live over the diner."

"That's no place to start a family." Granda holds up a finger. "I have already set aside a large section of acreage for each of you, so half of the acreage I set aside for Fin will be added to Buck's plot of land, and the other half added to Liam's—sorry, Fin's farm." Granda grins. "Everyone will have more than enough land to sustain themselves and make a good income."

The blotches on Buck's cheeks color bright red. "That's very generous, Granda."

"I set that land aside for you long ago." Granda holds out his hand, palm up. "Now, it's a matter of building a cabin."

"By April?" Buck blanches.

"We'll all pitch in and help," Liam says. "That's what we do in this family."

"Aunt Julianna. Uncle Liam. Granda. I…I can't believe…I can't thank you enough."

"You're more than welcome, Fin." Aunt Julianna smiles through her tears.

"Of course, come planting and harvest, we'll all be working very hard. And we'll help each other then, too." Liam rubs his hands together. "So, what do you say? Claire?"

"I'm so happy." Claire giggles. "It's like I'll be a real woman, taking care of my own home."

"Meg?"

When I turn to Meg, I'm surprised to see tears streaming down her face. She closes her eyes for a moment, her throat working, then leans forward, her elbows on her knees and her hands clasped before her. "I...don't know what to say."

Liam cocks his head. "Are you unhappy with the plan?"

She blinks, licking her lips. "I thought I'd never have anything. Not a family. Not a home. Not...children." She looks up and scans the faces around the room. "You've given me all that. And more. I..." She presses her lips together, swallowing. "I will never be able to express how much it means to me."

Granda leans back in his chair with a contented sigh. "You lost your family, but now you've gained a new one and will soon make one of your own."

I blurt, "Full circle."

"What?"

Emma nods her head toward me. "Tell them."

"I told Aunt Emma it feels like everything is coming full circle." A flood of warmth mixed with sorrow washes over me. "Buck and I are giving Mani the New Zealand farm, fulfilling Pa's mission to restore land to the Māori. You see? Full circle. Their life's work is finally completed, and the plans of the evil men who killed them are thwarted once and for all."

Liam gasps, slamming his fists on his knees. "You're what?"

A wistful smile flickers across Buck's lips. "It don't bring Ma and Pa back, but it sure feels like the right thing to do."

"Your pa worked long and hard to earn that land. And you want to give it away?" Liam throws up his hands, rolling his eyes. "You could sell the land, make a lot of money."

Buck snorts. "Who would we sell it to? The men who killed our parents because of their greed?" He shakes his head. "We'd rather Mani have it."

Liam's face softens as he sits back in his seat. "I see."

Taking a deep breath to collect myself, I rise and walk to stand beside Granda, laying my arm across his shoulders. "We've all gone through so much pain and lost so many. Our Ma and Pa, and our home. Granma Ester. Ian. Mac. Katie. We almost lost Buck, Tom, and Samuel, too. We lost so many friends in the war. And that doesn't count Granda's parents and sisters, and the Lakota family he lost before he met Granma." I gesture around the room. "I suppose, as a family, we're a little like Job."

Granda chuckles. "You're right about that. But in Job, God promises redemption." His face slackens as he gazes through the window at the misty blue mountains. "Ester was the redemption of my lost Lakota family, a blessing beyond measure. And from her came the rest of my redemption." Turning his eyes toward his family, he smiles. "All of you." He lowers his head, his hands kneading in his lap. "The blessing doesn't take away the grief, but it gives it a beautiful cushion to rest on."

Granda's words sink into my chest like soothing balm. "All those endings brought so much pain…"

"I was almost broken by it," Aunt Emma murmurs.

"…but we endured. We kept living. We strengthened each other. And now, God has brought us full circle."

"Granda?" Buck hesitates, his breath shaking as he struggles to fill his chest. "How did you handle losing Grandma?"

"I'm still working that out, son. Likely to be for a long time."

Buck grimaces. "I miss Ian terribly. Will this feeling—like a hole through my heart—will it ever go away?"

"I don't reckon it will. But there comes a time when the memories bring you a kind of poignant joy instead of pain." Granda closes his eyes with a sigh. "Truth be told, the hole you feel in your heart is real. A part of yourself died with Ian." His face breaks into a bittersweet smile. "But those you love who are still in your life, and the certain knowledge that you will one day see your loved ones again, can soothe the rough edges of that emptiness."

I wrap my arms around Granda's neck. "Thank you for giving us a home. For making us feel welcome and loved. For teaching us how to be good men. For everything."

"You're my family." Granda shrugs and pats my hand. "Besides, Ester and I gained a lot more than we gave in the bargain."

"Are family meetings always going to be like this?" Meg gives a rueful shake of her head. "This much sugar makes my teeth hurt."

Everyone chuckles, but I curl my lip and lift a brow, casting a sidelong glance at her. "Something tells me you're going to develop a sweet tooth, and quickly."

She cuts her eyes up to meet mine with a sly grin. "I think you're absolutely right."

ABOUT THE AUTHOR

Dr. Donna E. Lane is an award-winning, multi-genre author with a passion for exploring all aspects of the human experience. As a Christian counselor, retired professor of counseling, and spiritual director, Dr. Lane has dedicated herself to guiding individuals on their spiritual journeys, offering solace and wisdom through her integrated approach. Her 47 years of experience in this field provide insights that she seamlessly weaves into her writing, delving into the complexities of relationships and the depths of the human heart.

With a boundless imagination and a fervent devotion to Jesus, she crafts stories that resonate deeply with readers, offering them the opportunity to embark on unforgettable journeys to other times and other worlds.

A devoted wife of 47 years and mother of three, she now cherishes her role as a grandmother and mom to her sweet dog, a little white furball named Rosie Cotton.

Other Books by This Author

Fiction

The Interview
Sky Light Falls: Whisperers Book One
Sky Light Rises: Whisperers Book Two
Sky Light Ends: Whisperers Book Three
Time Forgotten
Infidel Wars
This Hallowed Ground
Scorched Earth
And Their Numbers Grew
And They Were Persuaded

Nonfiction

The Way of the Shepherd
Dwelling
Seeking Treasures
Strength in Adversity
Strength in Our Story
Wilderness Meditations
Restored Christianity

Professional

Please Share the Door: I'm Freezing–Creating Oneness in Marriage
Trauma Narrative Treatment
Gold Stone

How to Connect

Websites– https://thedoctorslane.com
https://donnaelane.com
https://codylanefoundation.com
Facebook– https://facebook.com/donnaelaneauthor
X - @doctordelane
Instagram–@doctordelane

www.ingramcontent.com/pod-product-compliance
Lightning Source LLC
LaVergne TN
LVHW100501110826
845146LV00002B/472

* 9 7 9 8 9 9 1 7 3 5 7 5 9 *